THE COLD EMBRACE

Weird Stories by Women

Introduced and Edited by

S. T. Joshi

Dover Publications, Inc., Mineola, New York

DOVER HORROR CLASSICS

Bibliographical Note

The Cold Embrace: Weird Stories by Women, first published by Dover Publications, Inc., in 2016, is a new compilation of short stories by women authors, selected and edited by S. T. Joshi. For information on the sources of the texts, see the Notes on the Authors section at the end of the book.

International Standard Book Number

ISBN-13: 978-0-486-80505-4
ISBN-10: 0-486-80505-0

Manufactured in the United States by RR Donnelley
80505001   2016
www.doverpublications.com

INTRODUCTION

S. T. Joshi

There is a certain artificiality in segregating literary or other artistic work by gender. Studies have repeatedly shown that readers are unable to tell the difference between work written by men and work written by women if the authors' names are concealed; and many attempts to identify characteristically "male" or "female" traits in writing have a tendency to descend to conventional stereotypes. That said, there is some virtue in focusing on the many distinguished women writers who have contributed to the development of the literature of horror and the supernatural, for they have been at the forefront of the field since its inception as a genre—perhaps more so than in any other literary genre.

The Gothic novels that appeared in their hundreds in the half-century following the publication of Horace Walpole's *The Castle of Otranto* (1764) could be said to have constituted the first instance of the emergence of "popular" fiction in English literature, and three writers took center stage in the movement: Ann Radcliffe, Matthew Gregory ("Monk") Lewis, and Charles Robert Maturin. But whereas Lewis (*The Monk*, 1796) and Maturin (*Melmoth the Wanderer*, 1820) came to be known for a single noteworthy work of Gothic fiction, Radcliffe wrote six novels, all of which were immense bestsellers, chief among them *The Mysteries of Udolpho* (1794), which in many ways came to define the Gothic novel. Its vivid setting in the Apennine Mountains of Italy, its classic portrayal of the "woman-in-peril" motif, and its mingling of historical fiction and terror were all copied by countless imitators, and "Mother Radcliffe" was arguably the most popular writer in the English-speaking world during the years 1790–1825. She wrote no short fiction, however, so she goes unrepresented in this volume. Moreover, her focus on the "explained supernatural"—the suggestion of the supernatural, later to be explained away as the result of trickery or misconstrual—was later rightly criticized by Sir Walter Scott as something of a disappointment and a copout, and subsequent ventures into "weird fiction" focused more clearly and unequivocally on the "reality" of the supernatural occurrence.

One of the more curious episodes in Gothic fiction was the now celebrated contest in 1816 that led to the writing of Mary Shelley's pioneering short novel *Frankenstein* (1818)—a work that not only fostered the development of weird fiction but also laid the groundwork for the later emergence of science fiction. Perhaps it is not surprising that for many decades thereafter it was believed that Mary's more famous husband, the poet Percy Bysshe Shelley, had helped her to write the book (even though his own early ventures into Gothic fiction, *Zastrossi* [1810] and *St. Irvyne* [1811], are almost laughably bad) or actually wrote it himself. Such speculations typify the denigration of female accomplishment that has dominated human history: it was no doubt offensive to many believers in male superiority that a woman barely twenty years old could write such a profound and compelling work while such of her more illustrious male counterparts, such as the poet Shelley and Lord Byron, produced next to nothing in the contest. (A fourth participant, Dr. John William Polidori, did write the notable novelette "The Vampyre" [1819].) Mary Shelley went on to write several other novels as well as a brace of weird stories, of which "Transformation" (1830) is something of a pendant to *Frankenstein* in some of its themes and motifs.

In the post-Gothic period, the one titanic literary figure to emerge was Edgar Allan Poe (1809–1849), who refined the outmoded Gothic tropes and rendered them imperishably potent in the compact mode of the short story. But, especially in England, the Victorian age saw the emergence of an array of women writers who focused on the "ghost story" to convey their fascination with the supernatural. There are, indeed, some faint supernatural episodes even in such novels as Charlotte Brontë's *Jane Eyre* (1847) and Emily Brontë's *Wuthering Heights* (1848); and a close friend of the Brontës, Elizabeth Gaskell, made frequent departures from her writing of novels of English domestic life to pen the occasional weird tale. And she was by no means alone: Mary Elizabeth Braddon, Amelia B. Edwards, Margaret Oliphant, and Mrs. J. H. Riddell followed in her wake, joining such male figures as Edward Bulwer-Lytton, J. Sheridan Le Fanu, Charles Dickens, Rudyard Kipling, and W. W. Jacobs in filling Victorian periodicals with tales of terror. Even the eminent Anglo-American novelist Henry James—who wrote an early and appreciative essay on Braddon—could not resist the tendency toward the weird, and his recurring work in the weird tale came to full flower in the short novel *The Turn of the Screw* (1898).

In America, the influence of Poe in the later nineteenth century was even more pronounced. His younger contemporary Fitz-James O'Brien led the way, although his early death in the Civil War no doubt deprived us of a number of weird tales along the lines of "What Was It?" and "The Diamond Lens." Another figure who fought in the Civil War, Ambrose Bierce (1842–1914?), became Poe's most notable disciple, adhering closely to his mentor's strictures on the "unity of effect" by writing stories whose austere compactness and focus on the psychological effects of terror rendered them almost unbearably intense. Bierce was an unabashed misygonist, but that did not stop him from promoting the work of his younger contemporary Gertrude Atherton, whose powerful weird stories are only a small portion of her prodigious work as novelist, short story writer, and chronicler of the history and topography of her native California.

Bierce and Atherton represent what might be called the "West Coast School" of supernatural writing in America during the period 1880–1940, a period that many have called the Golden Age of weird fiction. The East Coast School, dominated by Henry James and his colleague and disciple Edith Wharton, also generated fine work, but work that was perhaps more closely allied to the conventional "ghost story." In New England, Sarah Orne Jewett, Charlotte Perkins Gilman, and Mary E. Wilkins Freeman all took occasional respite from their focus on gritty realism to write weird tales whose power resides precisely in their evocation of the hard, unforgiving landscape of their native land and the dour, grizzled denizens it produces. Gilman's "The Yellow Wall Paper" (1892) seems to be a textbook case of the kind of psychological horror that can uniquely affect women—it was inspired by her own bout with post-partum depression—but a closer reading of the story suggests a supernatural undercurrent (the psychic possession of the hapless woman confined to the attic bedroom by a previous denizen of the place) that many critics have failed to detect.

Nearly all the Victorian writers mentioned above indulged in the supernatural only as a kind of hobby—a respite from their more recognized work in mainstream fiction. Even Le Fanu, who (aside from Poe) perhaps came closest to being a "professional" weird writer, confined the weird to his short stories and novellas; most of his novels, even the celebrated *Uncle Silas* (1864), do not involve the supernatural and rarely venture even into psychological or Gothic horror. Perhaps it was not possible to make a career out of weird writing at this juncture. E. Nesbit, who wrote two early collections of weird tales, achieved far greater success in writing children's books (some of which do involve elements of fantasy, if not the supernatural) than in weird fiction designed for adults.

But with the turn of the twentieth century there emerged, somewhat fortuitously, a cadre of towering figures who transformed weird fiction into a genre that could attain the highest aesthetic levels. It is no doubt an historical accident that all these writers—Arthur Machen, Lord Dunsany, Algernon Blackwood, M. R. James, and H. P. Lovecraft—are men; and even a good many of the second-tier figures who helped to make this era such a rich period of weird fiction—William Hope Hodgson, Walter de la Mare, L. P. Hartley, Robert Hichens—are also male. But, as before, mainstream writers dabbled in the weird to no little extent. Even putting aside the obscure American novelist and translator Edna W. Underwood, whose eccentric volume *A Book of Dear Dead Women* (1911) is only now gaining some attention, we can point to the highly regarded Southern writer Ellen Glasgow and to such British figures as Marjorie Bowen, May Sinclair, and, preeminently, Virginia Woolf as examples of the ineluctable attraction of the weird upon temperaments of a very different sort.

It should also be noted that, during the long history of *Weird Tales* (1923-54) and its fellow pulp magazines, women were a not insignificant presence: Francis Stevens (pseudonym of Gertrude Barrows Bennett), Everill Worrill, Leah Bodine Drake, Mary Elizabeth Counselman, and many other women made frequent appearances in the pulps and attracted a devoted following. During the 1950s and 1960s, weird fiction suffered something of an eclipse, as mystery fiction and science fiction came to the fore; but the mainstream writer Shirley Jackson elevated the weird to the highest literary status in such works as "The Lottery" (1948) and *The Haunting of Hill House* (1959).

The sudden and unexpected emergence of supernatural fiction as a bestselling phenomenon—begun with the publication of Ira Levin's *Rosemary's Baby* (1967), fostered by William Peter Blatty's *The Exorcist* (1971), and culminating in the many novels of Stephen King—might be said to be a largely male phenomenon, as such other writers as Peter Straub, Clive Barker, and Dean R. Koontz contributed to the immense popularity of the weird as a literary and media phenomenon; but no one would have expected Anne Rice, a predominantly mainstream writer whose *Interview with the Vampire* (1976) was initially published with little fanfare, to become the queen of the weird as she has become in the past few decades. Many other women writers who do not always attain bestseller status but whose work is second to none in quality—Caitlín R. Kiernan, Nancy Kilpatrick, Nancy A. Collins, Lois H. Gresh, Elizabeth Hand, Gemma Files, Kathe Koja, Kelly Link—have made the present era an inexhaustibly rich one for the expression of weird motifs and conceptions.

Is there any specifically "female" approach to the weird? It would be demeaning and stereotypical to say that women writers have focused more on the human emotions elicited by a weird scenario rather than the weird phenomenon itself, or even that women writers can portray women characters more emphatically and realistically than male writers can. All we can say is that women have contributed to the development of weird fiction in ways that perhaps can only be paralleled by the female dominance of the detective story with such writers as Agatha Christie, Margery Allingham, Ngaio Marsh, P. D. James, Ruth Rendell, Sue Grafton, and countless others. Let us be content to read the weird work of women—and men—and enjoy the pleasant shivers they can send up our spines.

CONTENTS

TRANSFORMATION

Mary Shelley

Forthwith this frame of mine was wrench'd
　　With a woful agony,
Which forced me to begin my tale,
　　And then it set me free.
Since then, at an uncertain hour,
　　That agony returns;
And till my ghastly tale is told
　　This heart within me burns.—COLERIDGE'S ANCIENT MARINER.

I HAVE HEARD it said, that, when any strange, supernatural, and necromantic adventure has occurred to a human being, that being, however desirous he may be to conceal the same, feels at certain periods torn up as it were by an intellectual earthquake, and is forced to bare the inner depths of his spirit to another. I am a witness of the truth of this, I have dearly sworn to myself never to reveal to human ears the horrors to which I once, in excess of fiendly pride, delivered myself over. The holy man who heard my confession, and reconciled me to the church, is dead. None knows that once——

Why should it not be thus? Why tell a tale of impious tempting of Providence, and soul-subduing humiliation? Why? answer me, ye who are wise in the secrets of human nature! I only know that so it is; and in spite of strong resolve—of a pride that too much masters me—of shame, and even of fear, so to render myself odious to my species—I must speak.

Genoa! my birth-place—proud city! looking upon the blue waves of the Mediterranean sea—dost thou remember me in my boyhood, when thy cliffs and promontories, thy bright sky and gay vineyards, were my world? Happy time! when to the young heart the narrow-bounded universe, which leaves, by its very limitation, free scope to the imagination, enchains our physical energies, and, sole period in our lives, innocence and enjoyment are united. Yet, who can look back to childhood, and not remember its sorrows and its harrowing fears? I was born with the most imperious, haughty, tameless spirit, with which ever mortal was gifted. I quailed before my father only; and

1

he, generous and noble, but capricious and tyrannical, at once fostered and checked the wild impetuosity of my character, making obedience necessary, but inspiring no respect for the motives which guided his commands. To be a man, free, independent; or, in better words, insolent and domineering, was the hope and prayer of my rebel heart.

My father had one friend, a wealthy Genoese noble, who in a political tumult was suddenly sentenced to banishment, and his property confiscated. The Marchese Torella went into exile alone. Like my father, he was a widower: he had one child, the almost infant Juliet, who was left under my father's guardianship. I should certainly have been an unkind master to the lovely girl, but that I was forced by my position to become her protector. A variety of childish incidents all tended to one point,—to make Juliet see in me a rock of refuge; I in her, one, who must perish through the soft sensibility of her nature too rudely visited, but for my guardian care. We grew up together. The opening rose in May was not more sweet than this dear girl. An irradiation of beauty was spread over her face. Her form, her step, her voice—my heart weeps even now, to think of all of relying, gentle, loving, and pure, that was enshrined in that celestial tenement. When I was eleven and Juliet eight years of age, a cousin of mine, much older than either—he seemed to us a man— took great notice of my playmate; he called her his bride, and asked her to marry him. She refused, and he insisted, drawing her unwillingly towards him. With the countenance and emotions of a maniac I threw myself on him—I strove to draw his sword—I clung to his neck with the ferocious resolve to strangle him: he was obliged to call for assistance to disengage himself from me. On that night I led Juliet to the chapel of our house: I made her touch the sacred relics—I harrowed her child's heart, and profaned her child's lips with an oath, that she would be mine, and mine only.

Well, those days passed away. Torella returned in a few years, and became wealthier and more prosperous than ever. When I was seventeen, my father died; he had been magnificent to prodigality; Torella rejoiced that my minority would afford an opportunity for repairing my fortunes. Juliet and I had been affianced beside my father's deathbed—Torella was to be a second parent to me.

I desired to see the world, and I was indulged. I went to Florence, to Rome, to Naples; thence I passed to Toulon, and at length reached what had long been the bourne of my wishes, Paris. There was wild work in Paris then. The poor king, Charles the Sixth, now sane, now mad, now a monarch, now an abject slave, was the very mockery of humanity. The queen, the dauphin, the Duke of Burgundy, alternately friends and foes—now meeting in prodigal feasts, now shedding blood in rivalry—were blind to the miserable state of their country, and the dangers that impended over it, and gave themselves wholly up to dissolute enjoyment or savage strife. My character still followed me. I was arrogant and self-willed; I loved display, and above all, I threw all control far from me. Who could control me in Paris? My young friends were eager to foster passions which furnished them with pleasures. I was deemed handsome—I was master of every knightly accomplishment. I was disconnected with any political party. I grew a favourite with all: my presumption and arrogance were pardoned in one so young: I became a spoiled child. Who could control me? not the letters and advice of Torella— only strong necessity visiting me in the abhorred shape of an empty purse. But there were means to refill this void. Acre after acre, estate after estate, I sold. My dress, my jewels, my horses and their caparisons, were almost unrivalled in gorgeous Paris, while the lands of my inheritance passed into possession of others.

The Duke of Orleans was waylaid and murdered by the Duke of Burgundy. Fear and terror possessed all Paris. The dauphin and the queen shut themselves up; every pleasure was suspended. I grew weary of this state of things, and my heart yearned for my boyhood's haunts. I was nearly a beggar, yet still I would go there, claim my bride, and rebuild my fortunes. A few happy ventures as a merchant would make me rich again. Nevertheless, I would not return in humble guise. My last act was to dispose of my remaining estate near Albaro for half its worth, for ready money. Then I despatched all kinds of artificers, arras, furniture of regal splendour, to fit up the last relic of my inheritance, my palace in Genoa. I lingered a little longer yet, ashamed at the part of the prodigal returned, which I feared I should play. I sent my horses. One matchless Spanish jennet I despatched to my promised bride; its caparisons flamed with jewels and cloth of gold. In every part I caused to be entwined the initials of Juliet and her Guido. My present found favour in hers and in her father's eyes.

Still to return a proclaimed spendthrift, the mark of impertinent wonder, perhaps of scorn, and to encounter singly the reproaches or taunts of my fellow-citizens, was no alluring prospect. As a shield between me and censure, I invited some few of the most reckless of my comrades to accompany me: thus I went armed against the world, hiding a rankling feeling, half fear and half penitence, by bravado and an insolent display of satisfied vanity.

I arrived in Genoa. I trod the pavement of my ancestral palace. My proud step was no interpreter of my heart, for I deeply felt that, though surrounded by every luxury, I was a beggar. The first step I took in claiming Juliet must widely declare me such. I read contempt or pity in the looks of all. I fancied, so apt is conscience to imagine what it deserves, that rich and poor, young and old, all regarded me with derision. Torella came not near me. No wonder that my second father should expect a son's deference from me in waiting first on him. But, galled and stung by a sense of my follies and demerit, I strove to throw the blame on others. We kept nightly orgies in Palazzo Carega. To sleepless, riotous nights, followed listless, supine mornings. At the Ave Maria we showed our dainty persons in the streets, scoffing at the sober citizens, casting insolent glances on the shrinking women. Juliet was not among them—no, no; if she had been there, shame would have driven me away, if love had not brought me to her feet.

I grew tired of this. Suddenly I paid the Marchese a visit. He was at his villa, one among the many which deck the suburb of San Pietro d'Arena. It was the month of May—a month of May in that garden of the world—the blossoms of the fruit trees were fading among thick, green foliage; the vines were shooting forth; the ground strewed with the fallen olive blooms; the fire-fly was in the myrtle hedge; heaven and earth wore a mantle of surpassing beauty. Torella welcomed me kindly, though seriously; and even his shade of displeasure soon wore away. Some resemblance to my father—some look and tone of youthful ingenuousness, lurking still in spite of my misdeeds, softened the good old man's heart. He sent for his daughter—he presented me to her as her betrothed. The chamber became hallowed by a holy light as she entered. Hers was that cherub look, those large, soft eyes, full dimpled cheeks, and mouth of infantine sweetness, that expresses the rare union of happiness and love. Admiration first possessed me; she is mine! was the second proud emotion, and my lips curled with haughty triumph. I had not been the *enfant gâté* of the beauties of France not to have learnt the art of pleasing the soft heart of woman. If towards men I was overbearing, the deference I paid to them was the more in contrast. I commenced my courtship by the display of a thousand gallantries to Juliet, who, vowed to me from infancy, had never admitted the devotion of others; and who, though accustomed to expressions of admiration, was uninitiated in the language of lovers.

For a few days all went well. Torella never alluded to my extravagance; he treated me as a favourite son. But the time came, as we discussed the preliminaries to my union with his daughter, when this fair face of things should be overcast. A contract had been drawn up in my father's lifetime. I had rendered this, in fact, void, by having squandered the whole of the wealth which was to have been shared by Juliet and myself. Torella, in consequence, chose to consider this bond as cancelled, and proposed another, in which, though the wealth he bestowed was immeasurably increased, there were so many restrictions as to the mode of spending it, that I, who saw independence only in free career being given to my own imperious will, taunted him as taking advantage of my situation, and refused utterly to subscribe to his conditions. The old man mildly strove to recall me to reason. Roused pride became the tyrant of my thought: I listened with indignation—I repelled him with disdain.

"Juliet, thou art mine! Did we not interchange vows in our innocent childhood? are we not one in the sight of God? and shall thy cold-hearted, cold-blooded father divide us? Be generous, my love, be just; take not away a gift, last treasure of thy Guido—retract not thy vows—let us defy the world, and setting at nought the calculations of age, find in our mutual affection a refuge from every ill."

Fiend I must have been, with such sophistry to endeavour to poison that sanctuary of holy thought and tender love. Juliet shrank from me affrighted. Her father was the best and kindest of men, and she strove to show me how, in obeying him, every good would follow. He would receive my tardy submission with warm affection; and generous pardon would follow my repentance. Profitless words for a young and gentle daughter to use to a man accustomed to make his will, law; and to feel in his own heart a despot so terrible and stern, that he could yield obedience to nought save his own imperious desires! My resentment grew with resistance; my wild companions were ready to add fuel to the flame. We laid a plan to carry off Juliet. At first it appeared to be crowned with success. Midway, on our return, we were overtaken by the agonized father and his attendants. A conflict ensued. Before the city guard came to decide the victory in favour of our antagonists, two of Torella's servitors were dangerously wounded.

This portion of my history weighs most heavily with me. Changed man as I am, I abhor myself in the recollection. May none who hear this tale ever have felt as I. A horse driven to fury by a rider armed with barbed spurs, was not more a slave than I, to the violent tyranny of my temper. A fiend possessed my soul, irritating it to madness. I felt the voice of conscience within me; but if I yielded to it for a brief interval, it was only to be a moment after torn, as by a whirlwind, away—borne along on the stream of desperate rage—the plaything of the storms engendered by pride. I was imprisoned, and, at the instance of Torella, set free. Again I returned to carry off both him and his child to France; which hapless country, then preyed on by freebooters and gangs of lawless soldiery, offered a grateful refuge to a criminal like me. Our plots were discovered. I was sentenced to banishment; and, as my debts were already enormous, my remaining property was put in the hands of commissioners for their payment. Torella again offered his mediation, requiring only my promise not to renew my abortive attempts on himself and his daughter. I spurned his offers, and fancied that I triumphed when I was thrust out from

Genoa, a solitary and penniless exile. My companions were gone: they had been dismissed the city some weeks before, and were already in France. I was alone—friendless; with nor sword at my side, nor ducat in my purse.

I wandered along the sea-shore, a whirlwind of passion possessing and tearing my soul. It was as if a live coal had been set burning in my breast. At first I meditated on what *I should do*. I would join a band of freebooters. Revenge!—the word seemed balm to me:—I hugged it—caressed it—till, like a serpent, it stung me. Then again I would abjure and despise Genoa, that little corner of the world. I would return to Paris, where so many of my friends swarmed; where my services would be eagerly accepted; where I would carve out fortune with my sword, and might, through success, make my paltry birth-place, and the false Torella, rue the day when they drove me, a new Coriolanus, from her walls. I would return to Paris—thus, on foot—a beggar—and present myself in my poverty to those I had formerly entertained sumptuously? There was gall in the mere thought of it.

The reality of things began to dawn upon my mind, bringing despair in its train. For several months I had been a prisoner: the evils of my dungeon had whipped my soul to madness, but they had subdued my corporeal frame. I was weak and wan. Torella had used a thousand artifices to administer to my comfort; I had detected and scorned them all—and I reaped the harvest of my obduracy. What was to be done?—Should I crouch before my foe, and sue for forgiveness?—Die rather ten thousand deaths!—Never should they obtain that victory! Hate—I swore eternal hate! Hate from whom?—to whom?— From a wandering outcast—to a mighty noble. I and my feelings were nothing to them: already had they forgotten one so unworthy. And Juliet!—her angel-face and sylph-like form gleamed among the clouds of my despair with vain beauty: for I had lost her—the glory and flower of the world! Another will call her his!—that smile of paradise will bless another!

Even now my heart fails within me when I recur to this rout of grim-visaged ideas. Now subdued almost to tears, now raving in my agony, still I wandered along the rocky shore, which grew at each step wilder and more desolate. Hanging rocks and hoar precipices overlooked the tideless ocean; black caverns yawned; and for ever, among the seaworn recesses, murmured and dashed the unfruitful waters. Now my way was almost barred by an abrupt promontory, now rendered nearly impracticable by fragments fallen from the cliff. Evening was at hand, when, seaward, arose, as if on the waving of a wizard's wand, a murky web of clouds, blotting the late azure sky, and darkening and disturbing the till now placid deep. The clouds had strange fantastic shapes; and they changed, and mingled, and seemed to be driven about by a mighty spell. The waves raised their white crests; the thunder first muttered, then roared from across the waste of waters, which took a deep purple dye, flecked with foam. The spot where I stood, looked, on one side, to the wide-spread ocean; on the other, it was barred by a rugged promontory. Round this cape suddenly came, driven by the wind, a vessel. In vain the mariners tried to force a path for her to the open sea—the gale drove her on the rocks. It will perish!—all on board will perish!—Would I were among them! And to my young heart the idea of death came for the first time blended with that of joy. It was an awful sight to behold that vessel struggling with her fate. Hardly could I discern the sailors, but I heard them. It was soon all over!—A rock, just covered by the tossing waves, and so unperceived, lay in wait for its prey. A crash of thunder broke over my head at the moment that, with a frightful shock, the skiff dashed upon her unseen enemy. In a brief space of time she went to pieces. There I stood in safety; and there were my fellow-creatures, battling, how hopelessly, with annihilation. Methought I saw them struggling—too truly did I hear their shrieks, conquering the barking surges in their shrill agony. The dark breakers threw hither and thither the fragments of the wreck: soon it disappeared. I had been fascinated to gaze till the end: at last I sank on my knees—I covered my face with my hands: I again looked up; something was floating on the billows towards the shore. It neared and neared. Was that a human form?—It grew more distinct; and at last a mighty wave, lifting the whole freight, lodged it upon a rock. A human being bestriding a sea-chest!—A human being!—Yet was it one? Surely never such had existed before—a misshapen dwarf, with squinting eyes, distorted features, and body deformed, till it became a horror to behold. My blood, lately warming towards a fellow-being so snatched from a watery tomb, froze in my heart. The dwarf got off his chest; he tossed his straight, straggling hair from his odious visage:

"By St. Beelzebub!" he exclaimed, "I have been well bested." He looked round and saw me. "Oh, by the fiend! here is another ally of the mighty one. To what saint did you offer prayers, friend—if not to mine? Yet I remember you not on board."

I shrank from the monster and his blasphemy. Again he questioned me, and I muttered some inaudible reply. He continued:—

"Your voice is drowned by this dissonant roar. What a noise the big ocean makes! Schoolboys bursting from their prison are not louder than these waves set free to play. They disturb me. I will no more of their ill-timed brawling.— Silence, hoary One!—Winds, avaunt!—to your homes!—Clouds, fly to the antipodes, and leave our heaven clear!"

As he spoke, he stretched out his two long lank arms, that looked like spider's claws, and seemed to embrace with them the expanse before him. Was it a miracle? The clouds became broken, and fled; the azure sky first peeped out, and then was spread a calm field of blue above us; the stormy gale was exchanged to the softly breathing west; the sea grew calm; the waves dwindled to riplets.

"I like obedience even in these stupid elements," said the dwarf. "How much more in the tameless mind of man! It was a well got up storm, you must allow—and all of my own making."

It was tempting Providence to interchange talk with this magician. But *Power*, in all its shapes, is venerable to man. Awe, curiosity, a clinging fascination, drew me towards him.

"Come, don't be frightened, friend," said the wretch: "I am good-humoured when pleased; and something does please me in your well-proportioned body and handsome face, though you look a little woebegone. You have suffered a land—I, a sea wreck. Perhaps I can allay the tempest of your fortunes as I did my own. Shall we be friends?"—And he held out his hand; I could not touch it. "Well, then, companions—that will do as well. And now, while I rest after the buffeting I underwent just now, tell me why, young and gallant as you seem, you wander thus alone and downcast on this wild sea-shore."

The voice of the wretch was screeching and horrid, and his contortions as he spoke were frightful to behold. Yet he did gain a kind of influence over me, which I could not master, and I told him my tale. When it was ended, he laughed long and loud: the rocks echoed back the sound: hell seemed yelling around me.

Oh, thou cousin of Lucifer!" said he; "so thou too hast fallen through thy pride; and, though bright as the son of Morning, thou art ready to give up thy good looks, thy bride, and thy well-being, rather than submit thee to the tyranny of good. I honour thy choice, by my soul!—So thou hast fled, and yield the day: and mean to starve on these rocks, and to let the birds peck out thy dead eyes, while thy enemy and thy betrothed rejoice in thy ruin. Thy pride is strangely akin to humility, methinks."

As he spoke, a thousand fanged thoughts stung me to the heart.

"What would you that I should do?" I cried.

"I!—Oh, nothing, but lie down and say your prayers before you die. But, were I you, I know the deed that should be done."

I drew near him. His supernatural powers made him an oracle in my eyes; yet a strange unearthly thrill quivered through my frame as I said—"Speak!—teach me—what act do you advise?"

"Revenge thyself, man!—humble thy enemies!—set thy foot on the old man's neck, and possess thyself of his daughter!"

"To the east and west I turn," cried I, "and see no means! Had I gold, much could I achieve; but, poor and single, I am powerless."

The dwarf had been seated on his chest as he listened to my story. Now he got off; he touched a spring; it flew open!—What a mine of wealth—of blazing jewels, beaming gold, and pale silver—was displayed therein. A mad desire to possess this treasure was born within me.

"Doubtless," I said, "one so powerful as you could do all things."

"Nay," said the monster, humbly, "I am less omnipotent than I seem. Some things I possess which you may covet; but I would give them all for a small share, or even for a loan of what is yours."

"My possessions are at your service," I replied, bitterly—"my poverty, my exile, my disgrace—I make a free gift of them all."

"Good! I thank you. Add one other thing to your gift, and my treasure is yours."

"As nothing is my sole inheritance, what besides nothing would you have?

"Your comely face and well-made limbs."

I shivered. Would this all-powerful monster murder me? I had no dagger. I forgot to pray—but I grew pale.

"I ask for a loan, not a gift," said the frightful thing: "lend me your body for three days—you shall have mine to cage your soul the while, and, in payment, my chest. What say you to the bargain?—Three short days."

We are told that it is dangerous to hold unlawful talk; and well do I prove the same. Tamely written down, it may seem incredible that I should lend any ear to this proposition; but, in spite of his unnatural ugliness, there was something fascinating in a being whose voice could govern earth, air, and sea. I felt a keen desire to comply; for with that chest I could command the world. My only hesitation resulted from a fear that he would not be true to his bargain. Then, I thought, I shall soon die here on these lonely sands, and the limbs he covets will be mine no more:—it is worth the chance. And, besides, I knew that, by all the rules of art-magic, there were formula and oaths which none of its practisers dared break. I hesitated to reply; and he went on, now displaying his wealth, now speaking of the petty price he demanded, till it seemed madness to refuse. Thus is it: place our bark in the current of the stream, and down, over fall and cataract it is hurried; give up our conduct to the wild torrent of passion, and we are away, we know not whither.

He swore many an oath, and I adjured him by many a sacred name; till I saw this wonder of power, this ruler of the elements, shiver like an autumn leaf before my words; and as if the spirit spake unwillingly and per force within him, at last, he, with broken voice, revealed the spell whereby he might be obliged, did he wish to play me false, to render up the unlawful spoil. Our warm life-blood must mingle to make and to mar the charm.

Enough of this unholy theme. I was persuaded the thing was done. The morrow dawned upon me as I lay upon the shingles, and I knew not my own shadow as it fell from me. I felt myself changed to a shape of horror, and cursed my easy faith and blind credulity. The chest was there—there the gold and precious stones for which I had sold the frame of flesh which nature had given me. The sight a little stilled my emotions: three days would soon be gone.

They did pass. The dwarf had supplied me with a plenteous store of food. At first I could hardly walk, so strange and out of joint were all my limbs; and my voice—it was that of the fiend. But I kept silent, and turned my face to the sun, that I might not see my shadow, and counted the hours, and ruminated on my future conduct. To bring Torella to my feet—to possess my Juliet in spite of him—all this my wealth could easily achieve. During dark night I slept, and dreamt of the accomplishment of my desires. Two suns had set—the third dawned. I was agitated, fearful. Oh expectation, what a frightful thing art thou, when kindled more by fear than hope! How dost thou twist thyself round the heart, torturing its pulsations! How dost thou dart unknown pangs all through our feeble mechanism, now seeming to shiver us like broken glass, to nothingness—now giving us a fresh strength, which can do nothing, and so torments us by a sensation, such as the strong man must feel who cannot break his fetters, though they bend in his grasp. Slowly paced the bright, bright orb up the eastern sky; long it lingered in the zenith, and still more slowly wandered down the west: it touched the horizon's verge—it was lost! Its glories were on the summits of the cliff—they grew dun and gray. The evening star shone bright. He will soon be here.

He came not!—By the living heavens, he came not!—and night dragged out its weary length, and, in its decaying age, "day began to grizzle its dark hair;"* and the sun rose again on the most miserable wretch that ever upbraided its light. Three days thus I passed. The jewels and the gold—oh, how I abhorred them!

Well, well—I will not blacken these pages with demoniac ravings. All too terrible were the thoughts, the raging tumult of ideas that filled my soul. At the end of that time I slept; I had not before since the third sunset; and I dreamt that I was at Juliet's feet, and she smiled, and then she shrieked—for she saw my transformation—and again she smiled, for still her beautiful lover knelt before her. But it was not I—it was he, the fiend, arrayed in my limbs, speaking with my voice, winning her with my looks of love. I strove to warn her, but my tongue refused its office; I strove to tear him from her,

* Byron, *Werner* III. iv. 152-3 (Ed.).

but I was rooted to the ground—I awoke with the agony. There were the solitary hoar precipices—there the plashing sea, the quiet strand, and the blue sky over all. What did it mean? was my dream but a mirror of the truth? was he wooing and winning my betrothed? I would on the instant back to Genoa—but I was banished. I laughed—the dwarf's yell burst from my lips—*I* banished! O, no! they had not exiled the foul limbs I wore; I might with these enter, without fear of incurring the threatened penalty of death, my own, my native city.

I began to walk towards Genoa, I was somewhat accustomed to my distorted limbs; none were ever so ill adapted for a straight-forward movement; it was with infinite difficulty that I proceeded. Then, too, I desired to avoid all the hamlets strewed here and there on the sea-beach, for I was unwilling to make a display of my hideousness. I was not quite sure that, if seen, the mere boys would not stone me to death as I passed, for a monster: some ungentle salutations I did receive from the few peasants or fishermen I chanced to meet. But it was dark night before I approached Genoa. The weather was so balmy and sweet that it struck me that the Marchese and his daughter would very probably have quitted the city for their country retreat. It was from Villa Torella that I had attempted to carry off Juliet; I had spent many an hour reconnoitring the spot, and knew each inch of ground in its vicinity. It was beautifully situated, embosomed in trees, on the margin of a stream. As I drew near, it became evident that my conjecture was right; nay, moreover, that the hours were being then devoted to feasting and merriment. For the house was lighted up; strains of soft and gay music were wafted towards me by the breeze. My heart sank within me. Such was the generous kindness of Torella's heart that I felt sure that he would not have indulged in public manifestations of rejoicing just after my unfortunate banishment, but for a cause I dared not dwell upon.

The country people were all alive and flocking about; it became necessary that I should study to conceal myself; and yet I longed to address some one, or to hear others discourse, or in any way to gain intelligence of what was really going on. At length, entering the walks that were in immediate vicinity to the mansion, I found one dark enough to veil my excessive frightfulness; and yet others as well as I were loitering in its shade. I soon gathered all I wanted to know—all that first made my very heart die with horror, and then boil with indignation. To-morrow Juliet was to be given to the penitent, reformed, beloved Guido—to-morrow my bride was to pledge her vows to a fiend from hell! And I did this!—my accursed pride—my demoniac violence and wicked self-idolatry had caused this act. For if I had acted as the wretch who had stolen my form had acted—if, with a mien at once yielding and dignified, I had presented myself to Torella, saying, I have done wrong, forgive me: I am unworthy of your angel-child, hut permit me to claim her hereafter, when my altered conduct shall manifest that I abjure my vices, and endeavour to become in some sort worthy of her. I go to serve against the infidels; and when my zeal for religion and my true penitence for the past shall appear to you to cancel my crimes, permit me again to call myself your son. Thus had he spoken; and the penitent was welcomed even as the prodigal son of scripture: the fatted calf was killed for him; and he, still pursuing the same path, displayed such open-hearted regret for his follies, so humble a concession of all his rights, and so ardent a resolve to reacquire them by a life of contrition and virtue, that he quickly conquered the kind, old man; and full pardon, and the gift of his lovely child, followed in swift succession.

O! had an angel from Paradise whispered to me to act thus! But now, what would be the innocent Juliet's fate) Would Cod permit the foul union—or, some prodigy destroying it, link the dishonoured name of Carega with the worst of crimes? To-morrow at dawn they were to be married: there was but one way to prevent this—to meet mine enemy, and to enforce the ratification of our agreement. I felt that this could only be done by a mortal struggle. I had no sword—if indeed my distorted arms could wield a soldier's weapon—but I had a dagger, and in that lay my every hope. There was no time for pondering or balancing nicely the question: I might die in the attempt; but besides the burning jealousy and despair of my own heart, honour, mere humanity, demanded that I should fall rather than not destroy the machinations of the fiend.

The guests departed—the lights began to disappear; it was evident that the inhabitants of the villa were seeking repose. I hid myself among the trees—the garden grew desert—the gates were closed—I wandered round and came under a window—ah! well did I know the same!—a soft twilight glimmered in the room—the curtains were half withdrawn. It was the temple of innocence and beauty. Its magnificence was tempered, as it were, by the slight disarrangements occasioned by its being dwelt in, and all the objects scattered around displayed the taste of her who hallowed it by her presence. I saw her enter with a quick light step—I saw her approach the window—she drew back the curtain yet further, and looked out into the night. Its breezy freshness played among her ringlets, and wafted them from the transparent marble of her brow. She clasped her hands, she raised her eyes to Heaven. I heard her voice. Guido! she softly murmured, Mine own Guido! and then, as if overcome by the fulness of her own heart, she sank on her knees:—her upraised eyes—her negligent but graceful attitude—the beaming thankfulness that lighted up her face—oh, these are tame words! Heart of mine, thou imagest ever, though thou canst not pourtray, the celestial beauty of that child of light and love.

I heard a step—a quick firm step along the shady avenue. Soon I saw a cavalier, richly dressed, young and, methought, graceful to look on, advance.—I hid myself yet closer.—The youth approached; he paused beneath the window. She arose, and again looking out she saw him, and said—I cannot, no, at this distant time I cannot record her terms of soft silver tenderness; to me they were spoken, but they were replied to by him.

"I will not go," he cried: "here where you have been, where your memory glides like some Heaven-visiting ghost, I will pass the long hours till we meet, never, my Juliet, again, day or night, to part. But do thou, my love, retire; the cold morn and fitful breeze will make thy cheek pale, and fill with languor thy love-lighted eyes. Ah, sweetest! could I press one kiss upon them, I could, methinks, repose."

And then he approached still nearer, and methought he was about to clamber into her chamber. I had hesitated, not to terrify her; now I was no longer master of myself. I rushed forward—I threw myself on him—I tore him away—I cried, "O loathsome and foul-shaped wretch!"

I need not repeat epithets, all tending, as it appeared, to rail at a person I at present feel some partiality for. A shriek rose from Juliet's lips. I neither heard nor saw—I *felt* only mine enemy, whose throat I grasped, and my dagger's hilt; he struggled, but could not escape: at length hoarsely he breathed these words: "Do!—strike home! destroy this body—you will still live: may your life be long and merry!"

The descending dagger was arrested at the word, and he, feeling my hold relax, extricated himself and drew his sword, while the uproar in the house, and flying of torches from one room to the other, showed that soon we should be separated—and I—oh! far better die: so that he did not survive, I cared not. In the midst of my frenzy there was much calculation:—fall I might, and so that he did not survive, I cared not for the death-blow I might deal against myself. While still, therefore, he thought I paused, and while I saw the villanous resolve to take advantage of my hesitation, in the sudden thrust he made at me, I threw myself on his sword, and at the same moment plunged my dagger, with a true desperate aim, in his side. We fell together, rolling over each other, and the tide of blood that flowed from the gaping wound of each mingled on the grass. More I know not—I fainted.

Again I returned to life: weak almost to death, I found myself stretched upon a bed—Juliet was kneeling beside it. Strange! my first broken request was for a mirror. I was so wan and ghastly, that my poor girl hesitated, as she told me afterwards; but, by the mass! I thought myself a right proper youth when I saw the dear reflection of my own well-known features. I confess it is a weakness, but I avow it, I do entertain a considerable affection for the countenance and limbs I behold, whenever I look at a glass; and have more mirrors in my house, and consult them oftener than any beauty in Venice. Before you too much condemn me, permit me to say that no one better knows than I the value of his own body; no one, probably, except myself, ever having had it stolen from him.

Incoherently I at first talked of the dwarf and his crimes, and reproached Juliet for her too easy admission of his love. She thought me raving, as well she might, and yet it was some time before I could prevail on myself to admit that the Guido whose penitence had won her back for me was myself; and while I cursed bitterly the monstrous dwarf, and blest the well-directed blow that had deprived him of life, I suddenly checked myself when I heard her say— Amen! knowing that him whom she reviled was my very self. A little reflection taught me silence—a little practice enabled me to speak of that frightful night without any very excessive blunder. The wound I had given myself was no mockery of one—it was long before I recovered—and as the benevolent and generous Torella sat beside me, talking such wisdom as might win friends to repentance, and mine own dear Juliet hovered near me, administering to my wants, and cheering me by her smiles, the work of my bodily cure and mental reform went on together. I have never, indeed, wholly recovered my strength—my cheek is paler since—my person a little bent. Juliet sometimes ventures to allude bitterly to the malice that caused this change, but I kiss her on the moment, and tell her all is for the best. I am a fonder and more faithful husband—and true is this—but for that wound, never had I called her mine.

I did not revisit the sea-shore, nor seek for the fiend's treasure; yet, while I ponder on the past, I often think, and my confessor was not backward in favouring the idea, that it might be a good rather than an evil spirit, sent by my guardian angel, to show me the folly and misery of pride. So well at least did I learn this lesson, roughly taught as I was, that I am known now by all my friends and fellow-citizens by the name of Guido il Cortese.

CURIOUS IF TRUE

Elizabeth Gaskell

(Extract from a Letter from Richard Whittingham, Esq.)

YOU WERE FORMERLY so much amused at my pride in my descent from that sister of Calvin's who married a Whittingham, Dean of Durham, that I doubt if you will be able to enter into the regard for my distinguished relation that has led me to France, in order to examine registers and archives, which I thought might enable me to discover collateral descendants of the great Reformer, with whom I might call cousins. I shall not tell you of my troubles and adventures in this research; you are not worthy to hear of them; but something so curious befell me one evening last August, that if I had not been perfectly certain I was wide awake, I might have taken it for a dream.

For the purpose I have named, it was necessary that I should make Tours my headquarters for a time. I had traced descendants of the Calvin family out of Normandy into the centre of France; but I found it was necessary to have a kind of permission from the bishop of the diocese before I could see certain family papers, which had fallen into the possession of the Church; and, as I had several English friends at Tours, I awaited the answer to my request to Monseigneur de——, at that town. I was ready to accept any invitation; but I received very few, and was sometimes a little at a loss what to do with my evenings. The *table d'hôte* was at five o'clock; I did not wish to go to the expense of a private sitting-room, disliked the dinnery atmosphere of the *salle à manger*, could not play either at pool or billiards, and the aspect of my fellow guests was unprepossessing enough to make me unwilling to enter into any *tête-à-tête* gamblings with them. So I usually rose from table early, and tried to make the most of the remaining light of the August evenings in walking briskly off to explore the surrounding country; the middle of the day was too hot for this purpose, and better employed in lounging on a bench in the boulevards, lazily listening to the distant band, and noticing with equal laziness the faces and figures of the women who passed by.

One Thursday evening—the 18th of August it was, I think—I had gone further than usual in my walk, and I found that it was later than I had imagined when I paused to turn back. I fancied I could make a round; I had enough notion of the direction in which I was, to see that by turning up a narrow straight lane to my left I should shorten my way back to Tours. And so I believe I should have done, could I have found an outlet at the right place, but field-paths are almost unknown in that part of France, and my lane, stiff and straight as any street, and marked into terribly vanishing perspective by the regular row of poplars on each side, seemed interminable. Of course night came on, and I was in darkness. In England I might have had a chance of seeing a light in some cottage only a field or two off, and asking my way from the inhabitants; but here I could see no such welcome sight; indeed, I believe French peasants go to bed with the summer daylight, so if there were any habitations in the neighbourhood I never saw them. At last—I believe I must have walked two hours in the darkness—I saw the dusky outline of a wood on one side of the weariful lane, and impatiently careless of all forest laws and penalties for trespassers, I made my way to it, thinking that, if the worst came to the worst, I could find some covert—some shelter where I could lie down and rest, until the morning light gave me a chance of finding my way back to Tours. But the plantation, on the outskirts of what appeared to me a dense wood, was of young trees, too closely planted to be more than slender stems growing up to a good height, with scanty foliage on their summits. On I went towards the thicker forest, and once there I slackened my pace, and began to look about me for a good lair. I was as dainty as Lochiel's grandchild, who made his grandsire indignant at the luxury of his pillow of snow: this brake was too full of brambles, that felt damp with dew; there was no hurry, since I had given up all hope of passing the night between four walls; and I went leisurely groping about, and trusting that there were no wolves to be poked up out of their summer drowsiness by my stick, when all at once I saw a château before me, not a quarter of a mile off, at the end of what seemed to be an ancient avenue (now overgrown and irregular), which I happened to be crossing, when I looked to my right, and saw the welcome sight. Large, stately, and dark was its outline against the dusky night-sky; there were pepperboxes and tourelles and what-not fantastically growing up into the dim starlight. And, more to the purpose still, though I could not see the details of the building that I was now facing, it was plain enough that there were lights in many windows, as if some great entertainment was going on.

"They are hospitable people, at any rate," thought I. "Perhaps they will give me a bed. I don't suppose French *propriétaires* have traps and horses quite as plentiful as English gentlemen; but they are evidently having a large party, and some of their guests may be from Tours, and will give me a cast back to the Lion d'Or. I am not proud, and I am dog-tired. I am not above hanging on behind, if need be."

So, putting a little briskness and spirit into my walk, I went up to the door, which was standing open, most hospitably, and showing a large lighted hall, all hung round with spoils of the chase, armour, etc., the details of which I had not time to notice, for the instant I stood on the threshold a huge porter appeared, in a strange, old-fashioned dress—a kind of livery which well befitted the general appearance of the house. He asked me, in French (so curiously pronounced that I thought I had hit upon a new kind of *patois*), my name, and whence I came. I thought he would not be much the wiser, still it was but civil to give it before I made my request for assistance; so, in reply, I said:

"My name is Whittingham—Richard Whittingham, an English gentleman, staying at——" To my infinite surprise, a light of pleased intelligence came over the giant's face; he made me a low bow, and said (still in the same curious dialect) that I was welcome, that I was long expected.

"Long expected!" What could the fellow mean? Had I stumbled on a nest of relations by John Calvin's side, who had heard of my genealogical inquiries, and were gratified and interested by them? But I was too much pleased to be under shelter for the night to think it necessary to account for my agreeable reception before I enjoyed it. Just as he was opening the great heavy *battants* of the door that led from the hall to the interior, he turned round and said:

"Apparently Monsieur le Géanquilleur is not come with you?"

"No! I am all alone. I have lost my way"—and I was going on with my explanation, when he, as if quite indifferent to it, led the way up a great stone staircase, as wide as many rooms, and having on each landing-place massive iron wickets in a heavy framework; these the porter unlocked with the solemn slowness of age. Indeed, a strange, mysterious awe of the centuries that had passed away since this château was built, came over me as I waited for the turning of the ponderous keys in the ancient locks. I could almost have fancied that I heard a mighty rushing murmur (like the ceaseless sound of a distant sea, ebbing and flowing for ever and for ever), coming forth from the great vacant galleries that opened out on each side of the broad staircase, and were to be dimly perceived in the darkness above us. It was as if the voices of generations of men yet echoed and eddied in the silent air. It was strange, too, that my friend the porter going before me, ponderously infirm, with his feeble old hands striving in vain to keep the tall flambeau he held steadily before him—strange, I say, that he was the only domestic I saw in the vast halls and passages, or met with on the great staircase. At length we stood before the gilded doors that led into the saloon where the family—or it might be the company, so great was the buzz of voices—was assembled. I would have remonstrated when I found he was going to introduce me, dusty and travel-smeared, in a morning costume that was not even my best, into this grand *salon*, with nobody knew how many ladies and gentlemen assembled; but the obstinate old man was evidently bent upon taking me straight to his master, and paid no heed to my words.

The doors flew open, and I was ushered into a saloon curiously full of pale light, which did not culminate on any spot, nor proceed from any centre, nor flicker with any motion of the air, but filled every nook and corner, making all things deliciously distinct; different from our light of gas or candle, as is the difference between a clear southern atmosphere and that of our misty England.

At the first moment, my arrival excited no attention, the apartment was so full of people, all intent on their own conversation. But my friend the porter went up to a handsome lady of middle age, richly attired in that antique manner which fashion has brought round again of late years, and, waiting first in an attitude of deep respect till her attention fell upon him, told her my name and something about me, as far as I could guess from the gestures of the one and the sudden glance of the eye of the other.

She immediately came towards me with the most friendly actions of greeting, even before she had advanced near enough to speak. Then—and was it not strange?—her words and accent were those of the commonest peasant of the country. Yet she herself looked high-bred, and would have been dignified had she been a shade less restless, had her countenance worn a little less lively and inquisitive expression. I had been poking a good deal about the old parts of Tours, and had had to understand the dialect of the people who dwelt in the Marché au Vendredi and similar places, or I really should not have understood my handsome hostess as she offered to present me to her husband, a henpecked, gentlemanly man, who was more quaintly attired than she in the very extreme of that style of dress. I thought to myself that in France, as in England, it is the provincials who carry fashion to such an excess as to become ridiculous.

However, he spoke (still in the *patois*) of his pleasure in making my acquaintance, and led me to a strange uneasy easy-chair, much of a piece with the rest of the furniture, which might have taken its place without any anachronism by the side of that in the Hôtel Cluny. Then again began the clatter of French voices, which my arrival had for an instant interrupted, and I had leisure to look about me. Opposite to me sat a very sweet-looking lady, who must have been a great beauty in her youth, I should think, and would be charming in old age, from the sweetness of her countenance. She was, however, extremely fat, and, on seeing her feet laid up before her on a cushion, I at once perceived that they were so swollen as to render her incapable of walking, which probably brought on her excessive *embonpoint*. Her hands were plump and small, but rather coarse-grained in texture, not quite so clean as they might have been, and altogether not so aristocratic-looking as the charming face. Her dress was of superb black velvet, ermine-trimmed, with diamonds thrown all abroad over it.

Not far from her stood the least little man I had ever seen, of such admirable proportions no one could call him a dwarf, because with that word we usually associate something of a deformity; but yet with an elfin look of shrewd, hard, worldly wisdom in his face that marred the impression which his delicate regular little features would otherwise have conveyed. Indeed, I do not think he was quite of equal rank with the rest of the company, for his dress was inappropriate to the occasion (and he apparently was an invited, while I was an involuntary guest); and one or two of his gestures and actions were more like the tricks of an uneducated rustic than anything else. To explain what I mean: his boots had evidently seen much service, and had been re-topped, re-heeled, re-soled to the extent of cobbler's powers. Why should he have come in them if they were not his best—his only pair? And what can be more ungenteel than poverty! Then, again, he had an uneasy trick of putting his hand up to his throat, as if he expected to find something the matter with it; and he had the awkward habit—which I do not think he could have copied from Dr Johnson, because most probably he had never heard of him— of trying always to retrace his steps on the exact boards on which he had trodden to arrive at any particular part of the room. Besides, to settle the question, I once heard him addressed as Monsieur Poucet, without any aristocratic "de" for a prefix; and nearly everyone else in the room was a marquis, at any rate.

I say "nearly everyone", for some strange people had the entrée; unless, indeed, they were, like me, benighted. One of the guests I should have taken for a servant, but for the extraordinary influence he seemed to have over the man I took for his master, and who never did anything without, apparently, being urged thereto by this follower. The master, magnificently dressed, but ill at ease in his clothes, as if they had been made for someone else, was a weak-looking, handsome man, continually sauntering about, and, I almost guessed, an object of suspicion to some of the gentlemen present, which, perhaps, drove him on the companionship of his follower, who was dressed something in the style of an ambassador's chasseur; yet it was not a chasseur's dress after all; it was something more thoroughly old-world; boots halfway up his ridiculously small legs, which clattered as he walked along, as if they were too large for his little feet; and a great quantity of grey fur, as trimming to coat, court-mantle, boots, cap—everything. You know the way in which certain countenances remind you perpetually of some animal, be it bird or beast! Well, this chasseur (as I will call him, for want of a better name) was exceedingly like the great Tom-cat that you have seen so often in my chambers, and laughed at almost as often for his uncanny gravity of demeanour. Grey whiskers has my Tom—grey whiskers had the chasseur; grey hair overshadows the upper lip of my Tom—grey mustachios hid that of the chasseur. The pupils of Tom's eyes dilate and contract as I had thought cats' pupils only could do, until I saw those of the chasseur. To be sure, canny as Tom is, the chasseur had the advantage in the more intelligent expression. He seemed to have obtained most complete sway over his master or patron, whose looks he watched, and whose steps he followed, with a kind of distrustful interest that puzzled me greatly.

There were several other groups in the more distant part of the saloon, all of the stately old school, all grand and noble, I conjectured from their bearing. They seemed perfectly well acquainted with each other, as if they were in the habit of meeting. But I was interrupted in my observations by the tiny little gentleman on the opposite side of the room coming across to take a place beside me. It is no difficult matter to a Frenchman to slide into conversation; and so gracefully did my pigmy friend keep up the character of the nation, that we were almost confidential before ten minutes had elapsed.

Now I was quite aware that the welcome which all had extended to me, from the porter up to the vivacious lady and meek lord of the castle, was intended for some other person. But it required either a degree of moral courage, of which I cannot boast, or the self-reliance and conversational powers of a bolder and cleverer man than I, to undeceive people who had fallen into so fortunate a mistake for me. Yet the little man by my side insinuated himself so much into my confidence that I had half a mind to tell him of my exact situation, and to turn him into a friend and an ally.

"Madame is perceptibly growing older," said he, in the midst of my perplexity, glancing at our hostess.

"Madame is still a very fine woman," replied I.

"Now, is it not strange," continued he, lowering his voice, "how women almost invariably praise the absent, or departed, as if they were angels of light? while as for the present, or the living"—here he shrugged up his little shoulders and made an expressive pause. "Would you believe it! Madame is always praising her late husband to monsieur's face; till, in fact, we guests are quite perplexed how to look: for, you know, the late M. de Retz's character was quite notorious—everybody has heard of him." All the world of Touraine, thought I, but I made an assenting noise.

At this instant, monsieur our host came up to me, and with a civil look of tender interest (such as some people put on when they inquire after your mother, about whom they do not care one straw), asked if I had heard lately how my cat was? "How my cat was!" What could the man mean? My cat! Could he mean the tail-less Tom, born in the Isle of Man, and now supposed to be keeping guard against the incursions of rats and mice into my chambers in London? Tom is, as you know, on pretty good terms with some of my friends, using their legs for rubbing posts without scruple, and highly esteemed by them for his gravity of demeanour, and wise manner of winking his eyes. But could his fame have reached across the Channel? However, an answer must be returned to the inquiry, as Monsieur's face was bent down to mine with a look of polite anxiety; so I, in my turn, assumed an expression of gratitude, and assured him that, to the best of my belief, my cat was in remarkably good health.

"And the climate agrees with her?"

"Perfectly," said I, in a maze of wonder at this deep solicitude in a tail-less cat who had lost one foot and half an ear in some cruel trap. My host smiled a sweet smile, and, addressing a few words to my neighbour, passed on.

"How wearisome those aristocrats are!" quoth my neighbour, with a slight sneer. "Monsieur's conversation rarely extends to more than two sentences to anyone. By that time his faculties are exhausted, and he needs the refreshment of silence. You and I, monsieur, are, at any rate, indebted to our own wits for our rise in the world!"

Here again I was bewildered! As you know, I am rather proud of my descent from families which, if not noble themselves, are allied to nobility— and as to my "rise in the world"—if I had risen, it would have been rather for balloon-like qualities than for mother-wit, to being unencumbered with heavy ballast either in my head or my pockets. However, it was my cue to agree: so I smiled again.

"For my part," said he, "if a man does not stick at trifles, if he knows how to judiciously add to, or withhold facts, and is not sentimental in his parade of humanity, he is sure to do well; sure to affix a *de* or *von* to his name, and end his days in comfort. There is an example of what I am saying"—and he glanced furtively at the weak-looking master of the sharp, intelligent servant, whom I have called the chasseur.

"Monsieur le Marquis would never have been anything but a miller's son, if it had not been for the talents of his servant. Of course you know his antecedents?"

I was going to make some remarks on the changes in the order of the peerage since the days of Louis XVI—going, in fact, to be very sensible and historical—when there was a slight commotion among the people at the other end of the room. Lacqueys in quaint liveries must have come in from behind the tapestry, I suppose (for I never saw them enter, though I sat right opposite to the doors), and were handing about the slight beverages and slighter viands which are considered sufficient refreshments, but which looked rather meagre to my hungry appetite. These footmen were standing solemnly opposite to a lady—beautiful, splendid, as the dawn, but—sound asleep in a magnificent settee. A gentleman, who showed so much irritation at her ill-timed slumbers, that I think he must have been her husband, was trying to awaken her with actions not far removed from shakings. All in vain; she was quite unconscious of his annoyance, or the smiles of the company, or the automatic solemnity of the waiting footman, or the perplexed anxiety of monsieur and madame.

My little friend sat down with a sneer, as if his curiosity was quenched in contempt.

"Moralists would make an infinity of wise remarks on that scene," said he. "In the first place, note the ridiculous position into which their superstitious reverence for rank and title puts all these people. Because monsieur is a reigning prince over some minute principality, the exact situation of which no one has as yet discovered, no one must venture to take their glass of *eau sucré* till Madame la Princesse awakens; and, judging from past experience, those poor lacqueys may have to stand for a century before that happens. Next— always speaking as a moralist, you will observe—note how difficult it is to break off bad habits acquired in youth!"

Just then the prince succeeded, by what means I did not see, in awaking the beautiful sleeper. But at first she did not remember where she was, and looking up at her husband with loving eyes, she smiled, and said:

"Is it you, my prince?"

But he was too conscious of the suppressed amusement of the spectators and his own consequent annoyance, to be reciprocally tender, and turned away with some little French expression, best rendered into English by "Pooh, pooh, my dear!"

After I had had a glass of delicious wine of some unknown quality, my courage was in rather better plight than before, and I told my cynical little neighbour—whom I must say I was beginning to dislike—that I had lost my way in the wood, and had arrived at the château quite by mistake.

He seemed mightily amused at my story; said that the same thing had happened to himself more than once; and told me that I had better luck than he had on one of these occasions, when, from his account, he must have been in considerable danger of his life. He ended his story by making me admire his boots, which he said he still wore, patched though they were, and all their excellent quality lost by patching, because they were of such a first-rate make for long pedestrian excursions. "Though, indeed," he wound up by saying, "the new fashion of railroads would seem to supersede the necessity for this description of boots."

When I consulted him as to whether I ought to make myself known to my host and hostess as a benighted traveller, instead of the guest whom they had taken me for, he exclaimed, "By no means! I hate such squeamish morality." And he seemed much offended by my innocent question, as if it seemed by implication to condemn something in himself. He was offended and silent; and just at this moment I caught the sweet, attractive eyes of the lady opposite—that lady whom I named at first as being no longer in the bloom of youth, but as being somewhat infirm about the feet, which were supported on a raised cushion before her. Her looks seemed to say, "Come here, and let us have some conversation together"; and, with a bow of silent excuse to my little companion, I went across to the lame old lady. She acknowledged my coming with the prettiest gesture of thanks possible; and, half-apologetically, said: "It is a little dull to be unable to move about on such evenings as this; but it is a just punishment to me for my early vanities. My poor feet, that were by nature so small, are now taking their revenge for my cruelty in forcing them into such little slippers.... Besides, monsieur," with a pleasant smile, "I thought it was possible you might be weary of the malicious sayings of your little neighbour. He has not borne the best character in his youth, and such men are sure to be cynical in their old age."

"Who is he?" asked I, with English abruptness.

"His name is Poucet, and his father was, I believe, a woodcutter, or charcoal-burner, or something of the sort. They do tell bad stories of connivance at murder, ingratitude, and obtaining money on false pretences—but you will think me as bad as he if I go on with my slanders. Rather let us admire the lovely lady coming up towards us, with the roses in her hand—I never see her without roses, they are so closely connected with her past history, as you are doubtless aware. Ah, beauty!" said my companion to the lady drawing near to us, "it is like you to come to me, now that I can no longer go to you." Then, turning to me, and gracefully drawing me into the conversation, she said, "You must know that, although we never met until we were both married, we have been almost like sisters ever since. There have been so many points of resemblance in our circumstances, and I think I may say in our characters. We had each two elder sisters—mine were but half-sisters, though—who were not so kind to us as they might have been."

"But have been sorry for it since," put in the other lady.

"Since we have married princes," continued the same lady, with an arch smile that had nothing of unkindness in it, "for we both have married far above our original station in life; we are both unpunctual in our habits, and, in consequence of this failing of ours, we have both had to suffer mortification and pain."

"And both are charming," said a whisper close behind me. "My lord the marquis, say it—say, 'And both are charming'."

"And both are charming," was spoken aloud by another voice. I turned, and saw the wily cat-like chasseur, prompting his master to make civil speeches.

The ladies bowed with that kind of haughty acknowledgement which shows that compliments from such a source are distasteful. But our trio of conversation was broken up, and I was sorry for it. The marquis looked as if he had been stirred up to make that one speech, and hoped that he would not be expected to say more; while behind him stood the chasseur, half-impertinent and half-servile in his ways and attitudes. The ladies, who were real ladies, seemed to be sorry for the awkwardness of the marquis, and addressed some trifling questions to him, adapting themselves to the subjects on which he could have no trouble in answering. The chasseur, meanwhile, was talking to himself in a growling tone of voice. I had fallen a little into the background at this interruption in a conversation which promised to be so pleasant, and I could not help hearing his words.

"Really, De Carabas grows more stupid every day. I have a great mind to throw off his boots, and leave him to his fate. I was intended for a court, and to a court I will go, and make my own fortune as I have made his. The emperor will appreciate my talents."

And such are the habits of the French, or such his forgetfulness of good manners in his anger, that he spat right and left on the parquetted floor.

Just then a very ugly, very pleasant-looking man, came towards the two ladies to whom I had lately been speaking, leading up to them a delicate, fair woman, dressed all in the softest white, as if she were *vouée au blanc*. I do not think there was a bit of colour about her. I thought I had heard her making, as she came along, a little noise of pleasure, not exactly like the singing of a tea-kettle, nor yet like the cooing of a dove, but reminding me of each sound.

"Madame de Mioumiou was anxious to see you," said he, addressing the lady with the roses, "so I have brought her across to give you a pleasure!" What an honest, good face! but oh! how ugly! And yet I liked his ugliness better than most persons' beauty. There was a look of pathetic acknowledgement of his ugliness, and a deprecation of your too hasty judgement, in his countenance, that was positively winning. The soft, white lady kept glancing at my neighbour the chasseur, as if they had had some former acquaintance, which puzzled me very much, as they were of such different rank. However, their nerves were evidently strung to the same tune, for at a sound behind the tapestry, which was more like the scuttering of rats and mice than anything else, both Madame de Mioumiou and the chasseur started with the most eager looks of anxiety on their countenances, and by their restless movements— madame's panting, and the fiery dilation of his eyes—one might see that commonplace sounds affected them both in a manner very different to the rest of the company. The ugly husband of the lovely lady with the roses now addressed himself to me.

"We are much disappointed," he said, "in finding that monsieur is not accompanied by his countryman—le grand Jean d'Angleterre; I cannot pronounce his name rightly"—and he looked at me to help him out.

"Le grand Jean d'Angleterre!" now who was le grand Jean d'Angleterre? John Bull? John Russell? John Bright?

"Jean—Jean"—continued the gentleman, seeing my embarrassment. "Ah, these terrible English names—'Jean de Géanquilleur'!"

I was as wise as ever. And yet the name struck me as familiar, but slightly disguised. I repeated it to myself. It was mighty like John the Giant-killer, only his friends always call that worthy "Jack". I said the name aloud.

"Ah, that is it!" said he. "But why has he not accompanied you to our little reunion tonight?"

I had been rather puzzled once or twice before, but this serious question added considerably to my perplexity. Jack the Giant-killer had once, it is true, been rather an intimate friend of mine, as far as (printer's) ink and paper can keep up a friendship, but I had not heard his name mentioned for years; and for aught I knew he lay enchanted with King Arthur's knights, who lie entranced until the blast of the trumpets of four mighty kings shall call them to help at England's need. But the question had been asked in serious earnest by that gentleman, whom I more wished to think well of me than I did any other person in the room. So I answered respectfully that it was long since I had heard anything of my countryman; but that I was sure it would have given him as much pleasure as it was doing myself to have been present at such an agreeable gathering of friends. He bowed, and then the lame lady took up the word.

"Tonight is the night when, of all the year, this great old forest surrounding the castle is said to be haunted by the phantom of a little peasant girl who once lived hereabouts; the tradition is that she was devoured by a wolf. In former days I have seen her on this night out of yonder window at the end of the gallery. Will you, ma belle, take monsieur to see the view outside by the moonlight (you may possibly see the phantom-child); and leave me to a little *tête-à-tête* with your husband?"

With a gentle movement the lady with the roses complied with the other's request, and we went to a great window, looking down on the forest, in which I had lost my way. The tops of the far-spreading and leafy trees lay motionless beneath us in that pale, wan light, which shows objects almost as distinct in form, though not in colour, as by day. We looked down on the countless avenues which seemed to converge from all quarters to the great old castle; and suddenly across one, quite near to us, there passed the figure of a little girl with the "capuchon" on, that takes the place of a peasant girl's bonnet in France. She had a basket on one arm, and by her, on the side to which her head was turned, there went a wolf. I could almost have said it was licking her hand, as if in penitent love, if either penitence or love had ever been a quality of wolves, but though not of living, perhaps it may be of phantom wolves.

"There, we have seen her!" exclaimed my beautiful companion. "Though so long dead, her simple story of household goodness and trustful simplicity still lingers in the hearts of all who have ever heard of her, and the country people about here say that seeing that phantom child on this anniversary brings good luck for the year. Let us hope that we shall share in the traditionary good fortune. Ah! here is Madame de Retz—she retains the name of her first husband, you know, as he was of higher rank than the present." We were joined by our hostess.

"If monsieur is fond of the beauties of nature and art," said she, perceiving that I had been looking at the view from the great window, "he will perhaps take pleasure in seeing the picture." Here she sighed, with a little affectation of grief. "You know the picture I allude to," addressing my companion, who bowed assent and smiled a little maliciously, as I followed the lead of madame.

I went after her to the other end of the saloon, noting by the way with what keen curiosity she caught up what was passing either in word or action on each side of her. When we stood opposite to the end wall, I perceived a full-length picture of a handsome peculiar-looking man, with—in spite of his good looks—a very fierce and scowling expression. My hostess clasped her hands together as her arms hung down in front, and sighed once more. Then, half in soliloquy, she said:

"He was the love of my youth; his stern yet manly character first touched this heart of mine. When—when shall I cease to deplore his loss?"

Not being acquainted with her enough to answer this question (if indeed it was not sufficiently answered by the fact of her second marriage), I felt awkward; and, by way of saying something, I remarked:

"The countenance strikes me as resembling something I have seen before—in an engraving from an historical picture, I think; only, it is there the principal figure in a group: he is holding a lady by her hair, and threatening her with his scimitar, while two cavaliers are rushing up the stairs, apparently only just in time to save her life."

"Alas, alas!" said she, "you too accurately describe a miserable passage in my life, which has often been represented in a false light. The best of husbands"—here she sobbed, and became slightly inarticulate with her grief—"will sometimes be displeased. I was young and curious, he was justly angry with my disobedience—my brothers were too hasty—the consequence is, I became a widow!"

After due respect for her tears, I ventured to suggest some commonplace consolation. She turned round sharply:

"No, monsieur; my only comfort is that I have never forgiven the brothers who interfered so cruelly, in such an uncalled-for manner, between my dear husband and myself. To quote my friend, Monsieur Sganarelle—'Ce sont petites choses qui sont de temps en temps nécessaires dans l'amitié, et cinq ou six coups d'épée entre gens qui s'aiment ne font que ragaillardir l'affection.' You observe the colouring is not quite what it should be?"

"In this light the beard is of rather a peculiar tint," said I.

"Yes; the painter did not do it justice. It was most lovely, and gave him such a distinguished air, quite different from the common herd. Stay, I will show you the exact colour, if you will come near this flambeau!" And going near the light, she took off a bracelet of hair, with a magnificent clasp of pearls. It was peculiar, certainly. I did not know what to say. "His precious lovely beard!" said she. "And the pearls go so well with the delicate blue!"

Her husband, who had come up to us, and waited till her eye fell upon him before venturing to speak, now said, "It is strange Monsieur Ogre is not yet arrived!"

"Not at all strange," said she, tartly. "He was always very stupid, and constantly falls into mistakes, in which he comes worse off; and it is very well he does, for he is a credulous and cowardly fellow. Not at all strange! If you will"—turning to her husband, so that I hardly heard her words, until I caught—"Then everybody would have their rights, and we should have no more trouble. Is it not, monsieur?" addressing me.

"If I were in England, I should imagine madame was speaking of the reform bill, or the millennium, but I am in ignorance."

And just as I spoke, the great folding-doors were thrown open wide, and everyone started to their feet to greet a little old lady, leaning on a thin black wand—and—

"Madame le Féemarraine," was announced by a chorus of sweet shrill voices.

And in a moment I was lying in the grass close by a hollow oak-tree, with the slanting glory of the dawning day shining full in my face, and thousands of little birds and delicate insects piping and warbling out their welcome to the ruddy splendour.

THE COLD EMBRACE

Mary Elizabeth Braddon

HE WAS AN artist—such things as happened to him happen sometimes to artists.

He was a German—such things as happened to him happen sometimes to Germans.

He was young, handsome, studious, enthusiastic, metaphysical, reckless, unbelieving, heartless.

And being young, handsome, and eloquent, he was beloved.

He was an orphan, under the guardianship of his dead father's brother, his uncle Wilhelm, in whose house he had been brought up from a little child; and she who loved him was his cousin—his cousin Gertrude, whom he swore he loved in return.

Did he love her? Yes, when he first swore it. It soon wore out, this passionate love; how threadbare and wretched a sentiment it became at last in the selfish heart of the student! But in its first golden dawn, when he was only nineteen, and had just returned from his apprenticeship to a great painter at Antwerp, and they wandered together in the most romantic outskirts of the city at rosy sunset, by holy moonlight, or bright and joyous morning, how beautiful a dream!

They keep it a secret from Wilhelm, as he has the father's ambition of a wealthy suitor for his only child—a cold and dreary vision beside the lover's dream.

So they are betrothed; and standing side by side when the dying sun and the pale rising moon divide the heavens, he puts the betrothal ring upon her finger, the white and taper finger whose slender shape he knows so well. This ring is a peculiar one, a massive golden serpent, its tail in its mouth, the symbol of eternity; it had been his mother's, and he would know it amongst a thousand. If he were to become blind tomorrow, he could select it from amongst a thousand by the touch alone.

He places it on her finger, and they swear to be true to each other for ever and ever—through trouble and danger—sorrow and change—in wealth or

29

poverty. Her father must needs be won to consent to their union by-and-by, for they were now betrothed, and death alone could part them.

But the young student, the scoffer at revelation, yet the enthusiastic adorer of the mystical asks:

'Can death part us? I would return to you from the grave, Gertrude. My soul would come back to be near my love. And you—you, if you died before me—the cold earth would not hold you from me; if you loved me, you would return, and again these fair arms would be clasped round my neck as they are now.'

But she told him, with a holier light in her deep-blue eyes than had ever shone in his—she told him that the dead who die at peace with God are happy in heaven, and cannot return to the troubled earth; and that it is only the suicide—the lost wretch on whom sorrowful angels shut the door of Paradise—whose unholy spirit haunts the footsteps of the living.

The first year of their betrothal is passed, and she is alone, for he has gone to Italy, on a commission for some rich man, to copy Raphaels, Titians, Guidos, in a gallery at Florence. He has gone to win fame, perhaps; but it is not the less bitter—he is gone!

Of course her father misses his young nephew, who has been as a son to him; and he thinks his daughter's sadness no more than a cousin should feel for a cousin's absence.

In the meantime, the weeks and months pass. The lover writes—often at first, then seldom—at last, not at all.

How many excuses she invents for him! How many times she goes to the distant little post-office, to which he is to address his letters! How many times she hopes, only to be disappointed! How many times she despairs, only to hope again!

But real despair comes at last, and will not be put off any more. The rich suitor appears on the scene, and her father is determined. She is to marry at once. The wedding-day is fixed—the fifteenth of June.

The date seems burnt into her brain.

The date, written in fire, dances for ever before her eyes.

The date, shrieked by the Furies, sounds continually in her ears.

But there is time yet—it is the middle of May—there is time for a letter to reach him at Florence; there is time for him to come to Brunswick, to take her away and marry her, in spite of her father—in spite of the whole world.

But the days and weeks fly by, and he does not write—he does not come. This is indeed despair which usurps her heart, and will not be put away.

It is the fourteenth of June. For the last time she goes to the little post-office; for the last time she asks the old question, and they give her for the last time the dreary answer, 'No, no letter.'

For the last time—for tomorrow is the day appointed for her bridal. Her father will hear no entreaties; her rich suitor will not listen to her prayers. They will not be put off a day—an hour; tonight alone is hers—this night, which she may employ as she will.

She takes another path than that which leads home; she hurries through some by-streets of the city, out on to a lonely bridge, where he and she had stood so often in the sunset, watching the rose-coloured light glow, fade, and die upon the river.

He returns from Florence. He had received her letter. That letter, blotted with tears, entreating, despairing—he had received it, but he loved her no longer. A young Florentine, who has sat to him for a model, had bewitched his fancy—that fancy which with him stood in place of a heart—and Gertrude had been half-forgotten. If she had a rich suitor, good; let her marry him; better for her, better far for himself. He had no wish to fetter himself with a wife. Had he not his art always?—his eternal bride, his unchanging mistress.

Thus he thought it wiser to delay his journey to Brunswick, so that he should arrive when the wedding was over—arrive in time to salute the bride.

And the vows—the mystical fancies—the belief in his return, even after death, to the embrace of his beloved? O, gone out of his life; melted away for ever, those foolish dreams of his boyhood.

So on the fifteenth of June he enters Brunswick, by that very bridge on which she stood, the stars looking down on her, the night before. He strolls across the bridge and down by the water's edge, a great rough dog at his heels, and the smoke from his short meerschaum pipe curling in blue wreaths fantastically in the pure morning air. He has his sketch-book under his arm, and attracted now and then by some object that catches his artist's eye, stops to draw: a few weeds and pebbles on the river's brink—a crag on the opposite shore—a group of pollard willows in the distance. When he has done, he admires his drawing, shuts his sketch-book, empties the ashes from his pipe, refills from his tobacco-pouch, sings the refrain of a gay drinking song, calls to his dog, smokes again, and walks on. Suddenly he opens his sketch-book again; this time that which attracts him is a group of figures: but what is it?

It is not a funeral, for there are no mourners.

It is not a funeral, but a corpse lying on a rough bier, covered with an old sail, carried between two bearers.

It is not a funeral, for the bearers are fishermen—fishermen in their everyday garb.

About a hundred yards from him they rest their burden on a bank—one stands at the head of the bier, the other throws himself down at the foot of it.

And thus they form a perfect group; he walks back two or three paces, selects his point of sight, and begins to sketch a hurried outline. He has finished it before they move; he hears their voices, though he cannot hear their words, and wonders what they can be talking of. Presently he walks on and joins them.

'You have a corpse there, my friends?' he says.

'Yes; a corpse washed ashore an hour ago.'

'Drowned?'

'Yes, drowned. A young girl, very handsome.'

'Suicides are always handsome,' says the painter; and then he stands for a little while idly smoking and meditating, looking at the sharp outline of the corpse and the stiff folds of the rough canvas covering.

Life is such a golden holiday for him—young, ambitious, clever—that it seems as though sorrow and death could have no part in his destiny.

At last he says that, as this poor suicide is so handsome, he should like to make a sketch of her.

He gives the fishermen some money, and they offer to remove the sailcloth that covers her features.

No; he will do it himself. He lifts the rough, coarse, wet canvas from her face. What face?

The face that shone on the dreams of his foolish boyhood; the face which once was the light of his uncle's home. His cousin Gertrude—his betrothed!

He sees, as in one glance, while he draws one breath, the rigid features—the marble arms—the hands crossed on the cold bosom; and, on the third finger of the left hand, the ring which had been his mother's—the golden serpent; the ring which, if he were to become blind, he could select from a thousand others by the touch alone.

But he is a genius and a metaphysician—grief, true grief, is not for such as he. His first thought is flight—flight anywhere out of that accursed city—anywhere far from the brink of that hideous river—anywhere away from remorse—anywhere to forget.

He is miles on the road that leads away from Brunswick before he knows that he has walked a step.

It is only when his dog lies down panting at his feet that he feels how exhausted he is himself, and sits down upon a bank to rest. How the landscape spins round and round before his dazzled eyes, while his morning's sketch of the two fishermen and the canvas-covered bier glares redly at him out of the twilight!

At last, after sitting a long time by the roadside, idly playing with his dog, idly smoking, idly lounging, looking as any idle, light-hearted travelling student might look, yet all the while acting over that morning's scene in his burning brain a hundred times a minute; at last he grows a little more composed, and tries presently to think of himself as he is, apart from his cousin's suicide. Apart from that, he was no worse off than he was yesterday. His genius was not gone; the money he had earned at Florence still lined his pocket-book; he was his own master, free to go whither he would.

And while he sits on the roadside, trying to separate himself from the scene of that morning—trying to put away the image of the corpse covered with the damp canvas sail—trying to think of what he should do next, where he should go, to be farthest away from Brunswick and remorse, the old diligence comes rumbling and jingling along. He remembers it; it goes from Brunswick to Aix-la-Chapelle.

He whistles to his dog, shouts to the postilion to stop, and springs into the *coupé*.

During the whole evening, through the long night, though he does not once close his eyes, he never speaks a word; but when morning dawns, and the other passengers awake and begin to talk to each other, he joins in the conversation. He tells them that he is an artist, that he is going to Cologne and to Antwerp to copy Rubenses, and the great picture by Quentin Matsys, in the museum. He remembered afterwards that he talked and laughed boisterously, and that when he was talking and laughing loudest, a passenger, older and graver than the rest, opened the window near him, and told him to put his head out. He remembered the fresh air blowing in his face, the singing of the birds in his ears, and the flat fields and roadside reeling before his eyes. He remembered this, and then falling in a lifeless heap on the floor of the diligence.

It is a fever that keeps him for six long weeks on a bed at a hotel in Aix-la-Chapelle.

He gets well, and, accompanied by his dog, starts on foot for Cologne. By this time he is his former self once more. Again the blue smoke from his short meerschaum curls upwards in the morning air—again he sings some old university drinking-song—again stops here and there, meditating and sketching.

He is happy, and has forgotten his cousin—and so on to Cologne.

It is by the great cathedral he is standing, with his dog at his side. It is night, the bells have just chimed the hour, and the clocks are striking eleven; the moonlight shines full upon the magnificent pile, over which the artist's eye wanders, absorbed in the beauty of form.

He is not thinking of his drowned cousin, for he has forgotten her and is happy.

Suddenly some one, something from behind him, puts two cold arms round his neck, and clasps its hands on his breast.

And yet there is no one behind him, for on the flags bathed in the broad moonlight there are only two shadows, his own and his dog's. He turns quickly round—there is no one—nothing to be seen in the broad square but himself and his dog; and though he feels, he cannot see the cold arms clasped round his neck.

It is not ghostly, this embrace, for it is palpable to the touch—it cannot be real, for it is invisible.

He tries to throw off the cold caress. He clasps the hands in his own to tear them asunder, and to cast them off his neck. He can feel the long delicate fingers cold and wet beneath his touch, and on the third finger of the left hand he can feel the ring which was his mother's—the golden serpent—the ring which he has always said he would know among a thousand by the touch alone. He knows it now!

His dead cousin's cold arms are round his neck—his dead cousin's wet hands are clasped upon his breast. He asks himself if he is mad. 'Up, Leo!' he shouts. 'Up, up, boy!' and the Newfoundland leaps to his shoulders—the dog's paws are on the dead hands, and the animal utters a terrific howl, and springs away from his master.

The student stands in the moonlight, the dead arms around his neck, and the dog at a little distance moaning piteously.

Presently a watchman, alarmed by the howling of the dog, comes into the square to see what is wrong.

In a breath the cold arms are gone.

He takes the watchman home to the hotel with him and gives him money; in his gratitude he could have given that man half his little fortune.

Will it ever come to him again, this embrace of the dead?

He tries never to be alone; he makes a hundred acquaintances, and shares the chamber of another student. He starts up if he is left by himself in the public room at the inn where he is staying, and runs into the street. People notice his strange actions, and begin to think that he is mad.

But, in spite of all, he is alone once more; for one night the public room being empty for a moment, when on some idle pretence he strolls into the street, the street is empty too, and for the second time he feels the cold arms round his neck, and for the second time, when he calls his dog, the animal slinks away from him with a piteous howl.

After this he leaves Cologne, still travelling on foot—of necessity now, for his money is getting low. He joins travelling hawkers, he walks side by side with labourers, he talks to every foot-passenger he falls in with, and tries from morning till night to get company on the road.

At night he sleeps by the fire in the kitchen of the inn at which he stops; but do what he will, he is often alone, and it is now a common thing for him to feel the cold arms around his neck.

Many months have passed since his cousin's death—autumn, winter, early spring. His money is nearly gone, his health is utterly broken, he is the shadow of his former self, and he is getting near to Paris. He will reach that city at the time of the Carnival. To this he looks forward. In Paris, in Carnival time, he need never, surely, be alone, never feel that deadly caress; he may even recover his lost gaiety, his lost health, once more resume his profession, once more earn fame and money by his art.

How hard he tries to get over the distance that divides him from Paris, while day by day he grows weaker, and his step slower and more heavy!

But there is an end at last; the long dreary roads are passed. This is Paris, which he enters for the first time—Paris, of which he has dreamed so much— Paris, whose million voices are to exorcise his phantom.

To him tonight Paris seems one vast chaos of lights, music, and confusion— lights which dance before his eyes and will not be still—music that rings in his ears and deafens him—confusion which makes his head whirls round and round.

But, in spite of all, he finds the opera-house, where there is a masked ball. He has enough money left to buy a ticket of admission, and to hire a domino to throw over his shabby dress. It seems only a moment after his entering the gates of Paris that he is in the very midst of all the wild gaiety of the opera-house ball.

No more darkness, no more loneliness, but a mad crowd, shouting and dancing, and a lovely Débardeuse hanging on his arm.

The boisterous gaiety he feels surely is his old light-heartedness come back. He hears the people round him talking of the outrageous conduct of some drunken student, and it is to him they point when they say this—to him, who has not moistened his lips since yesterday at noon, for even now he will not drink; though his lips are parched, and his throat burning, he cannot drink. His voice is thick and hoarse, and his utterance indistinct; but still this must be his old light-heartedness come back that makes him so wildly gay.

The little Débardeuse is wearied out—her arm rests on his shoulder heavier than lead—the other dancers one by one drop off.

The lights in the chandeliers one by one die out.

The decorations look pale and shadowy in that dim light which is neither night nor day.

A faint glimmer from the dying lamps, a pale streak of cold grey light from the new-born day, creeping in through half-opened shutters.

And by this light the bright-eyed Débardeuse fades sadly. He looks her in the face. How the brightness of her eyes dies out! Again he looks her in the face. How white that face has grown! Again—and now it is the shadow of a face alone that looks in his.

Again—and they are gone—the bright eyes, the face, the shadow of the face. He is alone; alone in that vast saloon.

Alone, and, in the terrible silence, he hears the echoes of his own footsteps in that dismal dance which has no music.

No music but the beating of his breast. For the cold arms are round his neck—they whirl him round, they will not be flung off, or cast away; he can no more escape from their icy grasp than he can escape from death. He looks behind him—there is nothing but himself in the great empty *salle*; but he can feel—cold, deathlike, but O, how palpable!—the long slender fingers, and the ring which was his mother's.

He tries to shout, but he has no power in his burning throat. The silence of the place is only broken by the echoes of his own footsteps in the dance from which he cannot extricate himself. Who says he has no partner? The cold hands are clasped on his breast, and now he does not shun their caress. No! One more polka, if he drops down dead.

The lights are all out, and, half an hour after, the *gendarmes* come in with a lantern to see that the house is empty; they are followed by a great dog that they have found seated howling on the steps of the theatre. Near the principal entrance they stumble over——

The body of a student, who has died from want of food, exhaustion, and the breaking of a blood-vessel.

AN ENGINEER'S STORY

Amelia B. Edwards

HIS NAME WAS Matthew Price; mine is Benjamin Hardy. We were born within a few days of each other; bred up in the same village; taught at the same school. I cannot remember the time when we were not close friends. Even as boys, we never knew what it was to quarrel. We had not a thought, we had not a possession, that was not in common. We would have stood by each other fearlessly, to the death. It was such a friendship as one reads about sometimes in books—fast and firm as the great Tors upon our native moorlands, true as the sun in the heavens.

The name of our village was Chadleigh. Lifted high above the pasture-flats which stretched away at our feet like a measureless green lake and melted into mist on the farthest horizon, it nestled, a tiny stone-built hamlet, in a sheltered hollow about midway between the plain and the plateau.

Above us, rising ridge beyond ridge, slope beyond slope, spread the mountainous moor-country, bare and bleak for the most part, with here and there a patch of cultivated field or hardy plantation, and crowned highest of all with masses of huge grey crag, abrupt, isolated, hoary, and older than the deluge. These were the Tors—Druids' Tor, King's Tor, Castle Tor, and the like; sacred places, as I have heard, in the ancient time, where crownings, burnings, human sacrifices, and all kinds of bloody heathen rites were performed.

Bones, too, had been found there, and arrowheads, and ornaments of gold and glass. I had a vague awe of the Tors in those boyish days, and would not have gone near them after dark for the heaviest bribe.

I have said that we were born in the same village. He was the son of a small farmer, named William Price, and the eldest of a family of seven; I was the only child of Ephraim Hardy, the Chadleigh blacksmith—a well-known man in those parts, whose memory is not forgotten to this day.

Just so far as a farmer is supposed to be a bigger man than a blacksmith, Mat's father might be said to have a better standing than mine; but William Price, with his small holding and his seven boys was, in fact, as poor as many a day-labourer; whilst the blacksmith, well-to-do, bustling, popular, and open-handed, was a person of some importance in the place.

All this, however, had nothing to do with Mat and myself. It never occurred to either of us that his jacket was out at elbows, or that our mutual funds came altogether from my pocket. It was enough for us that we sat on the same school-bench, conned our tasks from the same primer, fought each other's battles, screened each other's faults, fished, nutted, played truant, robbed orchards and birds' nests together, and spent every half hour, authorised or stolen, in each other's society.

It was a happy time; but it could not go on forever. My father, being prosperous, resolved to put me forward in the world. I must know more and do better than himself. The forge was not good enough, the little world of Chadleigh not wide enough, for me. Thus it happened that I was still swinging the satchel when Mat was whistling at the plough, and that at last, when my future course was shaped out, we were separated, as it then seemed to us, for life.

For, blacksmith's son as I was, furnace and forge, in some form or other, pleased me best. I chose to be a working engineer. So my father by-and-by apprenticed me to a Birmingham iron-master; and, having bidden farewell to Mat, and Chadleigh, and the grey old Tors in the shadow of which I had spent all the days of my life, I turned my face northward, and went over into 'the Black Country'.

I am not going to dwell on this part of my story. How I worked out the term of my apprenticeship; how, when I had served my full time and become a skilled workman, I took Mat from the plough and brought him over to the Black Country, sharing with him lodgings, wages, experience—all, in short, that I had to give; how he, naturally quick to learn and brimful of quiet energy, worked his way up a step at a time, and came by-and-by to be a 'first hand' in his own department; how, during all these years of change, and trial, and effort, the old boyish affection never wavered or weakened, but went on growing with our growth and strengthening with our strength—are facts which I need do no more than outline in this place.

About this time—it will be remembered that I speak of the days when Mat and I were on the bright side of thirty—it happened that our firm contracted to supply six first-class locomotives to run on the new line, then in progress of construction, between Turin and Genoa. It was the first Italian order we had taken.

We had had dealings with France, Holland, Belgium, Germany; but never with Italy. The connection, therefore, was new and valuable—all the more valuable because our Transalpine neighbours had but lately begun to lay down the iron roads, and would be safe to need more of our good English work as they went on. So the Birmingham firm set themselves to the contract with a will, lengthened our working hours, increased our wages, took on fresh hands, and determined, if energy and promptitude could do it, to place themselves at the head of the Italian labour-market, and stay there. They deserved and achieved success.

The six locomotives were not only turned out to time, but were shipped, despatched, and delivered with a promptitude that fairly amazed our Piedmontese consignee. I was not a little proud, you may be sure, when I found myself appointed to superintend the transport of the engines. Being allowed a couple of assistants, I contrived that Mat should be one of them; and thus we enjoyed together the first great holiday of our lives.

It was a wonderful change for two Birmingham operatives fresh from the Black Country. Genoa, that fairy city, with its crescent background of Alps; the port crowded with strange shipping; the marvellous blue sky and bluer sea; the painted houses on the quays; the quaint cathedral faced with black and white marble; the street of jewellers, like an Arabian Nights' bazaar; the street of palaces with its Moorish courtyards, its fountains and orange-trees; the women veiled like brides; the galley-slaves chained two and two, the processions of priests and friars; the everlasting clangour of bells; the babble of a strange tongue; the singular lightness and brightness of the climate—made, altogether, such a combination of wonders that we wandered about the first day in a kind of bewildered dream, like children at a fair. Before that week was ended, being tempted by the beauty of the place and the liberality of the pay, we had agreed to take service with the Turin and Genoa Railway Company, and to turn our backs upon Birmingham forever.

Then began a new life—a life so active and healthy, so steeped in fresh air and sunshine, that we sometimes marvelled how we could have endured the gloom of the Black Country. We were constantly up and down the line—now at Genoa, now at Turin, taking trial trips with the locomotives, and placing our old experience at the service of our new employers.

In the meanwhile we made Genoa our headquarters, and hired a couple of rooms over a small shop in a by-street sloping down to the quays. Such a busy little street—so steep and winding that no vehicles could pass through it, and so narrow that the sky looked like a mere strip of deep blue ribbon overhead! Every house in it, however, was a shop where the goods encroached on the footway, or were piled about the door, or hung like tapestry from the balconies; and all day long, from dawn till dusk, an incessant stream of passers-by poured up and down between the port and the upper quarter of the city.

Our landlady was the widow of a silver-worker, and lived by the sale of filigree ornaments, cheap jewellery, combs, fans, and toys in ivory and jet. She had an only daughter, named Gianetta, who served in the shop and was simply the most beautiful woman I ever beheld. Looking back across this weary chasm of years, and bringing her image before me (as I can and do) with all the vividness of life, I am unable, even now, to detect a flaw in her beauty. I do not attempt to describe her. I do not believe there is a poet living who could find the words to do it; but I once saw a picture that was somewhat like her (not half so lovely, but still like her), and for aught I know, that picture is still hanging where I last looked at it—upon the walls of the Louvre.

It represented a woman with brown eyes and golden hair, looking over her shoulder into a circular mirror held by a bearded man in the background. In this man, as I then understood, the artist had painted his own portrait; in her, the portrait of the woman he loved. No picture that I ever saw was half so beautiful, and yet it was not worthy to be named in the same breath with Gianetta Coneglia.

You may be certain the widow's shop did not want for customers. All Genoa knew how fair a face was to be seen behind that dingy little counter; and Gianetta, flirt as she was, had more lovers than she cared to remember, even by name. Gentle and simple, rich and poor, from the red-capped sailor buying his earrings or his amulet, to the nobleman carelessly purchasing half the filigrees in the window, she treated them all alike—encouraged them, laughed at them, led them on and turned them off at her pleasure. She had no more heart than a marble statue; as Mat and I discovered by-and-by, to our bitter cost.

I cannot tell to this day how it came about, or what first led me to suspect how things were going with us both; but long before the waning of that autumn a coldness had sprung up between my friend and myself. It was nothing that could have been put into words. It was nothing that either of us could have explained or justified, to save his life. We lodged together, ate together, worked together, exactly as before; we even took our long evening's walk together, when the day's labour was ended; and except, perhaps, that we were more silent than of old, no mere looker-on could have detected a shadow of change. Yet there it was, silent and subtle, widening the gulf between us every day.

It was not his fault. He was too true and gentle-hearted to have willingly brought about such a state of things between us. Neither do I believe—fiery as my nature is—that it was mine. It was all hers—hers from first to last—the sin, and the shame, and the sorrow.

If she had shown a fair and open preference for either of us, no real harm could have come of it. I would have put any constraint upon myself, and heaven knows! have borne any suffering, to see Mat really happy. I know that he would have done the same, and more if he could, for me. But Gianetta cared not one *bajocco* for either. She never meant to choose between us.

It gratified her vanity to divide us; it amused her to play with us. It would pass my power to tell how, by a thousand imperceptible shades of coquetry—by the lingering of a glance, the substitution of a word, the flitting of a smile—she contrived to turn our heads, and torture our hearts, and lead us on to love her. She deceived us both. She buoyed us both up with hope; she maddened us with jealousy; she crushed us with despair. For my part, when I seemed now and then to wake to a sudden sense of the ruin that was about our path, and saw how the truest friendship that ever bound two lives together was drifting on to wreck and ruin. I asked myself whether any woman in the world was worth what Mat had been to me and I to him. But this was not often. I was readier to shut my eyes upon the truth than to face it; and so lived on, wilfully, in a dream.

Thus the autumn passed away, and winter came—the strange, treacherous Genoese winter, green with olive and ilex, brilliant with sunshine, and bitter with storm. Still, rivals at heart and friends on the surface, Mat and I lingered on in our lodging in the Vicolo Balba. Still, Gianetta held us with her fatal wiles and her still more fatal beauty. At length there came a day when I felt I could bear the horrible misery and suspense of it no longer. The sun, I vowed, should not go down before I knew my sentence. She must choose between us. She must either take me or let me go. I was reckless. I was desperate. I was determined to know the worst or the best. If the worst, I would at once turn my back upon Genoa, upon her, upon all the pursuits and purposes of my past life, and begin the world anew. This I told her, passionately and sternly, standing before her in the little parlour at the back of the shop, one bleak December morning.

'If it's Mat whom you care for most,' I said, 'tell me so in one word, and I will never trouble you again. He is better worth your love. I am jealous and exacting; he is as trusting and unselfish as a woman. Speak, Gianetta; am I to bid you goodbye for ever and ever, or am I to write home to my mother in England, bidding her pray to God to bless the woman who has promised to be my wife?'

'You plead your friend's cause well,' she replied haughtily. 'Matteo ought to be grateful. This is more than he ever did for you.'

'Give me an answer, for pity's sake,' I exclaimed, 'and let me go!'

'You are free to go or stay, Signor Inglese,' she replied, 'I am not your gaoler.'

'Do you bid me leave you?'

'Beata Madre! not I.'

'Will you marry me, if I stay?'

She laughed aloud—such a merry, mocking, musical laugh, like a chime of silver bells!

'You ask too much,' she said.

'Only what you have led me to hope these five or six months past.'

'That is just what Matteo says. How tiresome you both are!'

'Oh, Gianetta,' I said, passionately, 'be serious for one moment! I am a rough fellow, it is true—not half good enough or clever enough for you; but I love you with my whole heart, and an emperor could do no more.'

'I am glad of it,' she replied; 'I do not want you to love me less.'

'Than you cannot wish to make me wretched! Will you promise me?'

'I promise nothing,' said she, with another burst of laughter; 'except that I will not marry Matteo!'

Except that she would not marry Matteo! Only that. Not a word of hope for myself. Nothing but my friend's condemnation. I might get comfort, and selfish triumph, and some sort of base assurance out of that, if I could. And so, to my shame, I did. I grasped at the vain encouragement, and, fool that I was! let her put me off again unanswered. From that day I gave up all effort at self-control, and let myself drift blindly on—to destruction.

At length things became so bad between Mat and myself that it seemed as if an open rupture must be at hand. We avoided each other, scarcely exchanged a dozen sentences in a day, and fell away from all our old familiar habits. At this time—I shudder to remember it!—there were moments when I felt that I hated him.

Thus, with the trouble deepening and widening between us day by day, another month or five weeks went by, and February came; and, with February, the carnival. They said in Genoa that it was a particularly dull carnival; and so it must have been, for, save a flag or two hung out in some of the principal streets, and a sort of *festa* look about the women, there were no special indications of the season. It was, I think, the second day of the carnival, when, having been on the line all the morning, I returned to Genoa at dusk, and to my surprise found Mat Price on the platform. He came up to me and laid his hand on my arm.

'You are in late,' he said. 'I have been waiting for you three-quarters-of-an-hour. Shall we dine together today?'

Impulsive as I am, this evidence of returning good will at once called up my better feelings.

'With all my heart, Mat,' I replied; 'shall we go to Gozzoli's?'

'No, no,' he said, hurriedly. 'Some quieter place—some place where we can talk. I have something to say to you.'

I noticed now that he looked pale and agitated, and an uneasy sense of apprehension stole upon me. We decided on The Pescatore, a little out-of-the-way *trattoria*, down near the Molo Vecchio. There, in a dingy salon frequented chiefly by seamen, and redolent of tobacco, we ordered our simple dinner. Mat scarcely swallowed a morsel, but, calling presently for a bottle of Sicilian wine, drank eagerly.

'Well, Mat,' I said, as the last dish was placed on the table, 'what news have you?'

'Bad.'

'I guessed that from your face.'

'Bad for you—bad for me. Gianetta——'

'What of Gianetta?'

He passed his hand nervously across his lips.

'Gianetta is false—worse than false,' he said in a hoarse voice. 'She values an honest man's heart just as she values a flower for her hair—wears it for a day, then throws it aside for ever. She has cruelly wronged us both.'

'In what way? Good heavens, speak out!'

'In the worst way that a woman can wrong those who love her. She has sold herself to the Marchese Loredano.'

The blood rushed to my head and face in a burning torrent. I could scarcely see, and dared not trust myself to speak.

'I saw her going towards the cathedral,' he went on, hurriedly. 'It was about three hours ago. I thought she might be going to confession, so I hung back and followed her at a distance. When she got inside, however, she went straight to the back of the pulpit, where this old man was waiting for her. You remember him—an old man who used to haunt the shop a month or two back. Well, seeing how deep in conversation they were, and how they stood close under the pulpit with their backs towards the church, I fell into a passion of anger and went straight up the aisle, intending to say or do something, I scarcely knew what; but, at all events, to draw her arm through mine, and take her home. When I came within a few feet, however, and found only a big pillar between myself and them, I paused. They could not see me, nor I them; but I could hear their voices distinctly, and—and I listened.'

'Well, and you heard——'

'The terms of a shameful bargain—beauty on the one side, gold on the other; so many thousand francs a year; a villa near Naples—pah! it makes me sick to repeat it.'

And with a shudder, he poured out another glass of wine and drank it at a draught.

'After that,' he said presently, 'I made no effort to bring her away. The whole thing was so cold-blooded, so deliberate, so shameful, that I felt I had only to wipe her out of my memory, and leave her to her fate. I stole out of the cathedral, and walked about here by the sea for ever so long, trying to get my thoughts straight. Then I remembered you, Ben; and the recollection of how this wanton had come between us and broken up our lives drove me wild. So I went up to the station and waited for you. I felt you ought to know it all; and—and I thought, perhaps, that we might go back to England together.'

'The Marchese Loredano!'

It was all that I could say; all that I could think. As Mat had just said of himself, I felt 'like one stunned.'

'There is one other thing I may as well tell you,' he added, reluctantly, 'if only to show you how false a woman can be. We—we were to have been married next month.'

'*We?* Who? What do you mean?'

'I mean that we were to have been married—Gianetta and I.'

A sudden storm of rage, of scorn, of incredulity swept over me at this, and seemed to carry my senses away.

'*You!*' I cried. 'Gianetta marry *you!* I don't believe it.'

'I wish I had not believed it,' he replied, looking up as if puzzled by my vehemence. 'But she promised me; and I thought when she promised it she meant it.'

'She told me weeks ago that she would never be your wife!'

His colour rose; his brow darkened; but when his answer came, it was as calm as the last.

'Indeed,' he said. 'Then it is only one baseness more. She told me that she had refused you; and that was why we kept our engagement secret.'

'Tell the truth, Mat Price,' I said, well-nigh beside myself with suspicion. 'Confess that every word of this is false! Confess that Gianetta will not listen to you, and that you are afraid I may succeed where you have failed. As perhaps I shall—as perhaps I shall, after all!'

'Are you mad?' he exclaimed. 'What do you mean?'

'That I believe it's just a trick to get me away to England—that I don't credit a syllable of your story. You're a liar, and I hate you!'

He rose, and laying one hand on the back of his chair, looked me sternly in the face.

'If you were not Benjamin Hardy,' he said, deliberately, 'I would thrash you within an inch of your life.'

The words had no sooner passed his lips than I sprang at him. I have never been able distinctly to remember what followed. A curse—a blow—a struggle—a moment of blind fury—a cry—a confusion of tongues—a circle of strange faces. Then I see Mat lying back in the arms of a bystander; myself trembling and bewildered—the knife dropping from my grasp; blood upon the floor; blood upon my hands; blood upon his shirt. And then I hear those dreadful words:

'Oh, Ben, you have murdered me!'

He did not die—at least, not there and then. He was carried to the nearest hospital, and lay for some weeks between life and death. His case, they said, was difficult and dangerous. The knife had gone in just below the collarbone, and pierced down into the lungs.

He was not allowed to speak or turn—scarcely to breathe with freedom. He might not even lift his head to drink. I sat by him day and night all through that sorrowful time. I gave up my situation on the railway; I quitted my lodging in the Vicolo Balba; I tried to forget that such a woman as Gianetta Coneglia had ever drawn breath.

I lived only for Mat; and he tried to live, more I believe for my sake than his own. Thus, in the bitter silent hours of pain and penitence, when no hand but mine approached his lips or smoothed his pillow, the old friendship came back with even more than its old trust and faithfulness. He forgave me fully and freely; and I would thankfully have given my life for him.

At length there came one bright spring morning, when, dismissed as convalescent, he tottered out through the hospital gates, leaning on my arm and feeble as an infant. He was not cured; neither, as I then learned to my horror and anguish, was it possible that he ever could be cured.

He might, with care, live for some years; but the lungs were injured beyond hope of remedy, and a strong or healthy man he could never be again. These, spoken aside to me, were the parting words of the chief physician, who advised me to take him further south without delay.

I took him to a little coast-town called Rocca, some thirty miles beyond Genoa—a sheltered lonely place along the Riviera, where the sea was even bluer than the sky, and the cliffs were green with strange tropical plants, cacti, and aloes, and Egyptian palms.

Here we lodged in the house of a small tradesman; and Mat, to use his own words, 'set to work at getting well in good earnest'. But, alas! it was a work which no earnestness could forward. Day after day he went down to the beach, and sat for hours drinking the sea-air and watching the sails that came and went in the offing. By-and-by he could go no further than the garden of the house in which we lived.

A little later, and he spent his days on a couch beside the open window, waiting patiently for the end. Ay, for the end! It had come to that. He was fading fast—waning with the waning summer, and conscious that the reaper was at hand. His whole aim now was to soften the agony of my remorse and prepare me for what must shortly come.

'I would not live longer if I could,' he said, lying on his couch one summer evening and looking up to the stars. 'If I had my choice at this moment, I would ask to go. I should like Gianetta to know that I forgave her.'

'She shall know it,' I said, trembling suddenly from head to foot.

He pressed my hand.

'And you'll write to father?'

'I will.'

I had drawn a little back, that he might not see the tears raining down my cheeks; but he raised himself on his elbow, and looked round.

'Don't fret, Ben,' he whispered; laid his head back wearily upon the pillow—and so died.

And this was the end of it. This was the end of all that made life life to me. I buried him there, in hearing of the wash of a strange sea on a strange shore. I stayed by the grave till the priest and the bystanders were gone. I saw the earth filled in to the last sod, and the gravedigger stamp it down with his feet.

Then, and not till then, I felt that I had lost him for ever—the friend I had loved, and hated, and slain. Then, and not till then, I knew that all rest, and joy, and hope were over for me. From that moment my heart hardened within me, and my life was filled with loathing. Day and night, land and sea, labour and rest, food and sleep, were alike hateful to me.

It was the curse of Cain, and that my brother had pardoned me made it lie none the lighter. Peace on earth was for me no more, and goodwill towards men was dead in my heart forever. Remorse softens some natures; but it poisoned mine. I hated all mankind, but above all mankind I hated the woman who had come between us two, and ruined both our lives.

He had bidden me seek her out, and be the messenger of his forgiveness. I had sooner have gone down to the port of Genoa and taken upon me the serge cap and shotted chain of any galley-slave at his toil in the public works; but for all that I did my best to obey him. I went back, alone and on foot. I went back, intending to say to her, 'Gianetta Coneglia, he forgave you—but God never will.' But she was gone.

The little shop was let to a fresh occupant. The neighbours only knew that mother and daughter had left the place quite suddenly, and that Gianetta was supposed to be under the 'protection' of the Marchese Loredano. How I made inquiries here and there—how I heard they had gone to Naples—and how, being restless and reckless of my time, I worked my passage in a French steamer, and followed her—how, having found the sumptuous villa that was now hers, I learned that she had left there some ten days and gone to Paris, where the Marchese was ambassador for the Two Sicilies—how, working my passage back again to Marseilles, and thence, in part by the river and in part by the rail, I made my way to Paris—how, day after day I paced the streets and the parks, watched at the ambassador's gates, followed his carriage, and, at last, after weeks of waiting, discovered her address—how, having written to request an interview, her servants spurned me from her door, and flung my letter in my face—how, looking up at her windows, I then, instead of forgiving, solemnly cursed her with the bitterest curses my tongue could devise—and how, this done, I shook the dust of Paris from my feet and became a wanderer upon the face of the earth, are facts which I have no space to tell.

The next six or eight years of my life were shifting and unsettled enough. A morose and restless man, I took employment here and there as opportunity offered, turning my hand to many things, and caring little what I earned, so long as the work was hard and the change incessant. First of all I engaged myself as chief engineer in one of the French steamers plying between Marseilles and Constantinople. At Constantinople I changed to one of the Austrian Lloyds' boats, and worked for some time to and from Alexandria, Jaffa, and those parts. After that, I fell in with a party of Mr Layard's men at Cairo, and so went up the Nile and took a turn at the excavations of the mound of Nimroud.

Then I became a working engineer on the new desert line between Alexandria and Suez; and by-and-by I worked my passage out to Bombay, and took service as an engine-fitter on one of the great Indian railways. I stayed a long time in India—that is to say, I stayed nearly two years, which was a long time for me; and I might not even have left so soon, but for the war that was declared just then with Russia. That tempted me. For I loved danger and hardship as other men love safety and ease; and as for my life, I had sooner have parted with it than have kept it any day. So I came straight back to England and betook myself to Portsmouth, where my testimonials at once procured me the sort of berth I wanted. I then went out to the Crimea in the engine-room of one of Her Majesty's war-steamers.

I served with the fleet, of course, while the war lasted; and when it was over, went wandering off again, rejoicing in my liberty. This time I went to Canada, and after working on a railway then in progress near the American frontier, I presently passed over into the States; journeyed from north to south; crossed the Rocky Mountains; tried a month or two of life in the gold country; and then, being seized with a sudden, aching, unaccountable longing to revisit that solitary grave so far away on the Italian coast, I turned my face once more towards Europe.

Poor little grave! I found it rank with weeds, the cross half shattered, the inscription half effaced. It was as if no one had loved him or remembered him.

I went back to the house in which we had lodged together. The same people were still living there, and made me kindly welcome. I stayed with them for some weeks. I weeded, and planted, and trimmed the grave with my own hands, and set up a fresh cross in pure white marble. It was the first season of rest that I had known since I laid him there; and when at last I shouldered my knapsack and set forth again to battle with the world, I promised myself that, God willing, I would creep back to Rocca when my days drew near to ending, and be buried by his side.

From hence, being, perhaps, a little less inclined than formerly for very distant parts, and willing to keep within reach of that grave, I went no further than Mantua, where I engaged myself as an engine-driver on the line, then not long completed, between that city and Venice. Somehow, although I had been trained to the working engineering, I preferred in these days to earn my bread by driving. I liked the excitement of it, the sense of power, the rush of the air, the roar of the fire, the flitting of the landscape. Above all, I enjoyed to drive a night-express. The worse the weather, the better it suited with my sullen temper. For I was as hard, and harder than ever. The years had done nothing to soften me. They had only confirmed all that was blackest and bitterest in my heart.

I continued pretty faithful to the Mantua line, and had been working on it steadily for more than seven months, when that which I am now about to relate took place.

It was in the month of March. The weather had been unsettled for some days past, and the nights stormy; and at one point along the line, near Ponte di Brenta, the waters had risen and swept away some seventy yards of embankment. Since this accident, the trains had all been obliged to stop at a certain spot between Padua and Ponte di Brenta, and the passengers, with their luggage, had thence to be transported in all kinds of vehicles, by a circuitous country-road, to the nearest station on the other side of the gap, where another train and engine awaited them. This, of course, caused great confusion and annoyance, put all our time-tables wrong, and subjected the public to a large amount of inconvenience.

In the meanwhile an army of navvies was drafted to the spot, and worked day and night to repair the damage. At this time I was driving two through-trains each day; namely, one from Mantua to Venice in the early morning, and a return train from Venice to Mantua in the afternoon—a tolerably full day's work, covering about one hundred and ninety miles of ground, and occupying between ten and eleven hours.

I was therefore not best pleased when, on the third or fourth day after the accident, I was informed that, in addition to my regular allowance of work, I should that evening be required to drive a special train to Venice. This special train, consisting of an engine, a single carriage, and a break-van, was to leave the Mantua platform at eleven; at Padua the passengers were to alight and find post-chaises waiting to convey them to Ponte di Brenta; at Ponte di Brenta another engine, carriage, and break-van were to be in readiness. I was charged to accompany them throughout.

'*Corpo di Bacco*,' said the clerk who gave me my orders, 'you need not look so black, man. You are certain of a handsome gratuity. Do you know who goes with you?'

'Not I.'

'Not you, indeed! Why, it's the Duca Loredano, the Neapolitan ambassador.'

'Loredano!' I stammered. 'What Loredano? There was a Marchese——'

'*Certo*. He was the Marchese Loredano some years ago; but he has come into his dukedom since then.'

'He must be a very old man by this time.'

'Yes, he is old; but what of that? He is as hale, and bright, and stately as ever. You have seen him before?'

'Yes,' I said, turning away; 'I have seen him—years ago.'

'You have heard of his marriage?'

I shook my head.

The clerk chuckled, rubbed his hands, and shrugged his shoulders.

'An extraordinary affair,' he said. 'Made a tremendous *esclandre* at the time. He married his mistress—quite a common, vulgar girl—a Genoese—very handsome; but not received of course. Nobody visits her.'

'Married her!' I exclaimed. 'Impossible.'

'True, I assure you.'

I put my hand to my head. I felt as if I had had a fall or a blow.

'Does she—does she go tonight?' I faltered.

'Oh dear, yes—goes everywhere with him—never lets him out of her sight. You'll see her—*la bella Duchessa*!'

With this my informant laughed and rubbed his hands again, and went back to his office.

They day went by, I scarcely know how, except that my whole soul was in a tumult of rage and bitterness. I returned from my afternoon's work about 7.25, and at 10.30 I was once again at the station. I had examined the engine, given instructions to the *Fochista*, or stoker, about the fire, seen to the supply of oil, and got all in readiness, when, just as I was about to compare my watch with the clock in the ticket-office, a hand was laid upon my arm, and a voice in my ear said:

'Are you the engine-driver who is going on with this special train?'

I had never seen the speaker before. He was a small, dark man, muffled up about the throat, with blue glasses, a large black beard, and his hat drawn low upon his eyes.

'You are a poor man, I suppose,' he said, in a quick, eager whisper, 'and, like other poor men, would not object to be better off. Would you like to earn a couple of thousand florins?'

'In what way?'

'Hush! You are to stop at Padua, are you not, and to go on again at Ponte di Brenta?'

I nodded.

'Suppose you did nothing of the kind. Suppose, instead of turning off the steam, you jump off the engine, and let the train run on?'

'Impossible. There are seventy yards of embankment gone, and——'

'*Basta!* I know that. Save yourself, and let the train run on. It would be nothing but an accident.'

I turned hot and cold! I trembled; my heart beat fast, and my breath failed.

'Why do you tempt me?' I faltered.

'For Italy's sake,' he whispered; 'for liberty's sake. I know you are no Italian; but for all that you may be a friend. This Loredano is one of his country's bitterest enemies. Stay, here are the two thousand florins.'

I thrust his hand back fiercely.

'No—no,' I said. 'No blood-money. If I do it, I do it neither for Italy nor for money; but for vengeance.'

'For vengeance?' he repeated.

At this moment a signal was given for backing up to the platform. I sprang to my place upon the engine without another word. When I again looked towards the spot where he had been standing, the stranger had gone.

I saw them take their places—duke and duchess, secretary and priest, valet and maid. I saw the station-master bow them into the carriage, and stand, bareheaded, beside the door. I could not distinguish their faces; the platform was too dusk, and the glare from the engine-fire too strong; but I recognised her stately figure, and the poise of her head. Had I not been told who she was, I should have known her by those traits alone. Then the guard's whistle shrilled out, and the station-master made his last bow; I turned the steam on, and we started.

My blood was on fire. I no longer trembled or hesitated. I felt as if every nerve was iron, and every pulse instinct with deadly purpose. She was in my power, and I would be revenged. She should die—she for whom I had stained my soul with my friend's blood! She should die in the plenitude of her wealth and her beauty, and no power on earth should save her!

The stations flew past. I put on more steam; I bade the fireman heap in the coke, and stir the blazing mass. I would have outstripped the wind, had it been possible. Faster and faster—hedges and trees, bridges and stations, flashing past—villages no sooner seen than gone—telegraph wires twisting, and dipping, and twining themselves in one, with the awful swiftness of our pace! Faster and faster, till the fireman at my side looks white and scared, and refuses to add more fuel to the furnace! Faster and faster till the wind rushes in our faces and drives the breath back upon our lips!

I would have scorned to save myself. I meant to die with the rest. Mad as I was—and I believe from my soul that I was utterly mad for the time—I felt a passing pang of pity for the old man and his suite. I would have spared the poor fellow at my side, too, if I could; but the pace at which we were going made escape impossible.

Vicenza was passed—a mere confused vision of lights. Pojana flew by. At Padua, but nine miles distant, our passengers were to alight. I saw the fireman's face turned upon me in remonstrance; I saw his lips move, though I could not hear a word; I saw his expression change suddenly from remonstrance to a deadly terror; and then—merciful heaven! then for the first time I saw that he and I were no longer alone upon the engine.

There was a third man—a third man standing on my right hand, as the fireman was standing on my left—a tall, stalwart man, with short curling hair, and a flat Scotch cap upon his head. As I fell back in my first shock of surprise he stepped forward, took my place at the engine, and turned the steam off. I opened my lips to speak to him. He turned his head slowly, and looked me in the face.

Matthew Price!

I uttered one long cry, flung my hands wildly up above my head, and fell as if I had been smitten with an axe.

I am prepared for the objections that may be made to my story. I expect, as a matter of course, to be told that this was an optical illusion; or that I was suffering from pressure on the brain; or even that I laboured under an attack of temporary insanity. I have heard all these arguments before, and, if I may be forgiven for saying so, I have no desire to hear them again. My own mind has been made up on the subject for many a year. All that I can say-all that I *know* is—that Matthew Price came back from the dead to save my soul and the lives of those whom I, in my guilty rage, would have hurried to destruction. I believe this as I believe in the mercy of heaven and the forgiveness of repentant sinners.

THE SECRET CHAMBER

Margaret Oliphant

[Dedicated to the inquirers in the Norman Tower.]

CHAPTER I.

CASTLE GOWRIE is one of the most famous and interesting in all Scotland. It is a beautiful old house, to start with,—perfect in old feudal grandeur, with its clustered turrets and walls that could withstand an army,—its labyrinths, its hidden stairs, its long mysterious passages—passages that seem in many cases to lead to nothing, but of which no one can be too sure what they lead to. The front, with its fine gateway and flanking towers, is approached now by velvet lawns, and a peaceful, beautiful old avenue, with double rows of trees, like a cathedral; and the woods out of which the grey towers rise, look as soft and rich in foliage, if not so lofty in growth, as the groves of the South. But this softness of aspect is all new to the place,—that is, new within the century or two which count for but little in the history of a dwelling-place, some part of which, at least, has been standing since the days when the Saxon Athelings brought such share of arts as belonged to them to solidify and regulate the original Celtic art which reared incised stones upon rude burial-places, and twined mystic knots on its crosses, before historic days. Even of this primitive decoration there are relics at Gowrie, where the twistings and twinings of Runic cords appear still on some bits of ancient wall, solid as rocks and almost as everlasting. From these to the graceful French turrets, which, recall many a grey chateau, what a long interval of years! But these are filled with stirring chronicles enough, besides the dim, not always decipherable records, which different developments of architecture have left on the old house. The Earls of Gowrie had been in the heat of every commotion that took place on or about the Highland line for more generations than any but a Celtic pen could record. Rebellions, revenges, insurrections, conspiracies, nothing in which blood was shed and lands lost, took place in Scotland, in which they had not had a share; and the anuals of the house are very full, and not without many a stain. They had been a bold and vigorous

53

race—with much evil in them, and some good; never, insignificant, whatever else they might be. It could not be said, however, that they are remarkable nowadays. Since the first Stuart rising, known in Scotland as the "Fifteen," they have not done much that has been worth recording; but yet their family history has always been of an unusual kind. The Randolphs could not be called eccentric in themselves: on the contrary, when you knew them, they were at bottom a respectable race, full of all the country gentleman virtues; and yet their public career, such as it was, had been marked by the strangest leaps and jerks of vicissitude. You would have said an impulsive, fanciful family — now making a grasp at some visionary advantage, now rushing into some wild speculation, now making a sudden sally into public life—but soon falling back into mediocrity, not able apparently, even when the impulse was purely selfish and mercenary, to keep it up. But this would not have been at all a true conception of the family character; their actual virtues were not of the imaginative order, and their freaks were a mystery to their friends. Nevertheless these freaks were what the general world was most aware of in the Randolph race. The late Earl had been a representative peer of Scotland (they had no English title), and had made quite a wonderful start, and for a year or two had seemed about to attain a very eminent place in Scotch affairs; but his ambition was found to have made use of some very equivocal modes of gaining influence, and he dropped accordingly at once and for ever from the political firmament. This was quite a common circumstance in the family. An apparently brilliant beginning, a discovery of evil means adopted for ambitious ends, a sudden subsidence, and the curious conclusion at the end of everything that this schemer, this unscrupulous speculator or politician, was a dull, good man after all—unambitious, contented, full of domestic kindness and benevolence. This family peculiarity made the history of the Randolphs a very strange one, broken by the oddest interruptions, and with no consistency in it. There was another circumstance, however, which attracted still more the wonder and observation of the public. For one who can appreciate such a recondite matter as family character, there are hundreds who are interested in a family secret, and this the house of Randolph possessed in perfection. It was a mystery which piqued the imagination and excited the interest of the entire country. The story went, that somewhere hid amid the massive walls and tortuous passages there was a secret chamber in Gowrie Castle. Everybody knew of its existence; but save the earl, his heir, and one other person, not of the family, but filling a confidential post in their service, no mortal knew where this mysterious hiding-place was. There had been countless guesses made at it, and expedients of all kinds invented to find it out. Every visitor who ever entered the old gateway, nay, even passing travellers who saw the turrets from the road, searched keenly for some trace of this mysterious chamber. But all guesses and researches were equally in vain.

I was about to say that no ghost story I ever heard of has been so steadily and long believed. But this would be a mistake, for nobody knew even with any certainty that there was a ghost connected with it. A secret chamber was nothing wonderful in so old a house. No doubt they exist in many such old houses, and are always curious and interesting—strange relics, more moving than any history, of the time when a man was not safe in his own house, and when it might be necessary to secure a refuge beyond the reach of spies or traitors at a moment's notice. Such a refuge was a necessity of life to a great medieval noble. The peculiarity about this secret chamber, however, was, that some secret connected with the very existence of the family was always understood to be involved in it. It was not only the secret hiding-place for an emergency, a kind of historical possession presupposing the importance of his race, of which a man might be honestly proud; but there was something hidden in it of which assuredly the race could not be proud. It is wonderful how easily a family learns to pique itself upon any distinctive possession. A ghost is a sign of importance not to be despised; a haunted room is worth as much as a small farm to the complacency of the family that owns it. And no doubt the younger branches of the Gowrie family—the light-minded portion of the race—felt this, and were proud of their unfathomable secret, and felt a thrill of agreeable awe and piquant suggestion go through them, when they remembered the mysterious something which they did not know in their familiar home. That thrill ran through the entire circle of visitors, and children, and servants, when the Earl peremptorily forbade a projected improvement, or stopped a reckless exploration. They looked at each other with a pleasurable shiver, "Did you hear?" they said. "He will not let Lady Gowrie have that closet she wants so much in that bit of wall. He sent the workmen about their business before they could touch it, though the wall is twenty feet thick if it is an inch: ah!" said the visitors, looking at each other; and this lively suggestion sent tinglings of excitement to their very finger-points; but even to his wife, mourning the commodious closet she had intended, the Earl made no explanations. For anything she knew, it might be there, next to her room, this mysterious lurking-place; and it may be supposed that this suggestion conveyed to Lady Gowrie's veins a thrill more keen and strange, perhaps too vivid to be pleasant. But she was not in the favoured or unfortunate number of those to whom the truth could be revealed.

I need not say what the different theories on the subject were. Some thought there had been a treacherous massacre there, and that the secret chamber was blocked by the skeletons of murdered guests,—a treachery no doubt covering the family with shame in its day, but so condoned by long softening of years as to have all the shame taken out of it. The Randolphs could not have felt their character affected by any such interesting historical record. They were not so morbidly sensitive. Some said, on the other hand, that Earl Robert, the wicked Earl, was shut op there in everlasting penance, playing cards with the devil for his soul. But it would have been too great a feather in the family cap to have thus got the devil, or even one of his angels, bottled up, as it were, and safely in hand, to make it possible that any lasting stigma could be connected with such a fact as this. What a thing it would be to know where to lay one's hand upon the Prince of Darkness, and prove him once for all, cloven foot and everything else, to the confusion of gainsayers!

So this was not to be received as a satisfactory solution, nor could any other be suggested which was more to the purpose. The popular mind gave it up, and yet never gave it up; and still everybody who visits Gowrie, be it as a guest, be it as a tourist, be it only as a gazer from a passing carriage, or from the flying railway train which just glimpses its turrets in the distance, daily and yearly spends a certain amount of curiosity, wonderment, and conjecture about the Secret Chamber—the most piquant and undiscoverable wonder which has endured unguessed and undeciphered to modern times.

This was how the matter stood when young John Randolph, Lord Lindores, came of age. He was a young man of great character and energy, not like the usual Randolph strain—for, as we have said, the type of character common in this romantically-situated family, notwithstanding the erratic incidents common to them, was that of dulness and honesty, especially in their early days. But young Lindores was not so. He was honest and honourable, but not dull. He had gone through almost a remarkable course at school and at the university—not perhaps in quite the ordinary way of scholarship, but enough to attract men's eyes to him. He had made more than one great speech at the Union. He was full of ambition, and force, and life, intending all sorts of great things, and meaning to make his position a stepping-stone to all that was excellent in public life. Not for him the country-gentleman existence which was congenial to his father. The idea of succeeding to the family honours and becoming a Scotch peer, either represented or representative, filled him with horror; and filial piety in his case was made warm by all the energy of personal hopes when he prayed that his father might live, if not for ever, yet longer than any Lord Gowrie had lived for the last century or two. He was as sure of his election for the county the next time there was a chance, as anybody can be certain of anything; and in the meantime he meant to travel, to go to America, to go no one could tell where, seeking for instruction and experience, as is the manner of high-spirited young men with parliamentary tendencies in the present day. In former times he would have gone "to the wars in the Hie Germanie," or on a crusade to the Holy Land; but the days of the crusaders and of the soldiers of fortune being over, Lindores followed the fashion of his time. He had made all his arrangements for his tour, which his father did not oppose. On the contrary, Lord Gowrie encouraged all those plans, though with an air of melancholy indulgence which his son could not understand. "It will do you good," he said, with a sigh. "Yes, yes, my boy; the best thing for you." This, no doubt, was true enough; but there was an implied feeling that the young man would require something to do him good—that he would want the soothing of change and the gratification of his wishes, as one might speak of a convalescent or the victim of some calamity. This tone puzzled Lindores, who, though he thought it a fine thing to travel and acquire information, was as scornful of the idea of being done good to as is natural to any fine young fellow fresh from Oxford and the triumphs of the Union. But be reflected that the old school had its own way of treating things, and was satisfied. All was settled accordingly for this journey, before he came home to go through the ceremonial performances of the coming of age, the dinner of the tenantry, the speeches, the congratulations, his father's banquet, his mother's ball. It was in summer, and the country was as gay as all the entertainments that were to be given in his honour. His friend who was going to accompany him on his tour, as he had accompanied him through a considerable portion of his life—Almeric Ffarrington, a young man of the same aspirations—came up to Scotland with him for these festivities. And as they rushed through the night on the Great Northern Railway, in the intervals of two naps, they had a scrap of conversation as to these birthday glories. "It will be a bore, but it will not last long," said Lindores. They were both of the opinion that anything that did not produce information or promote culture was a bore.

"But is there not a revelation to be made to you, among all the other things you have to go through!" said Ffarrington. "Have not you to be introduced to the secret chamber, and all that sort of thing? I should like to be of the party there, Lindores."

"Ah," said the heir, "I had forgotten that part of it," which, however, was not the case. "Indeed I don't know if I am to be told. Even family dogmas are shaken nowadays."

"Oh, I should insist on that," said Ffarrington, lightly. "It is not many who have the chance of paying such a visit—better than Home and all the mediums. I should insist upon that."

"I have no reason to suppose that it has any connection with Home or the mediums," said Lindores, slightly nettled. He was himself an *esprit fort*; but a mystery in one's own family is not like vulgar mysteries. He liked it to be respected.

"Oh, no offence," said his companion. "I have always thought that a railway train would be a great chance for the spirits. If one was to show suddenly in that vacant seat beside you, what a triumphant proof of their existence that would be! but they don't take advantage of their opportunities."

Lindores could not tell what it was that made him think at that moment of a portrait he had seen in a back room at the castle of old Earl Robert, the wicked Earl. It was a bad portrait—a daub—a copy made by an amateur of the genuine portrait, which, out of horror of Earl Robert and his wicked ways, had been removed by some intermediate lord from its place in the gallery. Lindores had never seen the original—nothing but this daub of a copy. Yet somehow this face occurred to him by some strange link of association—seemed to come into his eyes as his friend spoke. A slight shiver ran over him. It was strange. He made no reply to Ffarrington, but set himself to think how it could be that the latent presence in his mind of some anticipation of this approaching disclosure, touched into life by his friend's suggestion should have called out of his memory a momentary realisation of the acknowledged magician of the family. This sentence is full of long words; but unfortunately long words are required in such a case. And the process was very simple when you traced it out. It was the clearest case of unconscious cerebration. He shut his eyes by way of securing privacy while he thought it out; and being tired, and not at all alarmed by his unconscious cerebration, before he opened them again fell fast asleep.

And his birthday, which was the day following his arrival at Glenlyou, was a very busy day. He had not time to think of anything but the immediate occupations of the moment. Public and private greetings, congratulations, offerings, poured upon him. The Gowries were popular in this generation, which was far from being usual in the family. Lady Gowrie was kind and generous, with that kindness which comes from the heart, and which is the only kindness likely to impress the keen-sighted popular judgment; and Lord Gowrie had but little of the equivocal reputation of his predecessors. They could be splendid now and then on great occasions, though in general they were homely enough; all which the public likes. It was a bore, Lindores said; but yet the young man did not dislike the honours, and the adulation, and all the hearty speeches and good wishes. It is sweet to a young man to feel himself the centre of all hopes. It seemed very reasonable to him—very natural— that he should be so, and that the farmers should feel a pride of anticipation in thinking of his future speeches in Parliament. He promised to them with the sincerest good faith that he would not disappoint their expectations—

that he would feel their interest in him an additional spur. What so natural as that interest and these expectations? He was almost solemnised by his own position—so young, looked up to by so many people—so many hopes depending on him; and yet it was quite natural. His father, however, was still more solemnised than Lindores—and this was strange, to say the least. His face grew graver and graver as the day went on, till it almost seemed as if he were dissatisfied with his son's popularity, or had some painful thought weighing on his mind. He was restless and eager for the termination of the dinner, and to get rid of his guests; and as soon as they were gone, showed an equal anxiety that his son should retire too. "Go to bed at once, as a favour to me." Lord Gowrie said. "You will have a great deal of fatigue— to-morrow." "You need not be afraid for me, sir," said Lindores, half affronted; but he obeyed, being tired. He had not once thought of the secret to be disclosed to him, through all that long day. But when he woke suddenly with a start in the middle of the night, to find the candles all lighted in his room, and his father standing by his bedside, Lindores instantly thought of it, and in a moment felt that the leading event—the chief incident of all that had happened—was going to take place now.

CHAPTER II.

Lord Gowrie was very grave, and very pale. He was standing with his hand on his son's shoulder to wake him; his dress was unchanged from the moment they had parted. And the sight of this formal costume was very bewildering to the young man as he started up in his bed. But next moment he seemed to know exactly how it was, and, more than that, to have known it all his life. Explanation seemed unnecessary. At any other moment, in any other place, a man would be startled to be suddenly woke up in the middle of the night. But Lindores had no such feeling; he did not even ask a question, but sprang up, and fixed his eyes taking in all the strange circumstances, on his father's face.

"Get up, my boy," said Lord Gowrie, "and dress as quickly as you can; it is full time. I have lighted your candles, and your things are all ready. You have had a good long sleep."

Even now he did not ask. What is it? as under any other circumstances he would have done. He got up without a word, with an impulse of nervous speed and rapidity of movement such as only excitement can give, and dressed himself, his father helping him silently. It was a curious scene: the room gleaming with lights, the silence, the hurried toilet, the stillness of deep night all around. The house, though so full, and with the echoes of festivity but just over, was quiet as if there was not a creature within it—more quiet, indeed, for the stillness of vacancy is not half so impressive as the stillness of hushed and slumbering life.

Lord Gowrie went to the table when this first step was over, and poured out a glass of wine from a bottle which stood there,—a rich, golden-coloured, perfumy wine, which sent its scent through the room. "You will want all your strength," he said; "take this before you go. It is the famous Imperial Tokay; there is only a little left, and you will want all your strength."

Lindores took the wine; he had never drunk any like it before, and the peculiar fragrance remained in his mind, as perfumes so often do, with a whole world of association in them. His father's eyes dwelt upon him with a melancholy sympathy. "You are going to encounter the greatest trial of your life," he said; and taking the young man's hand into his, felt his pulse. "It is quick, but it is quite firm, and you have had a good long sleep." Then he did what it needs a great deal of pressure to induce an Englishman to do,—he kissed his son on the cheek. "God bless you!" he said, faltering. "Come, now, everything is ready, Lindores."

He took up in his hand a small lamp, which he had apparently brought with him, and led the way. By this time Lindores began to feel himself again, and to wake to the consciousness of all his own superiorities and enlightenments. The simple sense that he was one of the members of a family with a mystery, and that the moment of his personal encounter with this special power of darkness had come, had been the first thrilling, overwhelming thought. But now as he followed his father, Lindores began to remember that he himself was not altogether like other men; that there was that in him which would make it natural that he should throw some light, hitherto unthought of, upon this carefully-preserved darkness. What secret even there might be in it— secret of hereditary tendency, of psychic force, of mental conformation, or of some curious combination of circumstances at once more and less potent than these—it was for him to find out. He gathered all his forces about him, reminded himself of modern enlightenment, and bade his nerves be steel to all vulgar horrors. He too, felt his own pulse as he followed his father. To spend the night perhaps amongst the skeletons of that old-world massacre, and to repent the sins of his ancestors—to be brought within the range of some optical illusion believed in hitherto by all the generations, and which, no doubt, was of a startling kind, or his father would not look so serious—any of these he felt himself quite strong to encounter. His heart and spirit rose. A young man has but seldom the opportunity of distinguishing himself so early in his career; and his was such a chance as occurs to very few. No doubt it was something that would be extremely trying to the nerves and imagination.

He called up all his powers to vanquish both. And along with this call upon himself to exertion, there was the less serious impulse of curiosity: he would see at last what the Secret Chamber was, where it was, how it fitted into the labyrinths of the old house. This he tried to put in its due place as a most interesting object. He said to himself that he would willingly have gone a long journey at any time to be present at such an exploration; and there is no doubt that in other circumstances a secret chamber, with probably some unthought-of historical interest in it, would have been a very fascinating discovery. He tried very hard to excite himself about this; but it was curious how fictitious he felt the interest; and how conscious he was that it was an effort to feel any curiosity at all on the subject. The fact was, that the Secret Chamber was entirely secondary—thrown back, as all accessories are by a more pressing interest. The overpowering thought of what was in it drove aside all healthy, natural curiosity about itself.

It must not be supposed, however, that the father and son had a long way to go to have time for all these thoughts. Thoughts travel at lightning speed, and there was abundant leisure for this between the time they had left the door of Lindores' room and gone down the corridor, no further off than to Lord Gowrie's own chamber, naturally one of the chief rooms of the house. Nearly opposite this, a few steps further on, was a little neglected room devoted to lumber, with which Lindores had been familiar all his life. Why this nest of old rubbish, dust, and cobwebs should be so near the bedroom of the head of the house had been a matter of surprise to many people—to the guests who saw it while exploring, and to each new servant in succession who planned an attack upon its ancient stores, scandalised by finding it to have been neglected by their predecessors. All their attempts to clear it out had, however, been resisted, nobody could tell how, or indeed thought it worth while to inquire. As for Lindores, he had been used to the place from his childhood, and therefore accepted it as the most natural thing in the world. He had been in and out a hundred times in his play. And it was here, he remembered suddenly, that he had seen the bad picture of Earl Robert which had so curiously come into his eyes on his journeying here, by a mental movement which he had identified at once as unconscious cerebration. The first feeling in his mind, as his father went to the open door of this lumber-room, was a mixture of amusement and surprise. What was he going to pick up there? some old pentacle, some amulet or scrap of antiquated magic to act as armour against the evil one? But Lord Gowrie, going on and setting down the lamp on the table, turned round upon his son with a face of agitation and pain which barred all further amusement; he grasped him by the hand, crushing it between his own. "Now, my boy, my dear son," he said, in tones that were scarcely audible. His countenance was full of the dreary pain of a looker-on—one who has no share in the excitement of personal danger, but has the more terrible part of watching those who are in deadliest peril. He was a powerful man, and his large form shook with emotion; great beads of moisture stood upon his forehead. An old sword with a cross handle lay upon a dusty chair among other dusty and battered relics. "Take this with you," he said, in the same inaudible, breathless way—whether as a weapon, whether as a religious symbol Lindores could not guess. The young man took it mechanically. His father pushed open a door which it seemed to him he had never seen before, and led him into another vaulted chamber. Here even the limited powers of speech Lord Gowrie had retained seemed to forsake him, and his voice became a mere hoarse murmur in his throat. For want of speech he pointed to another door in the further corner of this small vacant room, gave hint to understand by a gesture that he was to knock there, and then went back into the lumber-room. The door into this was left open, and a faint glimmer of the lamp shed light into this little intermediate place—this debatable land between the seen and the unseen. In spite of himself, Lindores' heart began to beat. He made a breathless pause, feeling his head go round. He held the old sword in his hand, not knowing what it was. Then, summoning all his courage, he went forward and knocked at the closed door. His knock was not loud, but it seemed to echo all over the silent house. Would everybody hear and wake, and rush to see what had happened? This caprice of imagination seized upon him, ousting all the firmer thoughts, the steadfast calm of mind with which he ought to have encountered the mystery. Would they all rush in, in wild *déshabille*, in terror and dismay, before the door opened? How long it was of opening! He touched the panel with his hand again.—This time there was no delay. In a moment, as if thrown suddenly open by some one within, the door moved. It opened just wide enough to let him enter, stopping half-way as if some one invisible held it, wide enough for welcome, but no more, Lindores stepped across the threshold with a beating heart. What was he about to see? the skeletons of the murdered victims? a ghostly charnel-house full of bloody traces of crime? He seemed to be hurried and pushed in as he made that step. What was this world of mystery into which he was plunged—what was it he saw?

He saw—nothing—except what was agreeable enough to behold,—an antiquated room hung with tapestry, very old tapestry of rude design, its colours faded into softness and harmony; between its folds here and there a panel of carved wood, rude too in design, with traces of half-worn gilding; a table covered with strange instruments, parchments, chemical tubes, and curious machinery, all with a quaintness of form and dimness of material that spoke of age. A heavy old velvet cover, thick with embroidery faded almost out of all colour, was on the table; on the wall above it, something that looked like a very old Venetian mirror, the glass so dim and crusted that it scarcely reflected at all; on the floor an old soft Persian carpet, worn into a vague blending of all colors. This was all that he thought he saw. His heart, which had been thumping so loud as almost to choke him, stopped that tremendous upward and downward motion like a steam piston; and he grew calm. Perfectly still, dim, unoccupied: yet not so dim either; there was no apparent source of light, no windows, curtains of tapestry drawn everywhere—no lamp visible, no fire—and yet a kind of strange light which made everything quite clear. He looked round, trying to smile at his terrors, trying to say to himself that it was the most curious place he had ever seen—that he must show Ffarrington some of that tapestry—that he must really bring away a panel of that carving,— when he suddenly saw that the door was shut by which he had entered—nay, more than shut, undiscernible, covered like all the rest of the walls by that strange tapestry. At this his heart began to beat again in spite of him. He looked round once more, and woke up to more vivid being with a sudden start. Had his eyes been incapable of vision on his first entrance? Unoccupied? Who was that in the great chair?

It seemed to Lindores that he had seen neither the chair nor the man when he came in. There they were, however, solid and unmistakable; the chair carved like the panels, the man seated in front of the table. He looked at Lindores with a calm and open gaze, inspecting him. The young man's heart seemed in his throat fluttering like a bird, but he was brave, and his mind made one final effort to break this spell. He tried to speak, labouring with a voice that would not sound, and with lips too parched to form a word. "I see how it is," was what he wanted to say. It was Earl Robert's face that was looking at him; and startled as he was, he dragged forth his philosophy to support him. What could it be but optical delusions, unconscious cerebration, occult seizure by the impressed and struggling mind of this one countenance? But he could not hear himself speak any word as he stood convulsed, struggling with dry lips and choking voice.

The Appearance smiled, as if knowing his thoughts—not unkindly, not malignly—with a certain amusement mingled with scorn. Then he spoke, and the sound seemed to breathe through the room not like any voice that Lindores had ever heard, a kind of utterance of the place, like the rustle of the air or the ripple of the sea. "You will learn better tonight: this is no phantom of your brain; it is I."

"In God's name," cried the young man in his soul; he did not know whether the words ever got into the air or not, if there was any air;—"In God's name, who are you?"

The figure rose as if coming to him to reply; and Lindores, overcome by the apparent approach, struggled into utterance. A cry came from him—he heard it this time—and even in his extremity felt a pang the more to hear the terror in his own voice. But he did not flinch, he stood desperate, all his strength concentrated in the act; he neither turned nor recoiled. Vaguely gleaming through his mind came the thought that to be thus brought in contact with the unseen was the experiment to be most desired on earth, the final settlement of a hundred questions; but his faculties were not sufficiently under command to entertain it. He only stood firm, that was all.

And the figure did not approach him; after a moment it subsided back again into the chair—subsided, for no sound, not the faintest, accompanied its movements. It was the form of a man of middle age, the hair white, but the beard only crisped with grey, the features those of the picture—a familiar face, more or less like all the Randolphs, but with an air of domination and power altogether unlike that of the race. He was dressed in a long robe of dark colour, embroidered with strange lines and angles. There was nothing repellent or terrible in his air—nothing except the noiselessness, the calm, the absolute stillness, which was as much in the place as in him, to keep up the involuntary trembling of the beholder. His expression was full of dignity and thoughtfulness, and not malignant or unkind. He might have been the kindly patriarch of the house, watching over its fortunes in a seclusion he had chosen. The pulses that had been beating in Lindores were stilled. What was his panic for? a gleam even of self-ridicule took possession of him, to be standing there like an absurd hero of antiquated romance with the rusty, dusty sword—good for nothing, surely not adapted for use against this noble old magician—in his hand—

"You are right," said the voice, once more answering his thoughts: "what could you do with that sword against me, young Lindores? Put it by. Why should my children meet me like an enemy? You are my flesh and blood. Give me your hand."

A shiver ran through the young man's frame. The hand that was held out to him was large and shapely and white, with a straight line across the palm—a family token upon which the Randolphs prided themselves—a friendly hand; and the face smiled upon him, fixing him with those calm, profound, blue eyes. "Come," said the voice. The word seemed to fill the place, melting upon him from every corner, whispering round him with softest persuasion. He was lulled and calmed in spite of himself. Spirit or no spirit, why should not he accept this proffered courtesy? What harm could come of it? The chief thing that retained him was the dragging of the old sword, heavy and useless, which he held mechanically, but which some internal feeling—he could not tell what—prevented him from putting down. Superstition, was it?

"Yes, that is superstition," said his ancestor, serenely; "put it down and come."

"You know my thoughts," said Lindores; "I did not speak."

"Your mind spoke, and spoke justly. Put down that emblem of brute force and superstition together. Here it is the intelligence that is supreme. Come."

Lindores stood doubtful. He was calm; the power of thought was restored to him. If this benevolent venerable patriarch was all he seemed, why his father's terror? why the secrecy in which his being was involved? His own mind, though calm, did not seem to act in the usual way. Thoughts seemed to be driven across it as by a wind. One of these came to him suddenly now—

> "How there looked him in the face,
>   An angel beautiful and bright,
> And how he knew it was a fiend."

The words were not ended, when Earl Robert replied suddenly with impatience in his voice, "Fiends are of the fancy of men; like angels and other follies. I am your father. You know me; and you are mine, Lindores. I have power beyond what you can understand; but I want flesh and blood to reign and to enjoy. Come, Lindores!"

He put out his other hand. The action, the look, were those of kindness, almost of longing, and the face was familiar, the voice was that of the race. Supernatural! was it supernatural that this man should live here shut up for ages? and why? and how? Was there any explanation of it? The young man's brain began to reel. He could not tell which was real—the life he had left half an hour ago, or this. He tried to look round him, but could not; his eyes were caught by those other kindred eyes, which seemed to dilate and deepen as he looked at them, and drew him with a strange compulsion. He felt himself yielding, swaying towards the strange being who thus invited him. What might happen if he yielded? And he could not turn away, he could not tear himself from the fascination of those eyes. With a sudden strange impulse which was half despair and half a bewildering half-conscious desire to try one potency against another, he thrust forward the cross of the old sword between him and those appealing hands. "In the name of God!"

Lindores never could tell whether it was that he himself grew faint, and that the dimness of swooning came into his eyes after this violence and strain of emotion, or if it was his spell that worked. But there was an instantaneous change. Everything swam around him for the moment, a giddiness and blindness seized him, and he saw nothing but the vague outlines of the room, empty as when he entered it. But gradually his consciousness came back, and he found himself standing on the same spot as before, clutching the old sword, and gradually, as though a dream, recognised the same figure emerging out of the mist which—was it solely in his own eyes?—had enveloped everything. But it was no longer in the same attitude. The hands which had been stretched out to him were busy now with some of the strange instruments on the table, moving about, now in the action of writing, now as if managing the keys of a telegraph. Lindores felt that his brain was all atwist and set wrong; but he was still a human being of his century. He thought of the telegraph with a keen thrill of curiosity in the midst of his reviving sensations. What communication was this which was going on before his eyes? The magician worked on. He had his face turned towards his victim, but his hands moved with unceasing activity. And Lindores, as he grew accustomed to the position, began to weary—to feel like a neglected suitor waiting for an audience. To be wound up to such a strain of feeling, then left to wait, was intolerable; impatience seized upon him. What circumstances can exist, however horrible, in which a human being will not feel impatience? He made a great many efforts to speed before he could succeed. It seemed to him that his body felt more fear than he did—that his muscles were contracted, his throat parched, his tongue refusing its office, although his mind was unaffected and undismayed. At last he found an utterance in spite of all resistance of his flesh and blood.

"Who are you?" he said hoarsely. "You that live here and oppress this house?"

The vision raised its eyes full upon him, with again that strange shadow of a smile, mocking yet not unkind. "Do you remember me," he said, "on your journey here?"

"That was—a delusion." The young man gasped for breath.

"More like that you are a delusion. You have lasted but one-and-twenty years, and I—for centuries."

"How? For centuries—and why? Answer me—are you man or demon?" cried Lindores, tearing the words, as he felt, out of his own throat. "Are you living or dead?"

The magician looked at him with the same intense gaze as before. "Be on my side, and you shall know everything, Lindores. I want one of my own race. Others I could have in plenty; but I want *you*. A Randolph, a Randolph! and *you*. Dead! do I seem dead! You shall have everything—more than dreams can give—if you will be on my side."

Can he give what he has not? was the thought that ran through the mind of Lindores. But he could not speak it. Something that choked and stifled him was in his throat.

"Can I give what I have not? I have everything—power, the one thing worth having; and you shall have more than power, for you are young—my son! Lindores!"

To argue was natural, and gave the young man strength. "Is this life," he said, "here? What is all your power worth—here? To sit for ages, and make a race unhappy?"

A momentary convulsion came across the still face. "You scorn me," he cried, with an appearance of emotion, "because you do not understand how I move the world. Power! 'Tis more than fancy can grasp. And you shall have it!" said the wizard, with what looked like a show of enthusiasm. He seemed to come nearer, to grow larger. He put forth his hand again, this time so close that it seemed impossible to escape. And a crowd of wishes seemed to rush upon the mind of Lindores. What harm to try if this might be true? To try what it meant—perhaps nothing, delusions, vain show, and then there could be no harm; or perhaps there was knowledge to be had, which was power. Try, try, try! the air buzzed about him. The room seemed full of voices urging him. His bodily frame rose into a tremendous whirl of excitement, his veins seemed to swell to bursting, his lips seemed to force a yes, in spite of him, quivering as they came apart. The hiss of the s seemed in his ears. He changed it into the name which was a spell too, and cried "Help me, God!" not knowing why.

Then there came another pause—he felt as if he had been dropped from something that had held him, and had fallen, and was faint. The excitement had been more than he could bear. Once more everything swam around him, and he did not know where he was. Had he escaped altogether? was the first waking wonder of consciousness in his mind. But when he could think and see again, he was still in the same spot, surrounded by the old curtains and the carved panels—but alone. He felt, too, that he was able to move, but the strangest dual consciousness was in him throughout all the rest of his trial. His body felt to him as a frightened horse feels to a traveller at night—a thing separate from him, more frightened than he was—starting aside at every step, seeing more than its master. His limbs shook with fear and weakness, almost refusing to obey the action of his will, trembling under him with jerks aside when he compelled himself to move. The hair stood upright on his head—every finger trembled as with palsy—his lips, his eyelids, quivered with nervous agitation. But his mind was strong, stimulated to a desperate calm. He dragged himself round the room, he crossed the very spot where the magician had been—all was vacant, silent, clear. Had he vanquished the enemy? This thought came into his mind with an involuntary triumph. The old strain of feeling came back. Such efforts might be produced, perhaps, only by imagination, by excitement, by delusion——

Lindores looked up, by a sudden attraction he could not tell what: and the blood suddenly froze in his veins that had been so boiling and fermenting. Some one was looking at him from the old mirror on the wall. A face not human and life-like, like that of the inhabitant of this place, but ghostly and terrible, like one of the dead; and while he looked, a crowd of other faces came behind, all looking at him, some mournfully, some with a menace in their terrible eyes. The mirror did not change, but within its small dim space seemed to contain an innumerable company, crowded above and below, all with one gaze at him. His lips dropped apart with a gasp of horror. More and more and more! He was standing close by the table when this crowd came. Then all at once there was laid upon him a cold hand. He turned; close to his side, brushing him with his robe, holding him fast by the arm, sat Earl Robert in his great chair. A shriek came from the young man's lips. He seemed to hear it echoing away into unfathomable distance. The cold touch penetrated to his very soul.

"Do you try spells upon me, Lindores? That is a tool of the past. You shall have something better to work with. And are you so sure of whom you call upon? If there is such a one, why should He help you who never called on Him before?"

Lindores could not tell if these words were spoken; it was a communication rapid as the thoughts in the mind. And he felt as if something answered that was not all himself. He seemed to stand passive and hear the argument, "Does God reckon with a man in trouble, whether he has ever called to Him before? I call now" (now he felt it was himself that said): "go, evil spirit!—go, dead and cursed!—go in the name of God!"

He felt himself flung violently against the wall. A faint laugh, stifled in the throat, and followed by a groan, rolled round the room; the old curtains seemed to open here and there, and flutter, as if with comings and goings. Lindores leaned with his back against the wall, and all his senses restored to him. He felt blood trickle down his neck; and in this contact once more with the physical, his body, in its madness of fright, grew manageable. For the first time he felt wholly master of himself. Though the magician was standing in his place, a great, majestic, appalling figure, he did not shrink. "Liar!" he cried, in a voice that rang and echoed as in natural air—"clinging to miserable life like a worm—like a reptile; promising all things, having nothing, but this den, unvisited by the light of day. Is this your power—your superiority to men who die? is it for this that you oppress a race, and make a house unhappy? I vow, in God's name, your reign is over! You and your secret shall last no more."

There was no reply. But Lindores felt his terrible ancestor's eyes getting once more that mesmeric mastery over him which had already almost overcome his powers. He must withdraw his own, or perish. He had a human horror of turning his back upon that watchful adversary: to face him seemed the only safety; but to face him was to be conquered. Slowly, with a pang indescribable, he tore himself from that gaze: it seemed to drag his eyes out of their sockets, his heart out of his bosom. Resolutely, with the daring of desperation, he turned round to the spot where he entered—the spot where no door was,—hearing already in anticipation the step after him—feeling the grip that would crush and smother his exhausted life—but too desperate to care.

CHAPTER III.

How wonderful is the blue dawning of the new day before the sun! not rosy-fingered, like that Aurora of the Greeks who comes later with all her wealth; but still, dreamy, wonderful, stealing out of the unseen, abashed by the solemnity of the new birth. When anxious watchers see that first brightness come stealing upon the waiting skies, what mingled relief and renewal of misery is in it! another long day to toil through—yet another sad night over! Lord Gowrie sat among the dust and cobwebs, his lamp flaring idly into the blue morning. He had heard his son's human voice, though nothing more: and he expected to have him brought out by invisible hands, as had happened to himself, and left lying in long deathly swoon outside that mystic door. This was how it had happened to heir after heir, as told from father to son, one after another, as the secret came down. One or two bearers of the name of Lindores had never recovered; most of them had been saddened and subdued for life. He remembered sadly the freshness of existence which had never come back to himself; the hopes that had never blossomed again; the assurance with which never more he had been able to go about the world. And now his son would be as himself—the glory gone out of his living—his ambitions, his aspirations wrecked. He had not been endowed as his boy was—he had been a plain, honest man, and nothing more; but experience and life had given him wisdom enough to smile by times at the coquetries of mind in which Lindores indulged. Were they all over now, those freaks of young intelligence, those enthusiasms of the soul? The curse of the house had come upon him—the magnetism of that strange presence, ever living, ever watchful, present in all the family history. His heart was sore for his son; and yet along with this there was a certain consolation to him in having henceforward a partner in the secret—some one to whom he could talk of it as he had not been able to talk since his own father died. Almost all the mental struggles which Gowrie had known had been connected with this mystery; and he had been obliged to hide them in his bosom—to conceal them even when they rent him in two. Now he had a partner in his trouble. This was what he was thinking as he sat through the night. How slowly the moments passed! He was not aware of the daylight coming in. After a while even thought got suspended in listening. Was not the time nearly over? He rose and began to pace about the encumbered space, which was but a step or two in extent. There was an old cupboard in the wall, in which there were restoratives—pungent essences and cordials, and fresh water which he had himself brought—everything was ready; presently the ghastly body of his boy, half dead, would be thrust forth into his care.

But this was not how it happened. While he waited, so intent that his whole frame seemed to be capable of hearing, be heard the closing of the door, boldly shut with a sound that rose in muffled echoes through the house, and Lindores himself appeared, ghastly indeed as a dead man, but walking upright and firmly, the lines of his face drawn, and his eyes staring. Lord Gowrie uttered a cry. He was more alarmed by this unexpected return than by the helpless prostration of the swoon which he had expected. He recoiled from his son as if he too had been a spirit. "Lindores!" he cried; was it Lindores, or some one else in his place? The boy seemed as if he did not see him. "He went straight forward to where the water stood on the dusty table, and took a great draught, then turned to the door. "Lindores!" said his father, in miserable anxiety; "don't you know me?" Even then the young man only half looked at him, and put out a hand almost as cold as the hand that had clutched himself in the Secret chamber; a faint smile came upon his face. "Don't stay here," he whispered; "come! come!"

Lord Gowrie drew his son's arm within his own, and felt the thrill through and through him of nerves strained beyond mortal strength. He could scarcely keep up with him as he stalked along the corridor to his room, stumbling as if he could not see, yet swift as an arrow. When they reached his room he turned and closed and locked the door, then laughed as he staggered to the bed. "That will not keep him out, will it?" he said.

"Lindores," said his father, "I expected to find you unconscious. I am almost more frightened to find you like this. I need not ask if you have seen him——"

"Oh, I have seen him. The old liar! Father, promise to expose him, to turn him out—promise to clear out that accursed old nest! It is our own fault. Why have we left such a place shut out from the eye of day? Isn't there something in the Bible about those who do evil hating the light?"

"Lindores! you don't often quote the Bible."

"No, I suppose not; but there is more truth in—many things than we thought."

"Lie down," said the anxious father. "Take some of this wine—try to sleep."

"Take it away; give me no more of that devil's drink. Talk to me—that's better. Did you go through it all the same, poor papa?—and hold me fast. You are warm—you are honest!" he cried. He put forth his hands over his father's, warming them with the contact. He put his cheek like a child against his father's arm. He gave a faint laugh, with the tears in his eyes. "Warm and honest," he repeated. "Kind flesh and blood! and did you go through it all the same?"

"My boy!" cried the father, feeling his heart glow and swell over the son who had been parted from him for years by that development of young manhood and ripening intellect which so often severs and loosens the ties of home. Lord Gowrie had felt that Lindores half despised his simple mind and duller imagination; but this childlike clinging overcame him, and tears stood in his eyes. "I fainted, I suppose. I never knew how it ended. They made what they liked of me. But you, my brave boy, you came out of your own will."

Lindores shivered. "I fled!" he said. "No honour in that. I had not courage to face him longer. I will tell you by-and-by. But I want to know about you."

What an ease it was to the father to speak! For years and years this had been shut up in his breast. It had made him lonely in the midst of his friends.

"Thank God," he said, "that I can speak to you, Lindores. Often and often I have been tempted to tell your mother. But why should I make her miserable? She knows there is something; she knows when I see him, but she knows no more."

"When you see him?" Lindores raised himself, with a return of his first ghastly look, in his bed. Then he raised his clenched fist wildly, and shook it in the air. "Vile devil, coward, deceiver!"

"Oh hush, hush, hush, Lindores! God help us! what troubles you may bring!"

"And God help me, whatever troubles I bring," said the young man. "I defy him, father. An accursed being like that must be less, not more powerful, than we are—with God to back us. Only stand by me: stand by me——"

"Hush, Lindores! You don't feel it yet—never to get out of hearing of him all your life! He will make you pay for it—if not now, after; when you remember he is there, whatever happens, knowing everything! But I hope it will not be so bad with you as with me, my poor boy. God help you indeed if it is, for you have more imagination and more mind. I am able to forget him sometimes when I am occupied—when in the hunting-field, going across country. But you are not a hunting man, my poor boy," said Lord Gowrie, with a curious mixture of a regret, which was less serious than the other. Then he lowered his voice. "Lindores, this is what has happened to me since the moment I gave him my hand."

"I did not give him my hand."

"You did not give him your hand? God bless you, my boy! You stood out?" he cried, with tears again rushing to his eyes; "and they say—they say—but I don't know if there is any truth in it." Lord Gowrie got up from his son's side, and walked up and down with excited steps. "If there should be truth in it! Many people think the whole thing is a fancy. If there should be truth in it, Lindores!"

"In what, father?"

'They say, if he is once resisted his power is broken—once refused. *You* could stand against him—you! Forgive me, my boy, as I hope God will forgive me, to have thought so little of His best gift," cried Lord Gowrie, coming back with wet eyes; and stooping, he kissed his son's hand. "I thought you would be more shaken by being more mind than body," he said, humbly. "I thought if I could but have saved you from the trial; and *you* are the conqueror!"

"Am I the conqueror? I think all my bones are broken, father—out of their sockets," said the young man, in a low voice. "I think I shall go to sleep."

"Yes, rest, my boy. It is the best thing for you," said the father, though with a pang of momentary disappointment. Lindores fell back upon the pillow. He was so pale that there were moments when the anxious watcher thought him not sleeping but dead. He put his hand out feebly, and grasped his father's hand. "Warm—honest," he said, with a feeble smile about his lips, and fell asleep.

The daylight was full in the room, breaking through shutters and curtains, and mocking at the lamp that still flared on the table. It seemed an emblem of the disorders, mental and material, of this strange night; and, as such, it affected the plain imagination of Lord Gowrie, who would have fain got up to extinguish it, and whose mind returned again and again, in spite of him, to this symptom of disturbance. By-and-by, when Lindores' grasp relaxed, and he got his hand free, he got up from his son's bedside, and put out the lamp, putting it carefully out of the way. With equal care he put away the wine from the table, and gave the room its ordinary aspect, softly opening a window to let in the fresh air of the morning. The park lay fresh in the early sunshine, still, except for the twittering of the birds, refreshed with dews, and shining in that soft radiance of the morning which is over before mortal cares are stirring. Never, perhaps, had Gowrie looked out upon the beautiful world around his house without a thought of the weird existence which was going on so near to him, which had gone on for centuries, shut up out of sight of the sunshine. The Secret Chamber had been present with him since ever he saw it. He had never been able to get free of the spell of it. He had felt himself watched, surrounded, spied upon, day after day, since he was of the age of Lindores, and that was thirty years ago. He turned it all over in his mind, as he stood there and his son slept. It had been on his lips to tell it all to his boy, who had now come to inherit the enlightenment of his race. And it was a disappointment to him to have it all forced back again, and silence imposed upon him once more. Would be care to hear it when he woke? would he not rather, as Lord Gowrie remembered to have done himself, thrust the thought as far as he could away from him, and endeavour to forget for the moment—until the time came when he would not be permitted to forget? He had been like that himself, he recollected now. He had not wished to hear his own father's tale. "I remember," he said to himself; "I remember"—turning over everything in his mind—if Lindores might only be willing to hear the story when he woke! But then he himself had not been willing when he was Lindores, and he could understand his son, and could not blame him; but it would be a disappointment. He was thinking this when he heard Lindores' voice calling him. He went back hastily to his bedside. It was strange to see him in his evening dress with his worn face, in the fresh light of the morning, which poured in at every crevice. "Does my mother know?" said Lindores; "what will she think!"

"She knows something; she knows you have some trial to go through. Most likely she will be praying for us both; that's the way of women," said Lord Gowrie, with the tremulous tenderness which comes into a man's voice sometimes when he speaks of a good wife. "I'll go and ease her mind, and tell her all is well over—"

"Not yet. Tell me first," said the young man, putting his hand upon his father's arm.

What an ease it was! "I was not so good to my father," he thought to himself, with sudden penitence for the long-past, long-forgotten fault, which, indeed, he had never realised as a fault before. And then he told his son what had been the story of his life—how he bad scarcely ever sat alone without feeling, from some corner of the room, from behind some curtain, those eyes upon him; and how, in the difficulties of his life, that secret inhabitant of the house had been present, sitting by him and advising him. "Whenever there has been anything to do: when there has been a question between two ways, all in a moment I have seen him by me: I feel when he is coming. It does not matter where I am—here or anywhere—as soon as ever there is a question of family business; and always he persuades me to the wrong way, Lindores. Sometimes I yield to him, how can I help it? He makes everything so clear; he makes wrong seem right. If I have done unjust things in my day——"

"You have not, father."

"I have: there were these Highland people I turned out. I did not mean to do it, Lindores; but he showed me that it would be better for the family. And my poor sister that married Tweedside and was wretched all her life. It was his doing, that marriage; he said she would be rich, and so she was, poor thing, poor thing! and died of it. And old Macalister's lease——Lindores, Lindores!

when there is any business it makes my heart sick. I know he will come, and advise wrong, and tell me—something I will repent after."

"The thing to do is to decide beforehand, that, good or bad, you will not take his advice."

Lord Gowrie shivered. "I am not strong like you, or clever; I cannot resist. Sometimes I repent in time and don't do it; and then: But for your mother and you children, there is many a day I would not have given a farthing for my life."

"Father," said Lindores, springing from his bed, "two of us together can do many things. Give me your word to clear out this cursed den of darkness this very day."

"Lindores, hush, hush, for the sake of heaven!"

"I will not, for the sake of heaven! Throw it open—let everybody who likes see it—make an end of the secret—pull down everything, curtains, walls. What do you say?—sprinkle holy water? Are you laughing at me?"

"I did not speak," said Earl Gowrie, growing very pale, and grasping his son's arm with both his hands. "Hush, boy; do you think he does not hear?"

And then there was a low laugh close to them—so close that both shrank; a laugh no louder than a breath.

"Did you laugh—father?"

"No, Lindores." Lord Gowrie had his eyes fixed. He was as pale as the dead. He held his son tight for a moment; then his gaze and his grasp relaxed, and he fell back feebly in a chair.

"You see," he said; "whatever we do it will be the same; we are under his power."

And then there ensued the blank pause with which baffled men confront a hopeless situation. But at that moment the first faint stirrings of the house—a window being opened, a bar undone, a movement of feet, and subdued voices—became audible in the stillness of the morning. Lord Gowrie roused himself at once. "We must not be found like this," he said; "we must not show how we have spent the night. It is over, thank God! and oh, my boy, forgive me! I am thankful there are two of us to bear it; it makes the burden lighter—though I ask your pardon humbly for saying so. I would have saved you if I could, Lindores."

"I don't wish to have been saved; but *I* will not bear it. I will end it," the young man said, with an oath out of which his emotion took all profanity. His father said, "Hush, hush." With a look of terror and pain, he left him; and yet there was a thrill of tender pride in his mind. How brave the boy was! even after he had been *there*. Could it be that this would all come to nothing, as every other attempt to resist had done before?

"I suppose you. know all about it now, Lindores," said his friend Ffarrington, after breakfast; "luckily for us who are going over the house. What a glorious old place it is!"

"I don't think that Lindores enjoys the glorious old place to-day," said another of the guests under his breath. "How pale he is! He doesn't look as if he had slept."

"I will take you over every nook where I have ever been," said Lindores. He looked at his father with almost command in his eyes. "Come with me, all of you. We shall have no more secrets here."

"Are you mad?" said his father in his ear.

"Never mind," cried the young man. "Oh, trust me; I will do it with judgment. Is everybody ready?" There was an excitement about him that half frightened, half roused the party. They all rose; eager, yet doubtful. His mother came to him and took his arm.

"Lindores! you will do nothing to vex your father; don't make him unhappy. I don't know your secrets, you two; but look, he has enough to bear."

"I want you to know our secrets, mother. Why should we have secrets from you?"

"Why, indeed?" she said, with tears in her eyes. "But, Lindores, my dearest boy, don't make it worse for *him*."

"I give you my word, I will be wary," he said; and she left him to go to his father, who followed the party, with an anxious look upon his face.

"Are you coming, too?" he asked.

"I? No; I will not go: but trust him—trust the boy, John."

"He can do nothing; he will not be able to do anything," he said.

And thus the guests set out on their round—the son in advance, excited and tremulous, the father anxious and watchful behind. They began in the usual way, with the old state-rooms and picture-gallery; and in a short time the party had half-forgotten that there was anything unusual in the inspection. When, however, they were half-way down the gallery, Lindores stopped short with an air of wonder. "You have had it put back then?" he said. He was standing in front of the vacant space where Earl Robert's portrait ought to have been. "What is it?" they all cried, crowding upon him, ready for any marvel. But as there was nothing to be seen, the strangers smiled among themselves. "Yes, to be sure, there is nothing so suggestive as a vacant place," said a lady who was of the party. "Whose portrait ought to be there, Lord Lindores?"

He looked at his father, who made a slight assenting gesture, then shook his head drearily.

"Who put it there?" Lindores said, in a whisper.

"It is not there; but you and I see it," said Lord Gowrie, with a sigh.

Then the strangers perceived that something had moved the father and the son, and, notwithstanding their eager curiosity, obeyed the dictates of politeness, and dispersed into groups looking at the other pictures. Lindores set his teeth and clenched his hands. Fury was growing upon him—not the awe that filled his father's mind. "We will leave the rest of this to another time," he cried, turning to the others, almost fiercely. "Come, I will show you something more striking now." He made no further pretence of going systematically over the house. He turned and went straight up-stairs, and along the corridor. "Are we going over the bed-rooms?" some one said. Lindores led the way straight to the old lumber-room, a strange place for such a gay party. The ladies drew their dresses about them. There was not room for half of them. Those who could get in began to handle the strange things that lay about, touching them with dainty fingers, exclaiming how dusty they were. The window was half blocked up by old armour and rusty weapons; but this did not hinder the full summer daylight from penetrating in a flood of light. Lindores went in with fiery determination on his face. He went straight to the wall, as if he would go through, then paused with a blank gaze. "Where is the door?" he said.

"You are forgetting yourself," said Lord Gowrie, speaking over the heads of the others. "Lindores! you know very well there never was any door there; the wall is very thick; you can see by the depth of the window. There is no door there."

The young man felt it over with his hand. The wall was smooth, and covered with the dust of ages. With a groan he turned away. At this moment a suppressed laugh, low, yet distinct, sounded close by him. "You laughed?" he said fiercely, to Ffarrington, striking his hand upon his shoulder.

"I—laughed! Nothing was farther from my thoughts," said his friend, who was curiously examining something that lay upon an old carved chair. "Look here! what a wonderful sword, cross-hilted! Is it an Andrea? What's the matter, Lindores?"

Lindores had seized it from his hands; he dashed it against the wall with a suppressed oath. The two or three people in the room stood aghast.

"Lindores!" his father said, in a tone of warning. The young man dropped the useless weapon with a groan. "Then God help us!" he said; "but I will find another way!"

"There is a very interesting room close by," said Lord Gowrie, hastily—"this way! Lindores has been put out by—some changes that have been made without his knowledge," he said, calmly. "You must not mind him. He is disappointed. He is perhaps too much accustomed to have his own way."

But Lord Gowrie knew that no one believed him. He took them to the adjoining room, and told them some easy story of an apparition that was supposed to haunt it. "Have you ever seen it?" the guests said, pretending interest. "Not I; but we don't mind ghosts in this house," he answered, with a smile. And then they resumed their round of the old noble mystic house.

I cannot tell the reader what young Lindores has done to carry out his pledged word and redeem his family. It may not be known, perhaps, for another generation, and it will not be for me to write that concluding chapter: but when, in the ripeness of time, it can be narrated, no one will say that the mystery of Gowrie Castle his been a vulgar horror, though there are some who are disposed to think so now.

FROM THE DEAD

E. Nesbit

I.

"But true or not true, your brother is a scoundrel. No man—no decent man—tells such things."

"He did not tell me. How dare you suppose it? I found the letter in his desk; and since she was my friend and your sweetheart, I never thought there could be any harm in my reading anything she might write to my brother. Give me back the letter. I was a fool to tell you."

Ida Helmont held out her hand for the letter.

"Not yet," I said, and I went to the window. The dull red of a London sunset burned on the paper, as I read in the pretty handwriting I knew so well, and had kissed so often—

> "DEAR—I do—I do love you; but it's impossible. I must marry Arthur. My honour is engaged. If he would only set me free—but he never will. He loves me foolishly. But as for me—it is you I love—body, soul and spirit. There is no one in my heart but you. I think of you all day, and dream of you all night. And we must part. Goodbye—Yours, yours, yours,
>
> ELVIRA."

I had seen the handwriting, indeed, often enough. But the passion there was new to me. That I had not seen.

I turned from the window. My sitting-room looked strange to me. There were my books, my reading-lamp, my untasted dinner still on the table, as I had left it when I rose to dissemble my surprise at Ida Helmont's visit—Ida Helmont, who now sat looking at me quietly.

"Well—do you give me no thanks?"

"You put a knife in my heart, and then ask for thanks?"

"Pardon me," she said, throwing up her chin. "I have done nothing but show you the truth. For that one should expect no gratitude—may I ask, out of pure curiosity, what you intend to do?"

79

"Your brother will tell you—"

She rose suddenly, very pale, and her eyes haggard.

"You will not tell my brother?"

She came towards me—her gold hair flaming in the sunset light.

"Why are you so angry with me?" she said. "Be reasonable. What else could I do?"

"I don't know."

"Would it have been right not to tell you?"

"I don't know. I only know that you've put the sun out, and I haven't got used to the dark yet."

"Believe me," she said, coming still nearer to me, and laying her hands in the lightest touch on my shoulders, "believe me, she never loved you."

There was a softness in her tone that irritated and stimulated me. I moved gently back, and her hands fell by her sides.

"I beg your pardon," I said. "I have behaved very badly. You were quite right to come, and I am not ungrateful. Will you post a letter for me?"

I sat down and wrote—

"I give you back your freedom. The only gift of mine that can please you now.—

ARTHUR."

I held the sheet out to Miss Helmont, but she would not look at it. I folded, sealed, stamped, and addressed it.

"Good-bye," I said then, and gave her the letter. As the door closed behind her, I sank into my chair, and cried like a child, or a fool, over my lost plaything—the little, dark-haired woman who loved someone else with "body, soul, and spirit."

I did not hear the door, open or any foot on the floor, and therefore I started when a voice behind me said:

"Are you so very unhappy? Oh, Arthur, don't think I am not sorry for you!"

"I don't want anyone to be sorry for me, Miss Helmont," I said.

She was silent a moment. Then, with a quick, sudden, gentle movement she leaned down and kissed my forehead—and I heard the door softly close. Then I knew that the beautiful Miss Helmont loved me.

At first that thought only fleeted by—a light cloud against a grey sky—but the next day reason woke, and said:

"Was Miss Helmont speaking the truth? Was it possible that—"

I determined to see Elvira, to know from her own lips whether by happy fortune this blow came, not from her, but from a woman in whom love might have killed honesty.

I walked from Hampstead to Gower Street. As I trod its long length, I saw a figure in pink come out of one of the houses. It was Elvira. She walked in front of me to the corner of Store Street. There she met Oscar Helmont. They turned and met me face to face, and I saw all I needed to see. They loved each other. Ida Helmont had spoken the truth. I bowed and passed on. Before six months were gone, they were married, and before a year was over, I had married Ida Helmont.

What did it, I don't know. Whether it was remorse for having, even for half a day, dreamed that she could be so base as to forge a lie to gain a lover, or whether it was her beauty, or the sweet flattery of the preference of a woman who had half her acquaintance at her feet, I don't know; anyhow, my thoughts turned to her as to their natural home. My heart, too, took that road, and before very long I loved her as I never loved Elvira. Let no one doubt that I loved her—as I shall never love again—please God!

There never was anyone like her. She was brave and beautiful, witty and wise, and beyond all measure adorable. She was the only woman in the world. There was a frankness—a largeness of heart—about her that made all other women seem small and contemptible. She loved me and I worshipped her. I married her, I stayed with her for three golden weeks, and then I left her. Why?

Because she told me the truth. It was one night—late—we had sat all the evening in the verandah of our sea-side lodging, watching the moonlight on the water, and listening to the soft sound of the sea on the sand. I have never been so happy; I shall never be happy any more, I hope.

"My dear, my dear," she said, leaning her gold head against my shoulder, "how much do you love me?"

"How much?"

"Yes—how much? I want to know what place I hold in your heart. Am I more to you than anyone else?"

"My love!"

"More than yourself?"

"More than my life."

"I believe you," she said. Then she drew a long breath, and took my hands in hers. "It can make no difference. Nothing in heaven or earth can come between us now."

"Nothing," I said. "But, my dear one, what is it?"

For she was trembling, pale.

"I must tell you," she said; "I cannot hide anything now from you, because I am yours—body, soul and spirit."

The phrase was an echo that stung.

The moonlight shone on her gold hair, her soft, warm, gold hair, and on her pale face.

"Arthur," she said, "you remember my coming to Hampstead with that letter."

"Yes, my sweet, and I remember how you—"

"Arthur!" she spoke fast and low—"Arthur, that letter was a forgery. She never wrote it. I—"

She stopped, for I had risen and flung her hands from me, and stood looking at her. God help me! I thought it was anger at the lie I felt. I know now it was only wounded vanity that smarted in me. That I should have been tricked, that I should have been deceived, that I should have been led on to make a fool of myself. That I should have married the woman who had befooled me. At that moment she was no longer the wife I adored—she was only a woman who had forged a letter and tricked me into marrying her.

I spoke: I denounced her; I said I would never speak to her again. I felt it was rather creditable in me to be so angry. I said I would have no more to do with a liar and a forger.

I don't know whether I expected her to creep to my knees and implore forgiveness. I think I had some vague idea that I could by-and-by consent with dignity to forgive and forget. I did not mean what I said. No, oh no, no; I did not mean a word of it. While I was saying it, I was longing for her to weep and fall at my feet, that I might raise her and hold her in my arms again.

But she did not fall at my feet; she stood quietly looking at me.

"Arthur," she said, as I paused for breath, "let me explain—she—I—"

"There is nothing to explain," I said hotly, still with that foolish sense of there being something rather noble in my indignation, the kind of thing one feels when one calls one's self a miserable sinner. "You are a liar and a forger, that is enough for me. I will never speak to you again. You have wrecked my life—"

"Do you mean that?" she said, interrupting me, and leaning forward to look at me. Tears lay on her cheeks, but she was not crying now.

I hesitated. I longed to take her in my arms and say—"What does all that old tale matter now? Lay your head here, my darling, and cry here, and know how I love you."

But instead I said nothing.

"*Do* you mean it?" she persisted.

Then she put her hand on my arm. I longed to clasp it and draw her to me.

Instead, I shook it off, and said—

"Mean it? Yes—of course I mean it. Don't touch me, please. You have ruined my life."

She turned away without a word, went into our room, and shut the door.

I longed to follow her, to tell her that if there was anything to forgive, I forgave it.

Instead, I went out on the beach, and walked away under the cliffs.

The moonlight and the solitude, however, presently brought me to a better mind. Whatever she had done, had been done for love of me—I knew that. I would go home and tell her so—tell her that whatever she had done, she was my dear life, my heart's one treasure. True, my ideal of her was shattered, at least I felt I ought to think that it was shattered, but, even as she was, what was the whole world of women compared to her? And to be loved like that... was that not sweet food for vanity? To be loved more than faith and fair dealing, and all the traditions of honesty and honour? I hurried back, but in my resentment and evil temper I had walked far, and the way back was very long. I had been parted from her for three hours by the time I opened the door of the little house where we lodged. The house was dark and very still. I slipped off my shoes and crept up the narrow stairs, and opened the door of our room quite softly. Perhaps she would have cried herself to sleep, and I would lean over her and waken her with my kisses, and beg her to forgive me. Yes, it had come to that now.

I went into the room—I went towards the bed. She was not there. She was not in the room, as one glance showed me. She was not in the house, as I knew in two minutes. When I had wasted a precious hour in searching the town for her, I found a note on my pillow—

"Good-bye! Make the best of what is left of your life. I will spoil it no more."

She was gone, utterly gone. I rushed to town by the earliest morning train, only to find that her people knew nothing of her. Advertisement failed. Only a tramp said he had seen a white lady on the cliff, and a fisherman brought me a handkerchief, marked with her name, which he had found on the beach.

I searched the country far and wide, but I had to go back to London at last, and the months went by. I won't say much about those months, because even the memory of that suffering turns me faint and sick at heart. The police and detectives and the Press failed me utterly. Her friends could not help me, and were, moreover, wildly indignant with me, especially her brother, now living very happily with my first love.

I don't know how I got through those long weeks and months. I tried to write; I tried to read; I tried to live the life of a reasonable human being. But it was impossible. I could not endure the companionship of my kind. Day and night I almost saw her face—almost heard her voice. I took long walks in the country, and her figure was always just round the next turn of the road—in the next glade of the wood. But I never quite saw her, never quite heard her. I believe I was not altogether sane at that time. At last, one morning, as I was setting out for one of those long walks that had no goal but weariness, I met a telegraph boy, and took the red envelope from his hand.

On the pink paper inside was written—

> "Come to me at once I am dying you must come IDA
> Apinshaw Farm Mellor Derbyshire"

There was a train at twelve to Marple, the nearest station. I took it. I tell you there are some things that cannot be written about. My life for those long months was one of them, that journey was another. What had her life been for those months? That question troubled me, as one is troubled in every nerve by the sight of a surgical operation, or a wound inflicted on a being clear to one. But the overmastering sensation was joy— intense, unspeakable joy. She was alive. I should see her again. I took out the telegram and looked at it: "I am dying." I simply did not believe it. She could not die till she had seen me. And if she had lived all these months without me, she could live now, when I was with her again, when she knew of the hell I had endured apart from her, and the heaven of our meeting. She must live; I could not let her die.

There was a long drive over bleak hills. Dark, jolting, infinitely wearisome. At last we stopped before a long, low building, where one or two lights gleamed faintly. I sprang out.

The door opened. A blaze of light made me blink and draw back. A woman was standing in the doorway.

"Art thee Arthur Marsh?" she said.

"Yes."

"Then th'art ower late. She's dead."

II.

I went into the house, walked to the fire, and held out my hands to it mechanically, for though the night was May, I was cold to the bone. There were some folks standing round the fire, and lights flickering. Then an old woman came forward, with the northern instinct of hospitality.

"Thou'rt tired," she said, "and mazed-like. Have a sup o' tea."

I burst out laughing. I had travelled two hundred miles to see *her*. And she was dead, and they offered me tea. They drew back from me as if I had been a wild beast, but I could not stop laughing. Then a hand was laid on my shoulder and someone led me into a dark room, lighted a lamp, set me in a chair, and sat down opposite me. It was a bare parlour, coldly furnished with rush chairs and much-polished tables and presses. I caught my breath, and grew suddenly grave, and looked at the woman who sat opposite me.

"I was Miss Ida's nurse," said she, "and she told me to send for you. Who are you?"

"Her husband—"

The woman looked at me with hard eyes, where intense surprise struggled with resentment.

"Then may God forgive you!" she said. "What you've done I don't know, but it'll be hard work forgivin' you, even for *Him!*"

"Tell me," I said, "my wife—"

"Tell you!" The bitter contempt in the woman's tone did not hurt me. What was it to the self-contempt that had gnawed my heart all these months. "Tell you! Yes, I'll tell you. Your wife was that ashamed of you, she never so much as told me she was married. She let me think anything I pleased sooner than that. She just come 'ere, an' she said, 'Nurse, take care of me, for I am in mortal trouble. And don't let them know where I am,' says she. An' me being well married to an honest man, and well-to-do here, I was able to do it, by the blessing."

"Why didn't you send for me before?" It was a cry of anguish wrung from me.

"I'd *never* 'a sent for you. It was *her* doin'. Oh, to think as God A'mighty's made men able to measure out such-like pecks o' trouble for us womenfolk! Young man, I don't know what you did to 'er to make 'er leave you; but it muster bin something cruel, for she loved the ground you walked on. She useter sit day after day a-lookin' at your picture, an' talkin' to it, an' kissin' of it, when she thought I wasn't takin' no notice, and cryin' till she made me cry too. She useter cry all night 'most. An' one day, when I tells 'er to pray to God to 'elp 'er through 'er trouble, she outs with *your* putty face on a card, she does, an', says she, with her poor little smile, 'That's my god, Nursey,' she says."

"Don't!" I said feebly, putting out my hands to keep off the torture; "not any more. Not now."

"*Don't?*" she repeated. She had risen, and was walking up and down the room with clasped hands. "Don't, indeed! No, I won't; but I shan't forget you! I tell you, I've had you in my prayers time and again, when I thought you'd made a light-o'-love of my darling. I shan't drop you outer them now, when I know she was your own wedded wife, as you chucked away when you tired of her, and left 'er to eat 'er 'art out with longin' for you. Oh! I pray to God above us to pay you scot and lot for all you done to 'er. You killed my pretty. The price will be required of you, young man, even to the uttermost farthing. Oh God in Heaven, make him suffer! Make him feel it!"

She stamped her foot as she passed me. I stood quite still. I bit my lip till I tasted the blood hot and salt on my tongue.

"She was nothing to you," cried the woman, walking faster up and down between the rush chairs and the table; "any fool can see that with half an eye. You didn't love her, so you don't feel nothin' now; but some day you'll care for someone, and then you shall know what she felt—if there's any justice in Heaven."

I, too, rose, walked across the room, and leaned against the wall. I heard her words without understanding them.

"Can't you feel *nothin'*? Are you mader stone? Come an' look at 'er lyin' there so quiet. She don't fret arter the likes o' you no more now. She won't sit no more a-lookin' outer winder an' sayin' nothin'—only droppin' 'er tears one by one, slow, slow on her lap. Come an' see 'er; come an' see what you done to my pretty—an' then you can go. Nobody wants you 'ere. *She* don't want you now. But p'raps you'd like to see 'er safe under ground afore yer go? I'll be bound you'll put a big stone slab on 'er—to make sure she don't rise again."

I turned on her. Her thin face was white with grief and rage. Her claw-like hands were clenched.

"Woman," I said, "have mercy."

She paused and looked at me.

"Eh?" she said.

"Have mercy!" I said again.

"Mercy! You should 'a thought o' that before. You 'and't no mercy on 'er. She loved you—she died loving you. An' if I wasn't a Christian woman, I'd kill you for it— like the rat you are! That I would, though I 'ad to swing for it arterwards."

I caught the woman's hands and held them fast, though she writhed and resisted.

"Don't you understand?" I said savagely. "We loved each other. She died loving me. I have to live loving her. And it's *her* you pity. I tell you it was all a mistake—a stupid, stupid mistake. Take me to her, and for pity's sake, let me be left alone with her."

She hesitated; then said, in a voice only a shade less hard: "Well, come along, then."

We moved towards the door. As she opened it, a faint, weak cry fell on my ear. My heart stood still.

"What's that?" I asked, stopping on the threshold.

"Your child," she said shortly.

That too! Oh, my love! oh, my poor love! All these long months!

"She allus said she'd send for you when she'd got over her trouble," the woman said, as we climbed the stairs. "'I'd like him to see his little baby, nurse,' she says; 'our little baby. It'll be all right when the baby's born,' she says. 'I know he'll come to me then. You'll see.' And I never said nothin', not thinkin' you'd come if she was your leavin's, and not dreamin' you could be 'er 'usband an' could stay away from 'er a hour—'er bein' as she was. Hush!"

She drew a key from her pocket and fitted it to a lock. She opened the door, and I followed her in. It was a large, dark room, full of old-fashioned furniture and a smell of lavender, camphor, and narcissus.

The big four-post bed was covered with white. "My lamb—my poor, pretty lamb!" said the woman, beginning to cry for the first time as she drew back the sheet. "Don't she look beautiful?"

I stood by the bedstead. I looked down on my wife's face. Just so I had seen it lie on the pillow beside me in the early morning, when the wind and the dawn came up from beyond the sea. She did not look like one dead. Her lips were still red, and it seemed to me that a tinge of colour lay on her cheek. It seemed to me, too, that if I kissed her she would awaken, and put her slight hand on my neck, and lay her cheek against mine—and that we should tell each other everything, and weep together, and understand, and be comforted.

So I stooped and laid my lips to hers as the old nurse stole from the room.

But the red lips were like marble, and she did not waken. She will not waken now ever any more.

I tell you again there are some things that cannot be written.

III.

I lay that night in a big room, filled with heavy dark furniture, in a great four-poster hung with heavy, dark curtains—a bed, the counterpart of that other bed from whose side they had dragged me at last.

They fed me, I believe, and the old nurse was kind to me. I think she saw now that it is not the dead who are to be pitied most.

I lay at last in the big, roomy bed, and heard the household noises grow fewer and die out, the little wail of my child sounding latest. They had brought the child to me, and I had held it my arms, and bowed my head over its tiny face and frail fingers. I did not love it then. I told myself it has cost me her life. But my heart told me it was I who had done that. The tall clock at the stairhead sounded the hours—eleven, twelve, one, and still I could not sleep. The room was dark and very still.

I had not yet been able to look at my life quietly. I had been full of the intoxication of grief—a real drunkenness, more merciful than the sober calm that comes afterwards.

Now I lay still as the dead woman in the next room, and looked at what was left of my life. I lay still, and thought, and thought, and thought. And in those hours I tasted the bitterness of death. It must have been about three when I first became aware of a slight sound that was not the ticking of a clock. I say I first became aware, and yet I knew perfectly that I had heard that sound more than once before, and had yet determined not to hear it, *because it came from the next room*—the room where the corpse lay.

And I did not wish to hear that sound, because I knew it meant that I was nervous—miserably nervous—a coward, and a brute. It meant that I, having killed my wife as surely as though I had put a knife in her breast, had now sunk so low as to be afraid of her dead body—the dead body that lay in the next room to mine. The heads of the beds were placed against the same wall; and from that wall I had fancied that I heard slight, slight, almost inaudible sounds. So that when I say I became aware of them, I mean that I, at last, heard a sound so definite as to leave no room for doubt or question. It brought me to a sitting position in the bed, and the drops of sweat gathered heavily on my forehead and fell on my cold hands, as I held my breath and listened.

I don't know how long I sat there—there was no further sound—and at last my tense muscles relaxed, and I fell back on the pillow.

"You fool!" I said to myself; "dead or alive, is she not your darling, your heart's heart? Would you not go near to die of joy, if she came back to you? Pray God to let her spirit come back and tell you she forgives you!"

"I wish she would come," myself answered in words, while every fibre of my body and mind shrank and quivered in denial.

I struck a match, lighted a candle, and breathed more freely as I looked at the polished furniture—the common-place details of an ordinary room. Then I thought of her, lying alone so near me, so quiet under the white sheet. She was dead; she would not wake or move. But suppose she did move? Suppose she turned back the sheet and got up and walked across the floor, and turned the door-handle?

As I thought it, I heard—plainly, unmistakably heard—the door of the chamber of death open slowly. I heard slow steps in the passage, slow, heavy steps. I heard the touch of hands on my door outside, uncertain hands that felt for the latch.

Sick with terror, I lay clenching the sheet in my hands.

I knew well enough what would come in when that door opened—that door on which my eyes were fixed. I dreaded to look, yet dared not turn away my eyes. The door opened slowly, slowly, slowly, and the figure of my dead wife came in. It came straight towards the bed, and stood at the bed foot in its white grave-clothes, with the white bandage under its chin. There was a scent of lavender and camphor and white narcissus. Its eyes were wide open, and looked at me with love unspeakable.

I could have shrieked aloud.

My wife spoke. It was the same dear voice that I had loved so to hear, but it was very weak and faint now; and now I trembled as I listened.

"You aren't afraid of me, darling, are you, though I am dead? I heard all you said to me when you came, but I couldn't answer. But now I've come back from the dead to tell you. I wasn't really so bad as you thought me. Elvira had told me she loved Oscar. I only wrote the letter to make it easier for you. I was too proud to tell you when you were so angry, but I am not proud any more now. You'll love again now, won't you, now I am dead. One always forgives dead people."

The poor ghost's voice was hollow and faint. Abject terror paralysed me. I could answer nothing.

"Say you forgive me," the thin, monotonous voice went on; "say you love me again."

I had to speak. Coward as I was, I did manage to stammer—

"Yes; I love you. I have always loved you, God help me."

The sound of my own voice reassured me, and I ended more firmly than I began. The figure by the bed swayed a little, unsteadily.

"I suppose," she said wearily, "you would be afraid, now I am dead, if I came round to you and kissed you?"

She made a movement as though she would have come to me.

Then I did shriek aloud, again and again, and covered my face with the sheet and wound it round my head and body, and held it with all my force. There was a moment's silence. Then I heard my door close, and then a sound of feet and of voices, and I heard something heavy fall. I disentangled my head from the sheet. My room was empty. Then reason came back to me. I leaped from the bed.

"Ida, my darling, come back! I am not afraid! I love you. Come back! Come back!"

I sprang to my door and flung it open. Someone was bringing a light along the passage. On the floor, outside the door of the death chamber, was a huddled heap—the corpse, in its grave-clothes. Dead, dead, dead.

*

She is buried in Mellor churchyard, and there is no stone over her.

Now, whether it was catalepsy, as the doctor said, or whether my love came back, even from the dead, to me who loved her, I shall never know; but this I know, that if I had held out my arms to her as she stood at my bed-foot—if I had said, "Yes, even from the grave, my darling—from hell itself, come back, come back to me!"—if I had had room in my coward's heart for anything but the unreasoning terror that killed love in that hour, I should not now be here alone. I shrank from her—I feared her—I would not take her to my heart. And now she will not come to me anymore.

Why do I go on living?

You see, there is the child. It is four years old now, and it has never spoken and never smiled.

WALNUT-TREE HOUSE

Mrs. J. H. Riddell

Chapter One

THE NEW OWNER

MANY years ago there stood at the corner of a street leading out of Upper Kennington Lane a great red brick house, covering a goodly-area of ground, and surrounded by gardens magnificent in their proportions when considered in relation to the populous neighbourhood mentioned.

Originally a place of considerable pretention; a gentleman's seat in the country probably when Lambeth Marsh had not a shop in the whole of it; when Vauxhall Gardens were still *in nubibus*; when no Southwestern Railway was planned or thought of; when London was comparatively a very small place, and its present suburbs were mere country villages—hamlets lying quite remote from the heart of the city.

Once, the house in question had been surrounded by a small park, and at that time there were fish-ponds in the grounds, and quite a stretch of meadow-land within the walls. Bit by bit, however, the park had been cut up into building ground and let off on building leases; the meadows were covered with bricks and mortar, shops were run up where cows once chewed the cud, and the roar and rumble of London traffic sounded about the old house and the deserted garden, formerly quiet and silent as though situated in some remote part of the country.

Many a time in the course of the generations that had come and gone, been born and buried, since the old house was built, the freehold it covered changed hands. On most estates of this kind round London there generally is a residence, which passes like a horse from buyer to buyer. When it has served one man's need it is put up for sale and bid for by another. When rows and rows of houses, and line after line of streets, have obliterated all the familiar marks, it is impossible to cultivate a sentiment as regards property; and it is unlikely that the descendants of the first possessors of Walnut-Tree House who had grown to be country folk and lived in great state, oblivious of business people, and entertaining a great contempt for trade, knew that in a very undesirable part of London there still stood the residence where the first successful man of their family went home each day from his counting-house over against St. Mildred's Church, in The Poultry.

One very wet evening, in an autumn the leaves of which have been dead and gone this many a year, Walnut-Tree House, standing grim and lonely in the mournful twilight, looked more than ordinarily desolate and deserted.

There was not a sign of life about it; the shutters were closed—the rusty iron gates were fast locked—the approach was choked up with grass and weeds—through no chink did the light of a single candle flicker. For seven years it had been given over to rats and mice and blackbeetles; for seven years no one had been found to live in it; for seven years it had remained empty, while its owner wore out existence in fits of moody dejection or of wild frenzy in the madhouse close at hand; and now that owner was dead and buried and forgotten, and the new owner was returning to take possession. This new owner had written to his lawyers, or rather had written to the lawyers of his late relative, begging them to request the person in charge of the house to have rooms prepared for his arrival; and, when the train drew into the station at Waterloo, he was met by one of the clerks in Messrs. Timpson and Co.'s office, who, picking out Mr. Stainton, delivered to that gentleman a letter from the firm, and said he would wait and hear if there were any message in reply.

Mr. Stainton read the letter—looked at the blank flyleaf—and then, turning back to the first words, read what his solicitors had to say all through once again, this time aloud.

"The house has stood empty for more than seven years," he said, half addressing the clerk and half speaking to himself. "Must be damp and uninhabitable; there is no one living on the premises. Under these circumstances we have been unable to comply with your directions, and can only recommend you to go to an hotel till we are able personally to discuss future arrangements."

"Humph," said the new owner, after he had finished. "I'll go and take a look at the place, anyhow. Is it far from here, do you know?" he asked, turning to the young man from Timpsons'.

"No, sir; not very far."

"Can you spare time to come over there with me?" continued Mr. Stainton.

The young man believed that he could, adding, "If you want to go into the house we had better call for the key. It is at an estate agent's in the Westminster Bridge Road."

"I cannot say I have any great passion for hotels," remarked the new owner, as he took his seat in the cab.

"Indeed, sir?"

"No; either they don't suit me, or I don't suit them. I have led a wild sort of life: not much civilisation in the bush, or at the goldfields, I can tell you. Rooms full of furniture, houses where a fellow must keep to the one little corner he has hired, seem to choke me. Then I have not been well, and I can't stand noise and the trampling of feet. I had enough of that on board ship; and I used to lie awake at nights and think how pleasant it would be to have a big house all to myself, to do as I liked in."

"Yes, sir," agreed the clerk.

"You see, I have been used to roughing it, and I can get along very well for a night without servants."

"No doubt, sir."

"I suppose the house is in substantial repair—roof tight, and all that sort of thing?"

"I can't say, I am sure, sir."

"Well, if there is a dry corner where I can spread a rug, I shall sleep there to-night."

The clerk coughed. He looked out of the window, and then he looked at Messrs. Timpsons' client.

"I do not think——" he began, apologetically, and then stopped.

"You don't think what?" asked the other.

"You'll excuse me, sir, but I don't think—I really do not think, if I were you, I'd go to that house to-night."

"Why not?"

"Well, it has not been slept in for nearly seven years, and it must be blue mouldy with damp; and if you have been ill, that is all the more reason you should not run such a risk. And, besides—"

"Besides?" suggested Mr. Stainton. "Out with it! Like a postscript, no doubt, that 'besides' holds the marrow of the argument."

"The house has stood empty for years, sir, because—there is no use in making any secret of it—the place has a bad name."

"What sort of a bad name—unhealthy?"

"Oh, no!"

"Haunted?"

The clerk inclined his head. "You have hit it, sir," he said.

"And that is the reason no one has lived there?"

"We have been quite unable to let the house on that account."

"The sooner it gets unhaunted, then, the better," retorted Mr. Stainton. "I shall certainly stop there to-night. You are not disposed to stay and keep me company, I suppose?"

With a little gesture of dismay the clerk drew back. Certainly, this was one of the most unconventional of clients. The young man from Timpsons' did not at all know what to make of him.

"A rough sort of fellow," he said afterwards, when describing the new owner; "boorish; never mixed with good society, that sort of thing."

He did not in the least understand this rich man, who treated him as an equal, who objected to hotels, who didn't mind taking up his abode in a house where not even a drunken charwoman could be induced to stop, and who calmly asked a stranger on whom he had never set eyes before—a clerk in the respectable office of Timpson and Co., a young fellow anxious to rise in the world, careful as to his associates, particular about the whiteness of his shirts and the sit of his collar and the cut of his coats—to "rough" things with him in that dreadful old dungeon, where, perhaps, he might even be expected to light a fire.

Still, he did not wish to offend the new owner. Messrs. Timpson expected him to be a profitable client; and to that impartial firm the money of a boor would, he knew, seem as good as the money of a count.

"I am very sorry," he stammered; "should only have felt too much honoured; but the fact is—previous engagement——"

Mr. Stainton laughed.

"I understand," he said. "Adventures are quite as much out of your line as ghosts. And now tell me about this apparition. Does the 'old man' walk?"

"Not that I ever heard of," answered the other.

"Is it, then, the miserable beggar who tried to do for himself?"

"It is not the late Mr. Stainton, I believe," said the young man, in a tone which mildly suggested that reference to a client of Timpsons' as a "miserable beggar" might be considered bad taste.

"Then who on earth is it?" persisted Mr. Stainton.

"If you must know, sir, it is a child—a child who has driven every tenant in succession out of the house."

The new owner burst into a hearty laugh—a laugh which gave serious offence to Timpsons' clerk.

"That is too good a joke," said Mr. Stainton. "I do not know when I heard anything so delicious."

"It is a fact, whether it be delicious or not," retorted the young man, driven out of all his former propriety of voice and demeanour by the contemptuous ridicule this "digger" thought fit to cast on his story; "and I, for one, would not, after all I have heard about your house, pass a night in it—no, not if anybody offered me fifty pounds down."

"Make your mind easy, my friend," said the new owner, quietly. "I am not going to bid for your company. The child and I can manage, I'll be bound, to get on very comfortably by ourselves."

Chapter Two

THE CHILD

I T was later on in the same evening; Mr. Stainton had an hour previously taken possession of Walnut-Tree House, dismissed his cab, bidden Timpsons' clerk good evening, and, having ordered in wood and coals from the nearest green-grocer, besides various other necessary articles from various other tradesmen, he now stood by the front gate waiting the coming of the goods purchased.

As he waited, he looked up at the house, which in the uncertain light of the street lamps appeared gloomier and darker than had been the case even in the gathering twilight.

The long rows of shuttered windows, the silent solemnity of the great trees, remnants of a once goodly avenue that had served to give its name to Walnut-Tree House; the appalling silence of everything within the place, when contrasted with the noise of passing cabs and whistling street boys, and men trudging home with unfurled umbrellas and women scudding along with draggled petticoats, might well have impressed even an unimpressionable man, and Edgar Stainton, spite of his hard life and rough exterior, was impressionable and imaginative.

"It has an 'uncanny' look, certainly," he considered; "but is not so cheerless for a lonely man as the 'bush'; and though I am not overtired, I fancy I shall sleep more soundly in my new home than I did many a night at the goldfields. When once I can get a good fire up I shall be all right. Now, I wonder when those coals are coming!"

As he turned once again towards the road, he beheld on its way the sack of fuel with which the nearest greengrocer said he thought he could— indeed, said he would—"oblige" him. A ton—half a ton—quarter of a ton, the greengrocer affirmed would be impossible until the next day; but a sack— yes—he would promise that. Bill should bring it round; and Bill was told to put his burden on the truck, and twelve bundles of wood, "and we'll make up the rest to-morrow," added Bill's master, with the air of one who has conferred a favour.

In the distance Mr. Stainton descried a very grimy Bill, and a very small boy, coming along with the truck leisurely, as though the load had been Herculean.

Through the rain he watched the pair advancing and greeted Bill with a glad voice of welcome.

"So you've come at last; that's right. Better late than never. Bring them this way. I'll have this small lot shot in the kitchen for the night."

"Begging your pardon, sir," answered Bill, "I don't think you will—that is to say, not by me. As I told our governor, I'll take 'em to the house as you've sold 'em to the house, but I won't set a foot inside it."

"Do you mean to say you are going to leave them out on the pavement?" asked Mr. Stainton.

"Well, sir, I don't mind taking them to the front door if it'll be a convenience."

"That will do. You are a brave lot of people in these parts I must say."

"As for that," retorted Bill, with sack on back and head bent forward, "I dare say we're as brave about here as where you come from."

"It is not impossible," retorted Mr. Stainton; "there are plenty of cowards over there too."

With a feint of being very much afraid, Bill, after he had shot his coals on the margin of the steps, retreated from the door, which stood partly open, and when the boy who brought up the wood was again out with the truck, said, putting his knuckles to his eyebrows:

"Beg pardon, sir, but I suppose you couldn't give us a drop of beer? Very wet night, sir."

"No, I could not," answered Mr. Stainton, very decidedly. "I shall have to shovel these coals into the house myself; and, as for the night, it is as wet for me as it is for you."

Nevertheless, as Bill shuffled along the short drive—shuffling wearily—like a man who, having nearly finished one day's hard work, was looking forward to beginning another hard day in the morning, the new owner relented.

"Here," he said, picking out a sixpence to give him, "it isn't your fault, I suppose, that you believe in old women's tales."

"Thank you kindly, sir," Bill answered; "I am sure I am extremely obliged; but if I was in your shoes I wouldn't stop in that house—you'll excuse me, sir, meaning no offence—but I wouldn't; indeed I wouldn't."

"It seems to have got a good name, at any rate," thought Mr. Stainton, while retracing his steps to the banned tenement. "Let us see what effect a fire will have in routing the shadows."

He entered the house, and, striking a match, lighted some candles he had brought in with him from a neighbouring oil-shop.

Years previously the gas company, weary of receiving no profit from the house, had taken away their meter and cut off their connections. The water supply was in the same case, as Mr. Stainton, going round the premises before it grew quite dark, had discovered.

Of almost all small articles of furniture easily broken by careless tenants, easily removed by charwomen, the place was perfectly bare; and as there were no portable candlesticks in which to place the lights the new tenant was forced to make his illumination by the help of some dingy mirrors provided with sconces, and to seek such articles as he needed by the help of a guttering mould candle stuck in the neck of a broken bottle. After an inspection of the ground-floor rooms he decided to take up his quarters for the night in one which had evidently served as a library.

In the centre of the apartment there was the table covered with leather. Around the walls were bookcases, still well filled with volumes, too uninviting to borrow, too valueless in the opinion of the ignorant to steal. In one corner stood a bureau, where the man, who for so many years had been dead even while living, kept his letters and papers.

The floor was bare. Once a Turkey carpet had been spread over the centre of the polished oak boards, but it lay in its wonted place no longer; between the windows hung a convex mirror, in which the face of any human being looked horrible and distorted; whilst over the mantle-shelf, indeed, forming a portion of it, was a long, narrow glass, bordered by a frame ornamented with a tracery of leaves and flowers. The ceiling was richly decorated, and, spite of the dust and dirt and neglect of years, all the appointments of the apartment he had selected gave Edgar Stainton the impression that it was a good thing to be the owner of such a mansion, even though it did chance to be situated as much out of the way of fashionable London as the diggings whence he had come.

"And there is not a creature but myself left to enjoy it all," he mused, as he sat looking into the blazing coals. "My poor mother, how she would have rejoiced to-night, had she lived to be the mistress of so large a place! And my father, what a harbour this would have seemed after the storms that buffeted him! Well, they are better off, I know; and yet I cannot help thinking how strange it all is—that I, who went away a mere beggar, should come home rich, to be made richer, and yet stand so utterly alone that in the length and breadth of England I have not a relative to welcome me or to say I wish you joy of your inheritance."

He had eaten his frugal supper, and now, pushing aside the table on which the remains of his repast were spread, he began walking slowly up and down the room, thinking over the past and forming plans for the future.

As he was buried in reflection, the fire began to die down without his noticing the fact; but a sudden feeling of chilliness at length causing him instinctively to look towards the hearth, he threw some wood into the grate, and, while the flames went blazing up the wide chimney, piled on coals as though he desired to set the house alight.

While he was so engaged there came a knock at the door of the room—a feeble, hesitating knock, which was repeated more than once before it attracted Mr. Stainton's attention.

When it did, being still busy with the fire, and forgetting he was alone in the house, he called out, "Come in."

Along the panels there stole a rustling sort of touch, as if someone were feeling uncertainly for the handle—a curious noise, as of a weak hand fumbling about the door in the dark; then, in a similar manner, the person seeking admittance tried to turn the lock.

"Come in, can't you?" repeated Mr. Stainton; but even as he spoke he remembered he was, or ought to be, the sole occupant of the mansion.

He was not alarmed; he was too much accustomed to solitude and danger for that; but he rose from his stooping position and instinctively seized his revolver, which he had chanced, while unpacking some of his effects, to place on the top of the bureau.

"Come in, whoever you are," he cried; but seeing the door remained closed, though the intruder was evidently making futile efforts to open it, he strode half-way across the room, and then stopped, amazed.

For suddenly the door opened, and there entered, shyly and timidly, a little child—a child with the saddest face mortal ever beheld; a child with wistful eyes and long, ill-kept hair; a child poorly dressed, wasted and worn, and with the mournfullest expression on its countenance that face of a child ever wore.

"What a hungry little beggar," thought Mr. Stainton. "Well, young one, and what do you want here?" he added, aloud.

The boy never answered, never took the slightest notice of his questioner, but simply walked slowly round the room, peering into all the corners, as if looking for something. Searching the embrasures of the windows, examining the recesses beside the fire-place, pausing on the hearth to glance under the library table, and finally, when the doorway was reached once more, turning to survey the contents of the apartment with an eager and yet hopeless scrutiny.

"What *is* it you want, my boy?" asked Mr. Stainton, glancing as he spoke at the child's poor thin legs, and short, shabby frock, and shoes wellnigh worn out, and arms bare and lean and unbeautiful. "Is it anything I can get for you?"

Not a word—not a whisper; only for reply a glance of the wistful brown eyes.

"Where do you come from, and who do you belong to?" persisted Mr. Stainton

The child turned slowly away.

"Come, you shall not get off so easily as you seem to imagine," persisted the new owner, advancing towards his visitor. "You have no business to be here at all; and before you go you must tell me how you chance to be in this house, and what you expected to find in this room."

He was close to the doorway by this time, and the child stood on the threshold, with its back towards him.

Mr. Stainton could see every detail of the boy's attire—his little plaid frock, which he had outgrown, the hooks which fastened it; the pinafore, soiled and crumpled, tied behind with strings broken and knotted; in one place the skirt had given from the body, and a piece of thin, poor flannel showed that the child's under habiliments matched in shabbiness his exterior garments.

"Poor little chap," thought Mr. Stainton. "I wonder if he would like something to eat. Are you hungry, my lad?"

The child turned and looked at him earnestly, but answered never a word.

"I wonder if he is dumb," marvelled Mr. Stainton; and, seeing he was moving away, put out a hand to detain him. But the child eluded his touch, and flitted out into the hall and up the wide staircase with swift, noiseless feet.

Only waiting to snatch a candle from one of the sconces, Mr. Stainton pursued as fast as he could follow.

Up the easy steps he ran at the top of his speed; but, fast as he went, the child went faster. Higher and higher he beheld the tiny creature mounting, then, still keeping the same distance between them, it turned when it reached the top story and trotted along a narrow corridor with rooms opening off to right and left. At the extreme end of this passage a door stood ajar. Through this the child passed, Mr. Stainton still following.

"I have run you to earth at last," he said, entering and closing the door. "Why, where has the boy gone?" he added, holding the candle above his head and gazing round the dingy garret in which he found himself.

The room was quite empty. He examined it closely, but could find no possible outlet save the door, and a skylight which had evidently not been opened for years.

There was no furniture in the apartment, except a truckle bedstead, a rush-bottomed chair, and a rickety washstand. No wardrobe, or box or press where even a kitten might have lain concealed.

"It is very strange," muttered Mr. Stainton, as he turned away baffled. "Very strange!" he repeated, while he walked along the corridor. "I don't understand it at all," he decided, proceeding slowly down the topmost flight of stairs; but then all at once he stopped.

"IT IS THE CHILD!" he exclaimed aloud, and the sound of his own voice woke strange echoes through the silence of that desolate house. "IT IS THE CHILD!" And he descended the principal staircase very slowly, with bowed head, and his grave, thoughtful face graver and more thoughtful than ever.

Chapter Three

SEEKING FOR INFORMATION

IT was enough to make any man look grave; and as time went on the new owner of Walnut-Tree House found himself pondering continually as to what the mystery could be which attached to the child he had found in possession of his property, and who had already driven tenant after tenant out of the premises. Inclined at first to regard the clerk's story as a joke, and his own experience on the night of his arrival a delusion, it was impossible for him to continue incredulous when he found, even in broad daylight, that terrible child stealing down the staircase and entering the rooms, looking—looking, for something it never found.

Never after the first horror was over did Mr. Stainton think of leaving the house in consequence of that haunting presence which had kept the house tenantless. It would have been worse than useless, he felt. With the ocean stretching between, his spirit would still be in the old mansion at Lambeth— his mental vision would always be watching the child engaged in the weary search to which there seemed no end—that never appeared to produce any result.

At bed and at board he had company, or the expectation of it. No apartment in the building was secure from intrusion. It did not matter where he lay; it did not matter where he ate; between sleeping and waking, between breakfast and dinner, whenever the notion seized it, the child came gliding in, looking, looking, looking, and never finding; not lingering longer than was necessary to be certain the object of its search was absent, but wandering hither and thither, from garret to kitchen, from parlour to bed-chamber, in that quest which still seemed fresh as when first begun.

Mr. Stainton went to his solicitors as the most likely persons from whom to obtain information on the subject, and plunged at once into the matter.

"Who is the child supposed to be, Mr. Timpson?" he asked, making no secret that he had seen it.

"Well, that is really very difficult to say," answered Mr. Timpson.

"There *was* a child once, I suppose—a real child—flesh and blood?"

Mr. Timpson took off his spectacles and wiped them.

"There were two; yes, certainly, in the time of Mr. Felix Stainton—a boy and a girl."

"In that house?"

"In that house. They survived him."

"And what became of them?"

"The girl was adopted by a relation of her father's, and the—boy—died."

"Oh! the boy died, did he? Do you happen to know what he died of?"

"No; I really do not. There was nothing wrong about the affair, however, if that is what you are thinking of. There never was a hint of that sort."

Mr. Stainton sat silent for a minute; then he said:

"Mr. Timpson, I can't shake off the idea that somehow there has been foul play with regard to those children. Who were they?"

"Felix Stainton's grandchildren. His daughter made a low marriage, and he cast her adrift. After her death the two children were received at Walnut-Tree House on sufferance—fed and clothed, I believe, that was all; and when the old man died the heir-at-law permitted them to remain."

"Alfred Stainton?"

"Yes; the unhappy man who became insane. His uncle died intestate, and he consequently succeeded to everything but the personalty, which was very small, and of which these children had a share."

"There was never any suspicion, you say, of foul play on the part of the late owner?"

"Dear, dear! No; quite the contrary."

"Then can you throw the least light on the mystery?"

"Not the least; I wish I could."

For all that, Mr. Stainton carried away an impression Mr. Timpson knew more of the matter than he cared to tell; and was confirmed in this opinion by a chance remark from Mr. Timpson's partner, whom he met in the street almost immediately after.

"Why can't you let the matter rest, Mr. Stainton?" asked the Co. with some irritation of manner when he heard the object of their client's visit. "What is the use of troubling your head about a child who has been lying in Lambeth Churchyard these dozen years? Take my advise, have the house pulled down and let or sell the ground for building. You ought to get a pot of money for it in that neighbourhood. If there were a wrong done it is too late to set it right now."

"What wrong do you refer to?" asked Mr. Stainton eagerly, thinking he had caught Timpson's partner napping. But that gentleman was too sharp for him.

"I remarked *if* there were a wrong done—not that there had been one," he answered; and then, without a pause, added, "We shall hope to hear from you that you have decided to follow our advice."

But Mr. Stainton shook his head.

"I will not pull down the old house just yet," he said, and walked slowly away.

"There is a mystery behind it all," he considered. "I must learn more about these children. Perhaps some of the local tradespeople may recollect them."

But the local tradespeople for the most part were newcomers—or else had not supplied "the house."

"So far as ever I could understand," said one "family butcher," irascibly sharpening his knife as he spoke, "there was not much to supply. *That* custom was not worth speaking of. I hadn't it, so what I am saying is not said on my own account. A scrag end of neck of mutton—a bit of gravy beef—two pennyworth of sheep's liver—that was the sort of thing. Misers, sir, misers; the old gentleman bad, and the nephew worse. A bad business, first and last. But what else could be expected? When people as can afford to live on the fat of the land never have a sirloin inside their doors, why, worse must come of it. No, sir, I never set eyes on the children to my knowledge; I only knew there were children by hearing one of them was dead, and that it was the poorest funeral ever crossed a decent threshold."

"Poor little chap," thought Mr. Stainton, looking straight out into the street for a moment; then added, "lest the family misfortunes should descend to me, you had better send round a joint to Walnut-Tree House."

"Lor', sir, are you the gentleman as is living there? I beg your pardon, I am sure, but I have been so bothered with questions in regard of that house and those children that I forget my manners when I talk about them. A joint, sir—what would you please to have?"

The new owner told him; and while he counted out the money to pay for it Mr. Parker remarked:

"There is only one person I can think of, sir, likely to be able to give any information about the matter."

"And that is?"

"Mr. Hennings, at the "Pedlar's Dog." He had some aquaintance with the old lady as was housekeeper both to Mr. Felix Stainton and the gentleman that went out of his mind."

Following the advice, the new owner repaired to the "Pedlar's Dog," where (having on his first arrival at Walnut-Tree House ordered some creature comforts from that well-known public) he experienced a better reception than had been accorded to him by Mr. Parker.

"Do I know Walnut-Tree House, sir?" said Mr. Hennings, repeating his visitor's question. "Well, yes, rather. Why, you might as well ask me, do I know the "Pedlar's Dog." As boy and man I can remember the old house for close on five-and-fifty years. I remember Mr. George Stainton; he used to wear a skull-cap and knee-breeches. There was an orchard then where Stainton Street is now, and his whole time was taken up in keeping the boys out of it. Many a time I have run from him."

"Did you ever see anything of the boy and girl who were there, after Mr. Alfred succeeded to the property—Felix Stainton's grandchildren, I mean?" asked the new owner, when a pause in Mr. Henning's reminiscences enabled him to take his part in the conversation.

"Well, sir, I may have seen the girl, but I can't bring it to my recollection; the boy I do remember, however. He came over here two or three times with Mrs. Toplis, who kept house for both Mr. Staintons, and I took notice of him, both because he looked so peaky and old-fashioned, and also an account of the talk about him."

"There was talk about him, then?"

"Bless you, yes, sir; as much talk while he was living as since he died. Everybody thought he ought to have been the heir."

"Why?" enquired the new owner.

"Because there was a will made leaving the place to him."

Here was information. Mr. Stainton's heart seemed to stand still for a second and then leap on with excitement.

"Who made the will?"

"The grandfather, Felix Stainton, to be sure; who else should make it?"

"I did not mean that. Was it not drawn out by a solicitor?"

"Oh! Yes—now I understand you, sir. The will was drawn right enough by Mr. Quinance, in the Lambeth Road, a very clever lawyer."

"Not by Timpson, then? How was that?"

"The old man took the notion of making it late one night, and so Mrs. Toplis sent to the nearest lawyer she knew of."

"Yes; and then?"

"Well, the will was made and signed and witnessed, and everything regular; and from that day to this no one knows what has become of it."

"How very strange."

"Yes, sir, it is more than strange—unaccountable. At first Mr. Quinance was suspected of having given it up to Mr. Alfred; but Mrs. Toplis and Quinance's clerk—he has succeeded to the business now—say that old Felix insisted upon keeping it himself. So, whether he destroyed it or the nephew got hold of it, Heaven only knows; for no man living does, I think."

"And the child—the boy, I mean?"

"If you want to hear all about him, sir, Mrs. Toplis is the one to tell you. If you have a mind to give a shilling to a poor old lady who always did try to keep herself respectable, and who, I will say, paid her way honourable as long as she had a sixpence to pay it honourable with, you cannot do better than go and see Mrs. Toplis, who will talk to you for hours about the time she lived at Walnut-Tree House."

And with this delicate hint that his minutes were more valuable than the hours of Mrs. Toplis, Mr. Hennings would have closed the interview, but that his visitor asked where he should be able to find the housekeeper.

"A thousand pardons!" he answered, with an air; "forgetting the very cream and marrow of it, wasn't I? Mrs. Toplis, sir, is to be found in Lambeth Workhouse—and a pity, too."

Edgar Stainton turned away, heart-sick. Was this all wealth had done for his people and those connected with them?

No man seemed to care to waste a moment in speaking about their affairs; no one had a good word for or kindly memory of them. The poorest creature he met in the streets might have been of more use in the world then they. The house they had lived in mentioned as if a curse rested on the place; themselves only recollected as leaving everything undone which it befitted their station to do. An old servant allowed to end her days in the workhouse!

"Heaven helping me," he thought, "I will not so misuse the wealth which has been given me."

The slight put upon his family tortured and made him wince, and the face of the dead boy who ought to have been the heir seemed, as he hurried along the streets, to pursue and look on him with a wistful reproach.

"If I cannot lay that child I shall go mad," he said, almost audibly, "as mad, perhaps, as Alfred Stainton." And then a terrible fear took possession of him. The horror of that which is worse than any death made for the moment this brave, bold man more timid than a woman.

"God preserve my senses," he prayed, and then, determinedly putting that phantom behind him, he went on to the Workhouse.

Chapter Four

BROTHER AND SISTER

MR. STAINTON had expected to find Mrs. Toplis a decrepit crone, bowed with age and racked with rheumatism, and it was therefore like a gleam of sunshine streaming across his path to behold a woman, elderly, certainly, but carrying her years with ease, ruddy cheeked, clear eyed, upright as a dart, who welcomed him with respectful enthusiasm.

"And so you are Mr. Edgar, the son of the dear old Captain," she said, after the first greetings and explanations were over, after she had wiped her eyes and uttered many ejaculations of astonishment and expressions of delight. "Eh! I remember him coming to the house just after he was married, and telling me about the sweet lady his wife. I never heard a gentleman so proud; he never seemed tired of saying the words, 'My wife'."

"She was a sweet lady," answered the new owner.

"And so the house has come to you, sir? Well, I wish you joy. I hope you may have peace, and health, and happiness, and prosperity in it. And I don't see why you should not—no, indeed, sir."

Edgar Stainton sat silent for a minute, thinking how he should best approach his subject.

"Mrs. Toplis," he began at last, plunging into the very middle of the difficulty, "I want you to tell me about it. I have come here on purpose to ask you what it all means."

The old woman covered her face with her hands, and he could see that she trembled violently.

"You need not be afraid to speak openly to me," he went on. "I am quite satisfied there was some great wrong done in the house, and I want to put it right, if it lies in my power to do so. I am a rich man. I was rich when the news of this inheritance reached me, and I would gladly give up the property to-morrow if I could only undo whatever may have been done amiss."

Mrs. Toplis shook her head.

"Ah, sir; you can't do that," she said. "Money can't bring back the dead to life; and, if it could, I doubt if even you could prove as good a friend to the poor child sleeping in the churchyard yonder as his Maker did when He took him out of this troublesome world. It was just soul rending to see the boy the last few months of his life. I can't bear to think of it, sir! Often at night I wake in a fright, fancying I still hear the patter, patter of his poor little feet upon the stair."

"Do you know, it is a curious thing, but he doesn't frighten me," said Mr. Stainton; "that is when I am in the house; although when I am away from it the recollection seems to dog every step I take."

"What?" cried Mrs. Toplis. "*Have you, then, seen him too?* There! what am I talking about? I hope, sir, you will forgive my foolishness."

"I see him constantly," was the calm reply.

"I wonder what it means!—I wonder what it can mean!" exclaimed the housekeeper, wringing her hands in dire perplexity and dismay.

"I do not know," answered the new owner, philosophically; "but I want you to help me to find out. I suppose you remember the children coming there at first?"

"Well, sir—well, they were poor Miss Mary's son and daughter. She ran away, you know, with a Mr. Fenton—made a very poor match; but I believe he was kind to her. When they were brought to us, a shivering little pair, my master was for sending them here. Ay, and he would have done it, too, if somebody had not said he could be made to pay for their keep. You never saw brother and sister so fond of one another—never. They were twins. But, Lor'! the boy was more like a father to the little girl than aught else. He'd have kept an apple a month rather than eat it unless she had half; and the same with everything. I think it was seeing that—watching the love they had, he for her and she for him, coming upon them unsuspected, with their little arms round one another's necks, made the old gentleman alter his mind about leaving the place to Mr. Alfred; for he said to me, one day, thoughtful like, pointing to them, 'Wonderful fond, Toplis!' and I answered, 'Yes, sir; for all the world like the Babes in the Wood;' not thinking of how lonely that meant——

"Shortly afterwards he took to his bed; and while he was lying there, no doubt, better thoughts came to him, for he used to talk about his wife and Miss Mary, and the Captain, your father, sir, and ask if the children were gone to bed, and such like—things he never used to mention before.

"So when he made the will Mr. Quinance drew out I was not surprised— no, not a bit. Though before that time he always spoke of Mr. Alfred as his heir, and treated him as such."

"That will never was found," suggested Mr. Stainton, anxious to get at another portion of the narrative.

"Never, sir; we hunted for it high and low. Perhaps I wronged him, but I always thought Mr. Alfred knew what became of it. After the old gentleman's death the children were treated shameful—shameful. I don't mean beaten, or that like; but half-starved and neglected. He would not buy them proper clothes, and he would not suffer them to wear decent things if anybody else bought them. It was just the same with their food. I durs'n't give them even a bit of bread and butter unless it was on the sly; and, indeed, there was not much to give in that house. He turned regular miser. Hoarding came into the family with Mrs. Lancelot Stainton, Mr. Alfred's great grandmother, and they went on from bad to worse, each one closer and nearer than the last, begging your pardon for saying so, sir; but it is the truth."

"I fear so, Mrs. Toplis," agreed the man, who certainly was neither close nor near.

"Well, sir, at last, when the little girl was about six years old, she fell sick, and we didn't think she would get over the illness. While she was about at her worst, Mrs. May, her father's sister, chanced to be stopping up in London, and, as Mr. Alfred refused to let a doctor inside his doors, she made no more ado but wrapped the child up in blankets, sent for a cab, and carried her off to her own lodgings. Mr. Alfred made no objection to that. All he said as she went through the hall was:

" 'If you take her now, remember, you must keep her.' "

" 'Very well,' she replied, 'I will keep her.' "

"And the boy? the boy?" cried Mr. Stainton, in an agony of impatience.

"I am coming to him, sir, if you please. He just dwindled away after his sister and he were parted, and died in December, as she was taken away in the July."

"What did he die of?"

"A broken heart, sir. It seems a queer thing to say about a child; but if ever a heart was broken his was. At first he was always wandering about the house looking for her, but towards the end he used to go up to his room and stay there all by himself. At last I wrote to Mrs. May, but she was ill when the letter got to her, and when she did come up he was dead. My word, she talked to Mr. Alfred! I never heard any one person say so much to another. She declared he had first cheated the boy of his inheritance, and then starved him to death; but that was not true, the child broke his heart fretting after his sister."

"Yes; and when he was dead——"

"Sir, I don't like to speak of it, but as true as I am sitting here, the night he was put in his coffin he came pattering down just as usual, looking, looking for his sister. I went straight upstairs, and if I had not seen the little wasted body lying there still and quiet, I must have thought he had come back to life. We were never without him afterwards, never; that, and nothing else, drove Mr. Alfred mad. He used to think he was fighting the child and killing it. When the worst fits were on him he tried to trample it under foot or crush it up in a corner, and then he would sob and cry, and pray for *it* to be taken away. I have heard he recovered a little before he died, and said his uncle told him there was a will leaving all to the boy, but he never saw such a paper. Perhaps it was all talk, though, or that he was still raving."

"You are quite positive there was no foul play as regards the child?" asked Mr. Stainton, sticking to that question pertinaciously.

"Certain, sir; I don't say but Mr. Alfred wished him dead. That is not murder, though."

"I am not clear about that," answered Mr. Stainton.

Chapter Five

THE NEXT AFTERNOON

MR. STAINTON was trying to work off some portion of his perplexities by pruning the grimy evergreens in front of Walnut-Tree House, and chopping away at the undergrowth of weeds and couch grass which had in the course of years matted together beneath the shrubs, when his attention was attracted to two ladies who stood outside the great iron gate looking up at the house.

"It seems to be occupied now," remarked the elder, turning to her companion. "I suppose the new owner is going to live here. It looks just as dingy as ever; but you do not remember it, Mary."

"I think I do," was the answer. "As I look the place grows familiar to me. I do recollect some of the rooms, I am sure just like a dream, as I remember Georgie. What I would give to have a peep inside."

At this juncture the new owner emerged from amongst the bushes, and, opening the gate, asked if the ladies would like to look over the place.

The elder hesitated; whilst the younger whispered, "Oh, aunt, pray do!"

"Thank you," said Mrs. May to the stranger, whom she believed to be a gardener; "but perhaps Mr. Stainton might object."

"No; he wouldn't, I know," declared the new owner. "You can go through the house if you wish. There is no one in it. Nobody lives there except myself."

"Taking charge, I suppose?" suggested Mrs. May blandly.

"Something of that sort," he answered.

"I do not think he is a caretaker," said the girl, as she and her relative passed into the old house together.

"What do you suppose he is, then?" asked her aunt.

"Mr. Stainton himself."

"Nonsense, child!" exclaimed Mrs. May, turning, nevertheless, to one of the windows, and casting a curious glance towards the new owner, who was now, his hands thrust deep in his pockets, walking idly up and down the drive.

After they had been all over the place, from hall to garret, with a peep into this room and a glance into that, Mrs. May found the man who puzzled her leaning against one of the pillars of the porch, waiting, apparently, for their reappearance.

"I am sure we are very much obliged to you," she began, with a certain hesitation in her manner.

"Pray do not mention it," he said.

"This young lady has sad associations connected with the house," Mrs. May proceeded, still doubtfully feeling her way.

He turned his eyes towards the girl for a moment, and though her veil was down, saw she had been weeping.

"I surmised as much," he replied. "She is Miss Fenton, is she not?"

"Yes, certainly," was the answer; "and you are——"

"Edgar Stainton," said the new owner, holding out his hand.

"I am all alone here," he went on, after the first explanations were over. "But I can manage to give you a cup of tea. Pray do come in, and let me feel I am not entirely alone in England."

Only too well pleased, Mrs. May complied, and ten minutes later the three were sitting round a fire, the blaze of which leapt and flickered upon the walls and over the ceiling, casting bright lights on the dingy mirrors and the dark oak shelves.

"It is all coming back to me now," said the girl softly, addressing her aunt. "Many an hour Georgie and I have sat on that hearth seeing pictures in the fire."

But she did not see something which was even then standing close beside her, and which the new owner had witnessed approach with a feeling of terror that precluded speech.

It was the child! The child searching about no longer for something it failed to find, but standing at the girl's side still and motionless, with its eyes fixed upon her face, and its poor, wasted figure nestling amongst the folds of her dress.

"Thank Heaven she does not see it!" he thought, and drew his breath, relieved.

No; she did not see it—though its wan cheek touched her shoulder, though its thin hand rested on her arm, though through the long conversation which followed it never moved from her side, nor turned its wistful eyes from her face.

When she went away—when she took her fresh young beauty out of the house it seemed to gladden and light up—the child followed her to the threshold; and then in an instant it vanished, and Mr. Stainton watched for its flitting up the staircase all in vain.

But later on in the evening, when he was sitting alone beside the fire, with his eyes bent on the glowing coals, and perhaps seeing pictures there, as Mary said she and her brother had done in their lonely childhood, he felt conscious, even without looking round, that the boy was there once again.

And when he fell to thinking of the long, long years during which the dead child had kept faithful and weary watch for his sister, searching through the empty rooms for one who never came, and then bethought him of the sister to whom her dead brother had become but the vaguest of memories, of the summers and winters during the course of which she had probably forgotten him altogether, he sighed deeply; and heard his sigh echoed behind him in the merest faintest whisper.

More, when he, thinking deeply about his newly found relative and trying to recall each feature in her face, each tone of her voice, found it impossible to dissociate the girl grown to womanhood from the child he had pictured to himself as wandering about the old house in company with her twin brother, their arms twined together, their thoughts one, their sorrows one, their poor pleasures one—he felt a touch on his hand, and knew the boy was beside him, looking with wistful eyes into the firelight, too.

But when he turned he saw that sadness clouded those eyes no longer. She was found; the lost had come again to meet a living friend on the once desolate hearth, and up and down the wide, desolate staircase those weary little feet pattered no longer.

The quest was over, the search ended; into the darksome corners of that dreary house the child's glance peered no longer.

She was come! Through years he had kept faithful watch for her, but the waiting was ended now.

That night Edgar Stainton slept soundly; and yet when morning dawned he knew that once in the darkness he wakened suddenly and was conscious of a small, childish hand smoothing his pillow and touching his brow.

Sweet were the dreams which visited his rest subsequently; sweet as ought to be the dreams of a man who had said to his own soul—and meant to hold fast by words he had spoken:

"As I deal by that orphan girl, so may God deal with me!"

Chapter Six

THE MISSING WILL

ERE long there were changes in the old house. Once again Mrs. Toplis reigned there, but this time with servants under her—with maids she could scold and lads she could harass.

The larder was well plenished, the cellars sufficiently stocked; windows formerly closely shuttered now stood open to admit the air; and on the drive grass grew no longer—too many footsteps passed that way for weeds to flourish.

It was Christmas-time. The joints in the butchers' shops were gay with ribbons; the grocers' windows were tricked out to delight the eyes of the children, young and old, who passed along. In Mr. May's house up the Clapham

Road all was excitement, for the whole of the family—father, mother, grown-up sons and daughters—girls still in short frocks and boys in round jackets—were going to spend Christmas Eve with their newly-found cousin, whom they had adopted as a relation with a unanimity as rare as charming.

Cousin Mary also was going—Cousin Mary had got a new dress for the occasion, and was having her hair done up in a specially effective manner by Cissie May, when the toilette proceedings were interrupted by half a dozen young voices announcing:

"A gentleman in the parlour wants to see you, Mary. Pa says you are to make haste and come down immediately."

Obediently Mary made haste as bidden and descended to the parlour, to find there the clerk from Timpsons' who met Mr. Stainton on his arrival in London.

His business was simple, but important. Once again he was the bearer of a letter from Timpson and Co., this time announcing to Miss Fenton that the will of Mr. Felix Stainton had been found, and that under it she was entitled to the interest of ten thousand pounds, secured upon the houses in Stainton Street.

"Oh! aunt, Oh! uncle, how rich we shall be," cried the girl, running off to tell her cousins; but the uncle and aunt looked grave. They were wondering how this will might effect Edgar Stainton.

While they were still talking it over—after Timpsons' young man had taken his departure, Mr. Edgar Stainton himself arrived.

"Oh, it's all right!" he said, in answer to their questions. "I found the will in the room where Felix Stainton died. Walnut-Tree House and all the freeholds were left to the poor little chap who died, chargeable with Mary's ten thousand pounds, five hundred to Mrs. Toplis, and a few other legacies. Failing George, the property was to come to me. I have been to Quinance's successor, and found out the old man and Alfred had a grievous quarrel, and that in consequence he determined to cut him out altogether. Where is Mary? I want to wish her joy."

Mary was in the little conservatory, searching for a rose to put in her pretty brown hair.

He went straight up to her, and said:

"Mary, dear, you have had one Christmas gift to-night, and I want you to take another with it."

"What is it, Cousin Edgar?" she asked; but when she looked in his face she must have guessed his meaning, for she drooped her head, and began pulling her sweet rose to pieces.

He took the flower, and with it her fingers.

"Will you have me, dear?" he asked. "I am but a rough fellow, I know; but I am true, and I love you dearly."

Somehow, she answered him as he wished, and all spent a very happy evening in the old house.

Once, when he was standing close beside her in the familiar room, hand clasped in hand, Edgar Stainton saw the child looking at them.

There was no sorrow or yearning in his eyes as he gazed—only a great peace, a calm which seemed to fill and light them with an exquisite beauty.

IN DARK NEW ENGLAND DAYS

Sarah Orne Jewett

I.

THE last of the neighbors was going home; officious Mrs. Peter Downs had lingered late and sought for additional housework with which to prolong her stay. She had talked incessantly, and buzzed like a busy bee as she helped to put away the best crockery after the funeral supper, while the sisters Betsey and Hannah Knowles grew every moment more forbidding and unwilling to speak. They lighted a solitary small oil lamp at last, as if for Sunday evening idleness, and put it on the side table in the kitchen.

"We ain't intending to make a late evening of it," announced Betsey, the elder, standing before Mrs. Downs in an expectant, final way, making an irresistible opportunity for saying good-night. "I 'm sure we 're more than obleeged to ye,—ain't we, Hannah?—but I don't feel's if we ought to keep ye longer. We ain't going to do no more to-night, but set down a spell and kind of collect ourselves, and then make for bed."

Susan Downs offered one more plea. "I 'd stop all night with ye an' welcome; 't is gettin' late—an' dark," she added plaintively; but the sisters shook their heads quickly, while Hannah said that they might as well get used to staying alone, since they would have to do it first or last. In spite of herself Mrs. Downs was obliged to put on her funeral best bonnet and shawl and start on her homeward way.

"Closed-mouthed old maids!" she grumbled as the door shut behind her all too soon and denied her the light of the lamp along the footpath. Suddenly there was a bright ray from the window, as if some one had pushed back the curtain and stood with the lamp close to the sash. "That's Hannah," said the retreating guest. "She'd told me some-thin' about things, I know, if it had n't 'a' been for Betsey. Catch me workin' myself to pieces again for 'em." But, however grudgingly this was said, Mrs. Downs's conscience told her that the industry of the past two days had been somewhat selfish on her part; she had hoped that in the excitement of this unexpected funeral season she might for once be taken into the sisters' confidence. More than this, she knew that

113

they were certain of her motive, and had deliberately refused the expected satisfaction. " 'T ain't as if I was one o' them curious busy-bodies anyway," she said to herself pityingly; "they might 'a' neighbored with somebody for once, I do believe." Everybody would have a question ready for her the next day, for it was known that she had been slaving herself devotedly since the news had come of old Captain Knowles's sudden death in his bed from a stroke, the last of three which had in the course of a year or two changed him from a strong old man to a feeble, chair-bound cripple.

Mrs. Downs stepped bravely along the dark country road; she could see a light in her own kitchen window half a mile away, and did not stop to notice either the penetrating dampness, or the shadowy woods at her right. It was a cloudy night, but there was a dim light over the open fields. She had a disposition of mind towards the exciting circumstances of death and burial, and was in request at such times among her neighbors; in this she was like a city person who prefers tragedy to comedy, but not having the semblance within her reach, she made the most of looking on at real griefs and departures.

Some one was walking towards her in the road; suddenly she heard footsteps. The figure stopped, then it came forward again.

"Oh, 't is you, ain't it?" with a tone of disappointment. "I cal'lated you 'd stop all night, 't had got to be so late, an' I was just going over to the Knowles gals'; well, to kind o' ask how they be, an' "— Mr. Peter Downs was evidently counting on his visit.

"They never passed me the compliment," replied the wife. "I declare I did n't covet the walk home; I'm most beat out, bein' on foot so much. I was 'most put out with 'em for letten' of me see quite so plain that my room was better than my company. But I don't know's I blame 'em; they want to look an' see what they 've got, an' kind of git by theirselves, I expect. 'T was natural."

Mrs. Downs knew that her husband would resent her first statements, being a sensitive and grumbling man. She had formed a pacific habit of suiting her remarks to his point of view, to save an out-burst. He contented himself with calling the Knowles girls hoggish, and put a direct question as to whether they had let fall any words about their situation, but Martha Downs was obliged to answer in the negative.

"Was Enoch Holt there after the folks come back from the grave?"

"He wa'n't; they never give him no encouragement neither."

"He appeared well, I must say," continued Peter Downs. "He took his place next but one behind us in the procession, 'long of Melinda Dutch, an' walked to an' from with her, give her his arm, and then I never see him after we got back; but I thought he might be somewhere in the house, an' I was out about the barn an' so on."

"They was civil to him. I was by when he come, just steppin' out of the bedroom after we 'd finished layin' tho old Cap'n into his coffin. Hannah looked real pleased when she see Enoch, as if she had n't really expected him, but Betsey stuck out her hand 's if 't was an eend o' board, an' drawed her face solemner 'n ever. There, they had natural feelin's. He was their own father when all was said, the Cap'n was, an' I don't know but he was clever to 'em in his way, 'ceptin' when he disappointed Hannah about her marryin' Jake Good'in. She l'arned to respect the old Cap'n's foresight, too."

"Sakes alive, Marthy, how you do knock folks down with one hand an' set 'em up with t' other," chuckled Mr. Downs. They next discussed the Captain's appearance as he lay in state in the front room, a subject which, with its endless ramifications, would keep the whole neighborhood interested for weeks to come.

An hour later the twinkling light in the Downs house suddenly disappeared. As Martha Downs took a last look out of doors through her bedroom window she could see no other light; the neighbors had all gone to bed. It was a little past nine, and the night was damp and still.

II.

The Captain Knowles place was eastward from the Downs's, and a short turn in the road and the piece of hard-wood growth hid one house from the other. At this unwontedly late hour the elderly sisters were still sitting in their warm kitchen; there were bright coals under the singing tea-kettle which hung from the crane by three or four long pothooks. Betsey Knowles objected when her sister offered to put on more wood.

"Father never liked to leave no great of a fire, even though he slept right here in the bedroom. He said this floor was one that would light an' catch easy, you r'member."

"Another winter we can move down and take the bedroom ourselves—'t will be warmer for us," suggested Hannah; but Betsey shook her head doubtfully. The thought of their old father's grave, unwatched and undefended in the outermost dark field, filled their hearts with a strange tenderness. They had been his dutiful, patient slaves, and it seemed like disloyalty to have abandoned the poor shape; to be sitting there disregarding the thousand requirements and services of the past. More than all, they were facing a free future; they were their own mistresses at last, though past sixty years of age. Hannah was still a child at heart. She chased away a dread suspicion, when Betsey forbade the wood, lest this elder sister, who favored their father's looks, might take his place as stern ruler of the household.

"Betsey," said the younger sister suddenly, "we'll have us a cook stove, won't we, next winter? I expect we're going to have something to do with?"

Betsey did not answer; it was impossible to say whether she truly felt grief or only assumed it. She had been sober and silent for the most part since she routed neighbor Downs, though she answered her sister's prattling questions with patience and sympathy. Now, she rose from her chair and went to one of the windows, and, pushing back the sash curtain, pulled the wooden shutter across and hasped it.

"I ain't going to bed just yet," she explained. "I've been a-waiting to make sure nobody was coming in. I don't know's there'll be any better time to look in the chest and see what we've got to depend on. We never'll get no chance to do it by day."

Hannah looked frightened for a moment, then nodded, and turned to the opposite window and pulled that shutter with much difficulty; it had always caught and hitched and been provoking—a warped piece of red oak, when even-grained white pine would have saved strength and patience to three generations of the Knowles race. Then the sisters crossed the kitchen and opened the bedroom door. Hannah shivered a little as the colder air struck her, and her heart beat loudly. Perhaps it was the same with Betsey.

The bedroom was clean and orderly for the funeral guests. Instead of the blue homespun there was a beautifully quilted white coverlet which had been part of their mother's wedding furnishing, and this made the bedstead with its four low posts look unfamiliar and awesome. The lamplight shone through the kitchen door behind them, not very bright at best, but Betsey reached under the bed, and with all the strength she could muster pulled out the end of a great sea chest. The sisters tugged together and pushed, and made the most of their strength before they finally brought it through the narrow door into the kitchen. The solemnity of the deed made them both whisper as they talked, and Hannah did not dare to say what was in her timid heart—that she would rather brave discovery by daylight than such a feeling of being disapprovingly watched now, in the dead of night. There came a slight sound outside the house which made her look anxiously at Betsey, but Betsey remained tranquil.

"It's nothing but a stick falling down the woodpile," she answered in a contemptuous whisper, and the younger woman was reassured.

Betsey reached deep into her pocket and found a great key which was worn smooth and bright like silver, and never had been trusted willingly into even her own careful hands. Hannah held the lamp, and the two thin figures bent eagerly over the lid as it opened. Their shadows were waving about the low walls, and looked like strange shapes bowing and dancing behind them.

The chest was stoutly timbered, as if it were built in some ship-yard, and there were heavy wrought-iron hinges and a large escutcheon for the keyhole that the ship's blacksmith might have hammered out. On the top somebody had scratched deeply the crossed lines for a game of fox and geese, which had a trivial, irreverent look, and might have been the unforgiven fault of some idle ship's boy. The sisters had hardly dared look at the chest or to signify their knowledge of its existence, at unwary times. They had swept carefully about it year after year, and wondered if it were indeed full of gold as the neighbors used to hint; but no matter how much found a way in, little had found the way out. They had been hampered all their lives for money, and in consequence had developed a wonderful facility for spinning and weaving, mending and making. Their small farm was an early example of intensive farming; they were allowed to use its products in a niggardly way, but the money that was paid for wool, for hay, for wood, and for summer crops had all gone into the chest. The old captain was a hard master; he rarely commended and often blamed. Hannah trembled before him, but Betsey faced him sturdily, being amazingly like him, with a feminine difference; as like as a ruled person can be to a ruler, for the discipline of life had taught the man to aggress, the woman only to defend. In the chest was a fabled sum of prize-money, besides these slender earnings of many years; all the sisters' hard work and self-sacrifice were there in money and a mysterious largess besides. All their lives they had been looking forward to this hour of ownership.

There was a solemn hush in the house; the two sisters were safe from their neighbors, and there was no fear of interruption at such an hour in that hard-working community, tired with a day's work that had been early begun. If any one came knocking at the door, both door and windows were securely fastened.

The eager sisters bent above the chest, they held their breath and talked in softest whispers. With stealthy tread a man came out of the woods near by.

He stopped to listen, came nearer, stopped again, and then crept close to the old house. He stepped upon the banking, next the window with the warped shutter; there was a knothole in it high above the women's heads, towards the top. As they leaned over the chest, an eager eye watched them. If they had turned that way suspiciously, the eye might have caught the flicker of the lamp and betrayed itself. No, they were too busy: the eye at the shutter watched and watched.

There was a certain feeling of relief in the sisters' minds because the contents of the chest were so commonplace at first sight. There were some old belongings dating back to their father's early days of seafaring. They unfolded a waistcoat pattern or two of figured stuff which they had seen him fold and put away again and again. Once he had given Betsey a gay China silk handkerchief, and here were two more like it. They had not known what a store of treasures might be waiting for them, but the reality so far was disappointing; there was much spare room to begin with, and the wares within looked pinched and few. There were bundles of papers, old receipts, some letters in two not very thick bundles, some old account books with worn edges, and a blackened silver can which looked very small in comparison with their anticipation, being an heirloom and jealously hoarded and secreted by the old man. The women began to feel as if his lean angry figure were bending with them over the sea chest.

They opened a package wrapped in many layers of old soft paper — a worked piece of Indian muslin, and an embroidered red scarf which they had never seen before. "He must have brought them home to mother," said Betsey with a great outburst of feeling. "He never was the same man again; he never would let nobody else have them when he found she was dead, poor old father!"

Hannah looked wistfully at the treasures. She rebuked herself for selfishness, but she thought of her pinched girlhood and the delight these things would have been. Ah yes! it was too late now for many things besides the sprigged muslin. "If I was young as I was once there's lots o' things I'd like to do now I'm free," said Hannah with a gentle sigh; but her sister checked her anxiously — it was fitting that they should preserve a semblance of mourning even to themselves.

The lamp stood in a kitchen chair at the chest's end and shone full across their faces. Betsey looked intent and sober as she turned over the old man's treasures. Under the India mull was an antique pair of buff trousers, a waistcoat of strange old-fashioned foreign stuff, and a blue coat with brass buttons, brought home from over seas, as the women knew, for their father's wedding clothes. They had seen him carry them out at long intervals to hang them in the spring sunshine; he had been very feeble the last time, and Hannah remembered that she had longed to take them from his shaking hands.

"I declare for 't I wish 't we had laid him out in 'em, 'stead o' the robe," she whispered; but Betsey made no answer. She was kneeling still, but held herself upright and looked away. It was evident that she was lost in her own thoughts.

"I can't find nothing else by eyesight," she muttered. "This chest never 'd be so heavy with them old clothes. Stop! Hold that light down, Hannah; there's a place underneath here. Them papers in the till takes a shallow part. Oh, my gracious! See here, will ye? Hold the light, hold the light!"

There was a hidden drawer in the chest's side—a long, deep place, and it was full of gold pieces. Hannah had seated herself in the chair to be out of her sister's way. She held the lamp with one hand and gathered her apron on her lap with the other, while Betsey, exultant and hawk-eyed, took out handful after handful of heavy coins, letting them jingle and chink, letting them shine in the lamp's rays, letting them roll across the floor—guineas, dollars, doubloons, old French and Spanish and English gold!

Now, now! Look! The eye at the window!

At last they have found it all; the bag of silver, the great roll of bank bills, and the heavy weight of gold—the prize-money that had been like Robinson Crusoe's in the cave. They were rich women that night; their faces grew young again as they sat side by side and exulted while the old kitchen grew cold. There was nothing they might not do within the range of their timid ambitions; they were women of fortune now and their own mistresses. They were beginning at last to live.

The watcher outside was cramped and chilled. He let himself down softly from the high step of the winter banking, and crept toward the barn, where he might bury himself in the hay and think. His fingers were quick to find the peg that opened the little barn door; the beasts within were startled and stumbled to their feet, then went back to their slumbers. The night wore on; the light spring rain began to fall, and the sound of it on the house roof close down upon the sisters' bed lulled them quickly to sleep. Twelve, one, two o'clock passed by.

They had put back the money and the clothes and the minor goods and treasures and pulled the chest back into the bedroom so that it was out of sight from the kitchen; the bedroom door was always shut by day. The younger sister wished to carry the money to their own room, but Betsey disdained such precaution. The money had always been safe in the old chest, and there it should stay. The next week they would go to Riverport and put it into the bank; it was no use to lose the interest any longer. Because their father had lost some invested money in his early youth, it did not follow that every bank was faithless. Betsey's self-assertion was amazing, but they still whispered to each other as they got ready for bed. With strange forgetfulness Betsey had laid the chest key on the white coverlet in the bedroom and left it there.

III.

In August of that year the whole countryside turned out to go to court.

The sisters had been rich for one night; in the morning they waked to find themselves poor with a bitter pang of poverty of which they had never dreamed. They had said little, but they grew suddenly pinched and old. They could not tell how much money they had lost, except that Hannah's lap was full of gold, a weight she could not lift nor carry. After a few days of stolid misery they had gone to the chief lawyer of their neighborhood to accuse Enoch Holt of the robbery. They dressed in their best and walked solemnly side by side across the fields and along the road, the shortest way to the man of law. Enoch Holt's daughter saw them go as she stood in her doorway, and felt a cold shiver run through her frame as if in foreboding. Her father was not at home; he had left for Boston late on the afternoon of Captain Knowles's funeral. He had had notice the day before of the coming in of a ship in which he owned a thirty-second; there was talk of selling the ship, and the owners' agent had summoned him. He had taken pains to go to the funeral, because he and the old captain had been on bad terms ever since they had bought a piece of woodland together, and the captain declared himself wronged at the settling of accounts. He was growing feeble even then, and had left the business to the younger man. Enoch Holt was not a trusted man, yet he had never before been openly accused of dishonesty. He was not a professor of religion, but foremost on the secular side of church matters. Most of the men in that region were hard men; it was difficult to get money, and there was little real comfort in a community where the sterner, stingier, forbidding side of New England life was well exemplified.

The proper steps had been taken by the officers of the law, and in answer to the writ Enoch Holt appeared, much shocked and very indignant, and was released on bail which covered the sum his shipping interest had brought him. The weeks had dragged by; June and July were long in passing, and here was court day at last, and all the townsfolk hastening by high-roads and by-roads to the court-house. The Knowles girls themselves had risen at break of day and walked the distance steadfastly, like two of the three Fates: who would make the third, to cut the thread for their enemy's disaster? Public opinion was divided. There were many voices ready to speak on the accused man's side; a sharp-looking acquaintance left his business in Boston to swear that Holt was in his office before noon on the day following the robbery, and that he had spent most of the night in Boston, as proved by several minor details of their interview. As for Holt's young married daughter, she was a favorite with the townsfolk, and her husband was away at sea overdue these last few weeks. She sat on one of the hard court benches with a young child in her arms, born since its father sailed; they had been more or less unlucky, the Holt family, though Enoch himself was a man of brag and bluster.

All the hot August morning, until the noon recess, and all the hot August afternoon, fly-teased and wretched with the heavy air, the crowd of neighbors listened to the trial. There was not much evidence brought; everybody knew that Enoch Holt left the funeral procession hurriedly, and went away on horseback towards Boston. His daughter knew no more than this. The Boston man gave his testimony impatiently, and one or two persons insisted that they saw the accused on his way at nightfall, several miles from home.

As the testimony came out, it all tended to prove his innocence, though public opinion was to the contrary. The Knowles sisters looked more stern and gray hour by hour; their vengeance was not to be satisfied; their accusation had been listened to and found wanting, but their instinctive knowledge of the matter counted for nothing. They must have been watched through the knot-hole of the shutter; nobody had noticed it until, some years before, Enoch Holt himself had spoken of the light's shining through on a winter's night as he came towards the house. The chief proof was that nobody else could have done the deed. But why linger over *pros* and *cons?* The jury returned directly with a verdict of "not proven," and the tired audience left the court-house.

But not until Hannah Knowles with angry eyes had risen to her feet.

The sterner elder sister tried to pull her back; every one said that they should have looked to Betsey to say the awful words that followed, not to her gentler companion. It was Hannah, broken and disappointed, who cried in a strange high voice as Enoch Holt was passing by without a look:

"You stole it, you thief! You know it in your heart!"

The startled man faltered, then he faced the women. The people who stood near seemed made of eyes as they stared to see what he would say.

"I swear by my right hand I never touched it."

"Curse your right hand, then!" cried Hannah Knowles, growing tall and thin like a white flame drawing upward. "Curse your right hand, yours and all your folks' that follow you! May I live to see the day!"

The people drew back, while for a moment accused and accuser stood face to face. Then Holt's flushed face turned white, and he shrank from the fire in those wild eyes, and walked away clumsily down the courtroom. Nobody followed him, nobody shook hands with him, or told the acquitted man that they were glad of his release. Half an hour later, Betsey and Hannah Knowles took their homeward way, to begin their hard round of work again. The horizon that had widened with such glory for one night, had closed round them again like an iron wall.

Betsey was alarmed and excited by her sister's uncharacteristic behavior, and she looked at her anxiously from time to time. Hannah had become the harder-faced of the two. Her disappointment was the keener, for she had kept more of the unsatisfied desires of her girlhood until that dreary morning when they found the sea-chest rifled and the treasure gone.

Betsey said inconsequently that it was a pity she did not have that black silk gown that would stand alone. They had planned for it over the open chest, and Hannah's was to be a handsome green. They might have worn them to court. But even the pathetic facetiousness of her elder sister did not bring a smile to Hannah Knowles's face, and the next day one was at the loom and the other at the wheel again. The neighbors talked about the curse with horror; in their minds a fabric of sad fate was spun from the bitter words.

The Knowles sisters never had worn silk gowns and they never would. Sometimes Hannah or Betsey would stealthily look over the chest in one or the other's absence. One day when Betsey was very old and her mind had grown feeble, she tied her own India silk handkerchief about her neck, but they never used the other two. They aired the wedding suit once every spring as long as they lived. They were both too old and forlorn to make up the India mull. Nobody knows how many times they took everything out of the heavy old clamped box, and peered into every nook and corner to see if there was not a single gold piece left. They never answered any one who made bold to speak of their misfortune.

IV.

Enoch Holt had been a seafaring man in his early days, and there was news that the owners of a Salem ship in which he held a small interest wished him to go out as supercargo. He was brisk and well in health, and his son-in-law, an honest but an unlucky fellow, had done less well than usual, so that nobody was surprised when Enoch made ready for his voyage. It was nearly a year after the theft, and nothing had come so near to restoring him to public favor as his apparent lack of ready money. He openly said that he put great hope in his adventure to the Spice Islands, and when he said farewell one Sunday to some members of the dispersing congregation, more than one person wished him heartily a pleasant voyage and safe return. He had an insinuating tone of voice and an imploring look that day, and this fact, with his probable long absence and the dangers of the deep, won him much sympathy. It is a shameful thing to accuse a man wrongfully, and Enoch Holt had behaved well since the trial; and, what is more, had shown no accession to his means of living. So away he went, with a fair amount of good wishes, though one or two persons assured remonstrating listeners that they thought it likely Enoch would make a good voyage, better than common, and show himself forwarded when he came to port. Soon after his departure, Mrs. Peter Downs and an intimate acquaintance discussed the ever-exciting subject of the Knowles robbery over a friendly cup of tea.

They were in the Downs kitchen, and quite by themselves. Peter Downs himself had been drawn as a juror, and had been for two days at the county town. Mrs. Downs was giving herself to social interests in his absence, and Mrs. Forder, an asthmatic but very companionable person, had arrived by two o'clock that afternoon with her knitting work, sure of being welcome. The two old friends had first talked over varied subjects of immediate concern, but when supper was nearly finished, they fell back upon the lost Knowles gold, as has been already said.

"They got a dreadful blow, poor gals," wheezed Mrs. Forder, with compassion. " 'T was harder for them than for most folks; they 'd had a long stent with the ol' gentleman; very arbitrary, very arbitrary."

"Yes," answered Mrs. Downs, pushing back her tea-cup, then lifting it again to see if it was quite empty. "Yes, it took holt o' Hannah, the most. I should 'a' said Betsey was a good deal the most set in her ways an' would 'a' been most tore up, but 't wa'n't so."

"Lucky that Holt's folks sets on the other aisle in the meetin'-house, I do consider, so 't they need n't face each other sure as Sabbath comes round."

"I see Hannah an' him come face to face two Sabbaths afore Enoch left. So happened he dallied to have a word 'long o' Deacon Good'in, an' him an' Hannah stepped front of each other 'fore they knowed what they 's about. I sh'd thought her eyes 'd looked right through him. No one of 'em took the word; Enoch he slinked off pretty quick."

"I see 'em too," said Mrs. Forder; "made my blood run cold."

"Nothin' ain't come of the curse yit,"— Mrs. Downs lowered the tone of her voice,— "least, folks says so. It kind o' worries pore Phœbe Holt— Mis' Dow, I would say. She was narved all up at the time o' the trial, an' when her next baby come into the world, first thin' she made out t' ask me was whether it seemed likely, an' she gave me a pleadin' look as if I 'd got to tell her what she had n't heart to ask. 'Yes, dear,' says I, 'put up his little hands to me kind of wonted'; an' she turned a look on me like another creatur', so pleased an' contented."

"I s'pose you don't see no great of the Knowles gals?" inquired Mrs. Forder, who lived two miles away in the other direction.

"They stepped to the door yesterday when I was passin' by, an' I went in an' set a spell long of 'em," replied the hostess. "They 'd got pestered with that ol' loom o' theirn. 'Fore I thought, says I, ' 'T is all worn out, Betsey,' says I, 'Why on airth don't ye git somebody to git some o' your own wood an' season it well so 't won't warp, same 's mine done, an' build ye a new one?' But Betsey muttered an' twitched away; 't wa'n't like her, but they 're dis'p'inted at every turn, I s'pose, an' feel poor where they 've got the same 's ever to do with. Hannah's a-coughin' this spring's if somethin' ailed her. I asked her if she had bad feelin's in her pipes, an' she said yis, she had, but not to speak of 't before

Betsey. I 'm goin' to fix her up some hoarhound an' elecampane quick 's the ground 's nice an' warm an' roots livens up a grain more. They 're limp an' wizened 'long to the fust of the spring. Them would be service'ble, simmered away to a syrup 'long o' molasses; now don't you think so, Mis' Forder?"

"Excellent," replied the wheezing dame. "I covet a portion myself, now you speak. Nothin' cures my complaint, but a new remedy takes holt clever sometimes, an' eases me for a spell." And she gave a plaintive sigh, and began to knit again.

Mrs. Downs rose and pushed the supper-table to the wall and drew her chair nearer to the stove. The April nights were chilly.

"The folks is late comin' after me," said Mrs. Forder, ostentatiously. "I may 's well confess that I told 'em if they was late with the work they might let go o' fetchin' o' me an' I 'd walk home in the mornin'; take it easy when I was fresh. Course I mean ef 't would n't put you out: I knowed you was all alone, an' I kind o' wanted a change."

"Them words was in my mind to utter while we was to table," avowed Mrs. Downs, hospitably. "I ain't reelly afeared, but 't is sort o' creepy fastenin' up an' goin' to bed alone. Nobody can't help hearkin', an' every common noise starts you. I never used to give nothin' a thought till the Knowleses was robbed, though."

" 'T was mysterious, I do maintain," acknowledged Mrs. Forder. "Comes over me sometimes p'raps 't was n't Enoch; he 'd 'a' branched out more in course o' time. I 'm waitin' to see if he does extry well to sea 'fore I let my mind come to bear on his bein' clean handed."

"Plenty thought 't was the ole Cap'n come back for it an' sperited it away. Enough said that 't was n't no honest gains; most on 't was prize-money o' slave ships, an' all kinds o' devil's gold was mixed in. I s'pose you 've heard that said?"

"Time an' again," responded Mrs. Forder; "an' the worst on 't was simple old Pappy Flanders went an' told the Knowles gals themselves that folks thought the ole Cap'n come back an' got it, and Hannah done wrong to cuss Enoch Holt an' his ginerations after him the way she done."

"I think it took holt on her ter'ble after all she 'd gone through," said Mrs. Downs, compassionately. "He ain't near so simple as he is ugly, Pappy Flanders ain't. I 've seen him set here an' read the paper sober 's anybody when I 've been goin' about my mornin's work in the shed-room, an' when I 'd come in to look about he 'd twist it with his hands an' roll his eyes an' begin to git off some o' his gable. I think them wander-in' cheap-wits likes the fun on 't an' 'scapes stiddy work, an' gits the rovin' habit so fixed, it sp'iles 'em."

"My gran'ther was to the South Seas in his young days," related Mrs. Forder, impressively, "an' he said cussin' was common there. I mean sober spitin' with a cuss. He seen one o' them black folks git a gredge against another an' go an' set down an' look stiddy at him in his hut an' cuss him in his mind an' set there an' watch, watch, until the other kind o' took sick an' died, all in a fortnight, I believe he said; 't would make your blood run cold to hear gran'ther describe it, 't would so. He never done nothin' but set an' look, an' folks would give him somethin' to eat now an' then, as if they thought 't was all right, an' the other one 'd try to go an' come, an' at last he hived away altogether an' died. I don't know what you 'd call it that ailed him. There 's suthin' in cussin' that's bad for folks, now I tell ye, Mis' Downs."

"Hannah's eyes always makes me creepy now," Mrs. Downs confessed uneasily. "They don't look pleadin' an' childish same 's they used to. Seems to me as if she 'd had the worst on 't."

"We ain't seen the end on 't yit," said Mrs. Forder, impressively. "I feel it within me, Marthy Downs, an' it's a terrible thing to have happened right amon'st us in Christian times. If we live long enough we 're goin' to have plenty to talk over in our old age that's come o' that cuss. Some seed 's shy o' sproutin' till a spring when the s'ile 's jest right to breed it."

"There 's lobeely now," agreed Mrs. Downs, pleased to descend to prosaic and familiar levels. "They ain't a good crop one year in six, and then you find it in a place where you never observed none to grow afore, like 's not; ain't it so, reely? "And she rose to clear the table, pleased with the certainty of a guest that night. Their conversation was not reassuring to the heart of a timid woman, alone in an isolated farmhouse on a dark spring evening, especially so near the anniversary of old Captain Knowles's death.

V.

Later in these rural lives by many years two aged women were crossing a wide field together, following a footpath such as one often finds between widely separated homes of the New England country. Along these lightly traced thoroughfares, the children go to play, and lovers to plead, and older people to companion one another in work and pleasure, in sickness and sorrow; generation after generation comes and goes again by these country by-ways.

The footpath led from Mrs. Forder's to another farmhouse half a mile beyond, where there had been a wedding. Mrs. Downs was there, and in the June weather she had been easily persuaded to go home to tea with Mrs. Forder with the promise of being driven home later in the evening. Mrs. Downs's husband had been dead three years, and her friend's large family was scattered from the old nest; they were lonely at times in their later years, these old friends, and found it very pleasant now to have a walk together. Thin little Mrs. Forder, with all her wheezing, was the stronger and more active of the two; Mrs. Downs had grown heavier and weaker with advancing years.

They paced along the footpath slowly, Mrs. Downs rolling in her gait like a sailor, and availing herself of every pretext to stop and look at herbs in the pasture ground they crossed, and at the growing grass in the mowing fields. They discussed the wedding minutely, and then where the way grew wider they walked side by side instead of following each other, and their voices sank to the low tone that betokens confidence.

"You don't say that you really put faith in all them old stories?"

"It ain't accident altogether, noways you can fix it in your mind," maintained Mrs. Downs. "Need n't tell me that cussin' don't do neither good nor harm. I should n't want to marry amon'st the Holts if I was young ag'in! I r'member when this young man was born that's married to-day, an' the fust thing his poor mother wanted to know was about his hands bein' right. I said yes they was, but las' year he was twenty year old and come home from the frontier with one o' them hands — his right one — shot off in a fight. They say 't happened to sights o' other fellows, an' their laigs gone too, but I count 'em over on my fingers, them Holts, an' he 's the third. May say that 't was all an accident his mother's gittin' throwed out o' her waggin comin' home from meetin', an' her wrist not bein' set good, an' she, bein' run down at the time, 'most lost it altogether, but thar' it is, stiffened up an' no good to her. There was the second. An' Enoch Holt his-self come home from the Chiny seas, made a good passage an' a sight o' money in the pepper trade, jest's we expected, an' goin' to build him a new house, an' the frame gives a kind o' lurch when they was raisin' of it an' surges over on to him an' nips him under. 'Which arm?' says everybody along the road when they was comin' an' goin' with the doctor. 'Right one — got to lose it,' says the doctor to 'em, an' next time Enoch Holt got out to meetin' he stood up in the house o' God with the hymn-book in his left hand, an' no right hand to turn his leaf with. He knowed what we was all a-thinkin'."

"Well," said Mrs. Forder, very short-breathed with climbing the long slope of the pasture hill, "I don't know but I 'd as soon be them as the Knowles gals. Hannah never knowed no peace again after she spoke them words in the co't-house. They come back an' harnted her, an' you know, Miss Downs, better 'n I do, being door-neighbors as one may say, how they lived their lives out like wild beasts into a lair."

"They used to go out some by night to git the air," pursued Mrs. Downs with interest. "I used to open the door an' step right in, an' I used to take their yarn an' stuff 'long o' mine an' sell 'em, an' do for the poor stray creatur 's long's they'd let me. They'd be grateful for a mess o' early pease or potatoes as ever you see, an' Peter he allays favored 'em with pork, fresh an' salt, when we slaughtered. The old Cap'n kept 'em child'n long as he lived, an' then they was too old to I'arn different. I allays liked Hannah the best till that change struck her. Betsey she held out to the last jest about the same. I don't know, now I come to think of it, but what she felt it the most o' the two."

"They'd never let me 's much as git a look at 'em," complained Mrs. Forder. "Folks got awful stories a-goin' one time. I've heard it said, an' it allays creeped me cold all over, that there was somethin' come an' lived with 'em — a kind o' black shadder, a cobweb kind o' a man-shape that followed 'em about the house an' made a third to them; but they got hardened to it theirselves, only they was afraid't would follow if they went anywheres from home. You don't believe no such piece o' nonsense? — But there, I've asked ye times enough before."

"They'd got shadders enough, poor creatur's," said Mrs. Downs with reserve. "Was n't no kind o' need to make 'em up no spooks, as I know on. Well, here's these young folks a-startin'; I wish 'em well, I'm sure. She likes him with his one hand better than most gals likes them as has a good sound pair. They looked prime happy; I hope no curse won't foller 'em."

The friends stopped again — poor, short-winded bodies — on the crest of the low hill and turned to look at the wide landscape, bewildered by the marvelous beauty and the sudden flood of golden sunset light that poured out of the western sky. They could not remember that they had ever observed the wide view before; it was like a revelation or an outlook towards the celestial country, the sight of their own green farms and the countryside that bounded them. It was a pleasant country indeed, their own New England: their petty thoughts and vain imaginings seemed futile and unrelated to so fair a scene of things. But the figure of a man who was crossing the meadow below looked like a malicious black insect. It was an old man, it was Enoch Holt; time had worn and bent him enough to have satisfied his bitterest foe. The women could see his empty coat-sleeve flutter as he walked slowly and unexpectantly in that glorious evening light.

THE YELLOW WALL PAPER

Charlotte Perkins Gilman

IT is very seldom that mere ordinary people like John and myself secure ancestral halls for the summer.

A colonial mansion, a hereditary estate, I would say a haunted house, and reach the height of romantic felicity,—but that would be asking too much of fate!

Still I will proudly declare that there is something queer about it.

Else, why should it be let so cheaply? And why have stood so long untenanted?

John laughs at me, of course, but one expects that in marriage.

John is practical in the extreme. He has no patience with faith, an intense horror of superstition, and he scoffs openly at any talk of things not to be felt and seen and put down in figures.

John is a physician, and *perhaps*—(I would not say it to a living soul, of course, but this is dead paper and a great relief to my mind)—*perhaps* that is one reason I do not get well faster.

You see, he does not believe I am sick!

And what can one do?

If a physician of high standing, and one's own husband, assures friends and relatives that there is really nothing the matter with one but temporary nervous depression,—a slight hysterical tendency,—what is one to do?

My brother is also a physician, and also of high standing, and he says the same thing.

So I take phosphates or phosphites,—whichever it is,—and tonics, and journeys, and air, and exercise, and am absolutely forbidden to "work" until I am well again.

Personally I disagree with their ideas.

Personally I believe that congenial work, with excitement and change, would do me good.

But what is one to do?

I did write for a while in spite of them; but it *does* exhaust me a good deal—having to be so sly about it, or else meet with heavy opposition.

I sometimes fancy that in my condition if I had less opposition and more society and stimulus—but John says the very worst thing I can do is to think about my condition, and I confess it always makes me feel bad.

So I will let it alone and talk about the house.

The most beautiful place! It is quite alone, standing well back from the road, quite three miles from the village. It makes me think of English places that you read about, for there are hedges and walls and gates that lock, and lots of separate little houses for the gardeners and people.

There is a *delicious* garden! I never saw such a garden—large and shady, full of box-bordered paths, and lined with long grape-covered arbors with seats under them.

There were greenhouses, too, but they are all broken now.

There was some legal trouble, I believe, something about the heirs and co-heirs; anyhow, the place has been empty for years.

That spoils my ghostliness, I am afraid; but I don't care—there is something strange about the house—I can feel it.

I even said so to John one moonlight evening, but he said what I felt was a *draught*, and shut the window.

I get unreasonably angry with John sometimes. I'm sure I never used to be so sensitive. I think it is due to this nervous condition.

But John says if I feel so I shall neglect proper self-control; so I take pains to control myself,—before him, at least,—and that makes me very tired.

I don't like our room a bit. I wanted one downstairs that opened on the piazza and had roses all over the window, and such pretty, old-fashioned chintz hangings! but John would not hear of it.

He said there was only one window and not room for two beds, and no near room for him if he took another.

He is very careful and loving, and hardly lets me stir without special direction.

I have a schedule prescription for each hour in the day; he takes all care from me, and so I feel basely ungrateful not to value it more.

He said we came here solely on my account, that I was to have perfect rest and all the air I could get. "Your exercise depends on your strength, my dear," said he, "and your food somewhat on your appetite; but air you can absorb all the time." So we took the nursery, at the top of the house.

It is a big, airy room, the whole floor nearly, with windows that look all ways, and air and sunshine galore. It was nursery first and then playground and gymnasium, I should judge; for the windows are barred for little children, and there are rings and things in the walls.

The paint and paper look as if a boys' school had used it. It is stripped off—the paper—in great patches all around the head of my bed, about as far as I can reach, and in a great place on the other side of the room low down. I never saw a worse paper in my life.

One of those sprawling flamboyant patterns committing every artistic sin.

It is dull enough to confuse the eye in following, pronounced enough to constantly irritate, and provoke study, and when you follow the lame, uncertain curves for a little distance they suddenly commit suicide—plunge off at outrageous angles, destroy themselves in unheard-of contradictions.

The color is repellant, almost revolting; a smouldering, unclean yellow, strangely faded by the slow-turning sunlight.

It is a dull yet lurid orange in some places, a sickly sulphur tint in others.

No wonder the children hated it! I should hate it myself if I had to live in this room long.

There comes John, and I must put this away,—he hates to have me write a word.

WE have been here two weeks, and I haven't felt like writing before, since that first day.

I am sitting by the window now, up in this atrocious nursery, and there is nothing to hinder my writing as much as I please, save lack of strength.

John is away all day, and even some nights when his cases are serious.

I am glad my case is not serious!

But these nervous troubles are dreadfully depressing.

John does not know how much I really suffer. He knows there is no *reason* to suffer, and that satisfies him.

Of course it is only nervousness. It does weigh on me so not to do my duty in any way!

I meant to be such a help to John, such a real rest and comfort, and here I am a comparative burden already!

Nobody would believe what an effort it is to do what little I am able—to dress and entertain, and order things.

It is fortunate Mary is so good with the baby. Such a dear baby!

And yet I *cannot* be with him, it makes me so nervous.

I suppose John never was nervous in his life. He laughs at me so about this wall paper!

At first he meant to repaper the room, but afterwards he said that I was letting it get the better of me, and that nothing was worse for a nervous patient than to give way to such fancies.

He said that after the wall paper was changed it would be the heavy bedstead, and then the barred windows, and then that gate at the head of the stairs, and so on.

"You know the place is doing you good," he said, "and really, dear, I don't care to renovate the house just for a three months' rental."

"Then do let us go downstairs," I said, "there are such pretty rooms there."

Then he took me in his arms and called me a blessed little goose, and said he would go down cellar if I wished, and have it whitewashed into the bargain.

But he is right enough about the beds and windows and things.

It is as airy and comfortable a room as any one need wish, and, of course, I would not be so silly as to make him uncomfortable just for a whim.

I'm really getting quite fond of the big room, all but that horrid paper.

Out of one window I can see the garden, those mysterious deep-shaded arbors, the riotous old-fashioned flowers, and bushes and gnarly trees.

Out of another I get a lovely view of the bay and a little private wharf belonging to the estate. There is a beautiful shaded lane that runs down there from the house. I always fancy I see people walking in these numerous paths and arbors, but John has cautioned me not to give way to fancy in the least. He says that with my imaginative power and habit of story-making a nervous weakness like mine is sure to lead to all manner of excited fancies, and that I ought to use my will and good sense to check the tendency. So I try.

I think sometimes that if I were only well enough to write a little it would relieve the press of ideas and rest me.

But I find I get pretty tired when I try.

It is so discouraging not to have any advice and companionship about my work. When I get really well John says we will ask Cousin Henry and Julia down for a long visit; but he says he would as soon put fire-works in my pillow-case as to let me have those stimulating people about now.

I wish I could get well faster.

But I must not think about that. This paper looks to me as if it *knew* what a vicious influence it had!

There is a recurrent spot where the pattern lolls like a broken neck and two bulbous eyes stare at you upside-down.

I got positively angry with the impertinence of it and the everlasting-ness. Up and down and sideways they crawl, and those absurd, unblinking eyes are everywhere. There is one place where two breadths didn't match, and the eyes go all up and down the line, one a little higher than the other.

I never saw so much expression in an inanimate thing before, and we all know how much expression they have! I used to lie awake as a child and get more entertainment and terror out of blank walls and plain furniture than most children could find in a toy-store.

I remember what a kindly wink the knobs of our big old bureau used to have, and there was one chair that always seemed like a strong friend.

I used to feel that if any of the other things looked too fierce I could always hop into that chair and be safe.

The furniture in this room is no worse than inharmonious, however, for we had to bring it all from downstairs. I suppose when this was used as a playroom they had to take the nursery things out, and no wonder! I never saw such ravages as the children have made here.

The wall paper, as I said before, is torn off in spots, and it sticketh closer than a brother—they must have had perseverance as well as hatred.

Then the floor is scratched and gouged and splintered, the plaster itself is dug out here and there, and this great heavy bed, which is all we found in the room, looks as if it had been through the wars.

But I don't mind it a bit—only the paper.

There comes John's sister. Such a dear girl as she is, and so careful of me! I must not let her find me writing.

She is a perfect, an enthusiastic housekeeper, and hopes for no better profession. I verily believe she thinks it is the writing which made me sick!

But I can write when she is out, and see her a long way off from these windows.

There is one that commands the road, a lovely, shaded, winding road, and one that just looks off over the country. A lovely country, too, full of great elms and velvet meadows.

This wall paper has a kind of sub-pattern in a different shade, a particularly irritating one, for you can only see it in certain lights, and not clearly then.

But in the places where it isn't faded, and where the sun is just so, I can see a strange, provoking, formless sort of figure, that seems to sulk about behind that silly and conspicuous front design.

There's sister on the stairs!

WELL, the Fourth of July is over! The people are all gone and I am tired out. John thought it might do me good to see a little company, so we just had mother and Nellie and the children down for a week.

Of course I didn't do a thing. Jennie sees to everything now.

But it tired me all the same.

John says if I don't pick up faster he shall send me to Weir Mitchell in the fall.

But I don't want to go there at all. I had a friend who was in his hands once, and she says he is just like John and my brother, only more so!

Besides, it is such an undertaking to go so far.

I don't feel as if it was worth while to turn my hand over for anything, and I'm getting dreadfully fretful and querulous.

I cry at nothing, and cry most of the time.

Of course I don't when John is here, or anybody else, but when I am alone.

And I am alone a good deal just now. John is kept in town very often by serious cases, and Jennie is good and lets me alone when I want her to.

So I walk a little in the garden or down that lovely lane, sit on the porch under the roses, and lie down up here a good deal.

I'm getting really fond of the room in spite of the wall paper. Perhaps *because* of the wall paper.

It dwells in my mind so!

I lie here on this great immovable bed—it is nailed down, I believe—and follow that pattern about by the hour. It is as good as gymnastics, I assure you. I start, we'll say, at the bottom, down in the corner over there where it has not been touched, and I determine for the thousandth time that I *will* follow that pointless pattern to some sort of a conclusion.

I know a little of the principles of design, and I know this thing was not arranged on any laws of radiation, or alternation, or repetition, or symmetry, or anything else that I ever heard of.

It is repeated, of course, by the breadths, but not otherwise.

Looked at in one way, each breadth stands alone, the bloated curves and flourishes—a kind of "debased Romanesque "with *delirium tremens*—go waddling up and down in isolated columns of fatuity.

But, on the other hand, they connect diagonally, and the sprawling outlines run off in great slanting waves of optic horror, like a lot of wallowing seaweeds in full chase.

The whole thing goes horizontally, too, at least it seems so, and I exhaust myself in trying to distinguish the order of its going in that direction.

They have used a horizontal breadth for a frieze, and that adds wonderfully to the confusion.

There is one end of the room where it is almost intact, and there, when the cross-lights fade and the low sun shines directly upon it, I can almost fancy radiation, after all,—the interminable grotesques seem to form around a common centre and rush off in headlong plunges of equal distraction.

It makes me tired to follow it. I will take a nap, I guess.

I DON'T know why I should write this.

I don't want to.

I don't feel able.

And I know John would think it absurd. But I *must* say what I feel and think in some way—it is such a relief!

But the effort is getting to be greater than the relief.

Half the time now I am awfully lazy, and lie down ever so much.

John says I mustn't lose my strength, and has me take cod-liver oil and lots of tonics and things, to say nothing of ale and wine and rare meat.

Dear John! He loves me very dearly, and hates to have me sick. I tried to have a real earnest reasonable talk with him the other day, and tell him how I wished he would let me go and make a visit to Cousin Henry and Julia.

But he said I wasn't able to go, nor able to stand it after I got there; and I did not make out a very good case for myself, for I was crying before I had finished.

It is getting to be a great effort for me to think straight. Just this nervous weakness, I suppose.

And dear John gathered me up in his arms, and just carried me upstairs and laid me on the bed, and sat by me and read to me till he tired my head.

He said I was his darling and his comfort and all he had, and that I must take care of myself for his sake, and keep well.

He says no one but myself can help me out of it, that I must use my will and self-control and not let my silly fancies run away with me.

There's one comfort, the baby is well and happy, and does not have to occupy this nursery with the horrid wall paper.

If we had not used it that blessed child would have! What a fortunate escape! Why, I wouldn't have a child of mine, an impressionable little thing, live in such a room for worlds.

I never thought of it before, but it is lucky that John kept me here, after all. I can stand it so much easier than a baby, you see.

Of course I never mention it to them any more,—I am too wise,—but I keep watch of it all the same.

There are things in that paper that nobody knows but me, or ever will.

Behind that outside pattern the dim shapes get clearer every day.

It is always the same shape, only very numerous.

And it is like a woman stooping down and creeping about behind that pattern. I don't like it a bit. I wonder—I begin to think—I wish John would take me away from here!

It is so hard to talk with John about my case, because he is so wise, and because he loves me so.

But I tried it last night.

It was moonlight. The moon shines in all around, just as the sun does.

I hate to see it sometimes, it creeps so slowly, and always comes in by one window or another.

John was asleep and I hated to waken him, so I kept still and watched the moonlight on that undulating wall paper till I felt creepy.

The faint figure behind seemed to shake the pattern, just as if she wanted to get out.

I got up softly and went to feel and see if the paper *did* move, and when I came back John was awake.

"What is it, little girl?" he said. "Don't go walking about like that—you'll get cold."

I thought it was a good time to talk, so I told him that I really was not gaining here, and that I wished he would take me away.

"Why, darling!" said he, "our lease will be up in three weeks, and I can't see how to leave before.

"The repairs are not done at home, and I cannot possibly leave town just now. Of course if you were in any danger I could and would, but you really are better, dear, whether you can see it or not. I am a doctor, dear, and I know. You are gaining flesh and color, your appetite is better. I feel really much easier about you."

"I don't weigh a bit more," said I, "nor as much; and my appetite may be better in the evening, when you are here, but it is worse in the morning, when you are away."

"Bless her little heart!" said he with a big hug; "she shall be as sick as she pleases. But now let's improve the shining hours by going to sleep, and talk about it in the morning."

"And you won't go away?" I asked gloomily.

"Why, how can I, dear? It is only three weeks more and then we will take a nice little trip of a few days while Jennie is getting the house ready. Really, dear, you are better!"

"Better in body, perhaps"—I began, and stopped short, for he sat up straight and looked at me with such a stern, reproachful look that I could not say another word.

"My darling," said he, "I beg of you, for my sake and for our child's sake, as well as for your own, that you will never for one instant let that idea enter your mind! There is nothing so dangerous, so fascinating, to a temperament like yours. It is a false and foolish fancy. Can you not trust me as a physician when I tell you so?"

So of course I said no more on that score, and we went to sleep before long. He thought I was asleep first, but I wasn't,—I lay there for hours trying to decide whether that front pattern and the back pattern really did move together or separately.

On a pattern like this, by daylight, there is a lack of sequence, a defiance of law, that is a constant irritant to a normal mind.

The color is hideous enough, and unreliable enough, and infuriating enough, but the pattern is torturing.

You think you have mastered it, but just as you get well under way in following, it turns a back somersault, and there you are. It slaps you in the face, knocks you down, and tramples upon you. It is like a bad dream.

The outside pattern is a florid arabesque, reminding one of a fungus. If you can imagine a toadstool in joints, an interminable string of toadstools, budding and sprouting in endless convolutions,—why, that is something like it.

That is, sometimes!

There is one marked peculiarity about this paper, a thing nobody seems to notice but myself, and that is that it changes as the light changes.

When the sun shoots in through the east window—I always watch for that first long, straight ray—it changes so quickly that I never can quite believe it.

That is why I watch it always.

By moonlight—the moon shines in all night when there is a moon—I wouldn't know it was the same paper.

At night in any kind of light, in twilight, candlelight, lamplight, and worst of all by moonlight, it becomes bars! The outside pattern, I mean, and the woman behind it is as plain as can be.

I didn't realize for a long time what the thing was that showed behind,—that dim sub-pattern,—but now I am quite sure it is a woman.

By daylight she is subdued, quiet. I fancy it is the pattern that keeps her so still. It is so puzzling. It keeps me quiet by the hour.

I lie down ever so much now. John says it is good for me, and to sleep all I can.

Indeed, he started the habit by making me lie down for an hour after each meal.

It is a very bad habit, I am convinced, for, you see, I don't sleep.

And that cultivates deceit, for I don't tell them I'm awake,— oh, no!

The fact is, I am getting a little afraid of John.

He seems very queer sometimes, and even Jennie has an inexplicable look.

It strikes me occasionally, just as a scientific hypothesis, that perhaps it is the paper!

I have watched John when he did not know I was looking, and come into the room suddenly on the most innocent excuses, and I've caught him several times *looking at the paper!* And Jennie too. I caught Jennie with her hand on it once.

She didn't know I was in the room, and when I asked her in a quiet, a very quiet voice, with the most restrained manner possible, what she was doing with the paper she turned around as if she had been caught stealing, and looked quite angry—asked me why I should frighten her so!

Then she said that the paper stained everything it touched, that she had found yellow smooches on all my clothes and John's, and she wished we would be more careful!

Did not that sound innocent? But I know she was studying that pattern, and I am determined that nobody shall find it out but myself!

LIFE is very much more exciting now than it used to be. You see I have something more to expect, to look forward to, to watch. I really do eat better, and am more quiet than I was.

John is so pleased to see me improve! He laughed a little the other day, and said I seemed to be flourishing in spite of my wall paper.

I turned it off with a laugh. I had no intention of telling him it was *because* of the wall paper—he would make fun of me. He might even want to take me away.

I don't want to leave now until I have found it out. There is a week more, and I think that will be enough.

I'M feeling ever so much better! I don't sleep much at night, for it is so interesting to watch developments; but I sleep a good deal in the daytime.

In the daytime it is tiresome and perplexing.

There are always new shoots on the fungus, and new shades of yellow all over it. I cannot keep count of them, though I have tried conscientiously.

It is the strangest yellow, that wall paper! It makes me think of all the yellow things I ever saw—not beautiful ones like buttercups, but old foul, bad yellow things.

But there is something else about that paper—the smell! I noticed it the moment we came into the room, but with so much air and sun it was not bad. Now we have had a week of fog and rain, and whether the windows are open or not the smell is here.

It creeps all over the house.

I find it hovering in the dining-room, skulking in the parlor, hiding in the hall, lying in wait for me on the stairs.

It gets into my hair.

Even when I go to ride, if I turn my head suddenly and surprise it— there is that smell!

Such a peculiar odor, too! I have spent hours in trying to analyze it, to find what it smelled like.

It is not bad—at first, and very gentle, but quite the subtlest, most enduring odor I ever met.

In this damp weather it is awful. I wake up in the night and find it hanging over me.

It used to disturb me at first. I thought seriously of burning the house—to reach the smell.

But now I am used to it. The only thing I can think of that it is like is the *color* of the paper—a yellow smell!

There is a very funny mark on this wall, low down, near the mopboard. A streak that runs around the room. It goes behind every piece of furniture, except the bed, a long, straight, even *smooch*, as if it had been rubbed over and over.

I wonder how it was done and who did it, and what they did it for. Round and round and round—round and round and round—it makes me dizzy!

I REALLY have discovered something at last.

Through watching so much at night, when it changes so, I have finally found out.

The front pattern *does* move—and no wonder! The woman behind shakes it!

Sometimes I think there are a great many women behind, and sometimes only one, and she crawls around fast, and her crawling shakes it all over.

Then in the very bright spots she keeps still, and in the very shady spots she just takes hold of the bars and shakes them hard.

And she is all the time trying to climb through. But nobody could climb through that pattern—it strangles so; I think that is why it has so many heads.

They get through, and then the pattern strangles them off and turns them upside-down, and makes their eyes white!

If those heads were covered or taken off it would not be half so bad.

I THINK that woman gets out in the daytime!

And I'll tell you why—privately—I've seen her!

I can see her out of every one of my windows!

It is the same woman, I know, for she is always creeping, and most women do not creep by daylight.

I see her in that long shaded lane, creeping up and down. I see her in those dark grape arbors, creeping all around the garden.

I see her on that long road under the trees, creeping along, and when a carriage comes she hides under the blackberry vines.

I don't blame her a bit. It must be very humiliating to be caught creeping by daylight!

I always lock the door when I creep by daylight. I can't do it at night, for I know John would suspect something at once.

And John is so queer, now, that I don't want to irritate him. I wish he would take another room! Besides, I don't want anybody to get that woman out at night but myself.

I often wonder if I could see her out of all the windows at once.

But, turn as fast as I can, I can only see out of one at one time.

And though I always see her she *may* be able to creep faster than I can turn!

I have watched her sometimes away off in the open country, creeping as fast as a cloud shadow in a high wind.

IF only that top pattern could be gotten off from the under one! I mean to try it, little by little.

I have found out another funny thing, but I shan't tell it this time! It does not do to trust people too much.

There are only two more days to get this paper off, and I believe John is beginning to notice. I don't like the look in his eyes.

And I heard him ask Jennie a lot of professional questions about me. She had a very good report to give.

She said I slept a good deal in the daytime.

John knows I don't sleep very well at night, for all I'm so quiet!

He asked me all sorts of questions, too, and pretended to be very loving and kind.

As if I couldn't see through him!

Still, I don't wonder he acts so, sleeping under this paper for three months.

It only interests me, but I feel sure John and Jennie are secretly affected by it.

HURRAH! This is the last day, but it is enough. John is to stay in town over night, and won't be out until this evening.

Jennie wanted to sleep with me—the sly thing! I but I told her I should undoubtedly rest better for a night all alone.

That was clever, for really I wasn't alone a bit! As soon as it was moonlight, and that poor thing began to crawl and shake the pattern, I got up and ran to help her.

I pulled and she shook, I shook and she pulled, and before morning we had peeled off yards of that paper.

A strip about as high as my head and half around the room.

And then when the sun came and that awful pattern began to laugh at me I declared I would finish it today!

We go away to-morrow, and they are moving all my furniture down again to leave things as they were before.

Jennie looked at the wall in amazement, but I told her merrily that I did it out of pure spite at the vicious thing.

She laughed and said she wouldn't mind doing it herself, but I must not get tired.

How she betrayed herself that time!

But I am here, and no person touches this paper but me — not *alive!*

She tried to get me out of the room—it was too patent! But I said it was so quiet and empty and clean now that I believed I would lie down again and sleep all I could; and not to wake me even for dinner—I would call when I woke.

So now she is gone, and the servants are gone, and the things are gone, and there is nothing left but that great bedstead nailed down, with the canvas mattress we found on it.

We shall sleep downstairs to-night, and take the boat home to-morrow.

I quite enjoy the room, now it is bare again.

How those children did tear about here!

This bedstead is fairly gnawed!

But I must get to work.

I have locked the door and thrown the key down into the front path.

I don't want to go out, and I don't want to have anybody come in, till John comes.

I want to astonish him.

I've got a rope up here that even Jennie did not find. If that woman does get out, and tries to get away, I can tie her!

But I forgot I could not reach far without anything to stand on!

This bed will *not* move!

I tried to lift and push it until I was lame, and then I got so angry I bit off a little piece at one corner—but it hurt my teeth.

Then I peeled off all the paper I could reach standing on the floor. It sticks horribly and the pattern just enjoys it! All those strangled heads and bulbous eyes and waddling fungus growths just shriek with derision!

I am getting angry enough to do something desperate. To jump out of the window would be admirable exercise, but the bars are too strong even to try.

Besides, I wouldn't do it. Of course not. I know well enough that a step like that is improper and might be misconstrued.

I don't like to *look* out of the windows even—there are so many of those creeping women, and they creep so fast.

I wonder if they all come out of that wall paper, as I did?

But I am securely fastened now by my well-hidden rope—you don't get *me* out in the road there!

I suppose I shall have to get back behind the pattern when it comes night, and that is hard!

It is so pleasant to be out in this great room and creep around as I please!

I don't want to go outside. I won't, even if Jennie asks me to.

For outside you have to creep on the ground, and everything is green instead of yellow.

But here I can creep smoothly on the floor, and my shoulder just fits in that long smooch around the wall, so I cannot lose my way.

Why, there's John at the door!

It is no use, young man, you can't open it!

How he does call and pound!

Now he's crying for an axe.

It would be a shame to break down that beautiful door!

"John, dear!" said I in the gentlest voice, "the key is down by the front steps, under a plantain leaf!"

That silenced him for a few moments.

Then he said—very quietly indeed, "Open the door, my darling!"

"I can't," said I. "The key is down by the front door, under a plantain leaf!"

And then I said it again, several times, very gently and slowly, and said it so often that he had to go and see, and he got it, of course, and came in. He stopped short by the door.

"What is the matter?" he cried. "For God's sake, what are you doing?"

I kept on creeping just the same, but I looked at him over my shoulder.

"I've got out at last," said I, "in spite of you and Jane! And I've pulled off most of the paper, so you can't put me back!"

Now why should that man have fainted? But he did, and right across my path by the wall, so that I had to creep over him every time!

DEATH AND THE WOMAN

Gertrude Atherton

Her husband was dying, and she was alone with him. Nothing could exceed the desolation of her surroundings. She and the man who was going from her were in the third-floor-back of a New York boarding-house. It was summer, and the other boarders were in the country; all the servants except the cook had been dismissed, and she, when not working, slept profoundly on the fifth floor. The landlady also was out of town on a brief holiday.

The window was open to admit the thick unstirring air; no sound rose from the row of long narrow yards, nor from the tall deep houses annexed. The latter deadened the rattle of the streets. At intervals the distant Elevated lumbered protestingly along, its grunts and screams muffled by the hot suspended ocean.

She sat there plunged in the profoundest grief that can come to the human soul, for in all other agony hope flickers, however forlornly. She gazed dully at the unconscious breathing form of the man who had been friend, and companion, and lover, during five years of youth too vigorous and hopeful to be warped by uneven fortune. It was wasted by disease; the face was shrunken; the night garment hung loosely about a body which had never been disfigured by flesh, but had been muscular with exercise and full-blooded with health. She was glad that the body was changed; glad that its beauty, too, had gone some otherwhere than into the coffin. She had loved his hands as apart from himself; loved their strong warm magnetism. They lay limp and yellow on the quilt: she knew that they were already cold, and that moisture was gathering on them. For a moment something convulsed within her. *They* had gone too. She repeated the words twice, and, after them, *"for ever."* And the while the sweetness of their pressure came back to her.

She leaned suddenly over him. HE was in there still, somewhere. *Where?* If he had not ceased to breathe, the Ego, the Soul, the Personality, was still in the sodden clay which had shaped to give it speech. Why could it not manifest itself to her? Was it still conscious in there, unable to project itself through the disintegrating matter which was the only medium its Creator had vouchsafed it? Did it struggle there, seeing her agony, sharing it, longing for the complete disintegration which should put an end to its torment? She called his name, she even shook him slightly, mad to tear the body apart and find her mate, yet even in that tortured moment realising that violence would hasten his going.

The dying man took no notice of her, and she opened his gown and put her cheek to his heart, calling him again. There had never been more perfect union; how could the bond still be so strong if he were not at the other end of it? He was there, her other part; until dead he must be living. There was no intermediate state. Why should he be as entombed and unresponding as if the screws were in the lid? But the faintly beating heart did not quicken beneath her lips. She extended her arms suddenly, describing eccentric lines, above, about him, rapidly opening and closing her hands as if to clutch some escaping object; then sprang to her feet, and went to the window. She feared insanity. She had asked to be left alone with her dying husband, and she did not wish to lose her reason and shriek a crowd of people about her.

The green plots in the yards were not apparent, she noticed. Something heavy, like a pall, rested upon them. Then she understood that the day was over and that night was coming.

She returned swiftly to the bedside, wondering if she had remained away hours or seconds, and if he were dead. His face was still discernible, and Death had not relaxed it. She laid her own against it, then withdrew it with shuddering flesh, her teeth smiting each other as if an icy wind had passed.

She let herself fall back in the chair, clasping her hands against her heart, watching with expanding eyes the white sculptured face which, in the gathering dark, was becoming less defined of outline. Did she light the gas it would draw mosquitoes, and she could not shut from him the little air he must be mechanically grateful for. And she did not want to see the opening eye—the falling jaw.

Her vision became so fixed that at length she saw nothing, and closed her eyes and waited for the moisture to rise and relieve the strain. When she opened them his face had disappeared; the humid waves above the house-tops put out even the light of the stars, and night was come.

Fearfully, she approached her ear to his lips; he still breathed. She made a motion to kiss him, then threw herself back in a quiver of agony—they were not the lips she had known, and she would have nothing less.

His breathing was so faint that in her half-reclining position she could not hear it, could not be aware of the moment of his death. She extended her arm resolutely and laid her hand on his heart. Not only must she feel his going, but, so strong had been the comradeship between them, it was a matter of loving honour to stand by him to the last.

She sat there in the hot heavy night, pressing her hand hard against the ebbing heart of the unseen, and awaited Death. Suddenly an odd fancy possessed her. Where was Death? Why was he tarrying? Who was detaining him? From what quarter would he come? He was taking his leisure, drawing near with footsteps as measured as those of men keeping time to a funeral march. By a wayward deflection she thought of the slow music that was always turned on in the theatre when the heroine was about to appear, or something eventful to happen. She had always thought that sort of thing ridiculous and inartistic. So had He.

She drew her brows together angrily, wondering at her levity, and pressed her relaxed palm against the heart it kept guard over. For a moment the sweat stood on her face; then the pent-up breath burst from her lungs. He still lived.

Once more the fancy wantoned above the stunned heart. Death—*where* was he? What a curious experience: to be sitting alone in a big house—she knew that the cook had stolen out—waiting for Death to come and snatch her husband from her. No; he would not snatch, he would steal upon his prey as noiselessly as the approach of Sin to Innocence—an invisible, unfair, sneaking enemy, with whom no man's strength could grapple. If he would only come like a man, and take his chances like a man! Women had been known to reach the hearts of giants with the dagger's point. But he would creep upon her.

She gave an exclamation of horror. Something was creeping over the windowsill. Her limbs palsied, but she struggled to her feet and looked back, her eyes dragged about against her own volition. Two small green stars glared menacingly at her just above the sill; then the cat possessing them leaped downward, and the stars disappeared.

She realised that she was horribly frightened. "Is it possible?" she thought. "Am I afraid of Death, and of Death that has not yet come? I have always been rather a brave woman; *He* used to call me heroic; but then with him it was impossible to fear anything. And I begged them to leave me alone with him as the last of earthly boons. Oh, shame!"

But she was still quaking as she resumed her seat, and laid her hand again on his heart. She wished that she had asked Mary to sit outside the door; there was no bell in the room. To call would be worse than desecrating the house of God, and she would not leave him for one moment. To return and find him dead—gone alone!

Her knees smote each other. It was idle to deny it; she was in a state of unreasoning terror. Her eyes rolled apprehensively about; she wondered if she should see It when It came; wondered how far off It was now. Not very far; the heart was barely pulsing. She had heard of the power of the corpse to drive brave men to frenzy, and had wondered, having no morbid horror of the dead. But this! To wait—and wait—and wait—perhaps for hours—past the midnight—on to the small hours—while that awful, determined, leisurely Something stole nearer and nearer.

She bent to him who had been her protector, with a spasm of anger. Where was the indomitable spirit that had held her all these years with such strong and loving clasp? How could he leave her? How could he desert her? Her head fell back and moved restlessly against the cushion; moaning with the agony of loss, she recalled him as he had been. Then fear once more took possession of her, and she sat erect, rigid, breathless, awaiting the approach of Death.

Suddenly, far down in the house, on the first-floor, her strained hearing took note of a sound—a wary, muffled sound, as if some one were creeping up the stair, fearful of being heard. Slowly! It seemed to count a hundred between the laying down of each foot. She gave a hysterical gasp. Where was the slow music?

Her face, her body, were wet—as if a wave of death-sweat had broken over them. There was a stiff feeling at the roots of her hair; she wondered if it were really standing erect. But she could not raise her hand to ascertain. Possibly it was only the colouring matter freezing and bleaching. Her muscles were flabby, her nerves twitched helplessly.

She knew that it was Death who was coming to her through the silent deserted house; knew that it was the sensitive ear of her intelligence that heard him, not the dull coarse-grained ear of the body.

He toiled up the stair painfully, as if he were old and tired with much work. But how could he afford to loiter, with all the work he had to do? Every minute, every second, he must be in demand to hook his cold hard finger about a soul struggling to escape from its putrefying tenement. But probably he had his emissaries, his minions: for only those worthy of the honour did he come in person.

He reached the first landing and crept like a cat down the hall to the next stair, then crawled slowly up as before. Light as the footfalls were, they were squarely planted, unfaltering; slow, they never halted.

Mechanically she pressed her jerking hand closer against the heart; its beats were almost done. They would finish, she calculated, just as those footfalls paused beside the bed.

She was no longer a human being; she was an Intelligence and an EAR. Not a sound came from without, even the Elevated appeared to be temporarily off duty; but inside the big quiet house that footfall was waxing louder, louder, until iron feet crashed on iron stairs and echo thundered.

She had counted the steps—one—two—three—irritated beyond endurance at the long deliberate pauses between. As they climbed and clanged with slow precision she continued to count, audibly and with equal precision, noting their hollow reverberation. How many steps had the stair? She wished she knew. No need! The colossal trampling announced the lessening distance in an increasing volume of sound not to be misunderstood. It turned the curve; it reached the landing; it advanced—slowly—down the hall; it paused before her door. Then knuckles of iron shook the frail panels. Her nerveless tongue gave no invitation. The knocking became more imperious; the very walls vibrated. The handle turned, swiftly and firmly. With a wild instinctive movement she flung herself into the arms of her husband.

When Mary opened the door and entered the room she found a dead woman lying across a dead man.

A WEDDING CHEST

Vernon Lee

No. 428. A panel (five feet by two feet three inches) formerly the front of a *cassone* or coffer, intended to contain the garments and jewels of a bride. *Subject:* "The Triumph of Love." Umbrian School of the Fifteenth Century." In the right-hand corner is a half-effaced inscription: *Desider ... de Civitate Lac ... me ... ecit.* This valuable painting is unfortunately much damaged by damp and mineral corrosives, owing probably to its having contained at one time buried treasure. Bequeathed in 1878 by the widow of the Rev. Lawson Stone, late Fellow of Trinity College, Cambridge.[1]

By Ascension Day, Desiderio of Castiglione del Lago had finished the front panel of the wedding chest which Messer Troilo Baglioni had ordered of Ser Piero Bontempi, whose shop was situated at the bottom of the steps of St. Maxentius, in that portion of the ancient city of Perugia (called by the Romans Augusta in recognition of its great glory) which takes its name from the Ivory Gate built by Theodoric, King of the Goths. The said Desiderio had represented upon his panel the Triumph of Love as described in his poem by Messer Francesco Petrarca of Arezzo, certainly with the exception of that Dante, who saw the Vision of Hell, Purgatory, and Paradise, the only poet of recent times who can be compared to those doctissimi viri P. Virgilius, Ovidius of Sulmona, and Statius. And the said Desiderio had betaken himself in this manner. He had divided the panel into four portions or regions, intended to represent the four phases of the amorous passion: the first was a pleasant country, abundantly watered with twisting streams, of great plenty and joyousness, in which were planted many hedges of fragrant roses, both red and blue, together with elms, poplars, and other pleasant and profitable trees. The second region was somewhat mountainous, but showing large store of lordly castles and thickets of pine and oak, fit for hunting, which region, as being that of glorious love, was girt all round with groves of laurels. The third region—*aspera ac dura regio*—was barren of all vegetation save huge thorns and ungrateful thistles; and in it, on rocks, was shown the pelican, who

---

[1] Catalogue of the Smith Museum, Leeds.

tears his own entrails to feed his young, symbolical of the cruelty of love to true lovers. Finally, the fourth region was a melancholy cypress wood, among which roosted owls and ravens and other birds, of evil omen, in order to display the fact that all earthly love leads but to death. Each of these regions was surrounded by a wreath of myrtles, marvellously drawn, and with great subtlety of invention divided so as to meet the carved and gilded cornice, likewise composed of myrtles, which Ser Piero executed with singular skill with his own hand. In the middle of the panel Desiderio had represented Love, even as the poet has described; a naked youth, with wings of wondrous changing colours, enthroned upon a chariot, the axle and wheels of which were red gold, and covered with a cloth of gold of such subtle device that the whole chariot seemed really to be on fire; on his back hung a bow and a quiver full of dreadful arrows, and in his hands he held the reins of four snow-white coursers, trapped with gold, and breathing fire from their nostrils. Round his eyes was bound a kerchief fringed with gold, to show that Love strikes blindly; and from his shoulders floated a scroll inscribed with the words— "Sævus Amor hominum deorumque deliciæ." Round his car, some before, some behind, some on horseback, some on foot, crowded those who have been famous for their love. Here you might see, on a bay horse, with an eagle on his helmet, Julius Cæsar, who loved Cleopatra, the Queen of Egypt; Sophonisba and Massinissa, in rich and strange Arabian garments; Orpheus, seeking for Eurydice, with his lute; Phædra, who died for love of Hippolytus, her stepson; Mark Antony; Rinaldo of Montalbano, who loved the beautiful Angelica; Socrates, Tibullus, Virgilius and other poets, with Messer Francesco Petrarca and Messer Giovanni Boccaccio; Tristram, who drank the love-potion, riding on a sorrel horse; and near him, Isotta, wearing a turban of cloth of gold, and these lovers of Rimini, and many more besides, the naming of whom would be too long, even as the poet has described. And in the region of happy love, among the laurels, he had painted his own likeness, red-haired, with a green hood falling on his shoulders, and this because he was to wed, next St. John's Eve, Maddalena, the only daughter of his employer, Ser Piero. And among the unhappy lovers, he painted, at his request, Messer Troilo himself, for whom he was making this coffer. And Messer Troilo was depicted in the character of Troilus, the son of Priam, Emperor of Troy; he was habited in armour, covered with a surcoat of white cloth of silver embroidered with roses; by his side was his lance, and on his head a scarlet cap; behind him were those who carried his falcon and led his hack, and men-at-arms with his banner, dressed in green and yellow parti-coloured, with a scorpion embroidered on their doublet; and from his lance floated a pennon inscribed: "Troilus sum servus Amoris."

But Desiderio refused to paint among the procession Monna Maddalena, Piero's daughter, who was to be his wife; because he declared it was not fit that modest damsels should lend their face to other folk; and this he said because Ser Piero had begged him not to incense Messer Troilo; for in reality he had often portrayed Monna Maddalena (the which was marvellously lovely), though only, it is true, in the figure of Our Lady, the Mother of God.

And the panel was ready by Ascension Day, and Ser Piero had prepared the box, and the carvings and gildings, griffins and chimeras, and acanthus leaves and myrtles, with the arms of Messer Troilo Baglioni, a most beautiful work. And Mastro Cavanna of the gate of St. Peter had made a lock and a key, of marvellous workmanship, for the same coffer. And Messer Troilo would come frequently, riding over from his castle of Fratta, and see the work while it was progressing, and entertain himself lengthily at the shop, speaking with benignity and wisdom wonderful in one so young, for he was only nineteen, which pleased the heart of Ser Piero; but Desiderio did not relish, for which reason he was often gruff to Messer Troilo, and had many disputes with his future father-in-law.

For Messer Troilo Baglioni, called Barbacane, to distinguish him from another Troilo, his uncle, who was bishop of Spello, although a bastard, had cast his eyes on Maddalena di Ser Piero Bontempi. He had seen the damsel for the first time on the occasion of the wedding festivities of his cousin Grifone Baglioni, son of Ridolfo the elder, with Deianira degli Orsini; on which occasion marvellous things were done in the city of Perugia, both by the magnificent House of Baglioni and the citizens, such as banquets, jousts, horse races, balls in the square near the cathedral, bull fights, allegories, both Latin and vulgar, presented with great learning and sweetness (among which was the fable of Perseus, how he freed Andromeda, written by Master Giannozzo, Belli Rector venerabilis istæ universitatis), and triumphal arches and other similar devices, in which Ser Piero Bontempi made many beautiful inventions, in company with Benedetto Bonfigli, Messer Fiorenzo di Lorenzo and Piero de Castro Plebis, whom the Holiness of our Lord Pope Sixtus IV afterwards summoned to work in his chapel in Rome. On this occasion, I repeat, Messer Troilo Baglioni of Fratta, who was *unanimiter* declared to be a most beautiful and courteous youth, of singular learning and prowess, and well worthy of this magnificent Baglioni family, cast his eyes on Maddalena di Ser Piero, and sent her, through his squire, the knot of ribbons off the head of a ferocious bull, whom he had killed *singulari vi ac virtute*. Nor did Messer Troilo neglect other opportunities of seeing the damsel, such as at church and at her father's shop, riding over from his castle at Fratta on purpose, but always *honestis valde modibus*, as the damsel showed herself very coy, and refused all presents which he sent her. Neither did Ser Piero prevent his honestly conversing with the damsel, fearing the anger of the magnificent family of Baglioni. But Desiderio di Città del Lago, the which was affianced to Monna Maddalena, often had words with Ser Piero on the subject, and one day well-nigh broke the ribs of Messer Troilo's squire, whom he charged with carrying dishonest messages.

Now it so happened that Messer Troilo, as he was the most beautiful, benign, and magnanimous of his magnificent family, was also the most cruel thereof, and incapable of brooking delay or obstacles. And being, as a most beautiful youth—he was only turned nineteen, and the first down had not come to his cheeks, and his skin was astonishingly white and fair like a woman's—of a very amorous nature (of which many tales went, concerning the violence he had done to damsels and citizens' wives of Gubbio and Spello, and evil deeds in the castle of Fratta in the Apennines, some of which it is more beautiful to pass in silence than to relate), being, as I say, of an amorous nature, and greatly magnanimous and ferocious of spirit, Messer Troilo was determined to possess himself of this Maddalena di Ser Piero. So, a week after, having fetched away the wedding chest from Ser Piero's workshop (paying for it duly in Florentine lilies), he seized the opportunity of the festivities of St. John's Nativity, when it is the habit of the citizens to go to their gardens and vineyards to see how the country is prospering, and eat and drink in honest converse with their friends, in order to satisfy his cruel wishes. For it so happened that the said Ser Piero, who was rich and prosperous, possessing an orchard in the valley of the Tiber near San Giovanni, was entertaining his friends there, it being the eve of his daughter's wedding, peaceful and unarmed. And a serving wench, a Moor and a slave, who had been bribed by Messer Troilo, proposed to Monna Maddalena and the damsels of her company, to refresh themselves, after picking flowers, playing with hoops, asking riddles and similar girlish games, by bathing in the Tiber, which flowed at the bottom of the orchard. To this the innocent virgin, full of joyousness, consented. Hardly had the damsels descended into the river bed, the river being low and easy to ford on account of the summer, when behold, there swept from the opposite bank a troop of horsemen, armed and masked, who seized the astonished Maddalena, and hurried off with her, vainly screaming, like another Proserpina, to her companions, who, surprised, and ashamed at being seen with no garments, screamed in return, but in vain. The horsemen galloped off through Bastia, and disappeared long before Ser Piero and his friends could come to the rescue. Thus was Monna Maddalena cruelly taken from her father and bridegroom, through the amorous passion of Messer Troilo.

Ser Piero fell upon the ground fainting for grief, and remained for several days like one dead; and when he came to he wept, and cursed wickedly, and refused to take food and sleep, and to shave his beard. But being old and prudent, and the father of other children, he conquered his grief, well knowing that it was useless to oppose providence or fight, being but a handicraftsman, with the magnificent family of Baglioni, lords of Perugia since many years, and as rich and powerful as they were magnanimous and implacable. So that when people began to say that, after all, Monna Maddalena might have fled willingly with a lover, and that there was no proof that the masked horseman came from Messer Troilo (although those of Basita affirmed that they had seen the green and yellow colours of Fratta, and the said Troilo came not near the town for many months after,) he never contradicted such words out of prudence and fear. But Desiderio of Castiglione del Lago, hearing these words, struck the old man on the mouth till he bled.

And it came to pass, about a year after the disappearance of Monna Maddalena, and when (particularly as there had been a plague in the city, and many miracles had been performed by a holy nun of the convent of Sant' Anna, the which fasted seventy days, and Messer Ascanio Baglioni had raised a company of horses for the Florentine Signiory in their war against those of Siena) people had ceased to talk of the matter, that certain armed men, masked, but wearing the colours of Messer Troilo, and the scorpion on their doublets, rode over from Fratta, bringing with them a coffer, wrapped in black baize, which they deposited overnight on Ser Piero Bontempi's doorstep. And Ser Piero, going at daybreak to his workshop, found that coffer; and recognising it as the same which had been made, with a panel representing the Triumph of Love and many ingenious devices of sculpture and gilding, for Messer Troilo, called Barbacane, he trembled in all his limbs, and went and called Desiderio, and with him privily carried the chest into a secret chamber in his house, saying not a word to any creature. The key, a subtle piece of work of the smith Cavanna, was hanging to the lock by a green silk string, on to which was tied a piece of parchment containing these words: "To Master Desiderio; a wedding gift from Troilo Baglioni of Fratta"—an allusion, doubtless, *ferox atque cruenta facetia*, to the Triumph of Love, according to Messer Francesco Petrarca, painted upon the front of the coffer. The lid being raised, they came to a piece of red cloth, such as is used for mules; *etiam*, a fold of common linen; and below it, a coverlet of green silk, which, being raised, their eyes were met *(heu! infandum patri sceleratumque donus)* by the body of Monna Maddalena, naked as God had made it, dead with two stabs in the neck, the long golden hair tied with pearls but dabbed in blood; the which Maddalena was cruelly squeezed into that coffer, having on her breast the body of an infant recently born, dead like herself.

When he beheld this sight Ser Piero threw himself on the floor and wept, and uttered dreadful blasphemies. But Desiderio of Castiglione del Lago said nothing, but called a brother of Ser Piero, a priest and prior of Saint Severus, and with his assistance carried the coffer into the garden. This garden, within the walls of the city on the side of Porta Eburnea, was pleasantly situated, and abounding in flowers and trees, useful both for their fruit and their shade, and rich likewise in all such herbs as thyme, marjoram, fennel, and many others, that prudent housewives desire for their kitchen; all watered by stone canals, ingeniously constructed by Ser Piero, which were fed from a fountain where you might see a mermaid squeezing the water from her breasts, a subtle device of the same Piero, and executed in a way such as would have done honour to Phidias or Praxiteles, on hard stone from Monte Catria. In this place Desiderio of Castiglione del Lago dug a deep grave under an almond tree, the which grave he carefully lined with stones and slabs of marble which he tore up from the pavement, in order to diminish the damp, and then requested the priest, Ser Piero's brother, who had helped him in the work, to fetch his sacred vestments, and books, and all necessary for consecrating that ground. This the priest immediately did, being a holy man and sore grieved for the case of his niece. Meanwhile, with the help of Ser Piero, Desiderio tenderly lifted the body of Monna Maddalena out of the wedding chest, washed it in odorous waters, and dressed it in fine linen and bridal garments, not without much weeping over the poor damsel's sad plight, and curses upon the cruelty of her ravisher; and having embraced her tenderly, they laid her once more in the box painted with the Triumph of Love, upon folds of fine damask and brocade, her hands folded, and her head decently placed upon a pillow of silver cloth, a wreath of roses, which Desiderio himself plaited, on her hair, so that she looked like a holy saint or the damsel Julia, daughter of the Emperor Augustus Cæsar, who was discovered buried on the Appian Way, and incontinently fell into dust—a marvellous thing. They filled the chest with as many flowers as they could find, also sweet-scented herbs, bay leaves, orris powder, frankincense, ambergris, and a certain gum called in Syrian fizelis, and by the Jews barach, in which they say that the body of King David was kept intact from earthly corruption, and which the priest, the brother of Ser Piero, who was learned in all alchemy and astrology, had bought of certain Moors. Then, with many alases! and tears, they covered the damsel's face with an embroidered veil and a fold of brocade, and closing the chest, buried it in the hole, among great store of hay and straw and sand; and closed it up, and smoothed the earth; and to mark the place Desiderio planted a tuft of fennel under the almond tree. But not before having embraced the damsel many times, and taken a handful of earth from her grave, and eaten it, with many imprecations upon

Messer Troilo, which it were terrible to relate. Then the priest, the brother of Ser Piero, said the service for the dead, Desiderio serving him as acolyte; and they all went their way, grieving sorely. But the body of the child, the which had been found in the wedding chest, they threw down a place near Saint Herculanus, where the refuse and offal and dead animals are thrown, called the *Sardegna;* because it was the bastard of Ser Troilo, *et infamiæ scelerisque partum.*

Then, as this matter got abroad, and also Desiderio's imprecations against Ser Troilo, Ser Piero, who was an old man and prudent, caused him to depart privily from Perugia, for fear of the wrath of the magnificent Orazio Baglioni, uncle of Messer Troilo and lord of the town.

Desiderio of Castiglione del Lago went to Rome, where he did wonderful things and beautiful, among others certain frescoes in Saints Cosmas and Damian, for the Cardinal of Ostia; and to Naples, where he entered the service of the Duke of Calabria, and followed his armies long, building fortresses and making machines and models for cannon, and other ingenious and useful things. And thus for seven years, until he heard that Ser Piero was dead at Perugia of a surfeit of eels; and that Messer Troilo was in the city, raising a company of horses with his cousin Astorre Baglioni for the Duke of Urbino; and this was before the plague, and the terrible coming to Umbria of the Spaniards and renegade Moors, under Cæsar Borgia, *Vicarius Sanctæ Ecclesiæ, seu Flagellum Dei et novus Attila.* So Desiderio came back privily to Perugia, and put up his mule at a small inn, having dyed his hair black and grown his beard, after the manner of Easterns, saying he was a Greek coming from Ancona. And he went to the priest, prior of Saint Severus, and brother of Ser Piero, and discovered himself to him, who, although old, had great joy in seeing him and hearing of his intent. And Desiderio confessed all his sins to the priest and obtained absolution, and received the Body of Christ with great fervour and compunction; and the priest placed his sword on the altar, beside the gospel, as he said mass, and blessed it. And Desiderio knelt and made a vow never to touch food save the Body of Christ till he could taste the blood of Messer Troilo.

And for three days and three nights he watched him and dogged him, but Messer Troilo rarely went unaccompanied by his men, because he had offended so many honourable citizens by his amorous fury, and he knew that his kinsmen dreaded him and would gladly be rid of him, on account of his ferocity and ambition, and their desire to unite the Fief of Fratta to the other lands of the main line of the magnificent House of Baglioni, famous in arms.

But one day, towards dusk, Desiderio saw Messer Troilo coming down a steep lane near Saint Herculanus, alone, for he was going to a woman of light fame, called Flavia Bella, the which was very lovely. So Desiderio threw some ladders, from a neighbouring house which was being built, and sacks across the road, and hid under an arch that spanned the lane, which was greatly steep and narrow. And Messer Troilo came down, on foot, whistling and paring his nails with a small pair of scissors. And he was dressed in grey silk hose, and a doublet of red cloth and gold brocade, pleated about the skirts, and embroidered with seed pearl and laced with gold laces; and on his head he had a hat of scarlet cloth with many feathers; and his cloak and sword he carried under his left arm. And Messer Troilo was twenty-six years old, but seemed much younger, having no beard, and a face like Hyacinthus or Ganymede, whom Jove stole to be his cup-bearer on account of his beauty. And he was tall and very ferocious and magnanimous of spirit. And as he went, going to Flavia the courtesan, he whistled.

And when he came near the heaped-up ladders and the sacks, Desiderio sprang upon him and tried to run his sword through him. But although wounded, Messer Troilo grappled with him long, but he could not get at his sword, which was entangled in his cloak; and before he could free his hand and get at his dagger, Desiderio had him down, and ran his sword three times through his chest, exclaiming, "This is from Maddalena, in return for her wedding chest!"

And Messer Troilo, seeing the blood flowing out of his chest, knew he must die, and merely said—

"Which Maddalena? Ah, I remember, old Piero's daughter. She was always a cursed difficult slut," and died.

And Desiderio stooped over his chest, and lapped up the blood as it flowed; and it was the first food he tasted since taking the Body of Christ, even as he had sworn.

Then Desiderio went stealthily to the fountain under the arch of Saint Proxedis, where the women wash linen in the daytime, and cleansed himself a little from that blood. Then he fetched his mule and hid it in some trees near Messer Piero's garden. And at night he opened the door, the priest having given him the key, and went in, and with a spade and mattock he had brought dug up the wedding chest with the body of Monna Maddalena in it; the which, owing to those herbs and virtuous gums, had dried up and become much lighter. And he found the spot by looking for the fennel tuft under the almond tree, which was then in flower, it being spring. He loaded the chest, which was mouldy and decayed, on the mule, and drove the mule before him till he got to Castiglione del Lago, where he hid. And meeting certain horsemen, who asked him what he carried in that box (for they took him for a thief), he answered his sweetheart; so they laughed and let him pass. Thus he got safely on to the territory of Arezzo, an ancient city of Tuscany, where he stopped.

Now when they found the body of Messer Troilo, there was much astonishment and wonder. And his kinsmen were greatly wroth; but Messer Orazio and Messer Ridolfo, his uncles, said: " 'Tis as well; for indeed his courage and ferocity were too great, and he would have done some evil to us all had he lived." But they ordered him a magnificent burial. And when he lay on the street dead, many folk, particularly painters, came to look at him for his great beauty; and the women pitied him on account of his youth, and certain scholars compared him to Mars, God of War, so great was his strength and ferocity even in death. And he was carried to the grave by eight men-at-arms, and twelve damsels and youths dressed in white walked behind, strewing flowers, and there was much splendour and lamentation, on account of the great power of the magnificent House of Baglioni.

As regards Desiderio of Castiglioni del Lago, he remained at Arezzo till his death, preserving with him always the body of Monna Maddalena in the wedding chest painted with the Triumph of Love, because he considered she had died *odore magnæ sanctitatis*.

THE HALL BEDROOM

Mary E. Wilkins Freeman

My name is Mrs. Elizabeth Jennings. I am a highly respectable woman. I may style myself a gentlewoman, for in my youth I enjoyed advantages. I was well brought up, and I graduated at a young ladies' seminary. I also married well. My husband was that most genteel of all merchants, an apothecary. His shop was on the corner of the main street in Rockton, the town where I was born, and where I lived until the death of my husband. My parents had died when I had been married a short time, so I was left quite alone in the world. I was not competent to carry on the apothecary business by myself, for I had no knowledge of drugs, and had a mortal terror of giving poisons instead of medicines. Therefore I was obliged to sell at a considerable sacrifice, and the proceeds, some five thousand dollars, were all I had in the world. The income was not enough to support me in any kind of comfort, and I saw that I must in some way earn money. I thought at first of teaching, but I was no longer young, and methods had changed since my school days. What I was able to teach, nobody wished to know. I could think of only one thing to do: take boarders. But the same objection to that business as to teaching held good in Rockton. Nobody wished to board. My husband had rented a house with a number of bedrooms, and I advertised, but nobody applied. Finally my cash was running very low, and I became desperate. I packed my furniture, rented a large house in this town, and moved there. It was a venture attended with many risks. In the first place the rent was exorbitant; in the next I was entirely unknown. However, I am a person of considerable ingenuity, and have inventive power, and much enterprise when the occasion presses. I advertised in a very original manner, although that actually took my last penny, that is, the last penny of my ready money, and I was forced to draw on my principal to purchase my first supplies, a thing which I had resolved never on any account to do. But the great risk met with a reward, for I had several applicants within two days after my advertisement appeared in the paper. Within two weeks my boarding-house was well established, I became very successful, and my success would have been uninterrupted had it not been for the mysterious and bewildering occurrences which I am about to relate. I am now forced to leave the house and rent another. Some of my old boarders accompany me, some, with the most unreasonable nervousness, refuse to be longer associated in any way, however indirectly, with the terrible and uncanny happenings which I have to relate. It remains to be seen whether my ill luck in this house will follow me into another, and whether my whole prosperity in life will be forever shadowed by the Mystery of the Hall Bedroom. Instead of telling the strange story myself in my own words, I shall present the Journal of Mr. George H. Wheatcroft. I shall show you the portions beginning on January 18 of the present year, the date when he took up his residence with me. Here it is:

"*January 18, 1883*. Here I am established in my new boarding-house. I have, as befits my humble means, the hall bedroom, even the hall bedroom on the third floor. I have heard all my life of hall bedrooms, I have seen hall bedrooms, I have been in them, but never until now, when I am actually established in one, did I comprehend what, at once, an ignominious and sternly uncompromising thing a hall bedroom is. It proves the ignominy of the dweller therein. No man at thirty-six (my age) would be domiciled in a hall bedroom unless he were himself ignominious, at least comparatively speaking. I am proved by this means incontrovertibly to have been left far behind in the race. I see no reason why I should not live in this hall bedroom for the rest of my life, that is, if I have enough money to pay the landlady, and that seems probable, since my small funds are invested as safely as if I were an orphan-ward in charge of a pillar of a sanctuary. After the valuables have been stolen, I have most carefully locked the stable door. I have experienced the revulsion which comes sooner or later to the adventurous soul who experiences nothing but defeat and so-called ill luck. I have swung to the opposite extreme. I have lost in everything—I have lost in love, I have lost in money, I have lost in the struggle for preferment, I have lost in health and strength. I am now settled down in a hall bedroom to live upon my small income, and regain my health by mild potations of the mineral waters here, if possible; if not, to live here without my health—for mine is not a necessarily fatal malady—until Providence shall take me out of my hall bedroom. There is no one place more than another where I care to live. There is not sufficient motive to take me away, even if the mineral waters do not benefit me. So I am here and to stay in the hall bedroom. The landlady is civil, and even kind, as kind as a woman who has to keep her poor womanly eye upon the main chance can be. The struggle for money always injures the fine grain of a woman; she is too fine a thing to do it; she does not by nature belong with the gold grubbers, and it therefore lowers her; she steps from heights to claw and scrape and dig. But she cannot help it oftentimes, poor thing, and her deterioration thereby is to be condoned. The landlady is all she can be, taking her strain of adverse circumstances into consideration, and the table is good, even conscientiously so. It looks to me as if she were foolish enough to strive to give the boarders their money's worth, with the due regard for the main chance which is inevitable. However, that is of minor importance to me, since my diet is restricted.

"It is curious what an annoyance a restriction in diet can be even to a man who has considered himself somewhat indifferent to gastronomic delights. There was to-day a pudding for dinner, which I could not taste without penalty, but which I longed for. It was only because it looked unlike any other pudding that I had ever seen, and assumed a mental and spiritual significance. It seemed to me, whimsically no doubt, as if tasting it might give me a new sensation, and consequently a new outlook. Trivial things may lead to large results: why should I not get a new outlook by means of a pudding? Life here stretches before me most monotonously, and I feel like clutching at alleviations, though paradoxically, since I have settled down with the utmost acquiescence. Still, one cannot immediately overcome and change radically all one's nature. Now I look at myself critically and search for the keynote to my whole self, and my actions, I have always been conscious of a reaching out, an overweening desire for the new, the untried, for the broadness of further horizons, the seas beyond seas, the thought beyond thought. This characteristic has been the primary cause of all my misfortunes. I have the soul of an explorer, and in nine out of ten cases this leads to destruction. If I had possessed capital and sufficient push, I should have been one of the searchers after the North Pole. I have been an eager student of astronomy. I have studied botany with avidity, and have dreamed of new flora in unexplored parts of the world, and the same with animal life and geology. I longed for riches in order to discover the power and sense of possession of the rich. I longed for love in order to discover the possibilities of the emotions. I longed for all that the mind of man could conceive as desirable for man, not so much for purely selfish ends, as from an insatiable thirst for knowledge of a universal trend. But I have limitations, I do not quite understand of what nature—for what mortal ever did quite understand his own limitations, since a knowledge of them would preclude their existence?—but they have prevented my progress to any extent. Therefore behold me in my hall bedroom, settled at last into a groove of fate so deep that I have lost the sight of even my horizons. Just at present, as I write here, my horizon on the left, that is my physical horizon, is a wall covered with cheap paper. The paper is an indeterminate pattern in white and gilt. There are a few photographs of my own hung about, and on the large wall space beside the bed there is a large oil painting which belongs to my landlady. It has a massive tarnished gold frame, and, curiously enough, the painting itself is rather good. I have no idea who the artist could have been. It is of the conventional landscape type in vogue some fifty years since, the type so fondly reproduced in chromos—the winding river with the little boat occupied by a pair of lovers, the cottage nestled among trees on the right shore, the gentle slope of the hills and the church spire in the background—but still it is well done. It gives me the impression of an artist without the slightest originality of design, but much of technique. But for some inexplicable reason the picture frets me. I find myself gazing at it when I do not wish to do so. It seems to compel my attention like some intent face in the room. I shall ask Mrs. Jennings to have it removed. I will hang in its place some photographs which I have in a trunk.

"*January 26.* I do not write regularly in my journal. I never did. I see no reason why I should. I see no reason why anyone should have the slightest sense of duty in such a matter. Some days I have nothing which interests me sufficiently to write out, some days I feel either too ill or too indolent. For four days I have not written, from a mixture of all three reasons. Now, to-day I both feel like it and I have something to write. Also I am distinctly better than I have been. Perhaps the waters are benefiting me, or the change of air. Or possibly it is something else more subtle. Possibly my mind has seized upon something new, a discovery which causes it to react upon my failing body and serves as a stimulant. All I know is, I feel distinctly better, and am conscious of an acute interest in doing so, which is of late strange to me. I have been rather indifferent, and sometimes have wondered if that were not the cause rather than the result of my state of health. I have been so continually balked that I have settled into a state of inertia. I lean rather comfortably against my obstacles. After all, the worst of the pain always lies in the struggle. Give up and it is rather pleasant than otherwise. If one did not kick, the pricks would not in the least matter. However, for some reason, for the last few days, I seem to have awakened from my state of quiescence. It means future trouble for me, no doubt, but in the meantime I am not sorry. It began with the picture—the large oil painting. I went to Mrs. Jennings about it yesterday, and she, to my surprise—for I thought it a matter that could be easily arranged—objected to having it removed. Her reasons were two; both simple, both sufficient, especially since I, after all, had no very strong desire either way. It seems that the picture does not belong to her. It hung here when she rented the house. She says, if it is removed, a very large and unsightly discoloration of the wall paper will be exposed, and she does not like to ask for new paper. The owner, an old man, is travelling abroad, the agent is curt, and she has only been in the house a very short time. Then it would mean a sad upheaval of my room, which would disturb me. She also says that there is no place in the house where she can store the picture, and there is not a vacant space in another room for one so large. So I let the picture remain. It really, when I came to think of it, was very immaterial after all. But I got my photographs out of my trunk, and I hung them around the large picture. The wall is almost completely covered. I hung them yesterday afternoon, and last night I repeated a strange experience which I have had in some degree every night since I have been here, but was not sure whether it deserved the name of experience, but was not rather one of those dreams in which one dreams one is awake. But last night it came again, and now I know. There is something very singular about this room. I am very much interested. I will write down for future reference the events of last night. Concerning those of the preceding nights since I have slept in this room, I will simply say that they have been of a similar nature, but, as it were, only the preliminary stages, the prologue to what happened last night.

"I am not depending upon the mineral waters here as the one remedy for my malady, which is sometimes of an acute nature, and indeed constantly threatens me with considerable suffering unless by medicine I can keep it in check. I will say that the medicine which I employ is not of the class commonly known as drugs. It is impossible that it can be held responsible for what I am about to transcribe. My mind last night and every night since I have slept in this room was in an absolutely normal state. I take this medicine, prescribed by the specialist in whose charge I was before coming here, regularly every four hours while awake. As I am never a good sleeper, it follows that I am enabled with no inconvenience to take any medicine during the night with the same regularity as during the day. It is my habit, therefore, to place my bottle and spoon where I can put my hand upon them easily without lighting the gas. Since I have been in this room, I have placed the bottle of medicine upon my dresser at the side of the room opposite the bed. I have done this rather than place it nearer, as once I jostled the bottle and spilled most of the contents, and it is not easy for me to replace it, as it is expensive. Therefore I placed it in security on the dresser, and, indeed, that is but three or four steps from my bed, the room being so small. Last night I wakened as usual, and I knew, since I had fallen asleep about eleven, that it must be in the neighbourhood of three. I wake with almost clock-like regularity, and it is never necessary for me to consult my watch.

"I had slept unusually well and without dreams, and I awoke fully at once, with a feeling of refreshment to which I am not accustomed. I immediately got out of bed and began stepping across the room in the direction of my dresser, on which I had set my medicine bottle and spoon.

"To my utter amazement, the steps which had hitherto sufficed to take me across my room did not suffice to do so. I advanced several paces, and my outstretched hands touched nothing. I stopped and went on again. I was sure that I was moving in a straight direction, and even if I had not been I knew it was impossible to advance in any direction in my tiny apartment without coming into collision either with a wall or a piece of furniture. I continued to walk falteringly, as I have seen people on the stage: a step, then a long falter, then a sliding step. I kept my hands extended; they touched nothing. I stopped again. I had not the least sentiment of fear or consternation. It was rather the very stupefaction of surprise. 'How is this?' seemed thundering in my ears. 'What is this?'

"The room was perfectly dark. There was nowhere any glimmer, as is usually the case, even in a so-called dark room, from the walls, picture-frames, looking-glass or white objects. It was absolute gloom. The house stood in a quiet part of the town. There were many trees about; the electric street lights were extinguished at midnight; there was no moon and the sky was cloudy. I could not distinguish my one window, which I thought strange, even on such a dark night. Finally I changed my plan of motion and turned, as nearly as I could estimate, at right angles. Now, I thought, I must reach soon, if I kept on, my writing-table underneath the window; or, if I am going in the opposite direction, the hall door. I reached neither. I am telling the unvarnished truth when I say that I began to count my steps and carefully measure my paces after that, and I traversed a space clear of furniture at least twenty feet by thirty—a very large apartment. And as I walked I was conscious that my naked feet were pressing something which gave rise to sensations the like of which I had never experienced before. As nearly as I can express it, it was as if my feet pressed something as elastic as air or water, which was in this case unyielding to my weight. It gave me a curious sensation of buoyancy and stimulation. At the same time this surface, if surface be the right name, which I trod, felt cool to my feet with the coolness of vapour or fluidity, seeming to overlap the soles. Finally I stood still; my surprise was at last merging into a measure of consternation. 'Where am I?' I thought. 'What am I going to do?' Stories that I had heard of travellers being taken from their beds and conveyed into strange and dangerous places, Middle Age stories of the Inquisition flashed through my brain. I knew all the time that for a man who has gone to bed in a commonplace hall bedroom in a very commonplace little town such surmises were highly ridiculous, but it is hard for the human mind to grasp anything but a human explanation of phenomena. Almost anything seemed then, and seems now, more rational than an explanation bordering upon the supernatural, as we understand the supernatural. At last I called, though rather softly, 'What does this mean?' I said quite aloud, 'Where am I? Who is here? Who is doing this? I tell you I will have no such nonsense. Speak, if there is anybody here.' But all was dead silence. Then suddenly a light flashed through the open transom of my door. Somebody had heard me—a man who rooms next door, a decent kind of man, also here for his health. He turned on the gas in the hall and called to me. 'What's the matter?' he asked, in an agitated, trembling voice. He is a nervous fellow.

"Directly, when the light flashed through my transom, I saw that I was in my familiar hall bedroom. I could see everything quite distinctly—my tumbled bed, my writing-table, my dresser, my chair, my little washstand, my clothes hanging on a row of pegs, the old picture on the wall. The picture gleamed out with singular distinctness in the light from the transom. The river seemed actually to run and ripple, and the boat to be gliding with the current. I gazed fascinated at it, as I replied to the anxious voice:

"'Nothing is the matter with me,' said I. 'Why?'

"'I thought I heard you speak,' said the man outside, 'I thought maybe you were sick.'

"'No,' I called back. 'I am all right. I am trying to find my medicine in the dark, that's all. I can see now you have lighted the gas.'

"'Nothing is the matter?'

"'No; sorry I disturbed you. Good-night.'

"'Good-night.' Then I heard the man's door shut after a minute's pause. He was evidently not quite satisfied. I took a pull at my medicine bottle, and got into bed. He had left the hall gas burning. I did not go to sleep again for some time. Just before I did so, someone, probably Mrs. Jennings, came out in the hall and extinguished the gas. This morning when I awoke everything was as usual in my room. I wonder if I shall have any such experience to-night.

"*January 27.* I shall write in my journal every day until this draws to some definite issue. Last night my strange experience deepened, as something tells me it will continue to do. I retired quite early, at half-past ten. I took the precaution, on retiring, to place beside my bed, on a chair, a box of safety matches, that I might not be in the dilemma of the night before. I took my medicine on retiring; that made me due to wake at half-past two. I had not fallen asleep directly, but had had certainly three hours of sound dreamless slumber when I awoke. I lay a few minutes hesitating whether or not to strike a safety match and light my way to the dresser, whereon stood my medicine bottle. I hesitated, not because I had the least sensation of fear, but because of the same shrinking from a nerve shock that leads one at times to dread the plunge into an icy bath. It seemed much easier to me to strike that match and cross my hall bedroom to my dresser, take my dose, then return quietly to my bed, than to risk the chance of floundering about in some unknown limbo either of fancy or reality.

"At last, however, the spirit of adventure, which has always been such a ruling one for me, conquered. I rose. I took the box of safety matches in my hand, and started on, as I conceived, the straight course for my dresser, about five feet across from my bed. As before, I travelled and travelled and did not reach it. I advanced with groping hands extended, setting one foot cautiously before the other, but I touched nothing except the indefinite, unnameable surface which my feet pressed. All of a sudden, though, I became aware of something. One of my senses was saluted, nay, more than that, hailed, with imperiousness, and that was, strangely enough, my sense of smell, but in a hitherto unknown fashion. It seemed as if the odour reached my mentality first. I reversed the usual process, which is, as I understand it, like this: the odour when encountered strikes first the olfactory nerve, which transmits the intelligence to the brain. It is as if, to put it rudely, my nose met a rose, and then the nerve belonging to the sense said to my brain, 'Here is a rose.' This time my brain said, 'Here is a rose,' and my sense then recognized it. I say rose, but it was not a rose, that is, not the fragrance of any rose which I had ever known. It was undoubtedly a flower odour, and rose came perhaps the nearest to it. My mind realized it first with what seemed a leap of rapture. 'What is this delight?' I asked myself. And then the ravishing fragrance smote my sense. I breathed it in and it seemed to feed my thoughts, satisfying some hitherto unknown hunger. Then I took a step further and another fragrance appeared, which I liken to lilies for lack of something better, and then came violets, then mignonette. I cannot describe the experience, but it was a sheer delight, a rapture of sublimated sense. I groped further and further, and always into new waves of fragrance. I seemed to be wading breast-high through flower beds of Paradise, but all the time I touched nothing with my groping hands. At last a sudden giddiness as of surfeit overcame me. I realized that I might be in some unknown peril. I was distinctly afraid. I struck one of my safety matches, and I was in my hall bedroom, midway between my bed and my dresser. I took my dose of medicine and went to bed, and after a while fell asleep and did not wake till morning.

"*January 28*. Last night I did not take my usual dose of medicine. In these days of new remedies and mysterious results upon certain organizations, it occurred to me to wonder if possibly the drug might have, after all, something to do with my strange experience.

"I did not take my medicine. I put the bottle as usual on my dresser, since I feared if I interrupted further the customary sequence of affairs I might fail to wake. I placed my box of matches on the chair beside the bed. I fell asleep about quarter past eleven o'clock, and I waked when the clock was striking two—a little earlier than my wont. I did not hesitate this time. I rose at once, took my box of matches and proceeded as formerly. I walked what seemed a great space without coming into collision with anything. I kept sniffing for the wonderful fragrances of the night before, but they did not recur. Instead, I was suddenly aware that I was tasting something, some morsel of sweetness hitherto unknown, and, as in the case of the odour, the usual order seemed reversed, and it was as if I tasted it first in my mental consciousness. Then the sweetness rolled under my tongue. I thought involuntarily of 'Sweeter than honey or the honeycomb' of the Scripture. I thought of the Old Testament manna. An ineffable content as of satisfied hunger seized me. I stepped further, and a new savour was upon my palate. And so on. It was never cloying, though of such sharp sweetness that it fairly stung. It was the merging of a material sense into a spiritual one. I said to myself, 'I have lived my life and always have I gone hungry until now.' I could feel my brain act swiftly under the influence of this heavenly food as under a stimulant. Then suddenly I repeated the experience of the night before. I grew dizzy, and an indefinite fear and shrinking were upon me. I struck my safety match and was back in my hall bedroom. I returned to bed, and soon fell asleep. I did not take my medicine. I am resolved not to do so longer. I am feeling much better.

"*January 29*. Last night to bed as usual, matches in place; fell asleep about eleven and waked at half-past one. I heard the half-hour strike; I am waking earlier and earlier every night. I had not taken my medicine, though it was on the dresser as usual. I again took my match-box in hand and started to cross the room, and, as always, traversed strange spaces, but this night, as seems fated to be the case every night, my experience was different. Last night I neither smelled nor tasted, but I heard—my Lord, I heard! The first sound of which I was conscious was one like the constantly gathering and receding murmur of a river, and it seemed to come from the wall behind my bed where the old picture hangs. Nothing in nature except a river gives that impression of at once advance and retreat. I could not mistake it. On, ever on, came the swelling murmur of the waves; past and ever past they died in the distance. Then I heard above the murmur of the river a song in an unknown tongue which I recognized as being unknown, yet which I understood; but the understanding was in my brain, with no words of interpretation. The song had to do with me, but with me in unknown futures for which I had no images of comparison in the past; yet a sort of ecstasy as of a prophecy of bliss filled my whole consciousness. The song never ceased, but as I moved on I came into new sound-waves. There was the pealing of bells which might have been made of crystal, and might have summoned to the gates of heaven. There was music of strange instruments, great harmonies pierced now and then by small whispers as of love, and it all filled me with a certainty of a future of bliss.

"At last I seemed the centre of a mighty orchestra which constantly deepened and increased until I seemed to feel myself being lifted gently but mightily upon the waves of sound as upon the waves of a sea. Then again the terror and the impulse to flee to my own familiar scenes were upon me. I struck my match and was back in my hall bedroom. I do not see how I sleep at all after such wonders, but sleep I do. I slept dreamlessly until daylight this morning.

"*January 30.* I heard yesterday something with regard to my hall bedroom which affected me strangely. I cannot for the life of me say whether it intimidated me, filled me with the horror of the abnormal, or rather roused to a greater degree my spirit of adventure and discovery. I was down at the Cure, and was sitting on the veranda sipping idly my mineral water, when somebody spoke my name. 'Mr. Wheatcroft?' said the voice politely, interrogatively, somewhat apologetically, as if to provide for a possible mistake in my identity. I turned and saw a gentleman whom I recognized at once. I seldom forget names or faces. He was a Mr. Addison whom I had seen considerable of three years ago at a little summer hotel in the mountains. It was one of those passing acquaintances which signify little one way or the other. If never renewed, you have no regret; if renewed, you accept the renewal with no hesitation. It is in every way negative. But just now, in my feeble, friendless state, the sight of a face which beams with pleased remembrance is rather grateful. I felt distinctly glad to see the man. He sat down beside me. He also had a glass of the water. His health, while not as bad as mine, leaves much to be desired.

"Addison had often been in this town before. He had in fact lived here at one time. He had remained at the Cure three years taking the waters daily. He therefore knows about all there is to be known about the town, which is not very large. He asked me where I was staying, and when I told him the street, rather excitedly inquired the number. When I told him the number, which is 240, he gave a manifest start, and after one sharp glance at me sipped his water in silence for a moment. He had so evidently betrayed some ulterior knowledge with regard to my residence that I questioned him.

"'What do you know about 240 Pleasant Street?' said I.

"'Oh, nothing,' he replied, evasively, sipping his water.

"After a little while, however, he inquired, in what he evidently tried to render a casual tone, what room I occupied. 'I once lived a few weeks at 240 Pleasant Street myself,' he said. That house always was a boarding-house, I guess.'

"'It had stood vacant for a term of years before the present occupant rented it, I believe,' I remarked. Then I answered his question. 'I have the hall bedroom on the third floor,' said I. 'The quarters are pretty straitened, but comfortable enough as hall bedrooms go.'

"But Mr. Addison had showed such unmistakable consternation at my reply that then I persisted in my questioning as to the cause, and at last he yielded and told me what he knew. He had hesitated both because he shrank from displaying what I might consider an unmanly superstition, and because he did not wish to influence me beyond what the facts of the case warranted. 'Well, I will tell you, Wheatcroft,' he said. 'Briefly all I know is this: When last I heard of 240 Pleasant Street it was not rented because of foul play which was supposed to have taken place there, though nothing was ever proved. There were two disappearances, and—in each case—of an occupant of the hall bedroom which you now have. The first disappearance was of a very beautiful girl who had come here for her health and was said to be the victim of a profound melancholy, induced by a love disappointment. She obtained board at 240 and occupied the hall bedroom about two weeks; then one morning she was gone, having seemingly vanished into thin air. Her relatives were communicated with; she had not many, nor friends either, poor girl, and a thorough search was made, but the last I knew she had never come to light. There were two or three arrests, but nothing ever came of them. Well, that was before my day here, but the second disappearance took place when I was in the house—a fine young fellow who had overworked in college. He had to pay his own way. He had taken cold, had the grip, and that and the overwork about finished him, and he came on here for a month's rest and recuperation. He had been in that room about two weeks, a little less, when one morning he wasn't there. Then there was a great hullabaloo. It seems that he had let fall some hints to the effect that there was something queer about the room, but, of course, the police did not think much of that. They made arrests right and left, but they never found him, and the arrested were discharged, though some of them are probably under a cloud of suspicion to this day. Then the boarding-house was shut up. Six years ago nobody would have boarded there, much less occupied that hall bedroom, but now I suppose new people have come in, and the story has died out. I dare say your landlady will not thank me for reviving it.'

"I assured him that it would make no possible difference to me. He looked at me sharply, and asked bluntly if I had seen anything wrong or unusual about the room. I replied, guarding myself from falsehood with a quibble, that I had seen nothing in the least unusual about the room, as indeed I had not, and have not now, but that may come. I feel that that will come in due time. Last night I neither saw, nor heard, nor smelled, nor tasted, but I—felt. Last night, having started again on my exploration of, God knows what, I had not advanced a step before I touched something. My first sensation was one of disappointment. 'It is the dresser, and I am at the end of it now,' I thought. But I soon discovered that it was not the old painted dresser which I touched, but something carved, as nearly as I could discover with my unskilled fingertips, with winged things. There were certainly long keen curves of wings which seemed to overlay an arabesque of fine leaf and flower work. I do not know what the object was that I touched. It may have been a chest. I may seem to be exaggerating when I say that it somehow failed or exceeded in some mysterious respect of being the shape of anything I had ever touched. I do not know what the material was. It was as smooth as ivory, but it did not feel like ivory; there was a singular warmth about it, as if it had stood long in hot sunlight. I continued, and I encountered other objects I am inclined to think were pieces of furniture of fashions and possibly of uses unknown to me, and about them all was the strange mystery as to shape. At last I came to what was evidently an open window of large area. I distinctly felt a soft, warm wind, yet with a crystal freshness, blow on my face. It was not the window of my hall bedroom, that I know. Looking out, I could see nothing. I only felt the wind blowing on my face.

"Then suddenly, without any warning, my groping hands to the right and left touched living beings, beings in the likeness of men and women, palpable creatures in palpable attire. I could feel the soft silken texture of their garments which swept around me, seeming to half enfold me in clinging meshes like cobwebs. I was in a crowd of these people, whatever they were, and whoever they were, but, curiously enough, without seeing one of them I had a strong sense of recognition as I passed among them. Now and then a hand that I knew closed softly over mine; once an arm passed around me. Then I began to feel myself gently swept on and impelled by this softly moving throng; their floating garments seemed to fairly wind me about, and again a swift terror overcame me. I struck my match, and was back in my hall bedroom. I wonder if I had not better keep my gas burning to-night? I wonder if it be possible that this is going too far? I wonder what became of those other people, the man and the woman who occupied this room? I wonder if I had better not stop where I am?

"*January 31*. Last night I saw—I saw more than I can describe, more than is lawful to describe. Something which nature has rightly hidden has been revealed to me, but it is not for me to disclose too much of her secret. This much I will say, that doors and windows open into an out-of-doors to which the outdoors which we know is but a vestibule. And there is a river; there is something strange with respect to that picture. There is a river upon which one could sail away. It was flowing silently, for to-night I could only see. I saw that

I was right in thinking I recognized some of the people whom I encountered the night before, though some were strange to me. It is true that the girl who disappeared from the hall bedroom was very beautiful. Everything which I saw last night was very beautiful to my one sense that could grasp it. I wonder what it would all be if all my senses together were to grasp it? I wonder if I had better not keep my gas burning tonight? I wonder—"

This finishes the journal which Mr. Wheatcroft left in his hall bedroom. The morning after the last entry he was gone. His friend, Mr. Addison, came here, and a search was made. They even tore down the wall behind the picture, and they did find something rather queer for a house that had been used for boarders, where you would think no room would have been let run to waste. They found another room, a long narrow one, the length of the hall bedroom, but narrower, hardly more than a closet. There was no window, nor door, and all there was in it was a sheet of paper covered with figures, as if somebody had been doing sums. They made a lot of talk about those figures, and they tried to make out that the fifth dimension, whatever that is, was proved, but they said afterward they didn't prove anything. They tried to make out then that somebody had murdered poor Mr. Wheatcroft and hid the body, and they arrested poor Mr. Addison, but they couldn't make out anything against him. They proved he was in the Cure all that night and couldn't have done it. They don't know what became of Mr. Wheatcroft, and now they say two more disappeared from that same room before I rented the house.

The agent came and promised to put the new room they discovered into the hall bedroom and have everything new—papered and painted. He took away the picture; folks hinted there was something queer about that, I don't know what. It looked innocent enough, and I guess he burned it up. He said if I would stay he would arrange it with the owner, who everybody says is a very queer man, so I should not have to pay much if any rent. But I told him I couldn't stay if he was to give me the rent. That I wasn't afraid of anything myself, though I must say I wouldn't want to put anybody in that hall bedroom without telling him all about it; but my boarders would leave, and I knew I couldn't get any more. I told him I would rather have had a regular ghost than what seemed to be a way of going out of the house to nowhere and never coming back again. I moved, and, as I said before, it remains to be seen whether my ill luck follows me to this house or not. Anyway, it has no hall bedroom.

THE EYES

Edith Wharton

I

We had been put in the mood for ghosts, that evening, after an excellent dinner at our old friend Culwin's, by a tale of Fred Murchard's— the narrative of a strange personal visitation.

Seen through the haze of our cigars, and by the drowsy gleam of a coal fire, Culwin's library, with its oak walls and dark old bindings, made a good setting for such evocations; and ghostly experiences at first hand being, after Murchard's brilliant opening, the only kind acceptable to us, we proceeded to take stock of our group and tax each member for a contribution. There were eight of us, and seven contrived, in a manner more or less adequate, to fulfil the condition imposed. It surprised us all to find that we could muster such a show of supernatural impressions, for none of us, excepting Murchard himself and young Phil Frenham—whose story was the slightest of the lot had the habit of sending our souls into the invisible. So that, on the whole, we had every reason to be proud of our seven 'exhibits,' and none of us would have dreamed of expecting an eighth from our host.

Our old friend, Mr Andrew Culwin, who had sat back in his armchair, listening and blinking through the smoke circles with the cheerful tolerance of a wise old idol, was not the kind of man likely to be favoured with such contacts, though he had imagination enough to enjoy, without envying, the superior privileges of his guests. By age and by education he belonged to the stout Positivist tradition, and his habit of thought had been formed in the days of the epic struggle between physics and metaphysics. But he had been, then and always, essentially a spectator, a humorous detached observer of the immense muddled variety show of life, slipping out of his seat now and then for a brief dip into the convivialities at the back of the house, but never, as far as one knew, showing the least desire to jump on the stage and do a 'turn.'

Among, his contemporaries there lingered a vague tradition of his having, at a remote period, and in a romantic clime, been wounded in a duel; but this legend no more tallied with what we younger men knew of his character than my mother's assertion that he had once been 'a charming little man with nice eyes' corresponded to any possible reconstitution of his dry thwarted physiognomy.

'He never can have looked like anything but a bundle of sticks,' Murchard had once said of him. 'Or a phosphorescent log, rather,' some one else amended; and we recognised the happiness of this description of his small squat trunk, with the red blink of the eyes in a face like mottled bark. He had always been possessed of a leisure which he had nursed and protected, instead of squandering it in vain activities. His carefully guarded hours had been devoted to the cultivation of a fine intelligence and a few judiciously chosen habits; and none of the disturbances common to human experience seemed to have crossed his sky. Nevertheless, his dispassionate survey of the universe had not raised his opinion of that costly experiment, and his study of the human race seemed to have resulted in the conclusion that all men were superfluous, and women necessary only because some one had to do the cooking. On the importance of this point his convictions were absolute, and gastronomy was the only science which he revered as dogma. It must be owned that his little dinners were a strong argument in favour of this view, besides being a reason—though not the main one—for the fidelity of his friends.

Mentally he exercised a hospitality less seductive but no less stimulating. His mind was like a forum, or some open meeting-place for the exchange of ideas: somewhat cold and draughty, but light, spacious and orderly—a kind of academic grove from which all the leaves had fallen. In this privileged area a dozen of us were wont to stretch our muscles and expand our lungs; and, as if to prolong as much as possible the tradition of what we felt to be a vanishing institution, one or two neophytes were now and then added to our band.

Young Phil Frenham was the last, and the most interesting, of these recruits, and a good example of Murchard's somewhat morbid assertion that our old friend 'liked 'em juicy.' It was indeed a fact that Culwin, for all his mental dryness, specially tasted the lyric qualities in youth. As he was far too good an Epicurean to nip the flowers of soul which he gathered for his garden, his friendship was not a disintegrating influence: on the contrary, it forced the young idea to robuster bloom. And in Phil Frenham he had a fine subject for experimentation. The boy was really intelligent, and the soundness of his nature was like the pure paste under a delicate glaze. Culwin had fished him out of a thick fog of family dullness, and pulled him up to a peak in Darien; and the adventure hadn't hurt him a bit. Indeed, the skill with which Culwin had contrived to stimulate his curiosities without robbing them of their young bloom of awe seemed to me a sufficient answer to Murchard's ogreish metaphor. There was nothing hectic in Frenham's efflorescence, and his old friend had not laid even a finger-tip on the sacred stupidities. One wanted no better proof of that than the fact that Frenham still reverenced them in Culwin.

'There's a side of him you fellows don't see. *I* believe that story about the duel!' he declared; and it was of the very essence of this belief that it should impel him—just as our little party was dispersing— to turn back to our host with the absurd demand: 'And now you've got to tell us about *your* ghost!'

The outer door had closed on Murchard and the others; only Frenham and I remained; and the vigilant servant who presided over Culwin's destinies, having brought a fresh supply of soda-water, had been laconically ordered to bed.

Culwin's sociability was a night-blooming flower, and we knew that he expected the nucleus of his group to tighten around him after midnight. But Frenham's appeal seemed to disconcert him comically, and he rose from the chair in which he had just reseated himself after his farewells in the hall.

'*My* ghost? Do you suppose I'm fool enough to go to the expense of keeping one of my own, when there are so many charming ones in my friends' closets?—Take another cigar,' he said, revolving toward me with a laugh.

Frenham laughed too, pulling up his slender height before the chimney-piece as he turned to face his short bristling friend.

'Oh,' he said, 'you'd never be content to share if you met one you really liked.'

Culwin had dropped back into his armchair, his shock head embedded in its habitual hollow, his little eyes glimmering over a fresh cigar.

'Liked—*liked?* Good Lord!' he growled.

'Ah, you *have*, then!' Frenham pounced on him in the same instant, with a sidewise glance of victory at me; but Culwin cowered gnome-like among his cushions, dissembling himself in a protective cloud of smoke.

'What's the use of denying it? You've seen everything, so of course you've seen a ghost!' his young friend persisted, talking intrepidly into the cloud. 'Or, if you haven't seen one, it's only because you've seen two!'

The form of the challenge seemed to strike our host. He shot his head out of the mist with a queer tortoise-like motion he sometimes had, and blinked approvingly at Frenham.

'That's it,' he suddenly flung at us on a shrill jerk of laughter; 'it's only because I've seen two!'

The words were so unexpected that they dropped down and down into a fathomless silence, while we continued to stare at each other over Culwin's head, and Culwin stared at his ghosts. At length Frenham, without speaking, threw himself into the chair on the other side of the hearth, and leaned forward with his listening smile ...

II

'Oh, of course they're not show ghosts—a collector wouldn't think anything of them ... Don't let me raise your hopes ... their one merit is their numerical strength: the exceptional fact of their being *two*. But, as against this, I'm bound to admit that at any moment I could probably have exorcised them both by asking my doctor for a prescription, or my oculist for a pair of spectacles. Only, as I never could make up my mind whether to go to the doctor or the oculist—whether I was afflicted by an optical or a digestive delusion—I left them to pursue their interesting double life, though at times they made mine exceedingly comfortable....

'Yes—uncomfortable; and you know how I hate to be uncomfortable! But it was part of my stupid pride, when the thing began, not to admit that I could be disturbed by the trifling matter of seeing two.

'And then I'd no reason, really, to suppose I was ill. As far as I knew I was simply bored—horribly bored. But it was part of my boredom—I remember—that I was feeling, so uncommonly well, and didn't know how on earth to work off my surplus energy. I had come back from a long journey—down in South America and Mexico—and had settled down for the winter near New York, with an old aunt who had known Washington Irving and corresponded with N.P. Willis. She lived, not far from Irvington, in a damp Gothic villa, overhung by Norway spruces, and looking exactly like a memorial emblem done in hair. Her personal appearance was in keeping with this image, and her own hair—of which there was little left—might have been sacrificed to the manufacture of the emblem.

'I had just reached the end of an agitated year, with considerable arrears to make up in money and emotion; and theoretically it seemed as though my aunt's mild hospitality would be as beneficial to my nerves as to my purse. But the deuce of it was that as soon as I felt myself safe and sheltered my energy began to revive; and how was I to work it off inside of a memorial emblem? I had, at that time, the agreeable illusion that sustained intellectual effort could engage a man's whole activity; and I decided to write a great book—I forget about what. My aunt, impressed by my plan, gave up to me her Gothic library, filled with classics in black cloth and daguerrotypes of faded celebrities; and I sat down at my desk to make myself a place among their number. And to facilitate my task she lent me a cousin to copy my manuscript.

'The cousin was a nice girl, and I had an idea that a nice girl was just what I needed to restore my faith in human nature, and principally in myself. She was neither beautiful nor intelligent—poor Alice Nowell!—but it interested me to see any woman content to be so uninteresting, and I wanted to find out the secret of her content. In doing this I handled it rather rashly, and put it out of joint—oh, just for a moment! There's no fatuity in telling you this, for the poor girl had never seen any one but cousins....

'Well, I was sorry for what I'd done, of course, and confoundedly bothered as to how I should put it straight. She was staying in the house, and one evening, after my aunt had gone to bed, she came down to the library to fetch a book she'd mislaid, like any artless heroine on the shelves behind us. She was pink-nosed and flustered, and it suddenly occurred to me that her hair, though it was fairly thick and pretty, would look exactly like my aunt's when she grew older. I was glad I had noticed this, for it made it easier for me to do what was right; and when I had found the book she hadn't lost I told her I was leaving for Europe that week.

'Europe was terribly far off in those days, and Alice knew at once what I meant. She didn't take it in the least as I'd expected—it would have been easier if she had. She held her book very tight, and turned away a moment to wind up the lamp on my desk—it had a ground glass shade with vine leaves, and glass drops around the edge, I remember. Then she came back, held out her hand, and said: "Good bye." And as she said it she looked straight at me and kissed me. I had never felt anything as fresh and shy and brave as her kiss. It was worse than any reproach, and it made me ashamed to deserve a reproach from her. I said to myself: "I'll marry her, and when my aunt dies she'll leave us this house, and I'll sit here at the desk and go on with my book; and Alice will sit over there with her embroidery and look at me as she's looking now. And life will go on like that for any number of years." The prospect frightened me a little, but at the time it didn't frighten me as much as doing anything to hurt her; and ten minutes later she had my seal ring on my finger, and my promise that when I went abroad she should go with me.

'You'll wonder why I'm enlarging on this familiar incident. It's because the evening on which it took place was the very evening on which I first saw the queer sight I've spoken of. Being at that time an ardent believer in a necessary sequence between cause and effect I naturally tried to trace some kind of link between what had just happened to me in my aunt's library, and what was to happen a lew hours later on the same night; and so the coincidence between the two events always remained in my mind.

'I went up to bed with rather a heavy heart, for I was bowed under the weight of the first good action I had ever consciously committed; and young as I was, I saw the gravity of my situation. Don't imagine from this that I had hitherto been an instrument of destruction. I had been merely a harmless young man, who had followed his bent and declined all collaboration with Providence. Now I had suddenly undertaken to promote the moral order of the world, and I felt a good deal like the trustful spectator who has given his gold watch to the conjurer, and doesn't know in what shape he'll get it back when the trick is over.... Still, a glow of self righteousness tempered my fears, and I said to myself as I undressed that when I'd got used to being good it probably wouldn't make me as nervous as at did at the start. And by the time I was in bed, and had blown out my candle, I felt that I really was getting used to it, and that, as far as I'd got, it was not unlike sinking down into one of my aunt's very softest wool mattresses.

'I closed my eyes on this image, and when I opened them it must have been a good deal later, for my room had grown cold, and the night was intensely still. I was waked suddenly by the feeling we all know—the feeling that there was something near me that hadn't been there when I fell asleep. I sat up and strained my eyes into the darkness. The room was pitch black, and at first I saw nothing; but gradually a vague glimmer at the foot of the bed turned into two eyes staring back at me. I couldn't see the face attached to them—on account of the darkness, I imagined—but as I looked the eyes grew more and more distinct: they gave out a light of their own.

'The sensation of being thus gazed at was far from pleasant, and you might suppose that my first impulse would have been to jump out of bed and hurl myself on the invisible figure attached to the eyes. But it wasn't—my impulse was simply to lie still.... I can't say whether this was due to an immediate sense of the uncanny nature of the apparition—to the certainty that if I did jump out of bed I should hurl myself on nothing—or merely to the benumbing effect of the eyes themselves. They were the very worst eyes I've ever seen: a man's eyes—but what a man! My first thought was that he must be frightfully old. The orbits were sunk, and the thick red-lined lids hung over the eyeballs like blinds of which the cords are broken. One lid drooped a little lower than the other, with the effect of a crooked leer; and between these pulpy folds of flesh, with their scant bristle of lashes, the eyes themselves, small glassy disks with an agate-like rim about the pupils, looked like sea-pebbles in the grip of a starfish.

'But the age of the eyes was not the most unpleasant thing about them. What turned me sick was their expression of vicious security. I don't know how else to describe the fact that they seemed to belong to a man who had done a lot of harm in his life, but had always kept just inside the danger lines. They were not the eyes of a coward, but of some one much too clever to take risks; and my gorge rose at their look of base astuteness. Yet even that wasn't the worst; for as we continued to scan each other I saw in them a tinge of faint derision, and felt myself to be its object.

'At that I was seized by an impulse of rage that jerked me out of bed and pitched me straight on the unseen figure at its foot. But of course there wasn't any figure there, and my fists struck at emptiness. Ashamed and cold, I groped about for a match and lit the candles. The room looked just as usual—as I had known it would; and I crawled back to bed, and blew out the lights.

'As soon as the room was dark again the eyes reappeared; and I now applied myself to explaining them on scientific principles. At first I thought the illusion might have been caused by the glow of the last embers in the chimney; but the fire-place was on the other side of my bed, and so placed that the fire could not possibly be reflected in my toilet glass, which was the only mirror in the room. Then it occurred to me that I might have been tricked by the reflection of the embers in some polished bit of wood or metal; and though I couldn't discover any object of the sort in my line of vision, I got up again, groped my way to the hearth, and covered what was left of the fire. But as soon as I was back in bed the eyes were back at its foot.

'They were an hallucination, then: that was plain. But the fact that they were not due to any external dupery didn't make them a bit pleasanter to see. For if they were a projection of my inner consciousness, what the deuce was the matter with that organ? I had gone deeply enough into the mystery of morbid pathological states to picture the conditions under which an exploring mind might lay itself open to such a midnight admonition; but I couldn't fit it to my present case. I had never felt more normal, mentally and physically; and the only unusual fact in my situation—that of having assured the happiness of an amiable girl—did not seem of a kind to summon unclean spirits about my pillow. But there were the eyes still looking at me.

'I shut mine, and tried to evoke a vision of Alice Nowell's. They were not remarkable eyes, but they were as wholesome as fresh water, and if she had had more imagination—or longer lashes—their expression might have been interesting. As it was, they did not prove very efficacious, and in a few moments I perceived that they had mysteriously changed into the eyes at the foot of the bed. It exasperated me more to feel these glaring at me through my shut lids than to see them, and I opened my eyes again and looked straight into their hateful stare....

'And so it went on all night. I can't tell you what that night was, nor how long it lasted. I have you ever lain in bed, hopelessly wide awake, and tried to keep your eyes shut, knowing that if you opened 'em you'd see something you dreaded and loathed? It sounds easy, but it's devilish hard. Those eyes hung there and drew me, I had the *vertige de l'abîme*, and their red lids were the edge of my abyss. ... I had known nervous hours before: hours when I'd felt the wind of danger in my neck; but never this kind of strain. It wasn't that the eyes were so awful; they hadn't the majesty of the powers of darkness. But they had— how shall I say?—a physical effect that was the equivalent of a bad smell: their look left a smear like a snail's. And I didn't see what business they had with me, anyhow—and I stared and stared, trying to find out.

'I don't know what effect they were trying to produce; but the effect they *did* produce was that of making me pack my portmanteau and bolt to town early the next morning. I left a note for my aunt, explaining that I was ill and had gone to see my doctor; and as a matter of fact I did feel uncommonly ill— the night seemed to have pumped all the blood out of me. But when I reached town I didn't go to the doctor's. I went to a friend's rooms, and threw myself on a bed, and slept for ten heavenly hours. When I woke it was the middle of the night, and I turned cold at the thought of what might be waiting for me. I sat up, shaking, and stared into the darkness; but there wasn't a break in its blessed surface, and when I saw that the eyes were not there I dropped back into another long sleep.

'I had left no word for Alice when I fled, because I meant to go back the next morning. But the next morning I was too exhausted to stir. As the day went on the exhaustion increased, instead of wearing off like the lassitude left by an ordinary night of insomnia: the effect of the eyes seemed to be cumulative, and the thought of seeing them again grew intolerable. For two days I struggled with my dread; but on the third evening I pulled myself together and decided to go back the next morning. I felt a good deal happier as soon as I'd decided, for I knew that my abrupt disappearance, and the strangeness of my not writing, must have been very painful for poor Alice. That night I went to bed with an easy mind, and fell asleep at once; but in the middle of the night I woke, and there were the eyes....

'Well, I simply couldn't face them; and instead of going back to my aunt's I bundled a few things into a trunk and jumped onto the first steamer for England. I was so dead tired when I got on board that I crawled straight into my berth, and slept most of the way over; and I can't tell you the bliss it was to wake from those long stretches of dreamless sleep and look fearlessly into the darkness, *knowing*, that I shouldn't see the eyes....

'I stayed abroad for a year, and then I stayed for another; and during that time I never had a glimpse of them. That was enough reason for prolonging my stay if I'd been on a desert island. Another was, of course, that I had perfectly come to see, on the voyage over, the folly, complete impossibility, of my marrying Alice Nowell. The fact that I had been so slow in making this discovery annoyed me, and made me want to avoid explanations. The bliss of escaping at one stroke from the eyes, and from this other embarrassment, gave my freedom an extraordinary zest; and the longer I savoured it the better I liked its taste.

'The eyes had burned such a hole in my consciousness that for a long time I went on puzzling over the nature of the apparition, and wondering nervously if it would ever come back. But as time passed I lost this dread, and retained only the precision of the image. Then that faded in its turn.

'The second year found me settled in Rome, where I was planning, I believe, to write another great book—a definitive work on Etruscan influences in Italian art. At any rate, I'd found some pretext of the kind for taking a sunny apartment in the Piazza di Spagna and dabbling about indefinitely in the Forum; and there, one morning, a charming youth came to me. As he stood there in the warm light, slender and smooth and hyacinthine, he might have stepped from a ruined altar—one to Antinous, say; but he'd come instead from New York, with a letter (of all people) from Alice Nowell. The letter—the first I'd had from her since our break—was simply a line introducing her young cousin, Gilbert Noyes, and appealing to me to befriend him. It appeared, poor lad, that he "had talent," and "wanted to write"; and, an obdurate family having insisted that his calligraphy should take the form of double entry, Alice had intervened to win him six months' respite, during which he was to travel on a meagre pittance, and somehow prove his ultimate ability to increase it by his pen. The quaint conditions of the test struck me first: it seemed about as conclusive as a mediaeval "ordeal." Then I was touched by her having sent him to me. I had always wanted to do her some service, to justify myself in my own eyes rather than hers; and here was a beautiful embodiment of my chance.

'I imagine it's safe to lay down the general principle that predestined geniuses don't, as a rule, appear before one in the spring sunshine of the Forum looking like one of its banished gods. At any rate, poor Noyes wasn't a predestined genius. But he *was* beautiful to see, and charming as a comrade too. It was only when he began to talk literature that my heart failed me. I knew all the symptoms so well—the things he had "in him," and the things outside him that impinged! There's the real test, after all. It was always—punctually, inevitably, with the inexorableness of a mechanical law—it was *always* the wrong thing that struck him. I grew to find a certain grim fascination in deciding in advance exactly which wrong thing he'd select; and I acquired an astonishing skill at the game....

'The worst of it was that his *bêtise* wasn't of the too obvious sort. Ladies who met him at picnics thought him intellectual; and even at dinners he passed for clever. I, who had him under the microscope, fanceid now and then that he might develop some kind of a slim talent, something that he could make "do" and be happy on; and wasn't that, after all, what I was concerned with? He was so charming—he continued to be so charming—that he called forth all my charity in support of this argument; and for the first few months I really believed there was a chance for him....

'Those months were delightful. Noyes was constantly with me, and the more I saw of him the better I liked him. His stupidity was a natural grace—it was as beautiful, really, as his eye-lashes. And he was so gay, so affectionate, and so happy with me, that telling him the truth would have been about as pleasant as slitting the throat of some artless animal. At first I used to wonder what had put into that radiant head the detestable delusion that it held a brain. Then I began to see that it was simply protective mimicry—an instinctive ruse to get away from family life and an office desk. Not that Gilbert didn't—dear lad!—believe in himself. There wasn't a trace of hypocrisy in his composition. He was sure that his "call" was irresistible, while to me it was the saving grace of his situation that it *wasn't*, and that a little money, a little leisure, a little pleasure would have turned him into an inoffensive idler. Unluckily, however, there was no hope of money, and with the grim alternative of the office desk before him he couldn't postpone his attempt at literature. The stuff he turned out was deplorable, and I see now that I knew it from the first. Still, the absurdity of deciding a man's whole future on a first trial seemed to justify me in withholding my verdict, and perhaps even in encouraging him a little, on the ground that the human plant generally needs warmth to flower.

'At any rate, I proceeded on that principle, and carried it to the point of getting his term of probation extended. When I left Rome he went with me, and we idled away a delicious summer between Capri and Venice. I said to myself: "If he has anything in him, it will come out now," and it *did*. He was never more enchanting and enchanted. There were moments of our pilgrimage when beauty born of murmuring sound seemed actually to pass into his face— but only to issue forth in a shallow flood of the palest ink ...

'Well the time came to turn off the tap; and I knew there was no hand but mine to do it. We were back in Rome, and I had taken him to stay with me, not wanting him to be alone in his dismal *pension* when he had to face the necessity of renouncing his ambition. I hadn't, of course, relied solely on my own judgment in deciding to advise him to drop literature. I had sent his stuff to various people—editors and critics—and they had always sent it back with the same chilling lack of comment. Really there was nothing on earth to say.

'I confess I never felt more shabbily than I did on the day when I decided to have it out with Gilbert. It was well enough to tell myself that it was my duty to knock the poor boy's hopes into splinters—but I'd like to know what act of gratuitous cruelty hasn't been justified on that plea? I've always shrunk from usurping the functions of Providence, and when I have to exercise them I decidedly prefer that it shouldn't be on an errand of destruction. Besides, in the last issue, who was I to decide, even after a year's trial, if poor Gilbert had it in him or not?

'The more I looked at the part I'd resolved to play, the less I liked it; and I liked it still less when Gilbert sat opposite me, with his head thrown back in the lamplight, just as Phil's is now. ...I'd been going over his last manuscript, and he knew it, and he knew that his future hung on my verdict—we'd tacitly agreed to that. The manuscript lay between us, on my table—a novel, his first novel, if you please!—and he reached over and laid his hand on it, and looked up at me with all his life in the look.

'I stood up and cleared my throat, trying to keep my eyes away from his face and on the manuscript.

' "The fact is, my dear Gilbert," I began—

'I saw him turn pale, but he was up and facing me in an instant.

' "Oh, look here, don't take on so, my dear fellow! I'm not so awfully cut up as all that!" His hands were on my shoulders, and he was laughing down on me from his full height, with a kind of mortally-stricken gaiety that drove the knife into my side.

'He was too beautifully brave for me to keep up any humbug about my duty. And it came over me suddenly how I should hurt others in hurting him: myself first, since sending him home meant losing him; but more particularly poor Alice Nowell, to whom I had so uneasily longed to prove my good faith and my immense desire to serve her. It really seemed like failing her twice to fail Gilbert—

'But my intuition was like one of those lightning flashes that encircle the whole horizon, and in the same instant I saw what I might be letting myself in for if I didn't tell the truth. I said to myself: "I shall have him for life"—and I'd never yet seen any one, man or woman, whom I was quite sure of wanting on those terms. Well, this impulse of egotism decided me. I was ashamed of it, and to get away from it I took a leap that landed me straight in Gilbert's arms.

' "The thing's all right, and you're all wrong!" I shouted up at him; and as he hugged me, and I laughed and shook in his incredulous clutch, I had for a minute the sense of self-complacency that is supposed to attend the footsteps of the just. Hang it all, making people happy *has* its charms—

'Gilbert, of course, was for celebrating his emancipation in some spectacular manner; but I sent him away alone to explore his emotions, and went to bed to sleep off mine. As I undressed I began to wonder what their after-taste would be—so many of the finest don't keep! Still, I wasn't sorry, and I meant to empty the bottle, even if it *did* turn a trifle flat.

'After I got into bed I lay for a long time smiling at the memory of his eyes—his blissful eyes ... Then I fell asleep, and when I woke the room was deathly cold, and I sat up with a jerk—and there were *the other eyes*....

'It was three years since I'd seen them, but I'd thought of them so often that I fancied they could never take me unawares again. Now, with their red sneer on me, I knew that I had never really believed they would come back, and that I was as defenceless as ever against them.... As before, it was the insane irrelevance of their coming that made it so horrible. What the deuce were they after, to leap out at me at such a time? I had lived more or less carelessly in the years since I'd seen them, though my worst indiscretions were not dark enough to invite the searchings of their internal glare; but at this particular moment I was really in what might have been called a state of grace; and I can't tell you how the fact added to their horror....

'But it's not enough to say they were as bad as before: they were worse. Worse by just so much as I'd learned of life in the interval; by all the damnable implications my wider experience read into them. I saw now what I hadn't seen before: that they were eyes which had grown hideous gradually, which had built up their baseness coral-wise, bit by bit, out of a series of small turpitudes slowly accumulated through the industrious years. Yes—it came to me that what made them so bad was that they'd grown bad so slowly....

'There they hung in the darkness, their swollen lids dropped across the little watery bulbs rolling loose in the orbits, and the puff of fat flesh making a muddy shadow underneath—and as their filmy stare moved with my movements, there came over me a sense of their tacit complicity, of a deep hidden understanding between us that was worse than the first shock of their strangeness. Not that I understood them; but that they made it so clear that some day I should ... Yes, that was the worst part of it, decidedly; and it was the feeling that became stronger each time they came back....

'For they got into the damnable habit of coming back. They reminded me of vampires with a taste for young flesh, they seemed so to gloat over the taste of a good conscience. Every night for a month they came to claim their morsel of mine: since I'd made Gilbert happy they simply wouldn't loosen their fangs. The coincidence almost made me hate him, poor lad, fortuitous as I felt it to be. I puzzled over it a good deal, but couldn't find any hint of an explanation except in the chance of his association with Alice Nowell. But then the eyes had let up on me the moment I had abandoned her, so they could hardly be the emissaries of a woman scorned, even if one could have pictured poor Alice charging such spirits to avenge her. That set me thinking, and I began to wonder if they would let up on me if I abandoned Gilbert. The temptation was insidious, and I had to stiffen myself against it; but really, dear boy! he was too charming to be sacrificed to such demons. And so, after all, I never found out what they wanted....'

III

THE fire crumbled, sending up a flash which threw into relief the narrator's gnarled red face under its grey-black stubble. Pressed into the hollow of the dark leather armchair, it stood out an instant like an intaglio of yellowish red-veined stone, with spots of enamel for the eyes; then the fire sank and in the shaded lamp-light it became once more a dim Rembrandtish blur.

Phil Frenham, sitting in a low chair on the opposite side of the hearth, one long arm propped on the table behind him, one hand supporting his thrown-back head, and his eyes steadily fixed on his old trend's face, had not moved since the tale began. He continued to maintain his silent immobility after Culwin had ceased to speak, and it was I who, with a vague sense of disappointment at the sudden drop of the story, finally asked: 'But how long did you keep on seeing them?'

Culwin, so sunk into his chair that he seemed like a heap of his own empty clothes, stirred a little, as if in surprise at my question. He appeared to have half-forgotten what he had been telling us.

'How long? Oh, off and on all that winter. It was infernal. I never got used to them. I grew really ill.'

Frenham shifted his attitude silently, and as he did so his elbow snuck against a small mirror in a bronze frame standing on the table behind him. He turned and changed its angle slightly; then he resumed his former attitude, his dark head thrown back on his lifted palm, his eyes intent on Culwin's face. Something in his stare embarrassed me, and as it to divert attention from it I pressed on with another question:

'And you never tried sacrificing Noyes?'

'Oh, no. The fact is I didn't have to. He did it for me, poor infatuated boy!'

'Did it for you? How do you mean?'

'He wore me out—wore everybody out. He kept on pouring out his lamentable twaddle, and hawking it up and down the place till he became a thing of terror. I tried to wean him from writing—oh, ever so gently, you understand, by throwing him with agreeable people, giving him a chance to make himself felt, to come to a sense of what he *really* had to give. I'd foreseen this solution from the beginning—felt sure that, once the first ardour of authorship was quenched, he'd drop into his place as a charming parasitic thing, the kind of chronic Cherubino for whom, in old societies, there's always a seat at table, and a shelter behind the ladies' skirts. I saw him take his place as "the poet": the poet who doesn't write. One knows the type in every drawing-room. Living in that way doesn't cost much—I'd worked it all out in my mind, and felt sure that, with a little help, he could manage it for the next few years; and meanwhile he'd be sure to marry. I saw him married to a widow, rather older, with a good cook and a well-run house. And I actually had my eye on the widow. ... Meanwhile I did everything to facilitate the transition—lent him money to ease his conscience, introduced him to pretty women to make him forget his vows. But nothing would do him: he had but one idea in his beautiful obstinate head. He wanted the laurel and not the rose, and he kept on repeating Gautier's axiom, and battering and filing at his limp prose till he'd spread it out over Lord knows how many thousand sloppy pages. Now and then he would send a barrelful to a publisher, and of course it would always come back.

'At first it didn't matter—he thought he was "misunderstood." He took the attitudes of genius, and whenever an opus came home he wrote another to keep it company. Then he had a reaction of despair, and accused me of deceiving him, and Lord knows what. I got angry at that, and told him it was he who had deceived himself. He'd come to me determined to write, and I'd done my best to help him. That was the extent of my offence, and I'd done it for his cousin's sake, not his.

'That seemed to strike home, and he didn't answer for a minute. Then he said: "My time's up and my money's up. What do you think I'd better do?"

' "I think you'd better not be an ass," I said.

'He turned red, and asked: "What do you mean by being an ass?"

'I took a letter from my desk and held it out to him.

' "I mean refusing this offer of Mrs Ellinger's: to be her secretary at a salary of five thousand dollars. There may be a lot more in it than that."

'He flung out his hand with a violence that struck the letter from mine. "Oh, I know well enough what's in it!" he said, scarlet to the roots of his hair.

' "And what's your answer, if you know?" I asked.

'He made none at the minute, but turned away slowly to the door. There, with his hand on the threshold, he stopped to ask, almost under his breath; "Then you really think my stuff's no good?"

'I was tired and exasperated, and I laughed. I don't defend my laugh—it was in wretched taste. But I must plead in extenuation that the boy was a fool, and that I'd done my best for him—I really had.

'He went out of the room, shutting the door quietly after him. That afternoon I left for Frascati, where I'd promised to spend the Sunday with some friends. I was glad to escape from Gilbert, and by the same token, as I learned that night, I had also escaped from the eyes. I dropped into the same lethargic sleep that had come to me before when their visitations ceased; and when I woke the next morning, in my peaceful painted room above the ilexes, I felt the utter weariness and deep relief that always followed on that repairing slumber. I put in two blessed nights at Frascati, and when I got back to my rooms in Rome I found that Gilbert had gone. ... Oh, nothing tragic had happened—the episode never rose to *that*. He'd simply packed his manuscripts and left for America—for his family and the Wall Street desk. He left a decent little note to tell me of his decision, and behaved altogether, in the circumstances, as little like a fool as it's possible for a fool to behave....'

IV

Culwin paused again, and again Frenham sat motionless, the dusky contour of his young head reflected in the mirror at his back.

'And what became of Noyes afterward?' I finally asked, still disquieted by a sense of incompleteness, by the need of some connecting thread between the parallel lines of the tale.

Culwin twitched his shoulders. 'Oh, nothing became of him— because he became nothing. There could be no question of "becoming" about it. He vegetated in an office, I believe, and finally got a clerkship in a consulate, and married drearily in China. I saw him once in Hong Kong, years afterward. He was fat and hadn't shaved. I was told he drank. He didn't recognise me.'

'And the eyes?' I asked, after another pause which Frenham's continued silence made oppressive.

Culwin, stroking his chin, blinked at me meditatively through the shadows. 'I never saw them after my last talk with Gilbert. Put two and two together if you can. For my part, I haven't found the link.'

He rose stiffly, his hands in his pockets, and walked over to the table on which reviving drinks had been set out.

'You must be parched after this dry tale. Here, help yourself, my dear fellow. Here, Phil—' He turned back to the hearth.

Frenham still sat in his low chair, making no response to his host's hospitable summons. But as Culwin advanced toward him, their eyes met in a long look; after which, to my intense surprise, the young man, turning suddenly in his seat, flung his arms across the table, and dropped his face upon them.

Culwin, at the unexpected gesture, stopped short, a flush on his face.

'Phil—what the deuce? Why, have the eyes scared *you?* My dear boy—my dear fellow—I never had such a tribute to my literary ability, never!'

He broke into a chuckle at the thought, and halted on the hearthrug, his hands still in his pockets, gazing down in honest perplexity at the youth's bowed head. Then, as Frenham still made no answer, he moved a step or two nearer.

'Cheer up, my dear Phil! It's years since I've seen them—apparently I've done nothing lately bad enough to call them out of chaos. Unless my present evocation of them has made *you* see them; which would be their worst stroke yet!'

His bantering appeal quivered off into an uneasy laugh, and he moved still nearer, bending over Frenham, and laying his gouty hands on the lad's shoulders.

'Phil, my dear boy, really—what's the matter? Why don't you answer? *Have* you seen the eyes?'

Frenham's face was still pressed against his arms, and from where I stood behind Culwin I saw the latter, as if under the rebuff of this unaccountable attitude, draw back slowly from his friend. As he did so, the light of the lamp on the table fell full on his perplexed congested face, and I caught its sudden reflection in the mirror behind Frenham's head.

Culwin saw the reflection also. He paused, his face level with the mirror, as if scarcely recognising the countenance in it as his own. But as he looked his expression gradually changed, and for an appreciable space of time he and the image in the glass confronted each other with a glare of slowly gathering hate. Then Calwin let go of Frenham's shoulders, and drew back a step, covering his eyes with his hands....

Frenham, his face still hidden, did not stir.

THE PAINTER OF DEAD WOMEN

Edna W. Underwood

We were lingering over one of our honeymoon breakfasts in Naples, my husband dividing his attention between *Il Corriere di Napoli* and his coffee, and I planning for my favorite pastime, swimming, in that sea which looks like a liquid sapphire.

"'No clue to the mysterious disappearance of the Contessa Fabriani,'" he read. "'After a month's search, the police are baffled.'

"That does not sound particularly remarkable to you, I suppose. Women—and men, too, for that matter—have disappeared from other cities. But this adds another chapter to a mysterious, story of crime.

"For twenty-five years not only native Italian women, but visiting women of other nations have disappeared from Naples, and nothing has afterward been heard of them. The peculiar part about it is that they have all been young and beautiful, and women of the upper class."

I paid little heed to his words. I was thinking of other things. Besides, Luigi was a Neapolitan and interested in all the happenings of his native city. On my first visit to Naples I did not have time to interest myself in a sensational story such as I could read any morning in the London papers.

"You have not forgotten that to-night is the ball?" said my husband, consulting his watch and jumping up. "I want you to look particularly lovely. All my friends—and your old rivals—will be there. Business takes me from the city for the day, and in case I should not return in time to accompany you, I have arranged for Cousin Lucia to meet you at ten at the door of the Cinascalchi Palace. I shall come later—in time for part of the dancing. Tell Pietro to get you there at exactly ten," he called, after he had kissed me good-by.

When I took a last look at myself in the glass that night, I felt that I had obeyed my husband's instructions. I was looking particularly lovely. I had dressed with the purpose of appearing as unlike Italian women as possible.

My slim six feet of stature was arrayed in a plain white satin princess, from which the shoulders rose scarcely less white and satiny. My hair was the color of the upland furze, and my cheeks glowed like the roses of an English garden.

"Pietro!" I called, after we had driven what seemed to me a very long time. "Are you sure that you are going in the right direction? I did not suppose that it was outside the city."

He reassured me and drove on.

We entered the courtyard of a country estate. As I stepped from the carriage, I saw in the distance the grouped lights of Naples. Pietro whipped the horses and drove off before I had time to speak.

There were no other carriages in the yard. Could I have mistaken the time? Lucia was not there to meet me, either. "She is probably within," I reflected, "since the palace is bright with light."

Doors swung back softly and as if by magic. I entered. The blaze of light that rushed out all but blinded me. Words cannot express the horror of it nor the silence that accompanied it. There were no servants moving about. No one was in sight. I was alone.

Imagine a sweep of majestic rooms whose floors were polished to the surface consistency of stone; straight white walls of mirrored marble, and, blazing from walls and ceiling, prisms of cut crystal. Wherever you looked the glitter of light flashed back at you, confusing your eyes and dazing your brain. I did not suppose that light could hold such terror.

"There is surely some mistake," I whispered. "This is no place for dancing or merriment. It is more like a white and shining sepulchre. I would rather trust myself to the night outside," and I turned toward the door with the purpose of leaving. But the space behind, where I knew that I had entered, presented a smooth and evenly paneled surface. There was no door. Nor was there place for lock or knob. As I stood confused and hesitating, I learned to the full the demoniac power of light. The slightest motion of my body, my head, my breathing, even, sent from polished corners and cornice quivering arrows into my eyes. The mirrors and the shining marble reflected floor and ceiling until it was impossible to tell where one left off and the other began. It seemed, after a time, that I was floating head downward in a sea of light.

Then something righted me sharply. It was not sound nor was it thought. It appealed to subtler senses. It was as if the material body was endowed with a thinking machine and each pore contained a brain. It aroused some consciousness which the hypnotism of light had dulled. I knew then that I was standing, slim and white and frozen with terror, in the focus of the light.

I felt the cold diamonds shift their position upon my throat and breast and tremble as I breathed irregularly. I heard the sibilant slipping of the stiff satin as it fell into a changed position.

A powerful and dominant brain had touched my own. For one unconscious moment it had ruled it and set upon it the seal of its thought.

Such a passion of fear assailed me that it seemed as if I must choke. My fascinated eyes turned toward the end of the farthest room. From there the message came. There, I knew, was something compelling, something electric. Exactly in the center of that far room, and very erect, stood a man. He was coming toward me, too, slowly—very slowly. Yet I heard not the slightest sound. Evidently he was shod with rubber. He moved as I have seen a malevolent spider move toward a prisoned fly, enjoying the pleasure of motion because he knows that there is no escape for his victim. Just as gracefully and easily did he move toward me. And as he came, I knew that he read my soul, measured my strength and my power of resistance, and at the same time admired the white erectness of my body.

Fear, as with a bitter acid, etched his picture on my brain. He was very tall—taller than I by a good inch—and faultlessly attired; a patrician, but a degenerate patrician, the body alone having preserved its ancient dignity.

Ribboned decorations brightened his coat, and I saw a garter on his leg.

He was thinner than any one I ever saw and correspondingly supple. His movements had the fascination of a serpent. Thus might a serpent move, if its coiled length were poised erect. His head would have been beautiful, had not the features been so delicately chiseled that strength and nobility had been refined away, and in their place had come effeminacy and a certain cold and delicate cruelty.

He was an old man, too, and his heavy hair was white. His brows, however, were black and youthful, and from beneath looked out blue eyes. The eyes were the color of light when it shines through thick ice. They were the color of the sharp edge of fine steel when it is bared too quickly to the sun. In the same hard way the light ran across them.

But the strangest part was that there seemed to be no limit to their depth. However far you looked within, you could not find a person. You could not surprise a consciousness. There was no soul there. In its stead there was merely a keen and destructive intelligence.

I realized that the man coming toward me did not live by means of the physical acts of life. He had learned to live by his brain. He was a cerebral!

I sensed his dominant personality and struggled against it. I sensed, too, the presence of a numbing mental fluid that crippled my will and dulled me as does that sweet-smelling death which surgeons call the anæsthetic.

He had stripped himself of human attributes. He knew nothing of fear, pity, love.

"I have the honor of meeting, I believe, the bride of the Leopardi." He bowed and spoke in an even, unemotional voice.

I bowed in return. "How is it possible for you to know that? I do not remember having met you."

"It is not necessary to have met me. No beautiful woman comes to Naples whom I do not know. I," bowing again, "am Count Ponteleone, painter of dead women. You have probably heard of me."

"Who has not!" I exclaimed, somewhat reassured and wondering that this could be the man whose name was resounding through two continents.

"This intrusion—which I beg you to pardon—is due to the coachman's mistake. I am expected at the Cinascalchi ball. My husband and cousin await me there. If you will send me on in your carriage, I shall be grateful."

"Oh, no, your coachman made no mistake," calmly ignoring my request. "I brought him here and you, too, as I have brought other women—by this," tapping his forehead.

"You are graciously jesting to excuse my rudeness," I managed to stammer, summoning the ghost of a smile.

"Well, we may as well call it a jest if you wish. It is a jest which ought to flatter. I entertain only beautiful women here."

The glance that accompanied this enveloped me from head to foot. It was a glance of admiration, and yet in it there was none of the desire of would-be love. It was devoid of warmth and emotion. Nothing could be more impersonal. No mark of material beauty had escaped it. It was the trained glance of a connoisseur which measures accurately. I might have been a picture or a piece of furniture.

I felt that he knew my racial standing, my rank as a human animal, by the delicate roundness of my bones and the fine fiber of my flesh. I had been as glass to his intelligent gaze. Somehow, then, I felt that the body of me belonged to him because of this masterly penetration which substance could not resist.

"Since you are to be my guest, we might seek a more comfortable place to converse."

He led the way to the center of the great rooms where, touching an invisible spring, doors flew back, disclosing a drawing-room draped in red. As he bowed me to a seat, he remarked: "Here you look like a pearl dropped in a cup of blood."

I, too, thought that I had never seen so wicked a red nor one so suggestive of luxurious crime. The comparison jarred upon me and prickled me with fear.

As he sank back in an easy-chair opposite, I saw how the red walls touched with color the whiteness of his hair and sent occasional ruddy gleams into the depth of his eyes.

"You are an Englishwoman, too," he observed, with evident relish. "I knew it. Only the mists and rains of England can make color like yours. Did you notice how well we looked together as we walked along between the mirrors?

Are we not as if made for each other—tall and regal—both of us? What a picture we would make!"

It occurred to me then, with unpleasant appropriateness, that he was the painter of *dead women*.

"It is an English woman, too, that I lack for my collection," he mused meditatively.

"Collection! Have you a collection of women? That is certainly unique. I have heard of collections of bugs, birds,—but women, never. Perhaps you would like me to join it!"

"Indeed I should! I never saw a woman I admired so tremendously."

I drew back in fear, silenced by the ardor of his words.

"Oh, you need not be afraid. I am not like other men. I do not love as they love. I love only with my brain. While you have been sitting here, I have caressed you a thousand times, and you have not even suspected it. I do not want the bestial common pleasures which my coachman can have, or my scullion can buy with a *lira*. Why should not I be as much superior to them in my loves as in my life? If I am not, then I am not their superior in any way. My pleasures are those of another plane of life, of a brain touched to a keener fire, of nerves that have reached the highest point of pleasurable vibration. Besides, when I love, I love only dead women. Life reaches its perfection only when death comes. *Life is never real until then*," he added.

"Perhaps you would like to kill me for your amusement to-night," I replied, still trying to keep up the jest. "I have always flattered myself, however, that I was better alive."

No sooner were the words out than I regretted them. His face grew thin and trained like a bird-dog's on the scent. His lips became expressive of a terrible desire, and his frail hands trembled with anticipation.

As I looked, his pupils disappeared, and his eyes became two pools of blue and blazing light. Unwittingly I had hit upon his object. I had surprised his purpose in a jest.

Who could have dreamed of this! At the worst, I thought, I might be detained for two or three days, forced to serve him for a model, and cause worry to my husband and gossiping comment.

But whose imagination could have reached this! Strangely enough, the decree of death that I read in his face dissipated my fear. I became calm and collected. In an instant I was mistress of myself and ready to fight for life. The blood stopped pounding in my brain. I could think with normal clearness.

"The worst of it is," I reflected, "this man is not mad. If he were, I might be able to play upon some delusion for freedom. He has passed the point where madness begins. He has gone just so much too far the other way."

"Then you really think that you could love me if I were dead," I laughed, leaning toward him gayly. "Is it not rather a strange requisite for winning a woman's love? What would my reward be? Are you sure you could not endure me any other way?"

"Do not jest about sacred things! Death," he answered slowly and reprovingly, "is the thing most to be desired by beautiful women. It saves them from something worse—old age. An ugly woman can afford to live; a beautiful woman can not. The real object of life is to ripen the body to its limit of physical perfection, and then, just as you would a perfect fruit, pluck and preserve it. Death sets the definite seal upon its perfection, that is, if death can be controlled to prevent decay. And that is what I can do," he added proudly, getting up in his abstraction and pacing up and down the room. "And what difference does it make, what day it comes? All days march toward death."

I admired unreservedly the elegant intellectualized figure, now that I had thrown fear to the winds.

"Come," he pleaded, "let me kill you! It is because I love you that I ask you. It is because I think that your physical self is worth being preserved. Your future will be assured. You will never be less happy than now, less lovely, less triumphant. You will always be an object of admiration."

"What a magician you are to picture death attractively! But tell me more about it first."

Joy leaped up and sang in my heart at the prospect of the struggle. I felt as the racehorse feels when, knowing the strength and the suppleness of his limbs, he sees the long white track unfold before him.

"In ancient days my ancestors," he began, "were Roman Governors in Spain. At the court of one of them, Vitellius Ponteleone, lived a famous Jewish physician (in old Spanish days the Jews were the first of scientists), by name Ibn Ezra. He made a poison (poison is not the right word, I regret greatly its vulgar suggestiveness) from a mineral which has now vanished from the face of the earth. This poison causes a delicious, pleasureful death, and at the same time arrests physical decay. Now, if you will just let me inject one drop of it into that white arm of yours, you will be immortal—superior to time and change, indestructibly young. You do not seem to realize the greatness of the offer. For this honor I have selected you from all the women in Naples."

"It is an honor, of course; but, like a proposal of marriage, it seems to me important and to require consideration."

"Oh, no, it is not important. We have to prepare for life, but for death we are always ready. Besides, I am offering you a chance to choose your own death. How many can do that!"

"Do not think that I am ungrateful, good Count, but—"

"One little drop of the liquid will run through your veins like flame, cutting off thought and all centers of painful sensation. Only a dim sweet memory of pleasant things will remain. Gradually, then, cells and arteries and flesh will harden. In time your body will attain the hardness of a diamond and the whiteness of fine marble. But it is months, years, before the brain dies. I am not really sure that it ever dies. In it, like the iridescent reflections upon a soap bubble, live the shadows of past pleasures. There is no other immortality that can equal this which I offer. Every day that you live now lessens your beauty. In a way every day is a vulgar death. It coarsens and over-colors your skin, dulls the gold of your hair, makes this bodily line, or this, a bit too full. That is why I brought you here to-night, at the height of your beauty, just as love and life have crowned you."

"It must be a remarkable liquid. Let me see it. Is it with you?"

"No, indeed! It is kept in a vault which it takes an hour to open. It is guarded as are the crown jewels of Italy," he responded proudly.

"There is no immediate danger," I thought. "There is time. Now the road lies long before me."

"I suppose there is an antidote for this liquid. I will not call it poison, since you dislike the word so greatly."

"None that is known now. You see it destroys instantly what only patient nature can rebuild."

"I am greatly interested in it. Show me the other women upon whom you have tried it. I am eager to see its effect."

"I knew you would be. Come this way."

We ascended a staircase, where again I felt the sting of light. Upon a landing, halfway up, he paused and pointed to our reflected figures.

"Are we not as if made for each other—you and I? When I sleep the white liquid sleep, I shall arrange that it be beside you."

My death evidently was firmly determined upon.

At the top he unlocked a door, and we entered a room where some fifty women were dancing a minuet. Above them great crystal chandeliers swung, giving to their jewels and their shimmering silks and satins reflected life. Each one was in an attitude of arrested motion. It was as if they had been frozen in the maddest moment of a dance. But what a horrible sight—this dance of dead women, this mimic merriment of death!

"You know my picture of this scene, do you not?" said he, turning on more light. "They were perfect models, I can assure you. I can paint them for hours in any light.

"When I die I shall bequeath to Naples this art gallery. Will it not be a gift to be proud of? Nothing can surpass it in uniqueness. Then the bodies of these women will have attained the hardness and the whiteness of fine marble. They can in no way be distinguished from it except by their hair.

"Of course now, if the outside world knew of this, I should be punished as a murderer."

How firmly it is settled in his mind that the outside world is mine no more!

"But then I shall be revered as a scientist who preserved for posterity the most perfect human specimens of the age in which I lived. I shall be looked upon as a God. It is as great to preserve life as it is to make it."

The next room we entered was a luxurious boudoir. Before an exquisite French dressing-table sat a woman whose bronze hair swept the floor. On either side peacocks stood with outspread tails. Their backs served as a rest for a variety of jeweled hairpins, one of which she was in the act of picking up.

"That is the Contessa Fabriani. She is not dead yet. She hears every word we say, but she is unable to speak. I am painting her now. You can see the unfinished picture against the wall."

In an adjoining room a dark-skinned woman of the Orient, whose black and unbound hair showed purplish tints, was reclining upon the back of a Bengal tiger. Other Eastern women lay upon couches and divans.

"See, even in death, what enticing languor! See the arrested dreams in their dark eyes, deep as an Oriental night! These women I have loved very greatly. Sometimes I have a fancy that death cannot touch them. In them there is an electric energy, the stored-up indestructible ardor of the sun, which, I like to fancy, death cannot dissipate."

"Now here," said the Count, opening another door, "I will show you an effect I have tried for years to reproduce. This has been the desire of my life."

He flung back a row of folding windows, making the room on one side open to the sea.

"It is the effect of the blended radiance flung from the water here and the moon, upon dull silver, upon crystal, and the flesh of blond women."

He turned out the lights. The moon sent an eerie, shivering luster across the crystal and silver decorations, and touched three women in robes of white, who were standing in attitudes of dreaming indolence.

"This thin, ethereal, surface light, this *puissance de lumière*, is what I have tried in vain to prison. I have always been greedy of the difficult and the unattainable. If I could do this, I should be the prince of painters! It is a fact, a real thing, and yet it possesses the magic of dreams, the enchantment of the fleeting and the illusory.

"I wish to be the wizard of light. I wish to be the only one to prison its bright, defiant insubstantiality.

"Can you not see how wonderful it is? It is the dust of light. Reflected upon silver and clear crystal it is what shadow is to sound. Sometimes it seems to me like a thin, clear acid; then like some blue, sweet-smelling volatile liquid, eager again to join the air.

"Have you noticed how it penetrates blond flesh? It reveals, yet transfigures it. I wish you could watch its effect often. Sometimes the wind churns the sea-light into transparent foam. Then I love its curd-like, piled-up whiteness. Sometimes when there is no moon, and only a wan, tremulous luster from the water, the light of a tar star is focused on their satins, on their diamonds, struggles eerily among their laces, or flickers mournfully from a pearl. The room then is filled with a regretful, metallic radiance. The stars caress them. They have become impersonal, you see, and the eternal things love them.

"When the autumn moons are high, the light that fills the room is resonant and yellow. It tingles like a crystal. It gives their cold white satins the yellow richness of the peach's heart, and to the women the enticing languor of life. On such nights the moonlight is musical and makes the crystal vibrate.

"Now, to-night, the light is more like the vanishing ripple of the sea. Is it not wonderful? Look! It is the twin of silence, the ghost of light!"

In his excitement and exhilaration, his eyes shone like the moon-swept sea. I knew that in them, too, slept terrors inconceivable.

"This is the room I have in mind for you. You will queen it by a head over the other women. The color of your dress is right. Your gems, too, are white. Here, sometime, I promise to join you, and together we will be immortal.

"Excuse me just a moment. Wait here. Let me get the liquid and show it to you. You will be fascinated by it, just as other women have been. I never saw one who could resist it."

As he left, I heard the key turn in the lock. When we entered the other rooms, I remembered that he bolted the doors on the inside. This door, then, was the only one by which he could gain entrance. Swiftly I slipped the bolt. Now I was safe—for a time, unless there was a secret entrance.

It was not far from the window to the water. I laughed with delight. I had dived that distance many a time for pleasure. I was one of the best swimmers in England, and I had always longed for a plunge in this sapphire sea. Now was my chance and life as the goal to gain. I took off my satin gown as gayly as I had put it on. Like the Count of Ponteleone, I, too, admired the play of light on its piled-up whiteness. How merrily the sea-wind came! How it counseled courage!

I took the plunge. Down, down, down I went, cleaving the clear water. The distance up seemed interminable. It was like being born again when at last I saw the white foam feather my arms and felt my lungs expand with air. I swam in the direction of Naples. I could not reach the city, but I could easily reach some fisher's hut and there gain shelter.

Oh, the delight of that warm, bright water under the moon! I felt that the strength of my arms and my legs was inexhaustible. I exulted in the water as a bird exults in its natural element, the air.

After I had covered what I thought to be a safe distance, I turned on my back and floated. Then I caught sight of the window from which I had leaped. It was brilliantly lighted. Count Ponteleone was leaning from it, his white hair shining like a malevolent flame.

Despite the distance, I could feel the power of his wild blue eyes, which sparkled like the sea. Again I dived, lest they should reassert their power over me and draw me back.

I came up under the shadow of the shore, and made my way along until I reached a boat where Neapolitan fisherwomen were spreading their nets to dry.

They took me in, and for the doubled price of a good month's fishing brought me that night to Naples.

"Ah, Luigi," I sobbed, as he folded me in his arms, "little did I think, when you spoke of the dance this morning, that I should spend the night with the dead dancing women of Ponteleone."

"Nor I that you would solve Naples' mystery of crime."

THE SHADOWY THIRD

Ellen Glasgow

WHEN THE call came I remember that I turned from the telephone in a romantic flutter. Though I had spoken only once to the great surgeon, Roland Maradick, I felt on that December afternoon that to speak to him only once—to watch him in the operating-room for a single hour—was an adventure which drained the colour and the excitement from the rest of life. After all these years of work on typhoid and pneumonia cases, I can still feel the delicious tremor of my young pulses; I can still see the winter sunshine slanting through the hospital windows over the white uniforms of the nurses.

"He didn't mention me by name. Can there be a mistake?" I stood, incredulous yet ecstatic, before the superintendent of the hospital.

"No, there isn't a mistake, I was talking to him before you came down." Miss Hemphill's strong face softened while she looked at me. She was a big, resolute woman, a distant Canadian relative of my mother's, and the kind of nurse I had discovered in the month since I had come up from Richmond, that Northern hospital boards, if not Northern patients, appear instinctively to select. From the first, in spite of her hardness, she had taken a liking—I hesitate to use the word "fancy" for a preference so impersonal—to her Virginia cousin. After all, it isn't every Southern nurse, just out of training, who can boast a kinswoman in the superintendent of a New York hospital.

"And he made you understand positively that he meant me?" The thing was so wonderful that I simply couldn't believe it.

"He asked particularly for the nurse who was with Miss Hudson last week when he operated. I think he didn't even remember that you had a name. When I asked if he meant Miss Randolph, he repeated that he wanted the nurse who had been with Miss Hudson. She was small, he said, and cheerful-looking. This, of course, might apply to one or two of the others, but none of these was with Miss Hudson."

"Then I suppose it is really true?" My pulses were tingling. "And I am to be there at six o'clock?"

"Not a minute later. The day nurse goes off duty at that hour, and Mrs. Maradick is never left by herself for an instant."

"It is her mind, isn't it? And that makes it all the stranger that he should select me, for I have had so few mental cases."

"So few cases of any kind," Miss Hemphill was smiling, and when she smiled I wondered if the other nurses would know her. "By the time you have gone through the treadmill in New York, Margaret, you will have lost a good many things besides your inexperience. I wonder how long you will keep your sympathy and your imagination? After all, wouldn't you have made a better novelist than a nurse?"

"I can't help putting myself into my cases. I suppose one ought not to?"

"It isn't a question of what one ought to do, but of what one must. When you are drained of every bit of sympathy and enthusiasm, and have got nothing in return for it, not even thanks, you will understand why I try to keep you from wasting yourself."

"But surely in a case like this—for Doctor Maradick?"

"Oh, well, of course—for Doctor Maradick." She must have seen that I implored her confidence, for, after a minute, she let fall carelessly a gleam of light on the situation: "It is a very sad case when you think what a charming man and a great surgeon Doctor Maradick is."

Above the starched collar of my uniform I felt the blood leap in bounds to my cheeks. "I have spoken to him only once," I murmured, "but he is charming, and so kind and handsome, isn't he?"

"His patients adore him."

"Oh, yes, I've seen that. Everyone hangs on his visits." Like the patients and the other nurses, I also had come by delightful, if imperceptible, degrees to hang on the daily visits of Doctor Maradick. He was, I suppose, born to be a hero to women. From my first day in his hospital, from the moment when I watched, through closed shutters, while he stepped out of his car, I have never doubted that he was assigned to the great part in the play. If I had been ignorant of his spell—of the charm he exercised over his hospital—I should have felt it in the waiting hush, like a dawn breath, which followed his ring at the door and preceded his imperious footstep on the stairs. My first impression of him, even after the terrible events of the next year, records a memory that is both careless and splendid. At that moment, when, gazing through the chinks in the shutters, I watched him, in his coat of dark fur, cross the pavement over the pale streaks of sunshine, I knew beyond any doubt— I knew with a sort of infallible prescience—that my fate was irretrievably bound up with his in the future. I knew this, I repeat, though Miss Hemphill would still insist that my foreknowledge was merely a sentimental gleaning from indiscriminate novels. But it wasn't only first love, impressionable as my kinswoman believed me to be. It wasn't only the way he looked. Even more than his appearance—more than the shining dark of his eyes, the silvery brown of his hair, the dusky glow in his face—even more than his charm and his magnificence, I think, the beauty and sympathy in his voice won my heart. It was a voice, I heard someone say afterwards, that ought always to speak poetry.

So you will see why—if you do not understand at the beginning, I can never hope to make you believe impossible things!—so you will see why I accepted the call when it came as an imperative summons. I couldn't have stayed away after he sent for me. However much I may have tried not to go, I know that in the end I must have gone. In those days, while I was still hoping to write novels, I used to talk a great deal about "destiny" (I have learned since then how silly all such talk is), and I suppose it was my "destiny" to be caught in the web of Roland Maradick's personality. But I am not the first nurse to grow love-sick about a doctor who never gave her a thought.

"I am glad you got the call, Margaret. It may mean a great deal to you. Only try not to be too emotional." I remember that Miss Hemphill was holding a bit of rose-geranium in her hand while she spoke—one of the patients had given it to her from a pot she kept in her room, and the scent of the flower is still in my nostrils—or my memory. Since then—oh, long since then—I have wondered if she also had been caught in the web.

"I wish I knew more about the case." I was pressing for light. "Have you ever seen Mrs. Maradick?"

'Oh, dear, yes. They have been married only a little over a year, and in the beginning she used to come sometimes to the hospital and wait outside while the doctor made his visits. She was a very sweet-looking woman then—not exactly pretty, but fair and slight, with the loveliest smile, I think, I have ever seen. In those first months she was so much in love that we used to laugh about it among ourselves. To see her face light up when the doctor came out of the hospital and crossed the pavement to his car, was as good as a play. We never tired of watching her— I wasn't superintendent then, so I had more rime to look out of the window while I was on day duty. Once or twice she brought her little girl in to see one of the patients. The child was so much like her that you would have known them anywhere for mother and daughter."

I had heard that Mrs. Maradick was a widow, with one child, when she first met the doctor, and I asked now, still seeking an illumination I had not found, "There was a great deal of money, wasn't there?"

"A great fortune. If she hadn't been so attractive, people would have said, I suppose, that Doctor Maradick married her for her money. Only," she appeared to make an effort of memory, "I believe I've heard somehow that it was all left in trust away from Mrs. Maradick if she married again. I can't, to save my life, remember just how it was; but it was a queer will, I know, and

Mrs. Maradick wasn't to come into the money unless the child didn't live to grow up. The pity of it——"

A young nurse came into the office to ask for something—the keys, I think, of the operating-room, and Miss Hemphill broke off inconclusively as she hurried out of the door. I was sorry that she left off just when she did. Poor Mrs. Maradick! Perhaps I was too emotional, but even before I saw her I had begun to feel her pathos and her strangeness.

My preparations took only a few minutes. In those days I always kept a suitcase packed and ready for sudden calls; and it was not yet six o'clock when I turned from Tenth Street into Fifth Avenue, and stopped for a minute, before ascending the steps, to look at the house in which Doctor Maradick lived. A fine rain was falling, and I remember thinking, as I turned the corner, how depressing the weather must be for Mrs. Maradick. It was an old house, with damp-looking walls (though that may have been because of the rain) and a spindle-shaped iron railing which ran up the stone steps to the black door, where I noticed a dim flicker through the old-fashioned fanlight. Afterwards I discovered that Mrs. Maradick had been born in the house—her maiden name was Calloran—and that she had never wanted to live anywhere else. She was a woman—this I found out when I knew her better—of strong attachments to both persons and places; and though Doctor Maradick had tried to persuade her to move uptown after her marriage, she had clung, against his wishes, to the old house in lower Fifth Avenue. I dare say she was obstinate about it in spite of her gentleness and her passion for the doctor. Those sweet, soft women, especially when they have always been rich, are sometimes amazingly obstinate. I have nursed so many of them since—women with strong affections and weak intellects—that I have come to recognize the type as soon as I set eyes upon it.

My ring at the bell was answered after a little delay, and when I entered the house I saw that the hall was quite dark except for the waning glow from an open fire which burned in the library. When I gave my name, and added that I was the night nurse, the servant appeared to think my humble presence unworthy of illumination. He was an old negro butler, inherited perhaps from Mrs. Maradick's mother, who, I learned afterwards, was from South Carolina; and while he passed me on his way up the staircase, I heard him vaguely muttering that he "wa'n't gwinter tu'n on dem lights twel de chile had done playin'."

To the right of the hall, the soft glow drew me into the library, and crossing the threshold timidly, I stooped to dry my wet coat by the fire. As I bent there, meaning to start up at the first sound of a footstep, I thought how cosy the room was after the damp walls outside to which some bared creepers were clinging; and I was watching the strange shapes and patterns the firelight made on the old Persian rug, when the lamps of a slowly turning motor flashed on me through the white shades at the window. Still dazzled by the glare, I looked round in the dimness and saw a child's ball of red and blue rubber roll towards me out of the gloom of the adjoining room. A moment later, while I made a vain attempt to capture the toy as it spun past me, a little girl darted airily, with peculiar lightness and grace, through the doorway, and stopped quickly, as if in surprise at the sight of a stranger. She was a small child—so small and slight that her footsteps made no sound on the polished floor of the threshold; and I remember thinking while I looked at her that she had the gravest and sweetest face I had ever seen. She couldn't—I decided this afterwards—have been more than six or seven years old, yet she stood there with a curious prim dignity, like the dignity of an elderly person, and gazed up at me with enigmatical eyes. She was dressed in Scotch plaid, with a bit of red ribbon in her hair, which was cut in a fringe over her forehead and hung very straight to her shoulders. Charming as she was, from her uncurled brown hair to the white socks and black slippers on her little feet, I recall most vividly the singular look in her eyes, which appeared in the shifting light to be of an indeterminate colour. For the odd thing about this look was that it was not the look of childhood at all. It was the look of profound experience, of bitter knowledge.

"Have you come for your ball?" I asked; but while the friendly question was still on my lips, I heard the servant returning. In my confusion I made a second ineffectual grasp at the plaything, which had rolled away from me into the dusk of the drawing-room. Then, as I raised my head, I saw that the child also had slipped from the room; and without looking after her I followed the old negro into the pleasant study above, where the great surgeon awaited me.

Ten years ago, before hard nursing had taken so much out of me, I blushed very easily, and I was aware at the moment when I crossed Doctor Maradick's study that my cheeks were the colour of peonies. Of course, I was a fool—no one knows this better than I do—but I had never been alone, even for an instant, with him before, and the man was more than a hero to me, he was—there isn't any reason now why I should blush over the confession—almost a god. At that age I was mad about the wonders of surgery, and Roland Maradick in the operating-room was magician enough to have turned an older and more sensible head than mine. Added to his great reputation and his marvelous skill, he was, I am sure of this, the most splendid-looking man, even at forty-five, that one could imagine. Had he been ungracious—had he been positively rude to me, I should still have adored him; but when he held out his hand, and greeted me in the charming way he had with women, I felt that I would have died for him. It is no wonder that a saying went about the hospital that every woman he operated on fell in love with him. As for the nurses—well, there wasn't a single one of them who had escaped his spell—not even Miss Hemphill, who could have been scarcely a day under fifty.

"I am glad you could come, Miss Randolph. You were with Miss Hudson last week when I operated?"

I bowed. To save my life I couldn't have spoken without blushing the redder.

"I noticed your bright face at the time. Brightness, I think, is what Mrs. Maradick needs. She finds her day nurse depressing." His eyes rested so kindly upon me that I have suspected since that he was not entirely unaware of my worship. It was a small thing, heaven knows, to flatter his vanity—a nurse just out of a training-school—but to some men no tribute is too insignificant to give pleasure.

"You will do your best, I am sure." He hesitated an instant—just long enough for me to perceive the anxiety beneath the genial smile on his face—and then added gravely, "We wish to avoid, if possible, having to send her away."

I could only murmur in response, and after a few carefully chosen words about his wife's illness, he rang the bell and directed the maid to take me upstairs to my room. Not until I was ascending the stairs to the third storey did it occur to me that he had really told me nothing. I was as perplexed about the nature of Mrs. Maradick's malady as I had been when I entered the house.

I found my room pleasant enough. It had been arranged—at Doctor Maradick's request, I think—that I was to sleep in the house, and after my austere little bed at the hospital, I was agreeably surprised by the cheerful look at the apartment into which the maid led me. The walls were papered in roses, and there were curtains of flowered chintz at the window, which looked down on a small formal garden at the rear of the house. This the maid told me, for it was too dark for me to distinguish more than a marble fountain and a fir-tree, which looked old, though I afterwards learned that it was replanted almost every season.

In ten minutes I had slipped into my uniform and was ready to go to my patient; but for some reason—to this day I have never found out what it was that turned her against me at the start—Mrs. Maradick refused to receive me. While I stood outside her door I heard the day nurse trying to persuade her to let me come in. It wasn't any use, however, and in the end I was obliged to go back to my room and wait until the poor lady got over her whim and consented to see me. That was long after dinner—it must have been nearer eleven than ten o'clock—and Miss Peterson was quite worn out by the time she came for me.

"I'm afraid you'll have a bad night," she said as we went downstairs together. That was her way, I soon saw, to expect the worst of everything and everybody.

"Does she often keep you up like this?"

"Oh, no, she is usually very considerate. I never knew a sweeter character. But she still has this hallucination——"

Here again, as in the scene with Doctor Maradick, I felt that the explanation had only deepened the mystery. Mrs. Maradick's hallucination, whatever form it assumed, was evidently a subject for evasion and subterfuge in the household. It was on the tip of my tongue to ask, "What is her hallucination?"—but before I could get the words past my lips we had reached Mrs. Maradick's door, and Miss Peterson motioned me to be silent. As the door opened a little way to admit me, I saw that Mrs. Maradick was already in bed, and that the lights were out except for a night-lamp burning on a candle-stand beside a book and a carafe of water.

"I won't go in with you," said Miss Peterson in a whisper; and I was on the point of stepping over the threshold when I saw the little girl, in the dress of Scotch plaid, slip by me from the dusk of the room into the electric light of the hall. She held a doll in her arms, and as she went by she dropped a doll's work-basket in the doorway. Miss Peterson must have picked up the toy, for when I turned in a minute to look for it I found that it was gone. I remember thinking that it was late for a child to be up—she looked delicate, too—but, after all, it was no business of mine, and four years in a hospital had taught me never to meddle in things that do not concern me. There is nothing a nurse learns quicker than not to try to put the world to rights in a day.

When I crossed the floor to the chair by Mrs. Maradick's bed, she turned over on her side and looked at me with the sweetest and saddest smile.

"You are the night nurse," she said in a gentle voice; and from the moment she spoke I knew that there was nothing hysterical or violent about her mania—or hallucination, as they called it. "They told me your name, but I have forgotten it."

"Randolph—Margaret Randolph." I liked her from the start, and I think she must have seen it.

"You look very young, Miss Randolph."

"I am twenty-two, but I suppose I don't look quite my age. People usually think I am younger."

For a minute she was silent, and while I settled myself in the chair by the bed, I thought how strikingly she resembled the little girl I had seen first in the afternoon, and then leaving her room a few moments before. They had the same small, heart-shaped faces, coloured ever so faintly; the same straight, soft hair, between brown and flaxen; and the same large, grave eyes, set very far apart under arched eyebrows. What surprised me most, however, was that they both looked at me with that enigmatical and vaguely wondering expression— only in Mrs. Maradick's face the vagueness seemed to change now and then to a definite fear— a flash, I had almost said, of startled horror.

I sat quite still in my chair, and until the time came for Mrs. Maradick to take her medicine not a word passed between us. Then, when I bent over her with the glass in my hand, she raised her head from the pillow and said in a whisper of suppressed intensity:

"You look kind. I wonder if you could have seen my little girl?"

As I slipped my arm under the pillow I tried to smile cheerfully down on her. "Yes, I've seen her twice. I'd know her anywhere by her likeness to you."

A glow shone in her eyes, and I thought how pretty she must have been before illness took the life and animation out of her features. "Then I know you're good." Her voice was so strained and low that I could barely hear it. "If you weren't good you couldn't have seen her."

I thought this queer enough, but all I answered was, "She looked delicate to be sitting up so late."

A quiver passed over her thin features, and for a minute I thought she was going to burst into tears. As she had taken the medicine, I put the glass back on the candle-stand, and bending over the bed, smoothed the straight brown hair, which was as fine and soft as spun silk, back from her forehead. There was something about her—I don't know what it was—that made you love her as soon as she looked at you.

"She always had that light and airy way, though she was never sick a day in her life," she answered calmly after a pause. Then, groping for my hand, she whispered passionately, "You must not tell him—you must not tell any one that you have seen her!"

"I must not tell any one?" Again I had the impression that had come to me first in Doctor Maradick's study, and afterwards with Miss Peterson on the staircase, that I was seeking a gleam of light in the midst of obscurity.

"Are you sure there isn't any one listening—that there isn't any one at the door?" she asked, pushing aside my arm and raising herself on the pillows.

"Quite, quite sure. They have put out the lights in the hall."

"And you will not tell him? Promise me that you will not tell him." The startled horror flashed from the vague wonder of her expression. "He doesn't like her to come back, because he killed her."

"Because he killed her!" Then it was that light burst on me in a blaze. So this was Mrs. Maradick's hallucination! She believed that her child was dead—the little girl I had seen with my own eyes leaving her room; and she believed that her husband—the great surgeon we worshipped in the hospital—

had murdered her. No wonder they veiled the dreadful obsession in mystery! No wonder that even Miss Peterson had not dared to drag the horrid thing out into the light! It was the kind of hallucination one simply couldn't stand having to face.

"There is no use telling people things that nobody believes," she resumed slowly, still holding my hand in a grasp that would have hurt me if her fingers had not been so fragile. "Nobody believes that he killed her. Nobody believes that she comes back every day to the house. Nobody believes—and yet you saw her——"

"Yes, I saw her—but why should your husband have killed her?" I spoke soothingly, as one would speak to a person who was quite mad. Yet she was not mad, I could have sworn this while I looked at her.

For a moment she moaned inarticulately, as if the horror of her thoughts were too great to pass into speech. Then she flung out her thin, bare arm with a wild gesture.

"Because he never loved me!" she said. "He never loved me!"

"But he married you," I urged gently while I stroked her hair. "If he hadn't loved you, why should he have married you?"

"He wanted the money—my little girl's money. It all goes to him when I die."

"But he is rich himself. He must make a fortune from his profession."

"It isn't enough. He wanted millions." She had grown stern and tragic. "No, he never loved me. He loved someone else from the beginning—before I knew him."

It was quite useless, I saw, to reason with her. If she wasn't mad, she was in a state of terror and despondency so black that it had almost crossed the border-line into madness. I thought once that I would go upstairs and bring the child down from her nursery; but, after a moment's hesitation, I realized that Miss Peterson and Doctor Maradick must have long ago tried all these measures. Clearly, there was nothing to do except soothe and quiet her as much as I could; and this I did until she dropped into a light sleep which lasted well into the morning.

By seven o'clock I was worn out—not from work but from the strain on my sympathy—and I was glad, indeed, when one of the maids came in to bring me an early cup of coffee. Mrs. Maradick was still sleeping—it was a mixture of bromide and chloral I had given her—and she did not wake until Miss Peterson came on duty an hour or two later. Then, when I went downstairs, I found the dining-room deserted except for the old housekeeper, who was looking over the silver. Doctor Maradick, she explained to me presently, had his breakfast served in the morning-room on the other side of the house.

"And the little girl? Does she take her meals in the nursery?"

She threw me a startled glance. Was it, I questioned afterwards, one of distrust or apprehension?

"There isn't any little girl. Haven't you heard?"

"Heard? No. Why, I saw her only yesterday."

The look she gave me—I was sure of it now—was full of alarm.

"The little girl—she was the sweetest child I ever saw—died just two months ago of pneumonia"

"But she couldn't have died." I was a fool to let this out, but the shock had completely unnerved me. "I tell you I saw her yesterday."

The alarm in her face deepened. "That is Mrs. Maradick's trouble. She believes that she still sees her."

"But don't you see her?" I drove the question home bluntly.

"No." She set her lips tightly. "I never see anything."

So I had been wrong, after all, and the explanation, when it came, only accentuated the terror. The child was dead—she had died of pneumonia two months ago—and yet I had seen her, with my own eyes, playing ball in the library; I had seen her slipping out of her mother's room, with her doll in her arms.

"Is there another child in the house? Could there be a child belonging to one of the servants?" A gleam had shot through the fog in which I was groping.

"No, there isn't any other. The doctors tried bringing one once, but it threw the poor lady into such a state she almost died of it. Besides, there wouldn't be any other child as quiet and sweet-looking as Dorothea. To see her skipping along in her dress of Scotch plaid used to make me think of a fairy, though they say that fairies wear nothing but white or green."

"Has any one else seen her—the child, I mean—any of the servants?"

"Only old Gabriel, the coloured butler, who came with Mrs. Maradick's mother from South Carolina. I've heard that negroes often have a kind of second sight—though I don't know that that is just what you would call it. But they seem to believe in the supernatural by instinct, and Gabriel is so old and doty—he does no work except answer the door-bell and clean the silver—that nobody pays much attention to anything that he sees——"

"Is the child's nursery kept as it used to be?"

"Oh, no. The doctor had all the toys sent to the children's hospital. That was a great grief to Mrs. Maradick; but Doctor Brandon thought, and all the nurses agreed with him, that it was best for her not to be allowed to keep the room as it was when Dorothea was living."

"Dorothea? Was that the child's name?"

"Yes, it means the gift of God, doesn't it? She was named after the mother of Mrs. Maradick's first husband, Mr. Ballard. He was the grave, quiet kind— not the least like the doctor."

I wondered if the other dreadful obsession of Mrs. Maradick's had drifted down through the nurses or the servants to the housekeeper; but she said nothing about it, and since she was, I suspected, a garrulous person, I thought it wiser to assume that the gossip had not reached her.

A little later, when breakfast was over and I had not yet gone upstairs to my room, I had my first interview with Doctor Brandon, the famous alienist who was in charge of the case. I had never seen him before, but from the first moment that I looked at him I took his measure almost by intuition. He was, I suppose, honest enough—I have always granted him that, bitterly as I have felt towards him. It wasn't his fault that he lacked red blood in his brain, or that he had formed the habit, from long association with abnormal phenomena, of regarding all life as a disease. He was the sort of physician—every nurse will understand what I mean—who deals instinctively with groups instead of with individuals. He was long and solemn and very round in the face; and I hadn't talked to him ten minutes before I knew he had been educated in Germany, and that he had learned over there to treat every emotion as a pathological manifestation. I used to wonder what he got out of life—what any one got out of life who had analyzed away everything except the bare structure.

When I reached my room at last, I was so tired that I could barely remember either the questions Doctor Brandon had asked or the directions he had given me. I fell asleep, I know, almost as soon as my head touched the pillow; and the maid who came to inquire if I wanted luncheon decided to let me finish my nap. In the afternoon, when she returned with a cup of tea, she found me still heavy and drowsy. Though I was used to night nursing, I felt as if I had danced from sunset to daybreak. It was fortunate, I reflected, while I drank my tea, that every case didn't wear on one's sympathies as acutely as Mrs. Maradick's hallucination had worn on mine.

Through the day I did not see Doctor Maradick; but at seven o'clock when I came up from my early dinner on my way to take the place of Miss Peterson, who had kept on duty an hour later than usual, he met me in the hall and asked me to come into his study. I thought him handsomer than ever in his evening clothes, with a white flower in his buttonhole. He was going to some public dinner, the housekeeper told me, but, then, he was always going somewhere. I believe he didn't dine at home a single evening that winter.

"Did Mrs. Maradick have a good night?" He had closed the door after us, and turning now with the question, he smiled kindly, as if he wished to put me at ease in the beginning.

"She slept very well after she took the medicine. I gave her that at eleven o'clock."

For a minute he regarded me silently, and I was aware that his personality—his charm—was focussed upon me. It was almost as if I stood in the centre of converging rays of light, so vivid was my impression of him.

"Did she allude in any way to her—to her hallucination?" he asked.

How the warning reached me—what invisible waves of sense-perception transmitted the message—I have never known; but while I stood there, facing the splendour of the doctor's presence, every intuition cautioned me that the time had come when I must take sides in the household. While I stayed there I must stand either with Mrs. Maradick or against her.

"She talked quite rationally," I replied after a moment.

"What did she say?"

"She told me how she was feeling, that she missed her child, and that she walked a little every day about her room."

His face changed—how I could not at first determine.

"Have you seen Doctor Brandon?"

"He came this morning to give me his directions."

"He thought her less well to-day. He has advised me to send her to Rosedale."

I have never, even in secret, tried to account for Doctor Maradick. He may have been sincere. I tell you only what I know—not what I believe or imagine—and the human is sometimes as inscrutable, as inexplicable, as the supernatural.

While he watched me I was conscious of an inner struggle, as if opposing angels warred somewhere in the depths of my being. When at last I made my decision, I was acting less from reason, I knew, than in obedience to the pressure of some secret current of thought. Heaven knows, even then, the man held me captive while I defied him.

"Doctor Maradick," I lifted my eyes for the first time frankly to his, "I believe that your wife is as sane as I am—or as you are."

He started. "Then she did not talk freely to you?"

"She may be mistaken, unstrung, piteously distressed in mind"— I brought this out with emphasis—"but she is not—I am willing to stake my future on it—a fit subject for an asylum. It would be foolish—it would be cruel to send her to Rosedale."

"Cruel, you say?" A troubled look crossed his face, and his voice grew very gentle. "You do not imagine that I could be cruel to her?"

"No, I do not think that." My voice also had softened.

"We will let things go on as they are. Perhaps Doctor Brandon may have some other suggestion to make." He drew out his watch and compared it with the clock—nervously, I observed, as if his action were a screen for his discomfiture or perplexity. "I must be going now. We will speak of this again in the morning."

But in the morning we did not speak of it, and during the month that I nursed Mrs. Maradick I was not called again into her husband's study. When I met him in the hall or on the staircase, which was seldom, he was as charming as ever; yet, in spite of his courtesy, I had a persistent feeling that he had taken my measure on that evening, and that he had no further use for me.

As the days went by Mrs. Maradick seemed to grow stronger. Never, after our first night together, had she mentioned the child to me; never had she alluded by so much as a word to her dreadful charge against her husband. She was like any woman recovering from a great sorrow, except that she was sweeter and gentler. It is no wonder that everyone who came near her loved her; for there was a mysterious loveliness about her like the mystery of light, not of darkness. She was, I have always thought, as much of an angel as it is possible for a woman to be on this earth. And yet, angelic as she was, there were times when it seemed to me that she both hated and feared her husband. Though he never entered her room while I was there, and I never heard his name on her lips until an hour before the end, still I could tell by the look of terror in her face whenever his step passed down the hall that her very soul shivered at his approach.

During the whole month I did not see the child again, though one night, when I came suddenly into Mrs. Maradick's room, I found a little garden, such as children make out of pebbles and bits of box, on the window-sill. I did not mention it to Mrs. Maradick, and a little later, as the maid lowered the shades, I noticed that the garden had vanished. Since then I have often wondered if the child were invisible only to the rest of us, and if her mother still saw her. But there was no way of finding out except by questioning, and Mrs. Maradick was so well and patient that I hadn't the heart to question. Things couldn't have been better with her than they were, and I was beginning to tell myself that she might soon go out for an airing, when the end came so suddenly.

It was a mild January day—the kind of day that brings the foretaste of spring in the middle of winter, and when I came downstairs in the afternoon, I stopped a minute by the window at the end of the hall to look down on the box maze in the garden. There was an old fountain, bearing two laughing boys in marble, in the centre of the gravelled walk, and the water, which had been turned on that morning for Mrs. Maradick's pleasure, sparkled now like silver as the sunlight splashed over it. I had never before felt the air quite so soft and springlike in January; and I thought, as I gazed down on the garden, that it would be a good idea for Mrs. Maradick to go out and bask for an hour or so in the sunshine. It seemed strange to me that she was never allowed to get any fresh air except the air that came through her windows.

When I went into her room, however, I found that she had no wish to go out. She was sitting, wrapped in shawls, by the open window, which looked down on the fountain; and as I entered she glanced up from a little book she was reading. A pot of daffodils stood on the window-sill—she was very fond of flowers and we tried always to keep some growing in her room.

"Do you know what I am reading. Miss Randolph?" she asked in her soft voice; and she read aloud a verse while I went over to the candle-stand to measure out a dose of medicine.

" 'If thou hast two loaves of bread, sell one and buy daffodils, for bread nourisheth the body, but daffodils delight the soul. That is very beautiful, don't you think so?"

I said "Yes," that it was beautiful; and then I asked her if she wouldn't go downstairs and walk about in the garden.

"He wouldn't like it," she answered; and it was the first time she had mentioned her husband to me since the night I came to her. "He doesn't want me to go out."

I tried to laugh her out of the idea; but it was no use, and after a few minutes I gave up and began talking of other things. Even then it did not occur to me that her fear of Doctor Maradick was anything but a fancy. I could see, of course, that she wasn't out of her head; but sane persons, I knew, sometimes have unaccountable prejudices, and I accepted her dislike as a mere whim or aversion. I did not understand then and—I may as well confess this before the end comes—I do not understand any better to-day. I am writing down the things I actually saw, and I repeat that I have never had the slightest twist in the direction of the miraculous.

The afternoon slipped away while we talked—she talked brightly when any subject came up that interested her—and it was the last hour of day—that grave, still hour when the movement of life seems to droop and falter for a few precious minutes—that brought us the thing I had dreaded silently since my first night in the house. I remember that I had risen to close the window, and was leaning out for a breath of the mild air, when there was the sound of steps, consciously softened, in the hall outside, and Doctor Brandon's usual knock fell on my ears. Then, before I could cross the room, the door opened, and the doctor entered with Miss Peterson. The day nurse, I knew, was a stupid woman; but she had never appeared to me so stupid, so armoured and encased in her professional manner, as she did at that moment.

"I am glad to see that you arc taking the air." As Doctor Brandon came over to the window, I wondered maliciously what devil of contradictions had made him a distinguished specialist in nervous diseases.

"Who was the other doctor you brought this morning?" asked Mrs. Maradick gravely; and that was all I ever heard about the visit of the second alienist.

"Someone who is anxious to cure you."He dropped into a chair beside her and patted her hand with his long, pale fingers. "We are so anxious to cure you that we want to send you away to the country for a fortnight or so. Miss Peterson has come to help you to get ready, and I've kept my car waiting for you. There couldn't be a nicer day for a trip, could there?"

The moment had come at last. I knew at once what he meant, and so did Mrs. Maradick. A wave of colour flowed and ebbed in her thin cheeks, and I felt her body quiver when I moved from the window and put my arms on her shoulders. I was aware again, as I had been aware that evening in Doctor Maradick's study, of a current of thought that beat from the air around into my brain. Though it cost me my career as a nurse and my reputation for sanity, I knew that I must obey that invisible warning.

"You are going to take me to an asylum," said Mrs. Maradick.

He made some foolish denial or evasion; but before he had finished I turned from Mrs. Maradick and faced him impulsively. In a nurse this was flagrant rebellion, and I realized that the act wrecked my professional future. Yet I did not care—I did not hesitate. Something stronger than I was driving me on.

"Doctor Brandon," I said, "I beg you—I implore you to wait until tomorrow. There arc things I must tell you."

A queer look came into his face, and I understood, even in my excitement, that he was mentally deciding in which group he should place me—to which class of morbid manifestations I must belong.

"Very well, very well, we will hear everything," he replied soothingly; but I saw him glance at Miss Peterson, and she went over to the wardrobe for Mrs. Maradick's fur coat and hat

Suddenly, without warning, Mrs. Maradick threw the shawls away from her, and stood up. "If you send me away," she said, "I shall never come back. I shall never live to come back."

The grey of twilight was just beginning, and while she stood there, in the dusk of the room, her face shone out as pale and flower-like as the daffodils on the window-sill. "I cannot go away!" she cried in a sharper voice. "I cannot go away from my child!"

I saw her face clearly; I heard her voice; and then—the horror of the scene sweeps back over me!—I saw the door open slowly and the little girl run across the room to her mother. I saw the child lift her little arms, and I saw the mother stoop and gather her to her bosom. So closely locked were they in that passionate embrace that their forms seemed to mingle in the gloom that enveloped them.

"After this can you doubt?" I threw out the words almost savagely— and then, when I turned from the mother and child to Doctor Brandon and Miss Peterson, I knew breathlessly—oh, there was a shock in the discovery!—that they were blind to the child. Their blank faces revealed the consternation of ignorance, not of conviction. They had seen nothing except the vacant arms of the mother and the swift, erratic gesture with which she stooped to embrace some invisible presence. Only my vision— and I have asked myself since if the power of sympathy enabled me to penetrate the web of material fact and see the spiritual form of the child—only my vision was not blinded by the clay through which I looked.

"After this can you doubt?" Doctor Brandon had flung my words back to me. Was it his fault, poor man, if life had granted him only the eyes of flesh? Was it his fault if he could sec only half of the thing there before him?

But they couldn't see, and since they couldn't see I realized that it was useless to tell them. Within an hour they took Mrs. Maradick to the asylum; and she went quietly, though when the time came for parting from me she showed some faint trace of feeling. I remember that at the last, while we stood on the pavement, she lifted her black veil, which she wore for the child, and said: "Stay with her, Miss Randolph, as long as you can. I shall never come back."

Then she got into the car and was driven off, while I stood looking after her with a sob in my throat. Dreadful as I felt it to be, I didn't, of course, realize the full horror of it, or I couldn't have stood there quietly on the pavement. I didn't realize it, indeed, until several months afterwards when word came that she had died in the asylum. I never knew what her illness was, though I vaguely recall that something was said about "heart failure"—a loose enough term. My own belief is that she died simply of the terror of life.

To my surprise Doctor Maradick asked me to stay on as his office nurse after his wife went to Rosedale; and when the news of her death came there was no suggestion of my leaving. I don't know to this day why he wanted me in the house. Perhaps he thought I should have less opportunity to gossip if I stayed under his roof; perhaps he still wished to test the power of his charm over me. His vanity was incredible in so great a man. I have seen him flush with pleasure when people turned to look at him in the street, and I know that he was not above playing on the sentimental weakness of his patients. But he was magnificent, heaven knows! Few men, I imagine, have been the objects of so many foolish infatuations.

The next summer Doctor Maradick went abroad for two months, and while he was away I took my vacation in Virginia. When we came back the work was heavier than ever—his reputation by this time was tremendous—and my days were so crowded with appointments, and hurried flittings to emergency cases, that I had scarcely a minute left in which to remember poor Mrs. Maradick. Since the afternoon when she went to the asylum the child had not been in the house; and at last I was beginning to persuade myself that the little figure had been an optical illusion—the effect of shifting lights in the gloom of the old rooms—not the apparition I had once believed it to be. It does not take long for a phantom to fade from the memory—especially when one leads the active and methodical life I was forced into that winter. Perhaps— who knows?—(I remember telling myself) the doctors may have been right, after all, and the poor lady may have actually been out of her mind. With this view of the past, my judgment of Doctor Maradick insensibly altered. It ended, I think, in my acquitting him altogether. And then, just as he stood clear and splendid in my verdict of him, the reversal came so precipitately that I grow breathless now whenever I try to live it over again. The violence of the next turn in affairs left me, I often fancy, with a perpetual dizziness of the imagination.

It was in May that we heard of Mrs. Maradick's death, and exactly a year later, on a mild and fragrant afternoon, when the daffodils were blooming in patches around the old fountain in the garden, the housekeeper came into the office, where I lingered over some accounts, to bring me news of the doctor's approaching marriage.

"It is no more than we might have expected," she concluded rationally. "The house must be lonely for him—he is such a sociable man. But I can't help feeling," she brought out slowly after a pause in which I felt a shiver pass over me, "I can't help feeling that it is hard for that other woman to have all the money poor Mrs. Maradick's first husband left her."

"There is a great deal of money, then?" I asked curiously.

"A great deal." She waved her hand, as if words were futile to express the sum. "Millions and millions!"

"They will give up this house, of course?"

"That's done already, my dear. There won't be a brick left of it by this time next year. It's to be pulled down and an apartment-house built on the ground."

Again the shiver passed over me. I couldn't bear to think of Mrs. Maradick's old home falling to pieces.

"You didn't tell me the name of the bride," I said, "Is she someone he met while he was in Europe?"

"Dear me, no! She is the very lady he was engaged to before he married Mrs. Maradick, only she threw him over, so people said, because he wasn't rich enough. Then she married some lord or prince from over the water; but there was a divorce, and now she has turned again to her old lover. He is rich enough now, I guess, even for her!"

It was all perfectly true, I suppose; it sounded as plausible as a story out of a newspaper; and yet while she told me I felt, or dreamed that I felt, a sinister, an impalpable hush in the air. I was nervous, no doubt; I was shaken by the suddenness with which the housekeeper had sprung her news on me; but as I sat there I had quite vividly an impression that the old house was listening—that there was a real, if invisible, presence somewhere in the room or the garden. Yet, when an instant afterwards I glanced through the long window which opened down to the brick terrace, I saw only the faint sunshine over the deserted garden, with its maze of box, its marble fountain, and its patches of daffodils.

The housekeeper had gone—one of the servants, I think, came for her—and I was sitting at my desk when the words of Mrs. Maradick on that last evening floated into my mind. The daffodils brought her back to me; for I thought, as I watched them growing, so still and golden in the sunshine, how she would have enjoyed them. Almost unconsciously I repeated the verse she had read to me:

"If thou hast two loaves of bread, sell one and buy daffodils"—and it was at this very instant, while the words were still on my lips, that I turned my eyes to the box maze, and saw the child skipping rope along the gravelled path to the fountain. Quite distinctly, as clear as day, I saw her come, with what children call the dancing step, between the low box borders to the place where the daffodils bloomed by the fountain. From her straight brown hair to her frock of Scotch plaid and her little feet, which twinkled in white socks and black slippers over the turning rope, she was as real to me as the ground on which she trod or the laughing marble boys under the splashing water. Starting up from my chair, I made a single step to the terrace. If I could only reach her—only speak to her—I felt that I might at last solve the mystery. But with the first flutter of my dress on the terrace, the airy little form melted into the quiet dusk of the maze. Not a breath stirred the daffodils, not a shadow passed over the sparkling flow of the water; yet, weak and shaken in every nerve, I sat down on the brick step of the terrace and burst into tears. I must have known that something terrible would happen before they pulled down Mrs. Maradick's home.

The doctor dined out that night. He was with the lady he was going to marry, the housekeeper told me; and it must have been almost midnight when I heard him come in and go upstairs to his room. I was downstairs because I had been unable to sleep, and the book I wanted to finish I had left that afternoon in the office. The book—I can't remember what it was—had seemed to me very exciting when I began it in the morning; but after the visit of the child I found the romantic novel as dull as a treatise on nursing. It was impossible for me to follow the lines, and I was on the point of giving up and going to bed when Doctor Maradick opened the front door with his latch-key and went up the staircase. "There can't be a bit of truth in it" I thought over and over again as I listened to his even step ascending the stairs. "There can't be a bit of truth in it." And yet, though I assured myself that "there couldn't be a bit of truth in it," I shrank, with a creepy sensation, from *going* through the house to my room in the third storey. I was tired out after a hard day, and my nerves must have reacted morbidly to the silence and the darkness. For the first time in my life I knew what it was to be afraid of the unknown, of the unseen; and while I bent over my book, in the glare of the electric light, I became conscious presently that I was straining my senses for some sound in the spacious emptiness of the rooms overhead. The noise of a passing motor-car in the street jerked me back from the intense hush of expectancy; and I can recall the wave of relief that swept over me as I turned to my book again and tried to fix my distracted mind on its pages.

I was still sitting there when the telephone on my desk rang, with what seemed to my overwrought nerves a startling abruptness, and the voice of the superintendent told me hurriedly that Doctor Maradick was needed at the hospital. I had become so accustomed to these emergency calls in the night that I felt reassured when I had rung up the doctor in his room and had heard the hearty sound of his response. He had not yet undressed, he said, and would come down immediately while I ordered back his car, which must just have reached the garage.

"I'll be with you in five minutes!" he called as cheerfully as if I had summoned him to his wedding.

I heard him cross the floor of his room; and before he could reach the head of the staircase, I opened the door and went out into the hall in order that I might turn on the light and have his hat and coat waiting. The electric button was at the end of the hall, and as I moved towards it, guided by the glimmer that fell from the landing above, I lifted my eyes to the staircase, which climbed dimly, with its slender mahogany balustrade, as far as the third storey.

Then it was, at the very moment when the doctor, humming gaily, began his quick descent of the steps, that I distinctly saw—I will swear to this on my deathbed—a child's skipping rope lying loosely coiled, as if it had dropped from a careless little hand, in the bend of the staircase. With a spring I had reached the electric button, flooding the hall with light; but as I did so, while my arm was still outstretched behind me, I heard the humming voice change to a cry of surprise or terror, and the figure on the staircase tripped heavily and stumbled with groping hands into emptiness. The scream of warning died in my throat while I watched him pitch forward down the long flight of stairs to the floor at my feet. Even before I bent over him, before I wiped the blood from his brow and felt for his silent heart, I knew that he was dead.

Something—it may have been, as the world believes, a misstep in the dimness, or it may have been, as I am ready to bear witness, an invisible judgment—something had killed him at the very moment when he most wanted to live.

SCOURED SILK

Marjorie Bowen

This is a tale that might be told in many ways and from various points of view; it has to be gathered from here and there—a letter, a report, a diary, a casual reference; in its day the thing was more than a passing wonder, and it left a mark of abiding horror on the neighborhood.

The house in which Mr. Orford lived has finally been destroyed, the mural tablet in St. Paul's, Covent Garden, may be sought for in vain by the curious, but little remains of the old piazza where the quiet scholar passed on his daily walks, the very records of what was once so real have become blurred, almost incoherent in their pleadings with things forgotten; but this thing happened to real people, in a real London, not so long ago that the generation had not spoken with those who remembered some of the actors in this terrible drama.

It is round the person of Humphrey Orford that this tale turns, as, at the time, all the mystery and horror centered; yet until his personality was brought thus tragically into fame, he had not been an object of much interest to many; he had, perhaps, a mild reputation for eccentricity, but this was founded merely on the fact that he refused to partake of the amusements of his neighbors, and showed a dislike for much company.

But this was excused on the ground of his scholarly predilections; he was known to be translating, in a leisurely fashion, as became a gentleman, Ariosto's great romance into English couplets, and to be writing essays on recondite subjects connected with grammar and language, which were not the less esteemed because they had never been published.

His most authentic portrait, taken in 1733 and intended for a frontispiece for the Ariosto when this should come to print, shows a slender man with reddish hair, rather severely clubbed, a brown coat, and a muslin cravat; he looks straight out of the picture, and the face is long, finely shaped, and refined, with eyebrows rather heavier than one would expect from such delicacy of feature.

When this picture was painted Mr. Orford was living near Covent Garden, close to the mansion once occupied by the famous Dr. Radcliffe, a straight-fronted, dark house of obvious gentility, with a little architrave portico over the

219

door and a few steps leading up to it; a house with neat windows and a gloomy air, like every other residence in that street and most other streets of the same status in London.

And if there was nothing remarkable about Mr. Orford's dwelling place or person there was nothing, as far as his neighbors knew, remarkable about his history.

He came from a good Suffolk family, in which county he was believed to have considerable estates (though it was a known fact that he never visited them), and he had no relations, being the only child of an only child, and his parents dead; his father had purchased this town house in the reign of King William, when the neighborhood was very fashionable, and up to it he had come, twenty years ago—nor had he left it since.

He had brought with him an ailing wife, a house-keeper, and a man-servant, and to the few families of his acquaintance near, who waited on him, he explained that he wished to give young Mrs. Orford, who was of a mopish disposition, the diversion of a few months in town.

But soon there was no longer this motive for remaining in London, for the wife, hardly seen by anyone, fell into a short illness and died— just a few weeks after her husband had brought her up from Suffolk. She was buried very simply in St. Paul's, and the mural tablet set up with a draped urn in marble, and just her name and the date, ran thus:

> FLORA, WIFE OF HUMPHREY ORFORD, ESQ.,
> OF THIS PARISH,
> DIED NOVEMBER, 1713, AGED 27 YEARS.

Mr. Orford made no effort to leave the house; he remained, people thought, rather stunned by his loss, kept himself close in the house, and for a considerable time wore deep mourning.

But this was twenty years ago, and all had forgotten the shadowy figure of the young wife, whom so few had seen and whom no one had known anything about or been interested in, and all trace of her seemed to have passed out of the quiet, regular, and easy life of Mr. Orford, when an event that gave rise to some gossip caused the one-time existence of Flora Orford to be recalled and discussed among the curious. This event was none other than the sudden betrothal of Mr. Orford and the announcement of his almost immediate marriage.

The bride was one who had been a prattling child when the groom had first come to London: one old lady who was forever at her window watching the little humors of the street recollected and related how she had seen Flora

Orford, alighting from the coach that had brought her from the country, turn to this child, who was gazing from the railing of the neighboring house, and touch her bare curls lovingly and yet with a sad gesture.

And that was about the only time anyone ever did see Flora Orford, she so soon became ailing; and the next the inquisitive old lady saw of her was the slender brown coffin being carried through the dusk towards St. Paul's Church.

But that was twenty years ago, and here was the baby grown up into Miss Elisa Minden, a very personable young woman, soon to be the second Mrs. Humphrey Orford. Of course there was nothing very remarkable about the match; Elisa's father, Dr. Minden, had been Mr. Orford's best friend (as far as he could be said to have a best friend, or indeed any friend at all) for many a long year, both belonged to the same quiet set, both knew all about each other. Mr. Orford was not much above forty-five or so, an elegant, well-looking man, wealthy, with no vices and a calm, equable temper; while Miss Elisa, though pretty and well-mannered, had an insufficient dowry, no mother to fend for her, and the younger sisters to share her slender advantages. So what could anyone say save that the good doctor had done very well for his daughter, and that Mr. Orford had been fortunate enough to secure such a fresh, capable maiden for his wife?

It was said that the scholar intended giving up his bookish ways— that he even spoke of going abroad a while, to Italy, for preference; he was of course, anxious to see Italy, as all his life had been devoted to preparing the translation of an Italian classic.

The quiet betrothal was nearing its decorous conclusion when one day Mr. Orford took Miss Minden for a walk and brought her home round the piazza of Covent Garden, then took her across the cobbled street, past the stalls banked up with the first spring flowers (it was the end of March), under the portico built by the great Inigo Jones, and so into the church.

"I want to show you where my wife Flora lies buried," said Mr. Orford.

And that is really the beginning of the story.

Now, Miss Minden had been in this church every Sunday of her life and many weekdays, and had been used since a child to see that tablet to Flora Orford; but when she heard these words in the quiet voice of her lover and felt him draw her out of the sunlight into the darkness of the church, she experienced a great distaste that was almost fear.

It seemed to her both a curious and a disagreeable thing for him to do, and she slipped her arm out of his as she replied.

"Oh, please let us go home!" she said. "Father will be waiting for us, and your good Mrs. Boyd vexed if the tea is over-brewed."

"But first I must show this," he insisted, and took her arm again and led her down the church, past his seat, until they stood between his pew end and the marble tablet in the wall which was just a hand's space above their heads.

"That is to her memory," said Mr. Orford. "And you see there is nothing said as to her virtues."

Now, Elisa Minden knew absolutely nothing of her predecessor, and could not tell if these words were spoken in reverence or irony, so she said nothing but looked up rather timidly from under the shade of her Leghorn straw at the tall figure of her lover, who was staring sternly at the square of marble.

"And what have you to say to Flora Orford?" he asked sharply, looking down at her quickly.

"Why, sir, she was a stranger to me," replied Miss Minden.

Mr. Orford pressed her arm.

"But to me she was a wife," he said. "She is buried under your feet. Quite close to where you are standing. Why, think of that, Lizzie, if she could stand up and put out her hand she could catch hold of your dress—she is as near as that!"

The words and his manner of saying them filled Miss Minden with shuddering terror, for she was a sensitive and fanciful girl, and it seemed to her a dreadful thing to be thus standing over the bones of the poor creature who had loved the man who was now to be her husband, and horrible to think that the handful of decay so near them had once clung to this man and loved him.

"Do not tremble, my dear girl," said Mr. Orford. "She is dead."

Tears were in Elisa Minden's eyes, and she answered coldly;

"Sir, how can you speak so?"

"She was a wicked woman," he replied, "a very wicked woman."

The girl could not reply as to that; this sudden disclosing of a painful secret abashed her simple mind.

"Need we talk of this? "she asked; then, under her breath—"Need we be married in this church, sir?"

"Of course," he answered shortly, "everything is arranged. Tomorrow week."

Miss Minden did not respond; hitherto she had been fond of the church, now it seemed spoilt for her—tarnished by the thought of Flora Orford.

Her companion seemed to divine what reflection lay behind her silence.

"You need not be afraid," he said rather harshly. "She is dead. Dead."

And he reached out the light cane he wore and tapped on the stone above his wife's grave, and slowly smiled as the sound rang hollow in the vaults beneath.

Then he allowed Elisa to draw him away, and they returned to Mr. Orford's comfortable house, where in the upper parlor Dr. Minden was awaiting them together with his sister and her son, a soldier cousin whom the quick perceptions of youthful friends had believed to be devoted to Elisa Minden. They made a pleasant little party with the red curtains drawn, and the fire burning up between the polished andirons and all the service for tea laid out with scones and Naples cake, and Mrs. Boyd coming to and fro with plates and dishes. And everyone was cheerful and friendly and glad to be indoors together, with a snowstorm coming up and people hurrying home with heads bent before a cutting wind.

But to Elisa's mind had come an unbidden thought:

"I do not like this house—it is where Flora Orford died."

And she wondered in which room, and also why this had never occurred to her before, and glanced rather thoughtfully at the fresh young face of the soldier cousin as he stood by the fire in his scarlet and white, with his glance on the flames.

But it was a cheerful party, and Elisa smiled and jested with the rest as she reserved the dishes at tea.

There is a miniature of her painted about this time, and one may see how she looked with her bright brown hair and bright brown eyes, rosy complexion, pretty nose and mouth, and her best gown of lavender blue tabinet with a lawn tucker and a lawn cap fastened under the chin with frilled lappets, showing now the big Leghorn hat with the velvet strings was put aside.

Mr. Orford also looked well tonight; he did not look his full age in the ruddy candle glow, the grey did not show in his abundant hair nor the lines in his fine face, but the elegance of his figure, the grace of his bearing, the richness of his simple clothes, were displayed to full advantage; Captain Hoare looked stiff and almost clumsy by contrast.

But now and then Elisa Minden's eyes would rest rather wistfully on the fresh face of this young man who had no dead wife in his life. And something was roused in her meek youth and passive innocence, and she wondered why she had so quietly accepted her father's arrangement of a marriage with this elderly scholar, and why Philip Hoare had let her do it. Her thoughts were quite vague and amounted to no more than a confused sense that something was wrong, but she lost her satisfaction in the tea-drinking and the pleasant company, and the warm room with the drawn curtains, and the bright fire, and rose up saying they must be returning, as there was a great store of mending she had promised to help her aunt with; but Mrs. Hoare would not help her out, but protested, laughing, that there was time enough for that, and the good doctor, who was in a fine humor and in no mood to go out into the bleak streets even as far as his own door, declared that now was the time they must be shown over the house.

"Do you know, Humphrey," he said, "you have often promised us this, but never done it, and, all the years that I have known you, I have never seen but this room and the dining-room below; and as to your own particular cabinet——"

"Well," said Mr. Orford, interrupting in a leisurely fashion, "no one has been in there, save Mrs. Boyd now and then, to announce a visitor."

"Oh, you scholars!" smiled the doctor. "A secretive tribe—and a fortunate one; why, in my poor room I have had three girls running to and fro!"

The soldier spoke, not so pleasantly as his uncle.

"What have you so mysterious, sir, in this same cabinet, that it must be so jealously guarded?" he asked.

"Why, nothing mysterious," smiled the scholar; "only my books, and papers, and pictures."

"You will show them to me?" asked Elisa Minden, and her lover gave graceful consent; there was further amiable talk, and then the whole party, guided by Mr. Orford holding a candle, made a tour of the house and looked over the fine rooms.

Mrs. Hoare took occasion to whisper to the bride-to-be that there were many alterations needed before the place was ready for a lady's use, and that it was time these were put in hand—why, the wedding was less than a fortnight off!

And Elisa Minden, who had not had a mother to advise her in these matters, suddenly felt that the house was dreary and old-fashioned, and an impossible place to live in; the very rooms that had so pleased her good father—a set of apartments for a lady—were to her the most hateful in the house, for they, her lover told her, had been furnished and prepared for Flora Orford, twenty years ago.

She was telling herself that when she was married she must at once go away and that the house must be altered before she could return to it, when the party came crowding to the threshold of the library or private cabinet, and Mr. Orford, holding the candle aloft, led them in. Then as this illumination was not sufficient, he went very quickly and lit the two candles on the mantelpiece.

It was a pleasant apartment, lined with books from floor to ceiling, old, valuable, and richly bound books, save only in the space above the chimney piece, which was occupied by a portrait of a lady and the panel behind the desk; this was situated in a strange position, in the farthest corner of the room fronting the wall, so that anyone seated there would be facing the door with the space of the room between; the desk was quite close to the wall, so that there was only just space for the chair at which the writer would sit, and to accommodate this there were no bookshelves behind it, but a smooth panel of wood on which hung a small picture; this was a rough, dark painting, and represented a man hanging on a gallows on a wild heath; it was a subject out of keeping with the luxurious room with its air of ease and learning, and while Mr. Orford was showing his first editions, his Elzevirs and Aldines, Elisa Minden was staring at this ugly little picture.

As she looked she was conscious of such a chill of horror and dismay as nearly caused her to shriek aloud. The room seemed to her to be full of an atmosphere of terror and evil beyond expression.

Never had such a thing happened to her before; her visit to the tomb in the afternoon had been as nothing to this. She moved away, barely able to disguise an open panic. As she turned, she half-stumbled against a chair, caught at it, and noticed, hanging over the back, a skirt of peach-colored silk. Elisa, not being mistress of herself, caught at this garment.

"Why, sir," cried she hysterically, "what is this?" All turned to look at her; her tone, her obvious fright, were out of proportion to her discovery.

"Why, child," said Mrs. Hoare, "it is a silk petticoat, as all can see."

"A gift for you, my dear," said the cheerful doctor.

"A gift for me?" cried Elisa. "Why, this has been scoured, and turned, and mended, and patched a hundred times!"

And she held up the skirt, which had indeed become like tinder and seemed ready to drop to pieces.

The scholar now spoke.

"It belongs to Mrs. Boyd," he said quietly. "I suppose she had been in here to clean up, and has left some of her mending."

Now, two things about this speech made a strange impression on everyone; first, it was manifestly impossible that the good housekeeper would ever have owned such a garment as this, that was a lady's dress and such as would be worn for a ball; secondly, Mr. Orford had only a short while before declared that Mrs. Boyd only entered his room when he was in it, and then of a necessity and for a few minutes.

All had the same impression, that this was some garment belonging to his dead wife and as such cherished by him; all, that is, but Elisa, who had heard him call Flora Orford a wicked woman.

She put the silk down quickly (there was a needle sticking into it and a spool of cotton lying on the chair beneath) and looked up at the portrait above the mantelpiece.

"Is that Mrs. Orford?" she asked.

He gave her a queer look.

"Yes," he said.

In a strange silence all glanced up at the picture.

It showed a young woman in a white gown, holding a crystal heart that hung round her neck; she had dark hair and a pretty face; as Elisa looked at the pointed fingers holding the pretty toy, she thought of the tablet in St. Paul's Church and Mr. Orford's words—"She is so near to you that if she could stretch out her hand she could touch you," and without any remark about the portrait or the sitter, she advised her aunt that it was time to go home. So the four of them left, and Mr. Orford saw them out, standing framed in the warm light of the corridor and watching them disappear into the grey darkness of the street.

It was a little more than an hour afterwards when Elisa Minden came creeping down the stairway of her home and accosted her cousin, who was just leaving the house.

"Oh, Philip," said she, clasping her hands, "if your errand be not a very important one, I beg you to give me an hour of your time. I have been watching for you to go out, that I might follow and speak to you privately."

The young soldier looked at her keenly as she stood in the light of the hall lamp, and he saw that she was very agitated.

"Of course, Lizzie," he answered kindly, and led her into the little parlor off the hall where there was neither candles or fire, but leisure and quiet to talk.

Elisa, being a housekeeper, found a lamp and lit it, and apologized for the cold, but she would not return upstairs, she said, for Mrs. Hoare and the two girls and the doctor were all quiet in the great parlor, and she had no mind to disturb them.

"You are in trouble," said Captain Hoare quietly.

"Yes," replied she in a frightened way, "I want you to come with me now to Mr. Orford's house—I want to speak to his housekeeper."

"Why, what is this, Lizzie?"

She had no very good explanation; there was only the visit to the church that afternoon, her impression of horror in the cabinet, the discovery of the scoured silk.

"But I must know something of his first wife, Philip," she concluded. "I could never go on with it—if I did not—something has happened today—I hate that house, I almost hate—him."

"Why did you do it, Lizzie?" demanded the young soldier sternly. "This was a nice homecoming for me ... a man who might be your father ... a solitary ... one who frightens you."

Miss Minden stared at her cousin; she did not know why she had done it; the whole thing seemed suddenly impossible.

"Please, you must come with me now," she said.

So overwrought was she that he had no heart to refuse her, and they took their warm cloaks from the hall and went out into the dark streets.

It was snowing now and the ground slippery under foot, and Elisa clung to her cousin's arm. She did not want to see Mr. Orford or his house ever again, and by the time they reached the doorstep she was in a tremble; but she rang the bell boldly.

It was Mrs. Boyd herself who came to the door; she began explaining that the master was shut up in his cabinet, but the soldier cut her short.

"Miss Minden wishes to see you," he said, "and I will wait in the hall till she is ready."

So Elisa followed the housekeeper down to her basement sitting-room; the man-servant was out, and the two maids were quickly dismissed to the kitchen.

Mrs. Boyd, a placid soul, near seventy-years, waited for the young lady to explain herself, and Elisa Minden, flushing and paling by turns, and feeling foolish and timid, put forth the object of her coming.

She wanted to hear the story of Flora Orford—there was no one else whom she could ask—and she thought that she had a right to know.

"And I suppose you have, my dear," said Mrs. Boyd, gazing into the fire, "though it is not a pretty story for you to hear—and I never thought I should be telling it to Mr. Orford's second wife!"

"Not his wife yet." said Miss Minden.

"There, there, you had better ask the master yourself," replied Mrs. Boyd placidly; "not but that he would be fierce at your speaking of it, for I do not think a mention of it has passed his lips, and it's twenty years ago and best forgotten, my dear."

"Tell it to me and then I will forget," begged Miss Minden.

So then Mrs. Boyd, who was a quiet, harmless soul with no dislike to telling a tale (though no gossip, as events had proved, she having kept her tongue still on this matter for so long), told her story of Humphrey Orford's wife; it was told in very few words.

"She was the daughter of his gamekeeper, my dear, and he married her out of hand, just for her pretty face. But they were not very happy together that I could ever see; she was afraid of him and that made her cringe, and he hated that, and she shamed him with her ignorant ways. And then one day he found her with a lover, saving your presence, mistress, one of her own people, just a common man. And he was just like a creature possessed; he shut up the house and sent away all the servants but me, and brought his lady up to town, to this house here. And what passed between her and him no one will know, but she ever looked like one dying of terror. And then the doctor began to come, Dr.

Thursby, it was, that is dead now, and then she died, and no one was able to see her even she was in her coffin, nor to send a flower. 'Tis likely she died of grief, poor, fond wretch. But, of course, she was a wicked woman, and there was nothing to do but pity the master."

And this was the story of Flora Orford.

"And the man?" asked Miss Minden, after a little.

"The man she loved, my dear? Well, Mr. Orford had him arrested as a thief for breaking into his house, he was wild, that fellow, with not the best of characters—well, he would not say why he was in the house, and Mr. Orford, being a Justice of the Peace, had some power, so he was just condemned as a common thief. And there are few to this day know the truth of the tale, for he kept his counsel to the last, and no one knew from him why he had been found in the Squire's house."

"What was his end?" asked Miss Minden in a still voice.

"Well he was hanged," said Mrs. Boyd; "being caught red-handed, what could he hope for?"

"Then that is a picture of him in the cabinet!" cried Elisa, shivering for all the great fire; then she added desperately, "Tell me, did Flora Orford die in that cabinet?"

"Oh, no, my dear, but in a great room at the back of the house that has been shut up ever since."

"But the cabinet is horrible," said Elisa; "perhaps it is her portrait and that picture."

"I have hardly been in there," admitted Mrs. Boyd, "but the master lives there—he has always had his supper there, and he talks to that portrait my dear—'Flora, Flora' he says, 'how are you tonight?' and then he imitates her voice, answering."

Elisa Minden clapped her hand to her heart.

"Do not tell me these things or I shall think that you are hateful too, to have stayed in this dreadful house and endured them!"

Mrs. Boyd was surprised.

"Now, my dear, do not be put out," she protested.

"They were wicked people both of them and got their deserts, and it is an old story best forgotten; and as for the master, he has been just a good creature ever since we have been here, and he will not go talking to any picture when he has a sweet young wife to keep him company."

But Elisa Minden had risen and had her fingers on the handle of the door.

"One thing more," said she breathlessly; "that scoured silk—of a peach color——"

"Why, has he got that still? Mrs. Orford wore it the night he found her with her sweetheart. I mind I was with her when she bought it—fine silk at forty shillings the yard. If I were you, my dear, I should burn that when I was mistress here."

But Miss Minden had run upstairs to the cold hall.

Her cousin was not there; she heard angry voices overhead and saw the two maid-servants affrighted on the stairs; a disturbance was unknown in this household.

While Elisa stood bewildered, a door banged, and Captain Hoare came down red in the face and fuming; he caught his cousin's arm and hurried her out of the house.

In an angry voice he told her of the unwarrantable behavior of Mr. Orford, who had found him in the hall and called him "intruder" and "spy" without waiting for an explanation; the soldier had followed the scholar up to his cabinet and there had been an angry scene about nothing at all, as Captain Hoare said.

"Oh, Philip," broke out poor Elisa as they hastened through the cold darkness, "I can never, never marry him!"

And she told him the story of Flora Orford. The young man pressed her arm through the heavy cloak.

"And how came such a one to entangle thee?" he asked tenderly. "Nay, thou shalt not marry him."

They spoke no more, but Elisa, happy in the protecting and wholesome presence of her kinsman, sobbed with a sense of relief and gratitude. When they reached home they found they had been missed and there had to be explanations; Elisa said there was something that she had wished to say to Mrs. Boyd, and Philip told of Mr. Orford's rudeness and the quarrel that had followed.

The two elder people were disturbed and considered Elisa's behavior strange, but her manifest agitation caused them to forbear pressing her for an explanation; nor was it any use addressing themselves to Philip, for he went out to his delayed meeting with companions at a coffee-house.

That night Elisa Minden went to bed feeling more emotion than she had ever done in her life; fear and disgust of the man whom hitherto she had placidly regarded as her future husband, and a yearning for the kindly presence of her childhood's companion united in the resolute words she whispered into her pillow during that bitter night.

"I can never marry him now!"

The next day it snowed heavily, yet a strange elation was in Elisa's heart as she descended to the warm parlor, bright from the fire and light from the glow of the snow without.

She was going to tell her father that she could not carry out her engagement with Mr. Orford, and that she did not want ever to go into his house again.

They were all gathered round the breakfast-table when Captain Hoare came in late (he had been out to get a newsletter) and brought the news that was the most unlocked for they could conceive, and that was soon to startle all London.

Mr. Orford had been found murdered in his cabinet.

These tidings, though broken as carefully as possible, threw the little household into the deepest consternation and agitation; there were shrieks, and cryings, and running to and fro.

Only Miss Minden, though of a ghastly color, made no especial display of grief; she was thinking of Flora Orford.

When the doctor could get away from his agitated womenkind, he went with his nephew to the house of Mr. Orford.

The story of the murder was a mystery. The scholar had been found in his chair in front of his desk with one of his own bread-knives sticking through his shoulders; and there was nothing to throw any light as to how or through whom he had met his death.

The story, sifted from the mazed incoherency of Mrs. Boyd, the hysterics of the maids, the commentaries of the constables, and the chatter of the neighbors, ran thus:

At half-past nine the night before, Mrs. Boyd had sent one of the maids up with her master's supper; it was his whim to have it always thus, served on a tray in the cabinet. There had been wine and meat, bread and cheese, fruit and cakes—the usual plates and silver—among these the knife that had killed Mr. Orford.

When the servant left, the scholar had followed her to the door and locked it after her; this was also a common practice of his, a precaution against any possible interruption, for, he said, he did the best part of his work in the evening.

It was found next morning that his bed had not been slept in, and that the library door was still locked; as the alarmed Mrs. Boyd could get no answer to her knocks, the man-servant had sent for someone to force the lock, and Humphrey Orford had been found in his chair, leaning forward over his papers with the knife thrust up to the hilt between his shoulders; he must have died instantly, for there was no sign of any struggle, nor any disarrangement of his person or his papers. The first doctor to see him, a passer-by, attracted by the commotion about the house, said he must have been dead some hours—probably since the night before; the candles had all burnt down to the socket, and there were spillings of grease on the desk; the supper tray stood at the other end of the room, most of the food had been eaten, most of the wine drunk, the articles were all there in order excepting only the knife sticking between Mr. Orford's shoulder-blades.

When Captain Hoare had passed the house on his return from buying the newsletter he had seen the crowd and gone in and been able to say that he had been the last person to see the murdered man alive, as he had had his sharp encounter with Mr. Orford about ten o'clock, and he remembered seeing the supper things in the room. The scholar had heard him below, unlocked the door, and called out such impatient resentment of his presence that Philip had come angrily up the stairs and followed him into the cabinet; a few angry words had passed, when Mr. Orford had practically pushed his visitor out, locking the door in his face and bidding him take Miss Minden home.

This threw no light at all on the murder; it only went to prove that at ten o'clock Mr. Orford had been alive in his cabinet.

Now here was the mystery; in the morning the door was still locked, on the inside, the window was, as it had been since early evening, shuttered and fastened across with an iron bar, on the inside, and, the room being on an upper floor, access would have been in any case almost impossible by the window which gave on to the smooth brickwork of the front of the house.

Neither was there any possible place in the room where anyone might be hidden—it was just the square lined with the shallow bookshelves, the two pictures (that sombre little one looking strange now above the bent back of the dead man), the desk, one or two chairs and side tables; there was not so much as a cupboard or bureau—not a hiding-place for a cat.

How, then, had the murderer entered and left the room?

Suicide, of course, was out of the question, owing to the nature of the wound—but murder seemed equally out of the question; Mr. Orford sat so close to the wall that the handle of the knife touched the panel behind him. For anyone to have stood between him and the wall would have been impossible; behind the back of his chair was not space enough to push a walking-stick.

How, then, had the blow been delivered with such deadly precision and force?

Not by anyone standing in front of Mr. Orford, first because he must have seen him and sprung up; and secondly, because, even had he been asleep with his head down, no one, not even a very tall man, could have leaned over the top of the desk and driven in the knife, for experiment was made, and it was found that no arm could possibly reach such a distance.

The only theory that remained was that Mr. Orford had been murdered in some other part of the room and afterwards dragged to his present position.

But this seemed more than unlikely, as it would have meant moving the desk, a heavy piece of furniture that did not look as if it had been touched, and also because there was a paper under the dead man's hand, a pen in his fingers, a splutter of ink where it had fallen, and a sentence unfinished. The thing remained a complete and horrid mystery, one that seized the imagination of men; the thing was the talk of all the coffee-houses and clubs.

The murder seemed absolutely motiveless, the dead man was not known to have an enemy in the world, yet robbery was out of the question, for nothing had been even touched.

The early tragedy was opened out. Mrs. Boyd told all she knew, which was just what she had told Elisa Minden—the affair was twenty years ago, and the gallows bird had no kith or kin left.

Elisa Minden fell into a desperate state of agitation, a swift change from her first stricken calm; she wanted Mr. Orford's house pulled down—the library and all its contents burnt; her own wedding-dress did she burn, in frenzied silence, and none dare stop her; she resisted her father's entreaties that she should go away directly after the inquest; she would stay on the spot, she said, until the mystery was solved.

Nothing would content her but a visit to Mr. Orford's cabinet; she was resolved, she said wildly, to come to the bottom of this mystery and in that room, which she had entered once and which had affected her so terribly, she believed she might find some clue.

The doctor thought it best to allow her to go; he and her cousin escorted her to the house that now no one passed without a shudder and into the chamber that all dreaded to enter.

Good Mrs. Boyd was sobbing behind them; the poor soul was quite mazed with this sudden and ghastly ending to her orderly life; she spoke all incoherently, explaining, excusing, and lamenting in a breath; yet through all her trouble she showed plainly and artlessly that she had had no affection for her master, and that it was custom and habit that had been wounded, not love.

Indeed, it seemed that there was no one who did love Humphrey Orford; the lawyers were already busy looking for a next-of-kin; it seemed likely that this property and the states in Suffolk would go into Chancery.

"You should not go in, my dear, you should not go in," sobbed the old woman, catching at Miss Minden's black gown (she was in mourning for the murdered man) and yet peering with a fearful curiosity into the cabinet.

Elisa looked ill and distraught but also resolute.

"Tell me, Mrs. Boyd," said she, pausing on the threshold, "what became of the scoured silk?"

The startled housekeeper protested that she had never seen it again; and here was another touch of mystery—the old peach-colored silk skirt that four persons had observed in Mr. Orford's cabinet the night of his murder, had completely disappeared.

"He must have burnt it," said Captain Hoare, and though it seemed unlikely that he could have consumed so many yards of stuff without leaving traces in the grate, still it was the only possible solution.

"I cannot think why he kept it so long," murmured Mrs. Boyd, "for it could have been no other than Mrs. Orford's best gown."

"A ghastly relic," remarked the young soldier grimly.

Elisa Minden went into the middle of the room and stared about her; nothing in the place was changed, nothing disordered; the desk had been moved round to allow of the scholar being carried away, his chair stood back, so that the long panel on which hung the picture of the gallows, was fuller exposed to view.

To Elisa's agitated imagination this portion of the wall sunk in the surrounding bookshelves, long and narrow, looked like the lid of a coffin.

"It is time that picture came down," she said; "it cannot interest anyone any longer."

"Lizzie, dear," suggested her father gently, "had you not better come away?—this is a sad and awful place."

"No," replied she. "I must find out about it—we must know."

And she turned about and stared at the portrait of Flora Orford.

"He hated her, Mrs. Boyd, did he not? And she must have died of fear— think of that!—died of fear, thinking all the while of that poor body on the gallows. He was a wicked man and whoever killed him must have done it to revenge Flora Orford."

"My dear," said the doctor hastily, "all that was twenty years ago, and the man was quite justified in what he did, though I cannot say I should have been so pleased with the match if I had known this story."

"How did we ever like him?" muttered Elisa Minden. "If I had entered this room before I should never have been promised to him— there is something terrible in it."

"And what else can you look for, my dear," snivelled Mrs. Boyd, "in a room where a man has been murdered."

"But it was like this before," replied Miss Minden; "it frightened me.

She looked round at her father and cousin, and her face quite distorted.

"There is something here now," she said, "something in this room."

They hastened towards her, thinking that her over-strained nerves had given way; but she took a step forward.

Shriek after shriek left her lips.

With a quivering finger she pointed before her at the long panel behind the desk.

At first they could not tell at what she pointed; then Captain Hoare saw the cause of her desperate terror.

It was a small portion of faded, peach-colored silk showing above the ribbed line of the wainscot, protruding from the wall, like a garment of stuff shut in a door.

"She is in there!" cried Miss Minden. "In there!"

A certain frenzy fell on all of them; they were in a confusion, hardly knowing what they said or did. Only Captain Hoare kept some presence of mind and, going up to the panel, discerned a fine crack all round.

"I believe it is a door," he said, "and that explains how the murderer must have struck—from the wall."

He lifted the picture of the hanged man and found a small knob or button, which, as he expected, on being pressed sent the panel back into the wall, disclosing a secret chamber no larger than a cupboard.

And directly inside this hidden room that was dark to the sight and noisome to the nostrils, was the body of a woman, leaning against the inner wall with a white kerchief knotted tightly round her throat, showing how she had died; she wore the scoured silk skirt, the end of which had been shut in the panel, and an old ragged bodice of linen that was like a dirty parchment; her hair was grey and scanty, her face past any likeness to humanity, her body thin and dry.

The room, which was lit only by a window a few inches square looking onto the garden, was furnished with a filthy bed of rags and a stool with a few tattered clothes; a basket of broken bits was on the floor.

Elisa Minden crept closer.

"It is Flora Orford," she said, speaking like one in a dream.

They brought the poor body down into the room, and then it was clear that this faded and terrible creature had a likeness to the pictured girl who smiled from the canvas over the mantelpiece.

And another thing was clear and, for a moment, they did not dare speak to each other.

For twenty years this woman had endured her punishment in the wall chamber in that library that no one but her husband entered; for twenty years he had kept her there, behind the picture of her lover, feeding her on scraps, letting her out only when the household was abed, amusing himself with her torture—she mending the scoured silk she had worn for twenty years, sitting there, cramped in the almost complete dark, a few feet from where he wrote his elegant poetry.

"Of course she was crazy," said Captain Hoare at length, "but why did she never cry out?"

"For a good reason," whispered Dr. Minden, when he had signed to Mrs. Boyd to take his fainting daughter away, "He saw to that—she has got no tongue."

The coffin bearing the nameplate "Flora Orford" was exhumed, and found to contain only lead; it was substituted by another containing the wasted body of a woman who died by her own hand twenty years after the date on the mural tablet to her memory.

Why or how this creature, certainly become idiotic and dominated entirely by the man who kept her prisoner, had suddenly found the resolution and skill to slay her tyrant and afterwards take her own life (a thing she might have done any time before) was a question never solved.

It was supposed that he had formed the hideous scheme to complete his revenge by leaving her in the wall to die of starvation while he left with his new bride for abroad, and that she knew this and had forestalled him; or else that her poor, lunatic brain had been roused by the sound of a woman's voice as she handled the scoured silk which the captive was allowed to creep out and mend when the library door was locked. But over these matters and the details of her twenty years' suffering, it is but decent to be silent.

Lizzie Minden married her cousin, but not at St. Paul's, Covent Garden. Nor did they ever return to the neighborhood of Humphrey Orford's house.

THE DEATH MASK

Mrs. H. D. Everett

'Yes, that is a portrait of my wife. It is considered to be a good likeness. But of course she was older-looking towards the last.'

Enderby and I were on our way to the smoking-room after dinner, and the picture hung on the staircase. We had been chums at school a quarter of a century ago, and later on, at college; but I had spent the last decade out of England. I returned to find my friend a widower of four years' standing. And a good job too, I thought to myself when I heard of it, for I had no great liking for the late Gloriana. Probably the sentiment, or want of sentiment, had been mutual: she did not smile on me, but I doubt if she smiled on any of poor Tom Enderby's bachelor cronies. The picture was certainly like her. She was a fine woman, with aquiline features and a cold eye. The artist had done the features justice—and the eye, which seemed to keep a steely watch on all the comings and goings of the house out of which she had died.

We made only a brief pause before the portrait, and then went on. The smoking-room was an apartment built out at the back of the house by a former owner, and shut off by double doors to serve as a nursery. Mrs Enderby had no family, and she disliked the smell of tobacco. So the big room was made over to Tom's pipes and cigars; and if Tom's friends wanted to smoke, they must smoke there or not at all. I remembered the room and the rule, but I was not prepared to find it still existing. I had expected to light my after dinner cigar over the dessert dishes, now there was no presiding lady to consider.

We were soon installed in a couple of deep-cushioned chairs before a good fire. I thought Enderby breathed more freely when he closed the double doors behind us, shutting off the dull formal house, and the staircase and the picture. But he was not looking well; there hung about him an unmistakable air of depression. Could he be fretting after Gloriana? Perhaps during their married years, he had fallen into the way of depending on a woman to care for him. It is pleasant enough when the woman is the right sort; but I shouldn't myself have fancied being cared for by the late Mrs Enderby. And, if the fretting was a fact, it would be easy to find a remedy. Evelyn has a couple of pretty sisters, and we would have him over to stay at our place.

'You must run down and see us,' I said presently, pursuing this idea. 'I want to introduce you to my wife. Can you come next week?'

His face lit up with real pleasure.

"I should like it of all things,' he said heartily. But a qualification came after. The cloud settled back over him and he sighed. 'That is, if I can get away.'

'Why, what is to hinder you?'

'It may not seem much to stay for, but I—I have got in the way of stopping here—to keep things together.' He did not look at me, but leaned over to the fender to knock the ash off his cigar.

'Tell you what, Tom, you are getting hipped living by yourself. Why don't you sell the house, or let it off just as it is, and try a complete change?'

'I can't sell it. I'm only the tenant for life. It was my wife's.'

'Well, I suppose there is nothing to prevent you letting it? Or if you can't let it, you might shut it up.'

'There is nothing *legal* to prevent me—!' The emphasis was too fine to attract notice, but I remembered it after.

'Then, my dear fellow, why not? Knock about a bit, and see the world. But, to my thinking, the best thing you could do would be to marry again.'

He shook his head drearily.

'Of course it is a delicate matter to urge upon a widower. But you have paid the utmost ceremonial respect. Four years, you know. The greatest stickler for propriety would deem it ample.'

'It isn't that. Dick, I—I've a great mind to tell you rather a queer story.' He puffed hard at his smoke, and stared into the red coals in the pauses. 'But I don't know what you'd think of it. Or think of me.'

'Try me,' I said. 'I'll give you my opinion after. And you know I'm safe to confide in.'

'I sometimes think I should feel better if I told it. It's—it's queer enough to be laughable. But it hasn't been any laughing-matter to me.'

He threw the stump of his cigar into the fire, and turned to me. And then I saw how pale he was, and that a dew of perspiration was breaking out on his white face.

'I was very much of your opinion, Dick: I thought I should be happier if I married again. And I went so far as to get engaged. But the engagement was broken off, and I am going to tell you why.

'My wife was some time ailing before she died, and the doctors were in consultation. But I did not know how serious her complaint was till the last. Then they told me there was no hope, as coma had set in. But it was possible, even probable, that there would be a revival of consciousness before death, and for this I was to hold myself ready.

'I dare say you will write me down a coward, but I dreaded the revival: I was ready to pray that she might pass away in her sleep. I knew she held exalted views about the marriage tie, and I felt sure if there were any last words she would exact a pledge.

'I could not at such a moment refuse to promise, and I did not want to be tied. You will recollect that she was my senior. I was about to be left a widower in middle life, and in the natural course of things I had a good many years before me. You see?'

'My dear fellow, I don't think a promise so extorted ought to bind you. It isn't fair!'

'Wait and hear me. I was sitting here, miserable enough, as you may suppose, when the doctor came to fetch me to her room. Mrs Enderby was conscious and had asked for me, but he particularly begged me not to agitate her in any way, lest pain should return. She was lying stretched out in the bed, looking already like a corpse.

' "Tom," she said, "they tell me I am dying, and there is something I want you to—promise."

'I groaned in spirit. It was all up with me, I thought. But she went on. "When I am dead and in my coffin, I want you to cover my face with your own hands. Promise me this."

'It was not in the very least what I expected. Of course I promised.

' "I want you to cover my face with a particular handkerchief on which I set a value. When the time comes, open the cabinet to the right of the window, and you will find it in the third drawer from the top. You cannot mistake it, for it is the only thing in the drawer."

'That was every word she said, if you believe me, Dick. She just sighed and shut her eyes as if she was going to sleep, and she never spoke again. Three or four days later they came again to ask me if I wished to take a last look, as the undertaker's men were about to close the coffin.

'I felt a great reluctance, but it was necessary I should go. She looked as if made of wax, and was colder than ice to touch. I opened the cabinet, and there, just as she said, was a large handkerchief of very fine cambric, lying by itself. It was embroidered with a monogram device in all four corners, and was not of a sort I had ever seen her use. I spread it out and laid it over the dead face; and then what happened was rather curious. It seemed to draw down over the features and cling to them, to nose and mouth and forehead and the shut eyes, till it became a perfect mask. My nerves were shaken, I suppose; I was seized with horror, and flung back the covering sheet, hastily quitting the room. And the coffin was closed that night.

'Well, she was buried, and I put up a monument which the neighbourhood considered handsome. As you see, I was bound by no pledge to abstain from marriage; and, though I knew what would have been her wish, I saw no reason why I should regard it. And, some months after, a family of the name of Ashcroft came to live at The Leasowes, and they had a pretty daughter.

'I took a fancy to Lucy Ashcroft the first time I saw her, and it was soon apparent that she was well inclined to me. She was a gentle, yielding little thing; not the superior style of woman. Not at all like—'

(I made no comment, but I could well understand that in his new matrimonial venture Tom would prefer a contrast.)

'—but I thought I had a very good chance of happiness with her; and I grew fond of her: very fond of her indeed. Her people were of the hospitable sort, and they encouraged me to go to The Leasowes, dropping in when I felt inclined: it did not seem as if they would be likely to put obstacles in our way. Matters progressed, and I made up my mind one evening to walk over there and declare myself. I had been up to town the day before, and came back with a ring in my pocket: rather a fanciful design of double hearts, but I thought Lucy would think it pretty, and would let me put it on her finger. I went up to change into dinner things, making myself as spruce as possible, and coming to the conclusion before the glass that I was not such a bad figure of a man after all, and that there was not much grey in my hair. Ay, Dick, you may smile: it is a good bit greyer now.

'I had taken out a clean handkerchief, and thrown the one carried through the day crumpled on the floor. I don't know what made me turn to look there, but, once it caught my eye, I stood staring at it as if spellbound. The handkerchief was moving—Dick, I swear it—rapidly altering in shape, puffing up here and there as if blown by wind, spreading and moulding itself into the features of a face. And what face should it be but the death-mask of Gloriana, which I had covered in the coffin eleven months before!

'To say I was horror-stricken conveys little of the feeling that possessed me. I snatched up the rag of cambric and flung it on the fire, and it was nothing but a rag in my hand, and in another moment no more than blackened tinder on the bar of the grate. There was no face below.'

'Of course not,' I said. 'It was a mere hallucination. You were cheated by an excited fancy.'

'You may be sure I told myself all that, and more; and I went downstairs and tried to pull myself together with a dram. But I was curiously upset, and, for that night at least, I found it impossible to play the wooer. The recollection of the death-mask was too vivid; it would have come between me and Lucy's lips.

'The effect wore off, however. In a day or two I was bold again, and as much disposed to smile at my folly as you are at this moment. I proposed, and

Lucy accepted me; and I put on the ring. Ashcroft *père* was graciously pleased to approve of the settlements I offered, and Ashcroft *mère* promised to regard me as a son. And during the first forty-eight hours of our engagement, there was not a cloud to mar the blue.

'I proposed on a Monday, and on Wednesday I went again to dine and spend the evening with just their family party. Lucy and I found our way afterwards into the back drawing-room, which seemed to be made over to us by tacit understanding. Anyway, we had it to ourselves; and as Lucy sat on the settee, busy with her work, I was privileged to sit beside her, close enough to watch the careful stitches she was setting, under which the pattern grew.

'She was embroidering a square of fine linen to serve as a tea-cloth, and it was intended for a present to a friend; she was anxious, she told me, to finish it in the next few days, ready for despatch. But I was somewhat impatient of her engrossment in the work; I wanted her to look at me while we talked, and to be permitted to hold her hand. I was making plans for a tour we would take together after Easter; arguing that eight weeks spent in preparation was enough for any reasonable bride. Lucy was easily entreated; she laid aside the linen square on the table at her elbow. I held her fingers captive, but her eyes wandered from my face, as she was still deliciously shy.

'All at once she exclaimed. Her work was moving, there was growing to be a face in it: did I not see?

'I saw, indeed. It was the Gloriana death-mask, forming there as it had formed in my handkerchief at home: the marked nose and chin, the severe mouth, the mould of forehead, almost complete. I snatched it up and dropped it over the back of the couch. "It did look like a face," I allowed. "But never mind it, darling; I want you to attend to me." Something of this sort I said, I hardly know what, for my blood was running cold. Lucy pouted; she wanted to dwell on the marvel, and my impatient action had displeased her. I went on talking wildly, being afraid of pauses, but the psychological moment had gone by. I felt I did not carry her with me as before: she hesitated over my persuasions; the forecast of a Sicilian honeymoon had ceased to charm. By-and-by she suggested that Mrs Ashcroft would expect us to rejoin the circle in the other room. And perhaps I would pick up her work for her—still with a slight air of offence.

'I walked round the settee to recover the luckless piece of linen; but she turned also, looking over the back, so at the same instant we both saw.

'There again was the Face, rigid and severe; and now the corners of the cloth were tucked under, completing the form of the head. And that was not all. Some white drapery had been improvised and extended beyond it on the floor, presenting the complete figure laid out straight and stiff, ready for the grave. Lucy's alarm was excusable. She shrieked aloud, shriek upon shriek, and immediately an indignant family of Ashcrofts rushed in through the half-drawn *portières* which divided the two rooms, demanding the cause of her distress.

'Meanwhile I had fallen upon the puffed-out form, and destroyed it. Lucy's embroidery composed the head; the figure was ingeniously contrived out of a large Turkish bath-sheet, brought in from one of the bedrooms, no-one knew how or when. I held up the things protesting their innocence, while the family were stabbing me through and through with looks of indignation, and Lucy was sobbing in her mother's arms. She might have been foolish, she allowed; it did seem ridiculous now she saw what it was. But at the moment it was too dreadful: it looked so like—so like! And here a fresh sob choked her into silence.

'Peace was restored at last, but plainly the Ashcrofts doubted me. The genial father stiffened, and Mrs Ashcroft administered indirect reproofs. She hated practical joking, so she informed me; she might be wrong, and no doubt she was old-fashioned, but she had been brought up to consider it in the highest degree ill-bred. And perhaps I had not considered how sensitive Lucy was, and how easily alarmed. She hoped I would take warning for the future, and that nothing of this kind would occur again.

'Practical joking—oh, ye gods! As if it was likely that I, alone with the girl of my heart, would waste the precious hour in building up effigies of sham corpses on the floor! And Lucy ought to have known that the accusation was absurd, as I had never for a moment left her side. She did take my part when more composed; but the mystery remained, beyond explanation of hers or mine.

'As for the future, I could not think of that without a failing heart. If the Power arrayed against us were in truth what superstition feared, I might as well give up hope at once, for I knew there would be no relenting. I could see the whole absurdity of the thing as well as you do now; but, if you put yourself in my place, Dick, you will be forced to confess that it was tragic too.

'I did not see Lucy the next day, as I was bound to go again to town; but we had planned to meet and ride together on the Friday morning. I was to be at The Leasowes at a certain hour, and you may be sure I was punctual. Her horse had already been brought round, and the groom was leading it up and down. I had hardly dismounted when she came down the steps of the porch; and I noticed at once a new look on her face, a harder set about that red mouth of hers which was so soft and kissable. But she let me put her up on the saddle and settle her foot in the stirrup, and she was the bearer of a gracious message from her mother. I was expected to return to lunch, and Mrs Ashcroft begged us to be punctual, as a friend who had stayed the night with them, would be leaving immediately after.

' "You will be pleased to meet her, I think," said Lucy, leaning forward to pat her horse. "I find she knows you very well. It is Miss Kingsworthy."

'Now Miss Kingsworthy was a school friend of Gloriana's, who used now and then to visit us here. I was not aware that she and the Ashcrofts were acquainted; but, as I have said, they had only recently come into the neighbourhood as tenants of The Leasowes. I had no opportunity to express pleasure or the reverse, for Lucy was riding on; and putting her horse to a brisk pace. It was some time before she drew rein, and again admitted conversation. We were descending a steep hill, and the groom was following at a discreet distance behind, far enough to be out of earshot.

'Lucy looked very pretty on horseback; but this is by the way. The mannish hat suited her, and so did the habit fitting closely to her shape.

' "Tom," she said; and again I noticed that new hardness in her face. "Tom, Miss Kingsworthy tells me your wife did not wish you to marry again, and she made you promise her that you would not. Miss Kingsworthy was quite astonished to hear that you and I were engaged. Is this true?"

'I was able to tell her it was not: that my wife had never asked, and I had never given her, any such pledge. I allowed she disliked second marriages—in certain cases, and perhaps she had made some remark to that effect to Miss Kingsworthy; it was not unlikely. And then I appealed to her. Surely she would not let a mischief-maker's tittle-tattle come between her and me?

'I thought her profile looked less obdurate, but she would not let her eyes meet mine as she answered: "Of course not, if that was all. And I doubt if I would have heeded it, only that it seemed to fit in with—something else. Tom, it was very horrible, what we saw on Wednesday evening. And—and—don't be angry, but I asked Miss Kingsworthy what your wife was like. I did not tell her why I wanted to know."

' "What has that to do with it?" I demanded—stoutly enough; but, alas! I was too well aware.

' "She told me Mrs Enderby was handsome, but she had very marked features, and was severe-looking when she did not smile. A high forehead, a Roman nose, and a decided chin. Tom, the face in the cloth was just like that. Did you not see?"

'Of course I protested. "My darling, what nonsense! I saw it looked a little like a face, but I pulled it to pieces at once because you were frightened. Why, Lucy, I shall have you turning into a spiritualist if you take up these fancies."

' "No," she said, "I do not want to be anything foolish. I have thought it over, and if it happens only once I have made up my mind to believe it a mistake and to forget. But if it comes again—if it goes on coming!" Here she shuddered and turned white. "Oh Tom, I could not—I could not!"

'That was the ultimatum. She liked me as much as ever; she even owned to a warmer feeling; but she was not going to marry a haunted man. Well, I suppose I cannot blame her. I might have given the same advice in another fellow's case, though in my own I felt it hard.

'I am close to the end now, so I shall need to tax your patience very little longer. A single chance remained. Gloriana's power, whatever its nature and however derived, might have been so spent in the previous efforts that she could effect no more. I clung to this shred of hope, and did my best to play the part of the light-hearted lover, the sort of companion Lucy expected, who would shape himself to her mood; but I was conscious that I played it ill.

'The ride was a lengthy business. Lucy's horse cast a shoe, and it was impossible to change the saddle on to the groom's hack or my own mare, as neither of them had been trained to the habit. We were bound to return at a foot-pace, and did not reach The Leasowes until two o'clock. Lunch was over: Mrs Ashcroft had set out for the station driving Miss Kingsworthy; but some cutlets were keeping hot for us, so we were informed, and could be served immediately.

'We went at once into the dining-room, as Lucy was hungry; and she took off her hat and laid it on a side-table: she said the close fit of it made her head ache. The cutlets had been misrepresented: they were lukewarm; but Lucy made a good meal off them and the fruit-tart which followed, very much at her leisure. Heaven knows I would not have grudged her so much as a mouthful; but that luncheon was an ordeal I cannot readily forget.

'The servant absented himself, having seen us served; and then my troubles began. The tablecloth seemed alive at the corner which was between us; it rose in waves as if puffed up by wind, though the window was fast shut against any wandering airs. I tried to seem unconscious; tried to talk as if no horror of apprehension was filling all my mind, while I was flattening out the bewitched damask with a grasp I hardly dared relax. Lucy rose at last, saying she must change her dress. Occupied with the cloth, it had not occurred to me to look round, or keep watch on what might be going on in another part of the room. The hat on the side-table had been tilted over sideways, and in that position it was made to crown another presentation of the Face. What it was made of this time I cannot say; probably a serviette, as several lay about. The linen material, of whatever sort, was again moulded into the perfect form; but this time the mouth showed humour, and appeared to relax in a grim smile.

'Lucy shrieked, and dropped into my arms in a swoon: a real genuine fainting-fit, out of which she was brought round with difficulty, after I had summoned the help of doctors.

'I hung about miserably till her safety was assured, and then went as miserably home. Next morning I received a cutting little note from my mother-in-law elect, in which she returned the ring, and informed me the engagement must be considered at an end.

'Well, Dick, you know now why I do not marry. And what have you to say?'

A HAUNTED HOUSE

Virginia Woolf

Whatever hour you woke there was a door shutting. From room to room they went, hand in hand, lifting here, opening there, making sure—a ghostly couple.

'Here we left it,' she said. And he added, 'Oh, but here too!' 'It's upstairs,' she murmured, 'And in the garden,' he whispered. 'Quietly,' they said, 'or we shall wake them.'

But it wasn't that you woke us. Oh, no. 'They're looking for it; they're drawing the curtain,' one might say, and so read on a page or two. 'Now they've found it,' one would be certain, stopping the pencil on the margin. And then, tired of reading, one might rise and see for oneself, the house all empty, the doors standing open, only the wood pigeons bubbling with content and the hum of the threshing machine sounding from the farm. 'What did I come in here for? What did I want to find?' My hands were empty. 'Perhaps it's upstairs then?' The apples were in the loft. And so down again, the garden still as ever, only the book had slipped into the grass.

But they had found it in the drawing-room. Not that one could ever see them. The window-panes reflected apples, reflected roses; all the leaves were green in the glass. If they moved in the drawing-room, the apple only turned its yellow side. Yet, the moment after, if the door was opened, spread about the floor, hung upon the walls, pendant from ceiling—what? My hands were empty. The shadow of a thrush crossed the carpet; from the deepest wells of silence the wood pigeon drew its bubble of sound. 'Safe, safe, safe,' the pulse of the house beat softly. 'The treasure buried; the room ...' the pulse stopped short. Oh, was that the buried treasure?

A moment later the light had faded. Out in the garden then? But the trees spun darkness for a wandering beam of sun. So fine, so rare, coolly sunk beneath the surface the beam I sought always burnt behind the glass. Death was the glass; death was between us; coming to the woman first, hundreds of years ago, leaving the house, sealing all the windows; the rooms were darkened. He left it, left her, went North, went East, saw the stars turned in the Southern sky; sought the house, found it dropped beneath the Downs. 'Safe, safe, safe,' the pulse of the house beat gladly, 'The treasure yours.'

The wind roars up the avenue. Trees stoop and bend this way and that. Moonbeams splash and spill wildly in the rain. But the beam of the lamp falls straight from the window. The candle burns stiff and still. Wandering through the house, opening the windows, whispering not to wake us, the ghostly couple seek their joy.

'Here we slept,' she says. And he adds, 'Kisses without number.' 'Waking in the morning—' 'Silver between the trees—' 'Upstairs—' 'In the garden—' 'When summer came—' 'In winter snowtime—' The doors go shutting far in the distance, gently knocking like the pulse of a heart.

Nearer they come; cease at the doorway. The wind falls, the rain slides silver down the glass. Our eyes darken; we hear no steps beside us; we see no lady spread her ghostly cloak. His hands shield the lantern. 'Look,' he breathes. 'Sound asleep. Love upon their lips.'

Stooping, holding their silver lamp above us, long they look and deeply. Long they pause. The wind drives straightly; the flame stoops slightly. Wild beams of moonlight cross both floor and wall, and, meeting, stain the faces bent; the faces pondering; the faces that search the sleepers and seek their hidden joy.

'Safe, safe, safe,' the heart of the house beats proudly. 'Long years—'he sighs. 'Again you found me.' 'Here,' she murmurs, 'sleeping; in the garden reading; laughing, rolling apples in the loft. Here we left our treasure—' Stooping, their light lifts the lids upon my eyes. 'Safe! safe! safe!' the pulse of the house beats wildly. Waking, I cry 'Oh, is this *your*—buried treasure? The light in the heart.'

WHERE THEIR FIRE IS NOT QUENCHED

May Sinclair

There was nobody in the orchard. Harriott Leigh went out, carefully, through the iron gate into the field. She had made the latch slip into its notch without a sound.

The path slanted widely up the field from the orchard gate to the stile under the elder tree. George Waring waited for her there.

Years afterwards, when she thought of George Waring she smelt the sweet, hot, wine-scent of the elder flowers. Years afterwards, when she smelt elder flowers she saw George Waring, with his beautiful, gentle face, like a poet's or a musician's, his black-blue eyes, and sleek, olive-brown hair. He was a naval lieutenant.

Yesterday he had asked her to marry him and she had consented. But her father hadn't, and she had come to tell him that and say goodbye before he left her. His ship was to sail the next day.

He was eager and excited. He couldn't believe that anything could stop their happiness, that anything he didn't want to happen could happen.

'Well?' he said.

'He's a perfect beast, George. He won't let us. He says we're too young.'

'I was twenty last August,' he said, aggrieved.

'And I shall be seventeen in September.'

'And this is June. We're quite old, really. How long does he mean us to wait?'

'Three years.'

'Three years before we can be engaged even—Why, we might be dead.'

She put her arms round him to make him feel safe. They kissed; and the sweet, hot, wine-scent of the elderflowers mixed with their kisses. They stood, pressed close together, under the elder tree.

Across the yellow fields of charlock they heard the village clock strike seven. Up in the house a gong clanged.

'Darling, I must go,' she said.

'Oh stay—Stay *five* minutes.'

He pressed her close. It lasted five minutes, and five more. Then he was running fast down the road to the station, while Harriott went along the field-path, slowly, struggling with her tears.

'He'll be back in three months,' she said. 'I can live through three months.'

But he never came back. There was something wrong with the engines of his ship, the *Alexandra*. Three weeks later she went down in the Mediterranean, and George with her.

Harriott said she didn't care how soon she died now. She was quite sure it would be soon, because she couldn't live without him.

Five years passed.

The two lines of beech trees stretched on and on, the whole length of the Park, a broad green drive between. When you came to the middle they branched off right and left in the form of a cross, and at the end of the right arm there was a white stucco pavilion with pillars and a three-cornered pediment like a Greek temple. At the end of the left arm, the west entrance to the Park, double gates and a side door.

Harriott, on her stone seat at the back of the pavilion, could see Stephen Philpotts the very minute he came through the side door.

He had asked her to wait for him there. It was the place he always chose to read his poems aloud in. The poems were a pretext. She knew what he was going to say. And she knew what she would answer.

There were elder bushes in flower at the back of the pavilion, and Harriott thought of George Waring. She told herself that George was nearer to her now than he could ever have been, living. If she married Stephen she would not be unfaithful, because she loved him with another part of herself. It was not as though Stephen were taking George's place. She loved Stephen with her soul, in an unearthly way.

But her body quivered like a stretched wire when the door opened and the young man came towards her down the drive under the beech trees.

She loved him; she loved his slenderness, his darkness and sallow whiteness, his black eyes lighting up with the intellectual flame, the way his black hair swept back from his forehead, the way he walked, tiptoe, as if his feet were lifted with wings.

He sat down beside her. She could see his hands tremble. She felt that her moment was coming; it had come.

'I wanted to see you alone because there's something I must say to you. I don't quite know how to begin ...'

Her lips parted. She panted lightly.

'You've heard me speak of Sybill Foster?'

Her voice came stammering, 'N-no, Stephen. Did you?'

'Well, I didn't mean to, till I knew it was all right. I only heard yesterday.'

'Heard what?'

'Why, that she'll have me. Oh, Harriott—do you know what it's like to be terribly happy?'

She knew. She had known just now, the moment before he told her. She sat there, stone-cold and stiff, listening to his raptures; listening to her own voice saying she was glad.

Ten years passed.

Harriott Leigh sat waiting in the drawing-room of a small house in Maida Vale. She had lived there ever since her father's death two years before.

She was restless. She kept on looking at the clock to see if it was four, the hour that Oscar Wade had appointed. She was not sure that he would come, after she had sent him away yesterday.

She now asked herself, why, when she had sent him away yesterday, she had let him come today. Her motives were not altogether clear. If she really meant what she had said then, she oughtn't to let him come to her again. Never again.

She had shown him plainly what she meant. She could see herself, sitting very straight in her chair, uplifted by a passionate integrity, while he stood before her, hanging his head, ashamed and beaten; she could feel again the throb in her voice as she kept on saying that she couldn't, she couldn't; he must see that she couldn't; that no, nothing would make her change her mind; she couldn't forget he had a wife; that he must think of Muriel.

To which he had answered savagely: 'I needn't. That's all over. We only live together for the look of the thing.'

And she, serenely, with great dignity: 'And for the look of the thing, Oscar, we must leave off seeing each other. Please go.'

'Do you mean it?'

'Yes. We must never see each other again.'

And he had gone then, ashamed and beaten.

She could see him, squaring his broad shoulders to meet the blow. And she was sorry for him. She told herself she had been unnecessarily hard. Why shouldn't they see each other again, now he understood where they must draw the line? Until yesterday the line had never been very clearly drawn. Today she meant to ask him to forget what he had said to her. Once it was forgotten, they could go on being friends as if nothing had happened.

It was four o'clock. Half-past. Five. She had finished tea and given him up when, between the half-hour and six o'clock, he came.

He came as he had come a dozen times, with his measured, deliberate, thoughtful tread, carrying himself well braced, with a sort of held-in arrogance, his great shoulders heaving. He was a man of about forty, broad and tall, lean-flanked and short-necked, his straight, handsome features showing small and even in the big square face and in the flush that swamped it. The close-clipped, reddish-brown moustache bristled forwards from the pushed-out upper lip. His small, flat eyes shone, reddish-brown, eager and animal.

She liked to think of him when he was not there, but always at the first sight of him she felt a slight shock. Physically, he was very far from her admired ideal. So different from George Waring and Stephen Philpotts.

He sat down, facing her.

There was an embarrassed silence, broken by Oscar Wade.

'Well, Harriott, you said I could come.' He seemed to be throwing the responsibility on her. 'So I suppose you've forgiven me,' he said.

'Oh, yes, Oscar, I've forgiven you.'

He said she'd better show it by coming to dine with him somewhere that evening.

She could give no reason to herself for going. She simply went.

He took her to a restaurant in Soho. Oscar Wade dined well, even extravagantly, giving each dish its importance. She liked his extravagance. He had none of the mean virtues.

It was over. His flushed, embarrassed silence told her what he was thinking. But when he had seen her home he left her at her garden gate. He had thought better of it.

She was not sure whether she were glad or sorry. She had had her moment of righteous exaltation and she had enjoyed it. But there was no joy in the weeks that followed it. She had given up Oscar Wade because she didn't want him very much; and now she wanted him furiously, perversely, because she had given him up. Though he had no resemblance to her ideal, she couldn't live without him.

She dined with him again and again, till she knew Schnebler's Restaurant by heart, the white panelled walls picked out with gold; the white pillars, and the curling gold fronds of their capitals; the Turkey carpets, blue and crimson, soft under her feet; the thick crimson velvet cushions, that clung to her skirts; the glitter of silver and glass on the innumerable white circles of the tables. And the faces of the diners, red, white, pink, brown, grey and sallow, distorted and excited; the curled mouths that twisted as they ate; the convoluted electric bulbs pointing, pointing down at them, under the red, crinkled shades. All shimmering in a thick air that the red light stained as wine stains water.

And Oscar's face, flushed with his dinner. Always, when he leaned back from the table and brooded in silence she knew what he was thinking. His heavy eyelids would lift; she would find his eyes fixed on hers, wondering, considering.

She knew now what the end would be. She thought of George Waring, and Stephen Philpotts, and of her life, cheated. She hadn't chosen Oscar, she hadn't really wanted him; but now he had forced himself on her she couldn't afford to let him go. Since George died no man had loved her, no other man ever would. And she was sorry for him when she thought of him going from her, beaten and ashamed.

She was certain, before he was, of the end. Only she didn't know when and where and how it would come. That was what Oscar knew.

It came at the close of one of their evenings when they had dined in a private sitting-room. He said he couldn't stand the heat and noise of the public restaurant.

She went before him, up a steep, red-carpeted stair to a white door on the second landing.

From time to time they repeated the furtive, hidden adventure. Sometimes she met him in the room above Schnebler's. Sometimes, when her maid was out, she received him at her house in Maida Vale. But that was dangerous, not to be risked too often.

Oscar declared himself unspeakably happy. Harriott was not quite sure. This was love, the thing she had never had, that she had dreamed of, hungered and thirsted for; but now she had it she was not satisfied. Always she looked for something just beyond it, some mystic, heavenly rapture, always beginning to come, that never came. There was something about Oscar that repelled her. But because she had taken him for her lover, she couldn't bring herself to admit that it was a certain coarseness. She looked another way and pretended it wasn't there. To justify herself, she fixed her mind on his good qualities, his generosity, his strength, the way he had built up his engineering business. She made him take her over his works and show her his great dynamos. She made him lend her the books he read. But always, when she tried to talk to him, he let her see that *that* wasn't what she was there for.

'My dear girl, we haven't time,' he said. 'It's waste of our priceless moments.'

She persisted. 'There's something wrong about it all if we can't talk to each other.'

He was irritated. 'Women never seem to consider that a man can get all the talk he wants from other men. What's wrong is our meeting in this unsatisfactory way. We ought to live together. It's the only sane thing. I would, only I don't want to break up Muriel's home and make her miserable.'

'I thought you said she wouldn't care.'

'My dear, she cares for her home and her position and the children. You forget the children.'

Yes. She had forgotten the children. She had forgotten Muriel. She had left off thinking of Oscar as a man with a wife and children and a home.

He had a plan. His mother-in-law was coming to stay with Muriel in October and he would get away. He would go to Paris, and Harriott should come to him there. He could say he went on business. No need to lie about it; he *had* business in Paris.

He engaged rooms in an hotel in the rue de Rivoli. They spent two weeks there.

For three days Oscar was madly in love with Harriott and Harriott with him. As she lay awake she would turn on the light and look at him as he slept at her side. Sleep made him beautiful and innocent; it laid a fine, smooth tissue over his coarseness; it made his mouth gentle; it entirely hid his eyes.

In six days reaction had set in. At the end of the tenth day, Harriott, returning with Oscar from Montmartre, burst into a fit of crying. When questioned, she answered wildly that the Hotel Saint Pierre was too hideously ugly; it was getting on her nerves. Mercifully Oscar explained her state as fatigue following excitement. She tried hard to believe that she was miserable because her love was purer and more spiritual than Oscar's; but all the time she knew perfectly well she had cried from pure boredom. She was in love with Oscar, and Oscar bored her. Oscar was in love with her, and she bored him. At close quarters, day in and day out, each was revealed to the other as an incredible bore.

At the end of the second week she began to doubt whether she had ever been really in love with him.

Her passion returned for a little while after they got back to London. Freed from the unnatural strain which Paris had put on them, they persuaded themselves that their romantic temperaments were better fitted to the old life of casual adventure.

Then, gradually, the sense of danger began to wake in them. They lived in perpetual fear, face to face with all the chances of discovery. They tormented themselves and each other by imagining possibilities that they would never have considered in their first fine moments. It was as though they were beginning to ask themselves if it were, after all, worth while running such awful risks, for all they got out of it. Oscar still swore that if he had been free he would have married her. He pointed out that his intentions at any rate were regular. But she asked herself: Would I marry *him?* Marriage would be the Hotel Saint Pierre all over again, without any possibility of escape. But, if she wouldn't marry him, was she in love with him? That was the test. Perhaps it was a good thing he wasn't free. Then she told herself that these doubts were morbid, and that the question wouldn't arise.

One evening Oscar called to see her. He had come to tell her that Muriel was ill.

'Seriously ill?'

'I'm afraid so. It's pleurisy. May turn to pneumonia. We shall know one way or another in the next few days.'

A terrible fear seized upon Harriott. Muriel might die of her pleurisy; and if Muriel died, she would have to marry Oscar. He was looking at her queerly, as if he knew what she was thinking, and she could see that the same thought had occurred to him and that he was frightened too.

Muriel got well again; but their danger had enlightened them. Muriel's life was now inconceivably precious to them both; she stood between them and that permanent union, which they dreaded and yet would not have the courage to refuse.

After enlightenment the rupture.

It came from Oscar, one evening when he sat with her in her drawing-room.

'Harriott,' he said, 'do you know I'm thinking seriously of settling down?'

'How do you mean, settling down?'

'Patching it up with Muriel, poor girl … Has it never occurred to you that this little affair of ours can't go on for ever?'

'You don't want it to go on?'

'I don't want to have any humbug about it. For God's sake, let's be straight. If it's done, it's done. Let's end it decently.'

'I see. You want to get rid of me.'

'That's a beastly way of putting it.'

'Is there any way that isn't beastly? The whole thing's beastly. I should have thought you'd have stuck to it now you've made it what you wanted. When I haven't an ideal, I haven't a single illusion, when you've destroyed everything you didn't want.'

'What didn't I want?'

'The clean, beautiful part of it. The part *I* wanted.'

'My part at least was real. It was cleaner and more beautiful than all that putrid stuff you wrapped it up in. You were a hypocrite, Harriott, and I wasn't. You're a hypocrite now if you say you weren't happy with me.'

'I was never really happy. Never for one moment. There was always something I missed. Something you didn't give me. Perhaps you couldn't.'

'No. I wasn't spiritual enough,' he sneered.

'You were not. And you made me what you were.'

'Oh, I noticed that you were always very spiritual *after* you'd got what you wanted.'

'What I wanted?' she cried. 'Oh, my God—'

'If you ever knew what you wanted.'

'What—I—wanted,' she repeated, drawing out her bitterness.

'Come,' he said, 'why not be honest? Face facts. I was awfully gone on you. You were awfully gone on me—once. We got tired of each other and it's over. But at least you might own we had a good time while it lasted.'

'A good time?'

'Good enough for me.'

'For you, because for you love only means one thing. Everything that's high and noble in it you dragged down to that, till there's nothing left for us but that. *That's* what you made of love.'

Twenty years passed.

It was Oscar who died first, three years after the rupture. He did it suddenly one evening, falling down in a fit of apoplexy.

His death was an immense relief to Harriott. Perfect security had been impossible as long as he was alive. But now there wasn't a living soul who knew her secret.

Still, in the first moment of shock Harriott told herself that Oscar dead would be nearer to her than ever. She forgot how little she had wanted him to be near her, alive. And long before the twenty years had passed she had contrived to persuade herself that he had never been near to her at all. It was incredible that she had ever known such a person as Oscar Wade. As for their affair, she couldn't think of Harriott Leigh as the sort of woman to whom such a thing could happen. Schnebler's and the Hotel Saint Pierre ceased to figure among prominent images of her past. Her memories, if she had allowed herself to remember, would have clashed disagreeably with the reputation for sanctity which she had now acquired.

For Harriott at fifty-two was the friend and helper of the Reverend Clement Farmer, Vicar of St Mary the Virgin's, Maida Vale. She worked as a deaconess in his parish, wearing the uniform of a deaconess, the semi-religious gown, the cloak, the bonnet and veil, the cross and rosary, the holy smile. She was also secretary to the Maida Vale and Kilburn Home for Fallen Girls.

Her moments of excitement came when Clement Farmer, the lean, austere likeness of Stephen Philpotts, in his cassock and lace-bordered surplice, issued from the vestry, when he mounted the pulpit, when he stood before the altar rails and lifted up his arms in the Benediction; her moments of ecstasy when she received the Sacrament from his hands. And she had moments of calm happiness when his study door closed on their communion. All these moments were saturated with a solemn holiness.

And they were insignificant compared with the moment of her dying.

She lay dozing in her white bed under the black crucifix with the ivory Christ. The basins and medicine bottles had been cleared from the table by her pillow; it was spread for the last rites. The priest moved quietly about the room, arranging the candles, the Prayer Book and the Holy Sacrament. Then he drew a chair to her bedside and watched with her, waiting for her to come up out of her doze.

She woke suddenly. Her eyes were fixed upon him. She had a flash of lucidity. She was dying, and her dying made her supremely important to Clement Farmer.

'Are you ready?' he asked.

'Not yet. I think I'm afraid. Make me not afraid.'

He rose and lit the two candles on the altar. He took down the crucifix from the wall and stood it against the foot-rail of the bed.

She sighed. That was not what she had wanted.

'You will not be afraid now,' he said.

'I'm not afraid of the hereafter. I suppose you get used to it. Only it may be terrible just at first.'

'Our first state will depend very much on what we are thinking of at our last hour.'

'There'll be my—confession,' she said.

'And after it you will receive the Sacrament. Then you will have your mind fixed firmly upon God and your Redeemer ... Do you feel able to make your confession now, Sister? Everything is ready.'

Her mind went back over her past and found Oscar Wade there. She wondered: Should she confess to him about Oscar Wade? One moment she thought it was possible; the next she knew that she couldn't. She could not. It wasn't necessary. For twenty years he had not been part of her life. No. She wouldn't confess about Oscar Wade. She had been guilty of other sins.

She made a careful selection.

'I have cared too much for the beauty of this world...I have failed in charity to my poor girls. Because of my intense repugnance to their sin...I have thought, often, about—people I love, when I should have been thinking about God.'

After that she received the Sacrament.

'Now,' he said, 'there is nothing to be afraid of.'

'I won't be afraid if—if you would hold my hand.'

He held it. And she lay still a long time, with her eyes shut. Then he heard her murmuring something. He stooped close.

'This—is—dying. I thought it would be horrible. And it's bliss ... Bliss.'

The priest's hand slackened, as if at the bidding of some wonder. She gave a weak cry.

'Oh—don't let me go.'

His grasp tightened.

'Try,' he said, 'to think about God. Keep on looking at the crucifix.'

'If I look,' she whispered, 'you won't let go my hand?'

'I will not let you go.'

He held it till it was wrenched from him in the last agony.

She lingered for some hours in the room where these things had happened.

Its aspect was familiar and yet unfamiliar, and slightly repugnant to her. The altar, the crucifix, the lighted candles, suggested some tremendous and awful experience the details of which she was not able to recall. She seemed to remember that they had been connected in some way with the sheeted body on the bed; but the nature of the connection was not clear; and she did not associate the dead body with herself. When the nurse came in and laid it out, she saw that it was the body of a middle-aged woman. Her own living body was that of a young woman of about thirty-two.

Her mind had no past and no future, no sharp-edged, coherent memories, and no idea of anything to be done next.

Then, suddenly, the room began to come apart before her eyes, to split into shafts of floor and furniture and ceiling that shifted and were thrown by their commotion into different planes. They leaned slanting at every possible angle; they crossed and overlaid each other with a transparent mingling of dislocated perspectives, like reflections fallen on an interior seen behind glass.

The bed and the sheeted body slid away somewhere out of sight. She was standing by the door that still remained in position.

She opened it and found herself in the street, outside a building of yellowish-grey brick and freestone, with a tall slated spire. Her mind came together with a palpable click of recognition. This object was the Church of St Mary the Virgin, Maida Vale. She could hear the droning of the organ. She opened the door and slipped in.

She had gone back into a definite space and time, and recovered a certain limited section of coherent memory. She remembered the rows of pitch-pine benches, with their Gothic peaks and mouldings; the stone-coloured walls and pillars with their chocolate stencilling; the hanging rings of lights along the aisles of the nave; the high altar with its lighted candles, and the polished brass cross, twinkling. These things were somehow permanent and real, adjusted to the image that now took possession of her.

She knew what she had come there for. The service was over. The choir had gone from the chancel; the sacristan moved before the altar, putting out the candles. She walked up the middle aisle to a seat that she knew under the pulpit. She knelt down and covered her face with her hands. Peeping sideways through her fingers, she could see the door of the vestry on her left at the end of the north aisle. She watched it steadily.

Up in the organ loft the organist drew out the Recessional, slowly and softly, to its end in the two solemn, vibrating chords.

The vestry door opened and Clement Farmer came out, dressed in his black cassock. He passed before her, close, close outside the bench where she knelt. He paused at the opening. He was waiting for her. There was something he had to say.

She stood up and went towards him. He still waited. He didn't move to make way for her. She came close, closer than she had ever come to him, so close that his features grew indistinct. She bent her head back, peering, short-sightedly, and found herself looking into Oscar Wade's face.

He stood still, horribly still, and close, barring her passage.

She drew back; his heaving shoulders followed her. He leaned forward, covering her with his eyes. She opened her mouth to scream and no sound came.

She was afraid to move lest he should move with her. The heaving of his shoulders terrified her.

One by one the lights in the side aisles were going out. The lights in the middle aisle would go next. They had gone. If she didn't get away she would be shut up with him there, in the appalling darkness.

She turned and moved towards the north aisle, groping, steadying herself by the book ledge.

When she looked back, Oscar Wade was not there.

Then she remembered that Oscar Wade was dead. Therefore, what she had seen was not Oscar; it was his ghost. He was dead; dead seventeen years ago. She was safe from him for ever.

When she came out on to the steps of the church she saw that the road it stood in had changed. It was not the road she remembered. The pavement on this side was raised slightly and covered in. It ran under a succession of arches. It was a long gallery walled with glittering shop windows on one side; on the other a line of tall grey columns divided it from the street.

She was going along the arcades of the rue de Rivoli. Ahead of her she could see the edge of an immense grey pillar jutting out. That was the porch of the Hotel Saint Pierre. The revolving glass doors swung forward to receive her; she crossed the grey, sultry vestibule under the pillared arches. She knew it. She knew the porter's shining, wine-coloured mahogany pen on her left, and the shining wine-coloured mahogany barrier of the clerk's bureau on her right; she made straight for the great grey carpeted staircase; she climbed the endless flights that turned round and round the caged-in shaft of the well, past the latticed doors of the lift, and came up on to a landing that she knew, and into the long, ash-grey, foreign corridor lit by a dull window at one end.

It was there that the horror of the place came on her. She had no longer any memory of St Mary's Church, so that she was unaware of her backward course through time. All space and time were here.

She remembered she had to go to the left, the left.

But there was something there; where the corridor turned by the window; at the end of all the corridors. If she went the other way she would escape it.

The corridor stopped there. A blank wall. She was driven back past the stairhead to the left.

At the corner, by the window, she turned down another long ash-grey corridor on her right, and to the right again where the night-light sputtered on the table-flap at the turn.

This third corridor was dark and secret and depraved. She knew the soiled walls and the warped door at the end. There was a sharp-pointed streak of light at the top. She could see the number on it now, 107.

Something had happened there. If she went in it would happen again.

Oscar Wade was in the room waiting for her behind the closed door. She felt him moving about in there. She leaned forward, her ear to the key-hole, and listened. She could hear the measured, deliberate, thoughtful footsteps. They were coming from the bed to the door.

She turned and ran; her knees gave way under her; she sank and ran on, down the long grey corridors and the stairs, quick and blind, a hunted beast seeking for cover, hearing his feet coming after her.

The revolving doors caught her and pushed her out into the street.

The strange quality of her state was this, that it had no time. She remembered dimly that there had once been a thing called time; but she had forgotten altogether what it was like. She was aware of things happening and about to happen; she fixed them by the place they occupied, and measured their duration by the space she went through.

So now she thought: If I could only go back and get to the place where it hadn't happened.

To get back farther—

She was walking now on a white road that went between broad grass borders. To the right and left were the long raking lines of the hills, curve after curve, shimmering in a thin mist.

The road dropped to the green valley. It mounted the humped bridge over the river. Beyond it she saw the twin gables of the grey house pricked up over the high, grey garden wall. The tall iron gate stood in front of it between the ball-topped stone pillars.

And now she was in a large, low-ceilinged room with drawn blinds. She was standing before the wide double bed. It was her father's bed. The dead body, stretched out in the middle under the drawn white sheet, was her father's body.

The outline of the sheet sank from the peak of the upturned toes to the shin bone, and from the high bridge of the nose to the chin.

She lifted the sheet and folded it back across the breast of the dead man. The face she saw then was Oscar Wade's face, stilled and smoothed in the innocence of sleep, the supreme innocence of death. She stared at it, fascinated, in a cold, pitiless joy.

Oscar was dead.

She remembered how he used to lie like that beside her in the room in the Hotel Saint Pierre, on his back with his hands folded on his waist, his mouth half-open, his big chest rising and falling. If he was dead, it would never happen again. She would be safe.

The dead face frightened her, and she was about to cover it up again when she was aware of a light heaving, a rhythmical rise and fall. As she drew the sheet up tighter, the hands under it began to struggle convulsively, the broad ends of the fingers appeared above the edge, clutching it to keep it down. The mouth opened; the eyes opened; the whole face stared back at her in a look of agony and horror.

Then the body drew itself forwards from the hips and sat up, its eyes peering into her eyes; he and she remained for an instant motionless, each held there by the other's fear.

Suddenly she broke away, turned and ran, out of the room, out of the house.

She stood at the gate, looking up and down the road, not knowing by which way she must go to escape Oscar. To the right, over the bridge and up the hill and across the downs she would come to the arcades of the rue de Rivoli and the dreadful grey corridors of the hotel. To the left the road went through the village.

If she could get further back she would be safe, out of Oscar's reach. Standing by her father's deathbed she had been young, but not young enough.

She must get back to the place where she was younger still, to the Park and the green drive under the beech trees and the white pavilion at the cross. She knew how to find it. At the end of the village the high road ran right and left, east and west, under the Park walls; the south gate stood there at the top, looking down the narrow street.

She ran towards it through the village, past the long grey barns of Goodyer's farm, past the grocer's shop, past the yellow front and blue sign of the 'Queen's Head', past the post office, with its one black window blinking under its vine, past the church and the yew trees in the churchyard, to where the south gate made a delicate black pattern on the green grass.

These things appeared insubstantial, drawn back behind a sheet of air that shimmered over them like thin glass. They opened out, floated past and away from her; and instead of the high road and park walls she saw a London street of dingy white façades, and instead of the south gate the swinging glass doors of Schnebler's Restaurant.

The glass doors swung open and she passed into the restaurant. The scene beat on her with the hard impact of reality: the white and gold panels, the white pillars and their curling gold capitals, the white circles of the tables, glittering, the flushed faces of the diners, moving mechanically.

She was driven forward by some irresistible compulsion to a table in the corner, where a man sat alone. The table napkin he was using hid his mouth, and jaw, and chest; and she was not sure of the upper part of the face above the straight, drawn edge. It dropped; and she saw Oscar Wade's face. She came to him, dragged, without power to resist; she sat down beside him, and he leaned to her over the table; she could feel the warmth of his red, congested face; the smell of wine floated towards her on his thick whisper.

'I knew you would come.'

She ate and drank with him in silence, nibbling and sipping slowly, staving off the abominable moment it would end in.

At last they got up and faced each other. His long bulk stood before her, above her; she could almost feel the vibration of its power.

'Come,' he said. 'Come.'

And she went before him, slowly, slipping out through the maze of the tables, hearing behind her Oscar's measured, deliberate, thoughtful tread. The steep, red-carpeted staircase rose up before her.

She swerved from it, but he turned her back.

'You know the way,' he said.

At the top of the flight she found the white door of the room she knew. She knew the long windows guarded by drawn muslin blinds; the gilt looking-glass over the chimney-piece that reflected Oscar's head and shoulders grotesquely between two white porcelain babies with bulbous limbs and garlanded loins, she knew the sprawling stain on the drab carpet by the table, the shabby, infamous couch behind the screen.

They moved about the room, turning and turning in it like beasts in a cage, uneasy, inimical, avoiding each other.

At last they stood still, he at the window, she at the door, the length of the room between.

'It's no good your getting away like that,' he said.

'There couldn't be any other end to it—to what we did.'

'But that *was* ended.'

'Ended there, but not here.'

'Ended for ever. We've done with it for ever.'

'We haven't. We've got to begin again. And go on. And go on.'

'Oh, no. No. Anything but that.'

'There isn't anything else.'

'We can't. We can't. Don't you remember how it bored us?'

'Remember? Do you suppose I'd touch you if I could help it? … That's what we're here for. We must. We must.'

'No. No. I shall get away—now.'

She turned to the door to open it.

'You can't,' he said. 'The door's locked.'

'Oscar—what did you do that for?'

'We always did it. Don't you remember?'

She turned to the door again and shook it; she beat on it with her hands.

'It's no use, Harriott. If you got out now you'd only have to come back again. You might stave it off for an hour or so, but what's that in an immortality?'

'Immortality?'

'That's what we're in for.'

'Time enough to talk about immortality when we're dead … Ah—'

They were being drawn towards each other across the room, moving slowly, like figures in some monstrous and appalling dance, their heads thrown back over their shoulders, their faces turned from the horrible approach. Their arms rose slowly, heavy with intolerable reluctance; they stretched them out towards each other, aching, as if they held up an overpowering weight. Their feet dragged and were drawn.

Suddenly her knees sank under her; she shut her eyes; all her being went down before him in darkness and terror.

It was over. She had got away, she was going back, back, to the green drive of the Park, between the beech trees, where Oscar had never been, where he would never find her. When she passed through the south gate her memory became suddenly young and clean. She forgot the rue de Rivoli and the Hotel Saint Pierre; she forgot Schnebler's Restaurant and the room at the top of the stairs. She was back in her youth. She was Harriott Leigh going to wait for Stephen Philpotts in the pavilion opposite the west gate. She could feel herself, a slender figure moving fast over the grass between the lines of the great beech trees. The freshness of her youth was upon her.

She came to the heart of the drive where it branched right and left in the form of a cross. At the end of the right arm the white Greek temple, with its pediment and pillars, gleamed against the wood.

She was sitting on their seat at the back of the pavilion, watching the side door that Stephen would come in by.

The door was pushed open; he came towards her, light and young, skimming between the beech trees with his eager, tiptoeing stride. She rose up to meet him. She gave a cry.

'Stephen!'

It had been Stephen. She had seen him coming. But the man who stood before her between the pillars of the pavilion was Oscar Wade.

And now she was walking along the field-path that slanted from the orchard door to the stile; further and further back, to where young George Waring waited for her under the elder tree. The smell of the elder flowers came to her over the field. She could feel on her lips and in all her body the sweet, innocent excitement of her youth.

'George, oh, George!'

As she went along the field-path she had seen him. But the man who stood waiting for her under the elder tree was Oscar Wade.

'I told you it's no use getting away, Harriott. Every path brings you back to me. You'll find me at every turn.'

'But how did you get *here*?'

'As I got into the pavilion. As I got into your father's room, on to his death bed. Because I *was* there. I am in all your memories.'

'My memories are innocent. How could you take my father's place, and Stephen's, and George Waring's? You?'

'Because I did take them.'

'Never. My love for *them* was innocent.'

'Your love for me was part of it. You think the past affects the future. Has it never struck you that the future may affect the past? In your innocence there was the beginning of your sin. You *were* what you *were to be*.'

'I shall get away,' she said.

'And, this time, I shall go with you.'

The stile, the elder tree, and the field floated away from her. She was going under the beech trees down the Park drive towards the south gate and the village, slinking close to the right-hand row of trees. She was aware that Oscar Wade was going with her under the left-hand row, keeping even with her, step by step, and tree by tree. And presently there was grey pavement under her feet and a row of grey pillars on her right hand. They were walking side by side down the rue de Rivoli towards the hotel.

They were sitting together now on the edge of the dingy white bed. Their arms hung by their sides, heavy and limp, their heads drooped, averted. Their passion weighed on them with the unbearable, unescapable boredom of immortality.

'Oscar—how long will it last?'

'I can't tell you. I don't know whether *this* is one moment of eternity, or the eternity of one moment.'

'It must end some time,' she said. 'Life doesn't go on for ever. We shall die.'

'Die? We *have* died. Don't you know what this is? Don't you know where you are? This is death. We're dead, Harriott. We're in hell.'

'Yes. There can't be anything worse than this.'

'This isn't the worst. We're not quite dead yet, as long as we've life in us to turn and run and get away from each other; as long as we can escape into our memories. But when you've got back to the farthest memory of all and there's nothing beyond it—When there's no memory but this—In the last hell we shall not run away any longer; we shall find no more roads, no more passages, no more open doors. We shall have no need to look for each other.

'In the last death we shall be shut up in this room, behind that locked door, together. We shall lie here together, for ever and ever, joined so fast that even God can't put us asunder. We shall be one flesh and one spirit, one sin repeated for ever, and ever; spirit loathing flesh, flesh loathing spirit; you and I loathing each other.'

'Why? Why?' she cried.

'Because that's all that's left us. That's what you made of love.'

The darkness came down swamping, it blotted out the room. She was walking along a garden path between high borders of phlox and larkspur and lupin. They were taller than she was, their flowers swayed and nodded above her head. She tugged at the tall stems and had no strength to break them. She was a little thing.

She said to herself then that she was safe. She had gone back so far that she was a child again; she had the blank innocence of childhood. To be a child, to go small under the heads of the lupins, to be blank and innocent, without memory, was to be safe.

The walk led her out through a yew hedge on to a bright green lawn. In the middle of the lawn there was a shallow round pond in a ring of rockery cushioned with small flowers, yellow and white and purple. Goldfish swam in the olive brown water. She would be safe when she saw the goldfish swimming towards her. The old one with the white scales would come up first, pushing up his nose, making bubbles in the water.

At the bottom of the lawn there was a privet hedge cut by a broad path that went through the orchard. She knew what she would find there; her mother was in the orchard. She would lift her up in her arms to play with the hard red balls of the apples that hung from the tree. She had got back to the farthest memory of all; there was nothing beyond it.

There would be an iron gate in the wall of the orchard. It would lead into a field.

Something was different here, something that frightened her. An ash-grey door instead of an iron gate.

She pushed it open and came into the last corridor of the Hotel Saint Pierre.

NOTES ON THE AUTHORS

Gertrude Atherton (1857–1948) was a prolific and bestselling American novelist. Born Gertrude Horn, she married George Atherton in 1876; he died in 1887, and she never remarried. She was the author of such popular novels as *The Conqueror* (1902) and *Black Oxen* (1923). The latter novel focused on a controversial medical procedure—the directing of low-level X-rays into a woman's ovaries to stimulate hormone production—pioneered by Dr. Eugen Steinach, and which Atherton herself underwent; she claimed it rejuvenated her mentally and physically. A native Californian, she was friends with Ambrose Bierce, Jack London, and other West Coast writers. Scattered weird tales appeared in such of her collections as *The Bell and the Fog and Other Stories* (1905) and *The Foghorn* (1934). Her collected weird tales were gathered in *The Caves of Death and Other Stories* (2008). "Death and the Woman" was first published in the London *Vanity Fair* for January 14, 1893.

Marjorie Bowen (pseudonym of Gabrielle Long, 1885–1952) was a prolific British novelist and biographer. Born Gabrielle Campbell, she was married twice: first to Zefferino Costanza, and then to Arthur L. Long. She had two sons with each of her husbands. She wrote her first novel, *The Viper of Milan*, when she was sixteen; it became a bestseller when it was published in 1906. She went on to write dozens of novels and short story collections, some under the pseudonyms George Preedy and Joseph Shearing. Her weird short fiction is scattered throughout her various story collections; many of them were gathered in the posthumous volume *Kecksies and Other Twilight Tales* (1976). The novel *Black Magic* (1909) is an historical novel about Pope Joan (a female pope who purportedly reigned for a few years in the Middle Ages) with some incidental supernaturalism. "Scoured Silk," which fuses her interest in the historical tale, the detective story, and the supernatural, was first published in the *All-Story Weekly* (June 8, 1918) and gathered in her collection *Crimes of Old Ludlow* (1919).

Mary Elizabeth Braddon (1835–1915) was a popular and prolific British novelist. In 1860 she began living with the publisher John Maxwell, whose wife was confined to an asylum. Braddon only married Maxwell in 1874, after his wife died; she subsequently bore him six children. She published more than eighty novels, the most famous of which was *Lady Audley's Secret* (1862), which Henry James characterized as "a skilful combination of bigamy, arson, murder, and insanity." It initiated the genre of the "sensational novel"—a fast-paced thriller with all manner of dramatic incidents but with no inclusion of the supernatural. However, she wrote many supernatural stories in the course of her career; the most famous of which is perhaps "Good Lady Ducayne" (1896), a vampire story. "The Cold Embrace" was first published in the *Welcome Guest* (September 29, 1860).

Amelia B. Edwards (Amelia Ann Blanford Edwards, 1831–1892) was a British novelist and Egyptologist. She published her first poem at the age of seven and her first short story at twelve; her first novel, *My Brother's Wife*, appeared in 1855. In 1873-74 she undertook an extensive trip to Egypt, which she described in the travelogue *A Thousand Miles Up the Nile* (1877). She subsequently wrote one other book about Egypt (*Pharaohs, Fellahs, and Explorers* [1891]) and other books of travel. The volume *Monsieur Maurice and Other Stories* (1876) contains the title short novel (about the spirit of an Arab who acts as a kind of guardian angel) and many supernatural short stories. "An Engineer's Story" was first published in *All the Year Round* (Christmas 1866).

Mrs. H. D. Everett (Henrietta Dorothy Everett, 1851–1923) is a British writer about whom little is known. Under the pseudonym Theo Douglas, she published such novels as *Iras: A Mystery* (1896) and *A White Witch* (1908). Her single collection of weird tales, *The Death Mask and Other Ghosts*, appeared in 1920. "The Death Mask" first appeared in that volume.

Mary E. Wilkins Freeman (1852–1930), born Mary Ella (later Eleanor) Wilkins, was an American short story writer and novelist best known for regional writing based on her New England heritage. She worked predominantly in the short story, and her many tales were gathered in such collections as *A Humble Romance and Other Stories* (1887), *A New England Nun and Other Stories* (1901), and *The Fair Lavinia and Others* (1907). Nearly all her collections contain a few weird specimens; in 1902-03 she wrote a series of weird tales for *Everybody's Magazine*, collected in *The Wind in the Rose-bush and Other Stories of the Supernatural* (1903). She also wrote a play about the Salem witch trials, *Giles Corey, Yeoman* (1892), although it does not involve the supernatural. She married Charles Freeman in 1892; he died in 1923. "The Hall Bedroom" first appeared in *Collier's* (March 28, 1903).

Elizabeth Gaskell (1810–1865) was a British novelist and biographer. Born Elizabeth Cleghorn Stevenson, she married William Gaskell in 1832. She had four children; one other was stillborn and another died in infancy. She gained celebrity not only with her realistic novels of English rural life, such as *Mary Barton* (1848) and *Cranford* (1851–53), but by her well-regarded *Life of Charlotte Brontë* (1857). Her weird tales are scattered throughout her various story collections; many of them were gathered in *Mrs. Gaskell's Tales of Mystery and Horror* (1978). "Curious If True" was first published in *Cornhill Magazine* (February 1860).

Charlotte Perkins Gilman (1860–1935) was an American feminist, sociologist, and novelist. Born Charlotte Perkins, she married the artist Charles Walter Stetson in 1884; she had one child, Katharine. In 1888 she separated from Stetson and divorced him in 1894. She married her first cousin, Houghton Gilman, in 1900. Her story "The Yellow Wall Paper" (first published in *New England Magazine* for January 1892 and as a separate booklet in 1899) was written partly as a result of the rest cure she underwent to deal with the postpartum depression she experienced after the birth of her child. She published nearly 200 short stories, as well as such novels as the Utopian *Herland* (1915), and such works of nonfiction as *Women and Economics* (1898). Her autobiography appeared as *The Living of Charlotte Perkins Gilman* (1935).

Ellen Glasgow (1873–1945) was an American novelist and short story writer who wrote profoundly of her native Virginia and other locales in the South. Glasgow never married, although she was engaged twice and also apparently had a longterm affair with a married man. She was well acquainted with another celebrated Virginia writer, James Branch Cabell. Many of her novels are realistic depictions of Southern life following the Civil War, such as *The Battle-Ground* (1902) and *Barren Ground* (1925). The short story collection *The Shadowy Third and Other Stories* (1923) contains the bulk of her weird short fiction. "The Shadowy Third" was first published in *Scribner's Magazine* (December 1916).

Sarah Orne Jewett (1849–1909) was an American regional writer whose many short stories and novels reflect her upbringing in Maine. She published her first short story at the age of nineteen; her first story collection, *Deephaven*, appeared in 1877. She never married, but maintained a long friendship with

Annie Fields and her husband, the publisher James T. Fields; after James's death in 1881 she lived with Annie for the rest of her life. Her most famous book was *The Country of the Pointed Firs* (1896), a series of linked short stories. Many of her story collections include tales of the supernatural. "In Dark New England Days" was first published in *Century Magazine* (October 1890).

Vernon Lee (pseudonym of Violet Paget, 1856–1935) was a British essayist and short story writer. Born in France to British expatriate parents, she spent most of her life in Europe, especially Italy. A devotee of music, aesthetics, and travel, she published her first work, *Studies in the Eighteenth Century in Italy*, in 1880. Among her travel books are *Genius Loci* (1899) and *Ravenna and Her Ghosts* (1907). Much of her fiction is laced with weirdness and the supernatural, including the volumes *A Phantom Lover* (1886), *Hauntings: Fantastic Stories* (1890), and *For Maurice: Five Unlikely Stories* (1927). "A Wedding Chest" was first published in *Pope Jacynth and Other Fantastic Tales* (1904).

E. Nesbit (Edith Nesbit Bland, 1858–1924) was a British novelist best known for such children's books as *The Story of the Treasure Seekers* (1899), *The Would-begoods* (1901), *Five Children and It* (1902), and *The Enchanted Castle* (1907). These books contain some elements of fantasy and terror, but her purely weird tales were collected in two early volumes, *Grim Tales* (1893) and *Fear* (1910). She was married to the critic Hubert Bland and was acquainted with many of the leading British literary figures of the day, including H. G. Wells and Lord Dunsany. "From the Dead" was first published in the *Illustrated London News* (September 3, 1880) and collected in *Grim Tales* and *Fear*.

Margaret Oliphant (1828–1897) was a Scottish novelist and short story writer. She published her first novel at the age of twenty-one and went on to write dozens of other novels—domestic, historical, and a few involving the supernatural. She married her cousin Frank Wilson Oliphant in 1852, but he succumbed to tuberculosis in 1859 while Margaret and her three children were living in Italy. These children all eventually predeceased their mother, causing Oliphant to develop an interest in spiritualism as a means of re-establishing contact with them. Among her weird works are the short novel *A Beleaguered City* (1880) and the story collection *Tales of the Seen and the Unseen* (1899). "The Secret Chamber" first appeared in *Blackwood's Edinburgh Magazine* (December 1876).

Mrs. J. H. Riddell (1832–1906) was a prolific Anglo-Irish novelist and short story writer. Born Charlotte Eliza Lawson Cowan in Carrickfergus, Ireland, she married Joseph Hadley Riddell in 1857. Her first novel was published in 1856, and she went on to write more than fifty others. Her tales of the superantural are found in such volumes as *Weird Stories* (1882) and *Idle Tales* (1887). Several of her novels and short novels, such as *The Inhabitated House* (1875), also feature the supernatural. "Walnut-Tree House" was first published in *Weird Stories*.

Mary Shelley (1797–1851) was an English novelist, playwright, and short story writer. Born Mary Wollstonecraft Godwin, she was the daughter of the celebrated feminist writer Mary Wollstonecraft (*A Vindication of the Rights of Woman*, 1792) and the political philosopher William Godwin. She married the poet Percy Bysshe Shelley in 1814. She wrote *Frankenstein; or, The Modern Prometheus* in 1816, as part of a contest in which she, Percy Shelley, Lord Byron, and John William Polidori sought to write the most frightening Gothic tale; it was published in 1818, and a revised version appeared in 1831. After Percy Shelley's early death, she edited his poetical works. She also wrote several other novels, including the futuristic fantasy *The Last Man* (1826). "Transformation" was first published in the *Keepsake for 1831* (1830).

May Sinclair (pseudonym of Mary Amelia St. Clair, 1863–1946) was a British novelist, short story writer, and poet. Well connected with avant-garde literary circles in England, she was on familiar terms with such writers as the poet H. D., Ezra Pound, and Dorothy Richardson. She coined the term "stream of consciousness." Among her novels are *The Divine Fire* (1904) and *The Dark Night: A Novel in Unrhymed Verse* (1924). A devotee of spiritualism and a member of the Society for Psychical Research, Sinclair published two notable collections of weird tales, *Uncanny Tales* (1923) and *The Intercessor and Other Stories* (1931). "Where Their Fire Is Not Quenched" was first published in the *English Review* (October 1922).

Edna W. Underwood (1873–1961) was an American short story writer, novelist, poet, and translator. Born Edna Worthley in Maine, she grew up in Kansas, married Earl Underwood in 1897, and moved to New York City, where she wrote historical novels, a book of poetry (*The Garden of Desire*, 1913), and translations from Russian, Persian, Japanese, and other languages. Today she is largely remembered for the short story collection *A Book of Dear Dead Women* (1911), which contains several weird specimens. "The Painter of Dead Women" first appeared in the *Smart Set* (January 1910).

Edith Wharton (1862–1937) was a renowned American novelist and short story writer, known for her friendship with Henry James and for such novels as *The House of Mirth* (1905), *Ethan Frome* (1911), and *The Age of Innocence*

(1920), which won the Pulitzer Prize. Born Edith Newbold Jones, she married Edward Robbins Wharton in 1885, but his chronic depression led her to divorce him in 1913. She spent most of her life in New York or New England, but traveled widely in Europe. Her weird tales were collected in the early volume *Tales of Men and Ghosts* (1910) and in the posthumous *Ghosts* (1937). "The Eyes" was first published in *Scribner's Magazine* (June 1910).

Virginia Woolf (1882–1941) was a celebrated British novelist, short story writer, dramatist, and essayist. Born Adeline Virginia Stephen, the daughter of the well-known critic and philosopher Leslie Stephen, she spent most of her life in London, where she became associated with the Bloomsbury group of writers, including Vita Sackville-West (with whom Woolf had a sexual affair) and Lytton Strachey. She married Leonard Woolf in 1912 and with him established the Hogarth Press, which published the work of T. S. Eliot and other modernist writers. Among her novels are *Mrs. Dalloway* (1925), *To the Lighthouse* (1927), and *Orlando* (1928). She wrote several collections of essays, including *The Common Reader* (1925) and *A Room of One's Own* (1929). The brief vignette "A Haunted House" was first published in the story collection *Monday or Tuesday* (1921).

A CATALOG OF SELECTED DOVER
BOOKS IN ALL FIELDS OF INTEREST

100 BEST-LOVED POEMS, Edited by Philip Smith. "The Passionate Shepherd to His Love," "Shall I compare thee to a summer's day?" "Death, be not proud," "The Raven," "The Road Not Taken," plus works by Blake, Wordsworth, Byron, Shelley, Keats, many others. Includes 13 selections from the Common Core State Standards Initiative. 112pp.   0-486-28553-7

ABC BOOK OF EARLY AMERICANA, Eric Sloane. Artist and historian Eric Sloane presents a wondrous A-to-Z collection of American innovations, including hex signs, ear trumpets, popcorn, and rocking chairs. Illustrated, hand-lettered pages feature brief captions explaining objects' origins and uses. 64pp.   0-486-49808-5

ADVENTURES OF HUCKLEBERRY FINN, Mark Twain. Join Huck and Jim as their boyhood adventures along the Mississippi River lead them into a world of excitement, danger, and self-discovery. Humorous narrative, lyrical descriptions of the Mississippi valley, and memorable characters. 224pp.   0-486-28061-6

ALICE STARMORE'S BOOK OF FAIR ISLE KNITTING, Alice Starmore. A noted designer from the region of Scotland's Fair Isle explores the history and techniques of this distinctive, stranded-color knitting style and provides copious illustrated instructions for 14 original knitwear designs. 208pp.   0-486-47218-3

ALICE'S ADVENTURES IN WONDERLAND, Lewis Carroll. Beloved classic about a little girl lost in a topsy-turvy land and her encounters with the White Rabbit, March Hare, Mad Hatter, Cheshire Cat, and other delightfully improbable characters. 42 illustrations by Sir John Tenniel. A selection of the Common Core State Standards Initiative. 96pp.   0-486-27543-4

THE ARTHUR RACKHAM TREASURY: 86 Full-Color Illustrations, Arthur Rackham. Selected and Edited by Jeff A. Menges. A stunning treasury of 86 full-page plates span the famed English artist's career, from *Rip Van Winkle* (1905) to masterworks such as *Undine, A Midsummer Night's Dream,* and *Wind in the Willows* (1939). 96pp.   0-486-44685-9

THE AWAKENING, Kate Chopin. First published in 1899, this controversial novel of a New Orleans wife's search for love outside a stifling marriage shocked readers. Today, it remains a first-rate narrative with superb characterization. New introductory note. 128pp.   0-486-27786-0

BASEBALL IS . . .: Defining the National Pastime, Edited by Paul Dickson. Wisecracking, philosophical, nostalgic, and entertaining, these hundreds of quips and observations by players, their wives, managers, authors, and others cover every aspect of our national pastime. It's a great any-occasion gift for fans! 256pp.   0-486-48209-X

THE CALL OF THE WILD, Jack London. A classic novel of adventure, drawn from London's own experiences as a Klondike adventurer, relating the story of a heroic dog caught in the brutal life of the Alaska Gold Rush. Note. 64pp.   0-486-26472-6

CANDIDE, Voltaire. Edited by Francois-Marie Arouet. One of the world's great satires since its first publication in 1759. Witty, caustic skewering of romance, science, philosophy, religion, government — nearly all human ideals and institutions. A selection of the Common Core State Standards Initiative. 112pp.   0-486-26689-3

THE CARTOON HISTORY OF TIME, Kate Charlesworth and John Gribbin. Cartoon characters explain cosmology, quantum physics, and other concepts covered by Stephen Hawking's *A Brief History of Time.* Humorous graphic novel–style treatment, perfect for young readers and curious folk of all ages. 64pp.   0-486-49097-1

Browse over 10,000 books at www.doverpublications.com

THE CHERRY ORCHARD, Anton Chekhov. Classic of world drama concerns passing of semifeudal order in turn-of-the-century Russia, symbolized in the sale of the cherry orchard owned by Madame Ranevskaya. Showcases Chekhov's rich sensitivities as an observer of human nature. 64pp. 0-486-26682-6

A CHRISTMAS CAROL, Charles Dickens. This engrossing tale relates Ebenezer Scrooge's ghostly journeys through Christmases past, present, and future and his ultimate transformation from a harsh and grasping old miser to a charitable and compassionate human being. 80pp. 0-486-26865-9

CRIME AND PUNISHMENT, Fyodor Dostoyevsky. Translated by Constance Garnett. Supreme masterpiece tells the story of Raskolnikov, a student tormented by his own thoughts after he murders an old woman. Overwhelmed by guilt and terror, he confesses and goes to prison. A selection of the Common Core State Standards Initiative. 448pp. 0-486-41587-2

CYRANO DE BERGERAC, Edmond Rostand. A quarrelsome, hot-tempered, and unattractive swordsman falls hopelessly in love with a beautiful woman and woos her for a handsome but slow-witted suitor. A witty and eloquent drama. 144pp. 0-486-41119-2

A DOLL'S HOUSE, Henrik Ibsen. Ibsen's best-known play displays his genius for realistic prose drama. An expression of women's rights, the play climaxes when the central character, Nora, rejects a smothering marriage and life in "a doll's house." A selection of the Common Core State Standards Initiative. 80pp. 0-486-27062-9

DOOMED SHIPS: Great Ocean Liner Disasters, William H. Miller, Jr. Nearly 200 photographs, many from private collections, highlight tales of some of the vessels whose pleasure cruises ended in catastrophe: the *Morro Castle, Normandie, Andrea Doria, Europa,* and many others. 128pp. 0-486-45366-9

DUBLINERS, James Joyce. A fine and accessible introduction to the work of one of the 20th century's most influential writers, this collection features 15 tales, including a masterpiece of the short-story genre, "The Dead." 160pp. 0-486-26870-5

THE EARLY SCIENCE FICTION OF PHILIP K. DICK, Philip K. Dick. This anthology presents short stories and novellas that originally appeared in pulp magazines of the early 1950s, including "The Variable Man," "Second Variety," "Beyond the Door," "The Defenders," and more. 272pp. 0-486-49733-X

THE EARLY SHORT STORIES OF F. SCOTT FITZGERALD, F. Scott Fitzgerald. These tales offer insights into many themes, characters, and techniques that emerged in Fitzgerald's later works. Selections include "The Curious Case of Benjamin Button," "Babes in the Woods," and a dozen others. 256pp. 0-486-79465-2

ETHAN FROME, Edith Wharton. Classic story of wasted lives, set against a bleak New England background. Superbly delineated characters in a hauntingly grim tale of thwarted love. Considered by many to be Wharton's masterpiece. 96pp. 0-486-26690-7

FLATLAND: A Romance of Many Dimensions, Edwin A. Abbott. Classic of science (and mathematical) fiction — charmingly illustrated by the author — describes the adventures of A. Square, a resident of Flatland, in Spaceland (three dimensions), Lineland (one dimension), and Pointland (no dimensions). 96pp. 0-486-27263-X

FRANKENSTEIN, Mary Shelley. The story of Victor Frankenstein's monstrous creation and the havoc it caused has enthralled generations of readers and inspired countless writers of horror and suspense. With the author's own 1831 introduction. 176pp. 0-486-28211-2

THE GARGOYLE BOOK: 572 Examples from Gothic Architecture, Lester Burbank Bridaham. Dispelling the conventional wisdom that French Gothic architectural flourishes were born of despair or gloom, Bridaham reveals the whimsical nature of these creations and the ingenious artisans who made them. 572 illustrations. 224pp. 0-486-44754-5

Browse over 10,000 books at www.doverpublications.com

THE GIFT OF THE MAGI AND OTHER SHORT STORIES, O. Henry. Sixteen captivating stories by one of America's most popular storytellers. Included are such classics as "The Gift of the Magi," "The Last Leaf," and "The Ransom of Red Chief." Publisher's Note. A selection of the Common Core State Standards Initiative. 96pp. 0-486-27061-0

THE GOETHE TREASURY: Selected Prose and Poetry, Johann Wolfgang von Goethe. Edited, Selected, and with an Introduction by Thomas Mann. In addition to his lyric poetry, Goethe wrote travel sketches, autobiographical studies, essays, letters, and proverbs in rhyme and prose. This collection presents outstanding examples from each genre. 368pp. 0-486-44780-4

GREAT ILLUSTRATIONS BY N. C. WYETH, N. C. Wyeth. Edited and with an Introduction by Jeff A. Menges. This full-color collection focuses on the artist's early and most popular illustrations, featuring more than 100 images from *The Mysterious Stranger, Robin Hood, Robinson Crusoe, The Boy's King Arthur,* and other classics. 128pp. 0-486-47295-7

HAMLET, William Shakespeare. The quintessential Shakespearean tragedy, whose highly charged confrontations and anguished soliloquies probe depths of human feeling rarely sounded in any art. Reprinted from an authoritative British edition complete with illuminating footnotes. A selection of the Common Core State Standards Initiative. 128pp. 0-486-27278-8

THE HAUNTED HOUSE, Charles Dickens. A Yuletide gathering in an eerie country retreat provides the backdrop for Dickens and his friends — including Elizabeth Gaskell and Wilkie Collins — who take turns spinning supernatural yarns. 144pp. 0-486-46309-5

HEART OF DARKNESS, Joseph Conrad. Dark allegory of a journey up the Congo River and the narrator's encounter with the mysterious Mr. Kurtz. Masterly blend of adventure, character study, psychological penetration. For many, Conrad's finest, most enigmatic story. 80pp. 0-486-26464-5

THE HOUND OF THE BASKERVILLES, Sir Arthur Conan Doyle. A deadly curse in the form of a legendary ferocious beast continues to claim its victims from the Baskerville family until Holmes and Watson intervene. Often called the best detective story ever written. 128pp. 0-486-28214-7

THE HOUSE BEHIND THE CEDARS, Charles W. Chesnutt. Originally published in 1900, this groundbreaking novel by a distinguished African-American author recounts the drama of a brother and sister who "pass for white" during the dangerous days of Reconstruction. 208pp. 0-486-46144-0

HOW TO DRAW NEARLY EVERYTHING, Victor Perard. Beginners of all ages can learn to draw figures, faces, landscapes, trees, flowers, and animals of all kinds. Well-illustrated guide offers suggestions for pencil, pen, and brush techniques plus composition, shading, and perspective. 160pp. 0-486-49848-4

HOW TO MAKE SUPER POP-UPS, Joan Irvine. Illustrated by Linda Hendry. Super pop-ups extend the element of surprise with three-dimensional designs that slide, turn, spring, and snap. More than 30 patterns and 475 illustrations include cards, stage props, and school projects. 96pp. 0-486-46589-6

THE IMITATION OF CHRIST, Thomas à Kempis. Translated by Aloysius Croft and Harold Bolton. This religious classic has brought understanding and comfort to millions for centuries. Written in a candid and conversational style, the topics include liberation from worldly inclinations, preparation and consolations of prayer, and eucharistic communion. 160pp. 0-486-43185-1

CATALOG OF DOVER BOOKS

THE IMPORTANCE OF BEING EARNEST, Oscar Wilde. Wilde's witty and buoyant comedy of manners, filled with some of literature's most famous epigrams, reprinted from an authoritative British edition. Considered Wilde's most perfect work. A selection of the Common Core State Standards Initiative. 64pp. 0-486-26478-5

JANE EYRE, Charlotte Brontë. Written in 1847, *Jane Eyre* tells the tale of an orphan girl's progress from the custody of cruel relatives to an oppressive boarding school and its culmination in a troubled career as a governess. A selection of the Common Core State Standards Initiative. 448pp. 0-486-42449-9

JUST WHAT THE DOCTOR DISORDERED: Early Writings and Cartoons of Dr. Seuss, Dr. Seuss. Edited and with an Introduction by Rick Marschall. The Doctor's visual hilarity, nonsense language, and offbeat sense of humor illuminate this compilation of items from his early career, created for periodicals such as *Judge, Life, College Humor,* and *Liberty.* 144pp. 0-486-49846-8

KING LEAR, William Shakespeare. Powerful tragedy of an aging king, betrayed by his daughters, robbed of his kingdom, descending into madness. Perhaps the bleakest of Shakespeare's tragic dramas, complete with explanatory footnotes. 144pp. 0-486-28058-6

THE LADY OR THE TIGER?: and Other Logic Puzzles, Raymond M. Smullyan. Created by a renowned puzzle master, these whimsically themed challenges involve paradoxes about probability, time, and change; metapuzzles; and self-referentiality. Nineteen chapters advance in difficulty from relatively simple to highly complex. 1982 edition. 240pp. 0-486-47027-X

LEAVES OF GRASS: The Original 1855 Edition, Walt Whitman. Whitman's immortal collection includes some of the greatest poems of modern times, including his masterpiece, "Song of Myself." Shattering standard conventions, it stands as an unabashed celebration of body and nature. 128pp. 0-486-45676-5

LES MISÉRABLES, Victor Hugo. Translated by Charles E. Wilbour. Abridged by James K. Robinson. A convict's heroic struggle for justice and redemption plays out against a fiery backdrop of the Napoleonic wars. This edition features the excellent original translation and a sensitive abridgment. 304pp. 0-486-45789-3

LIGHT FOR THE ARTIST, Ted Seth Jacobs. Intermediate and advanced art students receive a broad vocabulary of effects with this in-depth study of light. Diagrams and paintings illustrate applications of principles to figure, still life, and landscape paintings. 144pp. 0-486-49304-0

LILITH: A Romance, George MacDonald. In this novel by the father of fantasy literature, a man travels through time to meet Adam and Eve and to explore humanity's fall from grace and ultimate redemption. 240pp. 0-486-46818-6

LINE: An Art Study, Edmund J. Sullivan. Written by a noted artist and teacher, this well-illustrated guide introduces the basics of line drawing. Topics include third and fourth dimensions, formal perspective, shade and shadow, figure drawing, and other essentials. 208pp. 0-486-79484-9

THE LODGER, Marie Belloc Lowndes. Acclaimed by *The New York Times* as "one of the best suspense novels ever written," this novel recounts an English couple's doubts about their boarder, whom they suspect of being a serial killer. 240pp. 0-486-78809-1

MACBETH, William Shakespeare. A Scottish nobleman murders the king in order to succeed to the throne. Tortured by his conscience and fearful of discovery, he becomes tangled in a web of treachery and deceit that ultimately spells his doom. A selection of the Common Core State Standards Initiative. 96pp. 0-486-27802-6

Browse over 10,000 books at www.doverpublications.com

MANHATTAN IN MAPS 1527–2014, Paul E. Cohen and Robert T. Augustyn. This handsome volume features 65 full-color maps charting Manhattan's development from the first Dutch settlement to the present. Each map is placed in context by an accompanying essay. 176pp. 0-486-77991-2

MEDEA, Euripides. One of the most powerful and enduring of Greek tragedies, masterfully portraying the fierce motives driving Medea's pursuit of vengeance for her husband's insult and betrayal. Authoritative Rex Warner translation. 64pp. 0-486-27548-5

THE METAMORPHOSIS AND OTHER STORIES, Franz Kafka. Excellent new English translations of title story (considered by many critics Kafka's most perfect work), plus "The Judgment," "In the Penal Colony," "A Country Doctor," and "A Report to an Academy." A selection of the Common Core State Standards Initiative. 96pp. 0-486-29030-1

METROPOLIS, Thea von Harbou. This Weimar-era novel of a futuristic society, written by the screenwriter for the iconic 1927 film, was hailed by noted science-fiction authority Forrest J. Ackerman as "a work of genius." 224pp. 0-486-79567-5

THE MYSTERIOUS MICKEY FINN, Elliot Paul. A multimillionaire's disappearance incites a maelstrom of kidnapping, murder, and a plot to restore the French monarchy. "One of the funniest books we've read in a long time." — *The New York Times.* 256pp. 0-486-24751-1

NARRATIVE OF THE LIFE OF FREDERICK DOUGLASS, Frederick Douglass. The impassioned abolitionist and eloquent orator provides graphic descriptions of his childhood and horrifying experiences as a slave as well as a harrowing record of his dramatic escape to the North and eventual freedom. A selection of the Common Core State Standards Initiative. 96pp. 0-486-28499-9

OBELISTS FLY HIGH, C. Daly King. Masterpiece of detective fiction portrays murder aboard a 1935 transcontinental flight. Combining an intricate plot and "locked room" scenario, the mystery was praised by *The New York Times* as "a very thrilling story." 288pp. 0-486-25036-9

THE ODYSSEY, Homer. Excellent prose translation of ancient epic recounts adventures of the homeward-bound Odysseus. Fantastic cast of gods, giants, cannibals, sirens, other supernatural creatures — true classic of Western literature. A selection of the Common Core State Standards Initiative. 256pp. 0-486-40654-7

OEDIPUS REX, Sophocles. Landmark of Western drama concerns the catastrophe that ensues when King Oedipus discovers he has inadvertently killed his father and married his mother. Masterly construction, dramatic irony. A selection of the Common Core State Standards Initiative. 64pp. 0-486-26877-2

OTHELLO, William Shakespeare. Towering tragedy tells the story of a Moorish general who earns the enmity of his ensign Iago when he passes him over for a promotion. Masterly portrait of an archvillain. Explanatory footnotes. 112pp. 0-486-29097-2

THE PICTURE OF DORIAN GRAY, Oscar Wilde. Celebrated novel involves a handsome young Londoner who sinks into a life of depravity. His body retains perfect youth and vigor while his recent portrait reflects the ravages of his crime and sensuality. 176pp. 0-486-27807-7

A PLACE CALLED PECULIAR: Stories About Unusual American Place-Names, Frank K. Gallant. From Smut Eye, Alabama, to Tie Siding, Wyoming, this pop-culture history offers a well-written and highly entertaining survey of America's most unusual place-names and their often-humorous origins. 256pp. 0-486-48360-6

PRIDE AND PREJUDICE, Jane Austen. One of the most universally loved and admired English novels, an effervescent tale of rural romance transformed by Jane Austen's art into a witty, shrewdly observed satire of English country life. A selection of the Common Core State Standards Initiative. 272pp. 0-486-28473-5

Browse over 10,000 books at www.doverpublications.com

THE RED BADGE OF COURAGE, Stephen Crane. Amid the nightmarish chaos of a Civil War battle, a young soldier discovers courage, humility, and, perhaps, wisdom. Uncanny re-creation of actual combat. Enduring landmark of American fiction. 112pp. 0-486-26465-3

RELATIVITY SIMPLY EXPLAINED, Martin Gardner. One of the subject's clearest, most entertaining introductions offers lucid explanations of special and general theories of relativity, gravity, and spacetime, models of the universe, and more. 100 illustrations. 224pp. 0-486-29315-7

THE ROAD NOT TAKEN AND OTHER POEMS, Robert Frost. A treasury of Frost's most expressive verse. In addition to the title poem: "An Old Man's Winter Night," "In the Home Stretch," "Meeting and Passing," "Putting in the Seed," many more. All complete and unabridged. Includes a selection from the Common Core State Standards Initiative. 64pp. 0-486-27550-7

ROMEO AND JULIET, William Shakespeare. Tragic tale of star-crossed lovers, feuding families and timeless passion contains some of Shakespeare's most beautiful and lyrical love poetry. Complete, unabridged text with explanatory footnotes. 96pp. 0-486-27557-4

SANDITON AND THE WATSONS: Austen's Unfinished Novels, Jane Austen. Two tantalizing incomplete stories revisit Austen's customary milieu of courtship and venture into new territory, amid guests at a seaside resort. Both are worth reading for pleasure and study. 112pp. 0-486-45793-1

THE SCARLET LETTER, Nathaniel Hawthorne. With stark power and emotional depth, Hawthorne's masterpiece explores sin, guilt, and redemption in a story of adultery in the early days of the Massachusetts Colony. A selection of the Common Core State Standards Initiative. 192pp. 0-486-28048-9

SELECTED POEMS, Emily Dickinson. Over 100 best-known, best-loved poems by one of America's foremost poets, reprinted from authoritative early editions. No comparable edition at this price. Includes 3 selections from the Common Core State Standards Initiative. 64pp. 0-486-26466-1

SIDDHARTHA, Hermann Hesse. Classic novel that has inspired generations of seekers. Blending Eastern mysticism and psychoanalysis, Hesse presents a strikingly original view of man and culture and the arduous process of self-discovery, reconciliation, harmony, and peace. 112pp. 0-486-40653-9

SKETCHING OUTDOORS, Leonard Richmond. This guide offers beginners step-by-step demonstrations of how to depict clouds, trees, buildings, and other outdoor sights. Explanations of a variety of techniques include shading and constructional drawing. 48pp. 0-486-46922-0

STAR LORE: Myths, Legends, and Facts, William Tyler Olcott. Captivating retellings of the origins and histories of ancient star groups include Pegasus, Ursa Major, Pleiades, signs of the zodiac, and other constellations. "Classic." — *Sky & Telescope*. 58 illustrations. 544pp. 0-486-43581-4

STRIP FOR MURDER, Max Allan Collins. Illustrated by Terry Beatty. Colorful characters with murderous motives populate this illustrated mystery, in which the heated rivalry between a pair of cartoonists ends in homicide and a stripper-turned-detective and her stepson-partner seek the killer. "Great fun." — *Mystery Scene*. 288pp. 0-486-79811-9

SURVIVAL HANDBOOK: The Official U.S. Army Guide, Department of the Army. This special edition of the Army field manual is geared toward civilians. An essential companion for campers and all lovers of the outdoors, it constitutes the most authoritative wilderness guide. 288pp. 0-486-46184-X

Browse over 10,000 books at www.doverpublications.com